GEORGE

by

JAMES H. RUSSELL

(WWW. browastuff72@ Yahoo.com)

message me if you like!

**Grosvenor House
Publishing Limited**

This book is published by
Grosvenor House Publishing Ltd
Link House
140 The Broadway, Tolworth, Surrey, KT6 7HT.
www.grosvenorhousepublishing.co.uk

This book is a work of fiction. Any resemblance to
people or events, past or present, is purely coincidental.

A CIP record for this book
is available from the British Library

ISBN 978-1-83975-615-3

Dedication

For my wife, Julie, who has always supported and
believed in me, no matter what.
And my four children:
Alex (now sadly departed) and his wife Susan.
Elizabeth and her husband Phil.
Robert and his wife Amira.
Richard and his partner Jen.
And for my three Grandsons:
Daniel (and partner Courtney),
Joshua (and partner Nancy)
and Liam (no partner yet but I'm sure it won't be long).

PREFACE

What are we hoping to achieve?

We Humans have a seemingly insatiable appetite for exploration and invention.

What is it that drives us to such limits that we are even prepared to put our lives at risk in pursuit of some previously unattainable goal?

We have a word for this uniquely Human behaviour. We call it achievement. It's a word that most of us use every day in some context or other.

The desire to achieve goes far beyond the needs of mere survival. It is as if we are constantly in search of something better, something more rewarding than what we have already.

Is there a purpose to all this progress? Do we instinctively know that there is?

Maybe we do, but the big question is: What is that purpose?

Perhaps we'll find out one day.

INTRODUCTION

It's that age-old question: What makes us human?

We talk about Man and Nature as if these are two different entities.

From the very beginning we have behaved like parasites. We take, but give nothing back. The definition of a successful parasite is one that does not end up killing its host. Our host is Planet Earth. Time will tell if we are successful parasites or not,

The question of our humanity is one that has troubled and puzzled us from the very start. Throughout the ages we have tried to find an answer in all manner of ways, most of them involving the creation of a supernatural being that has some kind of control over us. As Voltaire put it: "If God did not exist, it would be necessary to invent Him."

Our species is increasing in numbers exponentially. This is not part of Nature's plan. If we had stayed in the tropical rain forests where we belong, Nature would have ensured that our numbers would be controlled by the same regular culling that all other animals are subjected to, in the way of food limitation, disease and predation.

But we don't obey the laws of Nature. Many of our daily actions and habits are based on the experiences of previous generations and we faithfully re-enact them without question, guided by the idea that whatever enabled our forebears to survive should also be good enough for us. But we are beginning to realise that the world around us is changing so fast that the old ways are just not enough to sustain us any more. The balance is tipping, and not necessarily in our favour.

I am a dentist. I trained back in the 60's when dentists were in very high demand, thanks to an epidemic of tooth decay and gum disease. I was taught how to do extractions, make plastic and metal dentures, and restore decayed teeth using amalgam fillings, composed of silver mixed with mercury, itself a highly toxic substance which would never be allowed if it were introduced for the first time today. But back then it was all we had and we blindly pursued the use of it for many years to come.

The puzzle about our existence (which up until then I had never really thought about) suddenly came to me one day while I was using this silver amalgam to fill a very large cavity in a molar tooth. It was something I had done every single working day for the past thirty years, but it was only now, for the very first time, that I stopped to question what on Earth was going on. What had happened to we humans to make it necessary for me to be doing such a weird thing as this?

The usual answer to the causes of dental disease is poor oral hygiene and the over consumption of purified foods, particularly those with a high sugar content. But what is oral hygiene? Why are we the only animals that have to resort to it? What is it that we do, and other animals don't, to create this situation in the first place? The answer, I realised, was that we cook our food. I don't remember ever having been taught that fact in so many words at dental school, but I may be wrong.

Luckily for many of us, we have worked out a partial solution to the problem of tooth decay by the regular use of fluoride toothpaste, but we have to keep on using it and keep on buying it. When fluoride toothpaste was first introduced it was meant to act topically, i.e. directly on the tooth surface, and the hope was that it would reduce decay by five per cent or so. But it soon became apparent that the decay rate was dropping much faster than expected, due to the unforeseen fact that nearly everyone swallows a tiny amount of toothpaste each time they brush (small children even more so), and this was allowing fluoride to be incorporated directly in the formation of teeth: a happy accident.

Man is the only animal that cooks and prepares its food. This is not what Nature intended. Nature's toothbrush is already built into raw food, but cooking destroys it. If you don't believe me, try eating a raw Brussels sprout. It may not be the tastiest thing around but when you've finished eating it notice how clean and fresh your mouth feels. You won't get that effect from a cooked and mushy version of the same thing.

Cooking food is a double-edged sword. On the one hand it helps to reduce the chance of parasitic, bacterial and viral infestation and it also makes available many foods which are not palatable, or even poisonous in their raw form, e.g. potatoes, rice, wheat, etc. But on the other hand, cooking destroys or reduces much of the beneficial properties of raw food, such as vitamins and roughage, and by making meat more palatable it encourages us to eat far more of it than we would ever do in a natural environment. (In fact, we have gone so far in trying making our food even more palatable, that our kitchens have become more like chemistry labs, using a myriad of herbs and spices to drown out the less interesting flavour of the basic ingredient.)

Even though I've told you all this, you're still going to carry on cooking your food aren't you?

The point I am trying to make is that each time we go against the wishes of Nature there is a price to be paid. I'm sure we already know that, but we still go ahead anyway. Why?

What we do to food is only one small example of the many ways in which we have come to exploit the world around us. Maybe there's a hidden purpose to these seemingly destructive actions: a purpose leading us to some sort of end result that as yet we are unable to visualise. Perhaps that purpose is already written into our DNA, stealthily motivating us and controlling everything we do in its preconceived mandate to take us on to our destiny?

My story is a complete fantasy based on this idea. I apologise in advance for my poor writing skills. I am a dentist, not a writer, but I hope you can still get something useful out of my story.

GEORGE
PART ONE

Chapter 1

No two people see the same rainbow. The colours are the result of refraction followed by the reflection of sunlight through each droplet of water. The angle that the light hits your eye is not the same as that of the person standing right next to you and because of this, your rainbow is very slightly different from theirs.

It's the same with people. No two of us are exactly identical, even twins, because we all have our own way of thinking and looking at the world. So what? I hear you ask.

Well, I'll tell you what. It means that however well you think you know me, you don't. There are parts of my mind that will forever be known only to me. Shameful secrets that I keep to myself: secrets that I know would do me no good if I let them escape. I'm sure you have them too. But I have one particular secret that's not just about me. It's about you and me, all of us. You see, I know something that no one else on this planet knows, and what's more I intend to keep that 'something' a secret until the day I die.

Sorry to disappoint you! But sometime in the future, when I'm long gone, somebody somewhere will discover my secret and when they do, I promise you the world will be a different place. It'll be different because my secret has the power to bring us all together, make us one, probably for the only time since we humans first appeared on this Earth.

Perhaps it's time for me to introduce myself. My name is James Harcourt Russell. Harcourt was my mother's maiden name, which she didn't want to give up. Perhaps she was hoping I might use it in my surname one day. If I ever got to be posh, Harcourt-Russell would have suited me very well, but there's no chance of me ever being called posh. I was born in August 1949, so I'm getting on a bit now, 71 to be exact. Looking back over my life, I think I've done okay. Had a good career as a dentist which, despite early misgivings from both myself and my mother that I might be too squeamish to hack it, gave me the opportunity to meet all sorts of people from all walks of life, and at very close quarters too; something that almost no other career offers.

And the work was also surprisingly varied. One minute it was an 18-month-old toddler with teething problems and the next an 80-year-old pensioner getting a new set of dentures. In between these, there was every age and every type of person, all with their own individual dental problems. It was a great job for thinking on the move, and I must admit that, by and large, I enjoyed the whole experience. But now it's all finished, and I'm finally retired.

If you want to know what I look like, well okay, I'm not a pretty sight, having lost most of my hair which is now grey but was once bright ginger, and at one stage, back in the 1970s, was down to my shoulders. I've got that pale freckly skin that goes with the hair and which burns at the slightest sign of sun. I'm over six feet tall and to be honest, I could do with losing a couple of stone, but I enjoy my food a bit too much. I've got very large feet, size 14, and very large hands. The rumour is that big feet indicate that other anatomical parts may follow, but I can't possibly comment on that! By the way, you might think that large hands would be a disadvantage for a dentist, but I can tell you that that isn't so. In fact, we seldom actually put our fingers inside the mouth because it's all about the instruments, and, believe or not, in all my time on the job I've never been bitten!

I've been married twice. My second wife's name is Sarah. I am her first husband. We've been together for 40 years, and married for 32 of them. Sarah is nine years younger than me. She is only five feet tall and weighs practically nothing, despite seeming to eat practically everything. She's slim and very petite, which is quite the opposite of me. She's so tiny, that one of my party tricks is to put just one arm round her waist and lift her up to my height. Her hair is jet black and naturally straight, and she always wears it short, in a page-boy style (like Demi Moore in *Ghost*) which goes very well with her youthful rounded face. I love her skin, which I must admit was the first thing that attracted me to her, because it's so totally different from mine. It's always deliciously smooth and unblemished, and is of a pale olive colour, which, in the summertime, turns into a gorgeous golden brown. They say opposites attract, and that idea seems to work well for us. Sarah doesn't go out to work now, but she used to be a primary school teacher. She gave it up after having Gary, our son, who is 36 now and married to Emily. They have two children: Jack and Ava.

Well, that's enough about me and my family, but now I'd like to tell you a little bit about my secret and how it came to be.

It all started one Thursday evening in January 1999, nearly 22 years ago. It was the speech and prize-giving day at Gary's school. When I saw the event written in Sarah's bold handwriting on the calendar at the beginning of that week, I do admit to letting out a sigh, which I hoped she hadn't heard.

My dislike of school speech days probably stemmed from my own time at school, where I never really excelled at anything academic and consequently never won any prizes (although I could have won the detentions prize if there had been such a thing). Speech days therefore, meant sitting in one spot for two hours or more, listening to some boring old fart spouting on about something I had no interest in at all, and then having to endure the smug looks of the prize-winners as they trooped up on to the stage one by one to receive their bounty.

Anyway, Thursday came around all too soon, and as the evening approached I began to brace myself for the inevitable. I was, however, consoled this particular year by the fact that Gary had actually managed to win something: the first person in my entire family to do so. The prize was for physics, his favourite subject. The prize-winners' parents were always guaranteed a seat near the front for the event, so there was a double incentive to attend.

This time, I had no excuse. This time, I didn't need one. There was no way I was going to miss this proud moment. When Gary stepped onto the stage to receive his prize and shake hands with the local mayor, he suddenly looked so grown up and mature, dressed so uncharacteristically well in his grey suit and shiny shoes and with not a hair out of place. Was this the same person who normally slouched around at home wearing a scruffy, printed T-shirt and torn jeans, always with an unruly mop of hair? Seeing him there in that unique situation, I was surprised to find myself overwhelmed with pride, and for a moment, I felt quite weak, with that same warm and fuzzy feeling I get after an orgasm.

The prize-giving ceremony came and went, and once the initial congratulatory buzz had settled down, the headmaster returned to the podium. After a brief acknowledgement and suitable praise for the good work of teaching staff, he turned his attention to the guest speaker, who was introduced as Richard Grayson, whose speciality was the subject of Human Palaeontology. He had graduated from Oxford (or was it Cambridge?), followed by a doctorate in evolution at some other institution in London before becoming a professor there.

The expert, bespectacled, balding, with a small goatee beard and speaking with a strong Yorkshire accent, talked about his research into the origin of man and of the various fossil discoveries from all around the world that related to it. There were many of these, but it seemed to him and to many other experts that the most interesting and important discoveries were centred around a lake in Northern Kenya called Turkana, set slap bang in the middle of the Great Rift Valley, itself formed by constant tectonic and volcanic activity over millions of years and which was slowly and surely splitting Africa in two. Apparently, the coming and going of the waters of the lake had created ideal conditions for the formation and preservation of all sorts of animal fossils, including humans and pre-humans.

At times, the talk became quite technical, with lots of difficult scientific names that soon started to play on my very limited powers of concentration: words such as Pliocene and Pleistocene, Australopithecus and Homo habilis. I'm afraid I did what I nearly always manage to do under such circumstances: fall asleep. I tried my very best not to, knowing how annoyed Sarah would be if I did, but it was a losing battle, and I sank slowly but surely into a soporific trance of disinterest. Very soon, my drooping eyelids closed completely, enabling me to sleep peacefully through much of the talk.

I was far away, dreaming of some pleasant place on the shores of a lake, when I was suddenly brought back to life by a sharp dig in my side. It had been administered by the ever-vigilant Sarah who, conscious of my heavy breathing, was beginning to worry that I might start snoring. I sat up quickly from a slumped position and glanced sideways to see her glaring angrily at me with that same look of disapproval I had seen so many times before. I blinked a few times and stretched my eyes wide to shake off the sleep, then looked up at the stage to see what was happening. The wall clock said nine-fifty and the speaker appeared to be winding down at last.

It was his last few words that were the only ones I really remember: "Lake Turkana and the shores around it offer the most magical experience I have ever had on any of my travels around the world. The unspoilt isolation, the wildlife and the amazingly resilient inhabitants, few as they are, are really something to savour. And the blue-green waters of the lake are so strikingly coloured against the surrounding desert. This place is truly a one off. No wonder they call it the Jade Sea!"

At that point, he paused and took a moment to peer around at his audience, as if to ensure they were all paying attention. Satisfied that they were, he continued. "I promise you, if you ever get a chance to go to Turkana, you will not for a moment regret it. In fact, if you are anything like me, you will be blown away! Every time I go back there, I can't wait to get down to the water and take it all in again." He paused once more and leaned forward to rest both hands on the rostrum, surveying and capturing his audience with that same sweeping stare, before saying, "And you know something else? When I'm standing on that shoreline looking out across that huge lake, I get the most beautiful feeling that somehow, I've come home. It is little wonder to me that so many scientists believe this really *is* the birthplace of mankind!"

I'm not quite sure what it was, but something in his voice (passion, enthusiasm, soulfulness, or whatever it was) ignited a spark in me: a spark that I had seldom, if ever, felt before. I was now wide awake.

Chapter 2

The next morning at work went very slowly. As usual, I was very ably assisted by my very loyal nurse, Jodie: a very bubbly 30-year-old, who was a little on the chubby side and had shoulder-length, blonde hair which she kept in check with an Alice band. She smiled often and easily, revealing a beautiful set of naturally straight white teeth, which were not of my doing but nevertheless very good for business. Having worked with me for five years or so, she had a good feel for my moods. While she was cleaning up after the first patient, and without looking up, she said, "You seem different today. Is there something on your mind?"

I couldn't help but smile. Sometimes it seemed she knew me better than I knew myself. "You noticed!" I replied. "Yes, you're right as usual. To be honest, I think I'm ready for a holiday."

She stopped scrubbing and looked up at me with a cheeky smile on her face. "Well, go for it then, and we can both have a rest!"

I returned her smile and nodded. If I needed any encouragement at all, that was it.

That morning was much the same as any other: two or three families for check-ups, a couple of crown preps, a few fillings and then an awkward upper partial denture that took ages to fit. Busy as I was, the morning could not go quick enough, because after repeating Richard Grayson's last words over and over in my mind, I was impatient to get more information about the place he had spoken about so enthusiastically. Unusually, my morning session finished on time (I made sure of that), and I was out of the door even before the last patient had left.

My target was the library in the high street. I went straight to the travel section, took a few books down and spent the whole hour reading up. My first task was to get a fix on where the place was. The atlas showed it to be in a remote and relatively barren part of Northern Kenya, stretching up and over into the neighbouring country, Ethiopia. More reading told me that most of the human fossils had been found on the north-eastern shores and hinterland of the lake, a little way south of the border. Every article I read came up with the same conclusion as Grayson: that humanity had to start somewhere, and with so much evidence building up in its favour, this place seemed as good as any.

That lunch hour went by in a flash, and by now my brain was really buzzing as I tried desperately to assimilate all the facts. I remember shaking my head and smiling to myself as the thought occurred to me that before yesterday this kind of stuff was a long way from anything that had ever interested me. It was like history and geography all rolled into one, and I was never any good at either; probably, I reasoned, because both subjects had been taught by what I saw as very uninspiring teachers who seemed to have done their utmost to make the subject extremely boring and dull. Subjects like chemistry and biology were about witnessing a few explosions or watching earthworms and frogs being dissected. To me that was much more fun than trying to remember dates of the kings and queens of England or the capital cities of South America; places I couldn't at the time imagine I'd ever get to visit.

But now things were different. Now, I suddenly wished I knew all the capital cities not just of South America, but of Africa as well. At that moment, I decided it was time to put things right; time to do some much-needed homework.

By the time I got back to work I'd made up my mind that I simply *had* to go there and see the place that Grayson had spoken so passionately about: a place which before yesterday I had never even heard of. At that moment I made the decision that, come what may, our next family holiday would be discovering the shores of Lake Turkana for ourselves.

I couldn't wait to tell Jodie about it all. She listened attentively as I spelled out my plans for a three-week break as soon as my work schedule would allow, but even before I finished I saw that she was frowning. "What does Sarah think about it?" she asked. The question made me go cold for a moment. "I'm sure she's going to like it," I replied.

But to be truthful, I wasn't sure at all. I had to admit to myself that perhaps it was all a bit selfish. In the past, Sarah had always been up for every chance to get away, but as I thought about it more, I realised that our holidays usually involved a beach, blue sea and copious gin and tonics. This particular holiday was not going to be one of those. I could see by the frown on Jodie's face that she already knew I had a rocky road ahead. Yes, the whole adventure did seem a great idea, but my heart began to sink as I realised there was just one little problem: how was I going to convince Sarah?

Chapter 3

A lot of people are very scared of the word 'no'. I'm one of them. The thing is that 'no' is a rejection. Some people are so afraid of being rejected that they will go to any length to avoid a 'no' situation. My own theory about it is that we mistakenly think of it as a statement meaning 'I don't love you', when really it's nothing of the sort. People who have had more than enough love in their childhood are not at all scared of the word 'no', which I think makes them the ones most likely to succeed in business. The way I have come to deal with the problem is that if I have an issue that might be rejected, I go around the houses with it instead of just facing the issue head on. There's only one word I want to hear, so I invent all sorts of pathways that will eventually lead me to the door that says 'yes'.

I did not sleep at all well that night. For the first hour or so I just lay there in bed with my eyes wide open, staring into the nothingness of darkness. I was searching my mind, trying to come up with something that would make the whole idea of such an unconventional holiday seem more appealing to my wife, who was now sleeping peacefully beside me, her breathing very regular and deep. Eventually I drifted off as well, only to waken again an hour or so later. I played with my pillow to plump it up, and turned it over because it felt warm and very damp from my nervous sweat. "Must have had a nightmare," I thought, but as hard as I tried, I could remember nothing.

How strange are dreams? There's someone or something playing games right there inside our heads. Why is that? Who is that?

It seemed like a very long night. I woke at around six, still feeling tired. Daylight was beginning to creep in around the curtains. I sat up to rub the sleep out of my eyes and have a stretch and a yawn. Then, as the fuzziness began to clear, I had one of those light-bulb moments. From out of nowhere came the answer to my little problem, loud and clear, as if it had been there all the time. It probably had, but yesterday I was too stupid to see it.

I smiled to myself. It was quite obvious really. I had to offer her a carrot: a deal to encourage her to do something she really didn't want to do with the promise of something better to follow. I knew then that I'd have to do a trade. The answer was easy, but it was going to cost me. The price would be two weeks in the Maldives.

It was then that I realised that my brain, or at least some part of it, had not been asleep at all, but had been busy all night, finding me the answer to my problem. Amazing, I thought. There it is, sitting inside my head, yet even I don't know what it's up to much of the time.

Chapter 4

I came straight out with it over breakfast. Sipping at my tea, I watched Sarah shaking her usual oat cereal into a bowl. As she began to add the milk, I said: "I want to do a deal with you." She stopped pouring and looked up at me suspiciously. "What kind of a deal?" she asked. At that moment I made the decision that it would be best to use the carrot first. I took a deep breath and took hold of her hand. "How would you like to go on that holiday you're always on about?"

Her face lit up with a huge smile. "The Maldives?" she cried. "Do you really mean it?"

"Yes," I said calmly, trying hard not to show my relief. I paused and took another deep breath. "But there's a catch."

The smile disappeared and was replaced with a frown. "Okay, what's that?"

I swallowed hard. "I-I want us to go somewhere else first," I stammered, fearing the worst.

But her response completely threw me. Instead of the expected reproach, she got up from her chair, put her arms around me and then with her lips right by my ear, whispered: "And I know where that is."

"You do?" I asked.

Without giving an answer, she sat back down and fixed me with a look of amusement. There was a twinkle in her eyes: that bedroom twinkle I knew so well.

Much as the idea of unscheduled nooky attracted me, I knew it was necessary to keep up the momentum.

A session in the bedroom would be more than good, but it wasn't what I was negotiating right now. And then, just when I thought I'd blown it, she said: "Turkana! You want to go to Turkana, don't you?"

I was not ready for that. I stared at her, open-mouthed. Seeing the look of surprise on my face, she started to laugh. "Funnily enough, so do I," she said. "And don't worry about the Maldives just yet. They can wait for a year or two."

I can't quite explain the feeling I had at that moment. It was a strange mixture of complete surprise, overwhelming joy and immense relief, all rolled into one. I leaped from my chair, nearly tipping it up in my haste to give her a hug. I could still hardly believe it. "Do you really mean it?" I asked again.

"Yes!" she assured. "Of course I mean it. I've known all along what you wanted to do, because you keep talking about it. I knew that sooner or later you'd bring it up, and anyway, after that speech day I got hooked, the same as you. It'll be fun doing something completely different for a change!"

"I thought you liked sun, sea and s—"

"Yes, I do," she interrupted, "but you can have too much of a good thing, and anyway, we can take Gary with us. I think he'll enjoy the adventure. You know how bored he gets on those beach holidays."

I went off to work that morning on a high such as I hadn't known for ages. Suddenly, the world seemed like a different place, and as I skipped along to the station that morning, I found myself smiling at anyone and everyone, most of them returning my efforts with the dispassionate stares one might give a madman.

Chapter 5

Quite a big slice of a holiday in prospect is the planning of it and the anticipation of the excitement to come. This one was certainly no exception, with the added bonus of a huge element of uncertainty. We knew right from the outset that this would be an adventure quite unlike anything we had ever done before. Most of our previous holidays had been arranged while sitting in front of a travel agent's desk, discussing various points, such as would four hotel stars be good enough, how far it was from the beach, which seats on the plane were best for my long legs, etc.

But this time, none of the travel agents we approached had packages such as the one we were contemplating. This time we were going to have to plan it all by ourselves, but with the prospect of Gary's next lot of exams coming up in May, we knew we had time on our side. There was no way we could go away before the end of July, so we had more than six months after the coming Christmas to plan things out and get used to the idea of travelling to somewhere so different.

Sarah's birthday is on 14 February, Valentine's Day. That coincidence was a very good bonus for me, because it makes the occasion very hard to forget. That particular birthday was extra special, because it was her fiftieth. I suspect that men can probably deal with reaching that age a lot more easily than women can. I may be wrong, but at the same time, I realised that it would be very important to buy her the right present: one that would give her something to look forward to and help to show that there is a life after 50.

Her birthstone is Amethyst, and most years I've resorted to buying her a piece of such jewellery as an easy (if somewhat expensive) answer to the gift problem. I've begun to notice, though, that she hardly ever wears Amethyst when we dress up, or on any other occasion for that matter, so this year I decided it was time to break the habit and use a bit of lateral thinking.

It didn't take long to come up with the answer. With the prospect of a special holiday in mind, and also having overheard her talking about the subject with our technophile son, I decided that one of these new-fangled digital cameras would be the way to go. Nowadays, digital cameras are everywhere, with almost everyone owning one (whether in a mobile phone or as an actual camera) but back then, in 1999, digital cameras were very much a new novelty, and also very expensive. They were not nearly as sophisticated as they are now, and consequently still viewed with a degree of suspicion by some, if not most.

So, I splashed out and bought a Nikon Coolpix 700, which was pretty much state of the art for such a thing in those days. I can't remember how much I paid for it, but I do remember thinking that a nice Amethyst necklace would have been much cheaper.

She was absolutely delighted with it! I remember holding my breath as I watched her tearing open the birthday wrapping paper, scared that once again I had done the wrong thing. But I needn't have worried. When she saw the large bold print on the box, revealing the contents, she let out the loudest whoop of joy I've ever heard from her (and that includes from the bedroom).

We, of course, had a family get together that day; probably around 14 of us altogether, including a few friends and her sister's family. It didn't take Sarah long to get that camera working, and she seemed to be snapping every time I looked. Even though I knew roughly how it worked, I still hadn't got used to the idea that there wasn't any expensive film inside being used up. There was, however, a memory card for storage, which only held eight megabytes, enough for about 12 or so photos, so it soon became apparent that only the best pictures could be saved before another card had to be installed. Luckily, I had thought to include a couple of replacement cards, so there were plenty of good photos that day.

That camera was built like a brick, and was almost as heavy, but we both agreed it was going to be a great asset to take on our trip. I made a mental note there and then to stock up on a few more of those memory cards. I had a feeling we were going to need them.

Chapter 6

One big concern about exploring new places, particularly somewhere in the tropics such as Kenya, is health. Endemic to these regions are all sorts of nasty microorganisms and parasites, which can't survive in the colder climates such as ours. Sarah had taken it upon herself to carry out a thorough search of what diseases we needed to protect ourselves against. The list was frighteningly long: hepatitis A and B, rabies, typhoid, yellow fever, etc. I can't remember exactly which ones we finally decided to get cover for, because the potential risk level goes up and down depending on area and seasonal factors, such as rainfall, etc., but there were at least two lots of injections for each of us (for which I had to pay a not inconsiderable amount), and we were also stocked up with antimalarial tablets, to help guard against the biggest killer of all.

We had arranged the flight for the last week in July. Not really the best time to travel if you have any choice because, with the UK academic year finishing then, everyone has the same idea and the prices seem to magically treble overnight.

Our early morning eight-hour flight from Heathrow finally landed at Nairobi just as the sun was beginning to disappear over the horizon. We were booked in at a place called The Safari Park Hotel. I chose it because the name seemed appropriate, but also because it was on the north side of Nairobi and near to the main A2 road, which headed out of town towards Thika, in the direction we wanted to go

That first evening, after checking in and settling into our rooms, we went down for dinner at the very well appointed restaurant. Gary was both relieved and delighted to find that most items on the menu were recognisable to him, including a list of hamburgers, one of which he chose for himself. I think Sarah had fish of some sort, and I had an amazingly succulent steak. After the meal, there was a floor show featuring dances and displays by a local African tribe. Very exhilarating and very noisy! We slept well that night. It had been a very long and tiring day.

The next morning, we were taken on a pre-booked tour of Nairobi, taking us past the main sights in town and included stops at a couple of museums which gave us the chance to get a brief insight into Kenyan culture. After a break for lunch, we were taken to a place called Bomas of Kenya, which is a cultural centre presenting the different features of Kenyan lifestyle. There was a large auditorium where we heard more tribal songs accompanied by dancing, during which we were invited to take part. I felt a bit like a fish out of water, but no doubt the locals were used to seeing ungainly European bodies making themselves look just a bit ridiculous. There were also some spectacular acrobatic displays to round the afternoon off.

This brief taste of Kenyan lifestyle and culture convinced us that we must come back at some later date and explore Nairobi in more depth, but for now, we were more concerned with concentrating our minds on the adventure ahead. An early night was called for.

Chapter 7

We had found a tour company that hired out vehicles and drivers who could act as guides. Loaded up with luggage, we took an early morning taxi to the depot. Sitting in front of the main office was a Land Rover, which appeared to be fully loaded and all set up and ready. Polishing the windscreen was an African man who, as we approached, stopped what he was doing and came over to greet us. He had a broad smile on his face. "Hello, folks." He said, in a strong local accent. "My name is Joseph. You must be Mister and Missus Russell?" I nodded and shook his outstretched hand, before introducing Sarah and Gary.

I liked Joseph almost as soon as I met him. He seemed to have a naturally cheerful demeanour, and he had greeted us with the warmest of smiles, somehow not self-conscious of a missing front tooth spoiling an otherwise perfect occlusion (as we dentists would say). I also noticed that his teeth bore signs of that same patchy yellow mottling I had seen in other Africans at the airport, telling me that there were water supplies somewhere in this country that must have contained excess amounts of natural fluoride.

"Welcome to Kenya!" he added. It was then that his smile disappeared, to be replaced by a look of puzzlement. "So, you really want to go to Turkana, eh?" He said, frowning. "You know, that's very unusual. Not many people wanna go up that way. They only ever seem to wanna go to the big game reserves that they've seen on TV or in the movies."

Suddenly, I felt sick. At this stage of the game, those words were not the ones I wanted to hear. "I gotta tell you now that Turkana is very different from all those other places," he said. "It's not like the rest of Kenya. There's not so many animals and it's very dry and barren, and there's no swimming pool or TV like you get in those big hotels. Are you sure you've done your homework?"

The words sent a chill down my spine, but I tried not to show my concern as I glanced back at the other two. From the doubtful looks on their faces, I knew they were thinking the same thing. Was it all a big mistake? If it was, then this was the time to pull out and go somewhere else; somewhere all the other tourists go.

I opened my mouth to try and say something positive, but Joseph beat me to it.

"They don't know what they're missing," he remarked with a smile.

"Who don't?" I asked.

"Those other tourist sheep: they just wanna stay in the flock and be safe, but you know, they're all really missing something. I really love going to Turkana!"

"You don't know how glad I am you said that!" I said, trying really hard not to sound too relieved.

"No, really, I think it's a very good choice! I think we're gonna have a really good time up there!"

"I hope so," I replied.

"Oh yes, sir, we will," assured Joseph. "Trust me; there's no place on Earth quite like Turkana!"

Those words were like music to my ears, dispersing a cloud of uncertainty that had been bothering me all along. At last there was something to smile about. Maybe this wasn't such a crazy idea after all. I let out a chuckle and grinned back at Joseph. "Well in that case," I said, "let's get going!"

Watching Joseph move around the vehicle, carrying out the last-minute checks, I had the chance to study him closer. He was of average height but a little overweight, with a slight paunch, which hung over his belt. But he had sturdy, muscular arms and a strong grip, which I had already experienced with that first handshake. His wiry hair, which was cut short, had the slightest hint of grey at the sides and was receding at the temples. To go with it, he sported a neatly trimmed moustache, balanced by a close-cropped beard. He wore a red football shirt with the universally recognised Manchester United badge, emblazoned with the number seven and the name 'Beckham' on the back. Plenty of opportunity for discussion later, I thought. Already, with his easy confident manner, Joseph was beginning to instil a sense of trust. He seemed to smile at every little thing, and he hummed quietly to himself almost constantly as he went about his business.

Having satisfied myself about Joseph, I thought it a good chance to check out the vehicle we were going to spend the next three weeks relying on.

The Land Rover was by no means new. In fact, it looked more like it had been around the world a few times. The bodywork showed signs of previous close encounters and was liberally scarred with minor dents and scrapes, but all the tyres looked good, and the engine, which Joseph had left running for the air conditioning, sounded very sweet to my untrained ear. I opened the tailgate door to start packing our luggage and was immediately shocked to find that there was very little spare room. It was already loaded with the full safari package: camping equipment, water and fuel canisters, first aid, etc. There was even a flare gun, which I could not, at this stage in the proceedings, imagine a use for. There were two spare wheels, one bolted to the tailgate and the other carried as luggage. Sarah had come over to join my inspection and I glanced back at her, pulling one of my impending doom faces as I pointed first to our luggage and then to the boot. For a moment, I thought I saw a look of horror on her face, but then true to form, she started to laugh. "I'll just have to unpack a few essentials," she joked, "like the hair dryer and my three sets of high heels. Don't worry, Jim. We can do it."

That's another thing that I find so attractive about my wife. She never makes a mountain out of a molehill. If there's an issue to be resolved, she always seems to find a shortcut to the answer; a quality that I've never been able to master for myself. I get there in the end, but it always seems to be by the long way round.

Anyway, we had a good sort-out of our belongings to decide what was essential and what was not, and the final result meant that we could only take about a third of what we had turned up with. We left two whole suitcases with the girl in the office and loaded the Land Rover with just one collapsible holdall for all three of us.

Hopefully Joseph would turn out to be a better driver than the one we had yesterday. That 40-minute journey from the airport to the hotel had been like nothing we had ever experienced before. The 12-seater transit bus had been driven by a very skinny and very young-looking African man who, for most of the journey, had only one hand on the wheel, the other being used to hold his mobile phone up to his ear while he had what seemed to be a very heated argument with someone on the other end. I had no idea what was being said, as the language was not one I recognised (probably Swahili), but from the level of discordant emotion involved I assumed that the other party had to be a wife or lover.

Then there were the Matutu buses. These things seemed to be everywhere. They were privately run and quite illegal but judging by their numbers it was obvious that a small thing like the law didn't stop them. After all, this was the only form of transport that most working locals could afford. Matutu buses came in all shapes and sizes, from neat 12-seaters to poorly converted pickup trucks. They were usually grossly overloaded, to the extent that they often became unstable on cornering, and it was not unusual to see the aftermath of a too-close encounter when goods, or even passengers, spilled out on to the road; such events added even more chaos to the already manic traffic. Despite all of this, our party had arrived at the hotel in one piece, and the only real signs of the ordeal were the sweat marks on my T-shirt.

After one final double check on our belongings, we climbed into the Land Rover and settled into our seats. I took the co-pilot's front seat, along with a couple of maps and my own conventional camera, while Sarah, armed with a book and two bottles of water, sat herself behind Joseph. Gary had already made it clear that it didn't matter where he sat, as long as he had his games console and earphones to hand.

We headed north out of Nairobi on the Thika Road, now very busy with the early morning rush-hour traffic.

As in any other big city, there were vehicles of all ages, shapes and sizes; a myriad of trucks and vans competed for space with all manner of two-wheeled vehicles, from motorbikes to mopeds, down to plain and simple pushbikes.

And everywhere there was noise: grinding gears and squealing brakes accompanied by a constant cacophony of hooters, sounded either as a warning of presence or just as a signal of aggression. And then, of course, there were those Matutu buses again, all crammed full because this was rush hour. Those who could not afford the fare (and there were many of them) were on foot, forming a straggling, broken, thin line along the side of the highway, heading towards the factories and warehouses up ahead.

The Kenyan sky was as blue as ever, and the sun was already climbing. To get a better look at it, I fought off my seat belt and peered up through the windscreen. I remember smiling to myself as I saw there was not one cloud in the sky; so very different from the grey skies and drizzle we had left behind in England.

This unaccustomed heat was making me sweat already. I dried my leaking forehead with a tissue from the dashboard and glanced across at Joseph, who seemed to be showing no signs of discomfort at all. He saw me looking at him and started to smile. "Hope you're not feeling too hot already," he laughed, "cos where we're goin', it gets much hotter than this! Close the window, *bwana*, and I'll turn up the air-con." I needed no encouragement. Very soon, the warm air became a deliciously cool breeze. Screwing up my soggy tissue, I had to admit to myself that I was a temperate: an alien in these tropical parts.

With heavy traffic on both sides, I noticed that Joseph seemed to be concentrating extra hard. He started to hum, and started shifting his body around in his seat while gripping the wheel tightly as if setting himself up for a conflict.   There was a roundabout up ahead, and our clump of vehicles seemed to be in a race to get to it first. Our Land Rover was in pole position, and from the look on Joseph's face, he wanted to keep it that way. Looking round, I immediately saw why. To our right side was a huge pallet truck going much too fast for its high stacked load which Joseph had already pointed out was much too unstable. The very inadequate-looking rope tethering the cargo was badly frayed and did not seem to be doing its job at all, causing the load to shift alarmingly at every slight twitch in the road. This was definitely not a vehicle to be following.

Perhaps the truck driver knew that his load was unstable, or maybe he was just still half asleep, but whatever it was, something made him try to straighten out the curves of the roundabout by stealing a yard of the inside lane without warning, suddenly crowding us out. Aware of the danger, Joseph reacted quickly, hitting the brakes and pulling hard on his wheel, making the Land Rover lurch violently to one side and away from the truck, which continued on its chosen course as if nothing had happened. Somehow, the two vehicles emerged from the roundabout unscathed but with the truck now half a length in front. Joseph put his foot on the gas to draw level, punched the horn with his fist and shouted through his now-open window at the other driver. "*Mjinga, Mjinga*!" he screamed. "You stupid fool!" There was no response. The truck driver's eyes were firmly fixed on the road ahead, showing that he was either completely deaf or just plain guilty, and he knew it. After uttering a few more Swahili epithets through the window, Joseph settled back down to the routine.

That incident, dangerous as it might have been, made me feel good. As a passive witness to Joseph's handling of the situation, I suddenly became much more confident in his ability to see the project through. This had always been my biggest concern. How experienced was Joseph? Did he know the area well enough? How was his driving? These were critical factors when it came to the safety of my family. But now I felt so much happier.

Chapter 8

As the journey went on and the traffic outside began to thin out, there was not so much to see. I noticed that Gary had reverted back to what he usually did on long journeys: play with that infernal game machine. I went to say something, but changed my mind when I saw his fingers twitching away. I knew full well from past experience that there would be absolutely no point talking to him in this situation. There would be no response. It was as if that machine had the power to hypnotise him into a trance-like state, which only *it* could release him from.

Another 20 minutes or so went by, when suddenly there was a loud clack as Gary shut the lid down, lifting his head and uttering a deep sigh as he did so. For a few minutes, he just sat motionless, staring straight ahead at nothing in particular. "I guess you didn't win?" his mother ventured.

Gary let out a muted grunt, which said everything. After that, nobody spoke for a while. From past experience, we both knew that the best thing was just to let him be until the cloud lifted.

I know he's my son and I'm bound to be biased, but Gary was always a bright student. Despite his apparent addiction to computer games, he was performing very well at school; not only academically, but also physically. Apart from winning the physics prize, he also excelled in athletics, where, thanks (in part, at least) to the fact that he had inherited his father's height, he won the senior high jump and was only just beaten in the javelin. Already, at the age of 16, he was only a couple of inches shorter than me, and that was despite having such a tiny mother. But she did contribute to many of his other features, including his hair, which was almost as dark as hers. He wore it quite long, to the nape of his neck, and it hung over his forehead like a shiny black curtain. So long was it that he had developed a habit of flicking his head back to clear it from his eyes; bright green eyes that contrasted so vividly against that pale olive skin. Little wonder that his school friends were as many female as male.

Up until now, the steady drone of the diesel engine had been accompanied by chatter from Joseph, involving all sorts of subjects, from Kenyan politics and the economy, to various people he knew, as well as stories about his family life and his children. For a while I enjoyed listening to him, but it wasn't long before the weariness of travelling started to catch up with me and all I really wanted to do was close my eyes and drift off. I glanced back to see that Sarah had already done just that. Joseph must have noticed, because he stopped talking. Shortly after that, I dropped off. I'm not sure how long for, but I was woken abruptly as Joseph slammed his foot hard on the brake to avoid colliding with a couple of stray cattle wandering across the road. No such thing as fences in these parts.

Now I was wide awake again, thanks to the very real possibility of another similar incident happening again. I decided to use this time as a chance to think of anything we might have forgotten to bring. I was reminded of other holidays where silly little things, like

JAMES H. RUSSELL

a bottle opener or a corkscrew, could make all the difference, but not on this particular trip. On this trip it would be more useful to have something like a Swiss army knife and maybe a spare first aid kit. That thought made me sit up straight from my slouch, as I suddenly felt a pang of guilt. I remember looking back just then at the other two, Sarah dozing with her head lolling to one side and Gary back on his game once again with his earphones on and totally lost into his electronic world, and thinking what have I done? These two have both put so much faith in me, but to be truthful, I don't know any more than they do whether it's going to be endless fun or just a huge disaster. How much safer it would have been on the beach or by a swimming pool, or even a conventional safari to the Massai Mara or somewhere similar, like all the other tourists do.

Chapter 9

Our first stop was at a place called Maragua. It was at a gas station with a restaurant attached. The owner was a friend of Joseph, and the two of them joined us for lunch. For much of it they chatted away in their own language but every now and again switched to English so as to include us in the conversation. Somehow it did not seem at all rude to do that. This was, after all, their country._Our final destination for that day was a town called Nanyuki, where we stayed for the night. The road was tarmacked all the way, and by the time we arrived it was getting dark. Being so close to the equator there is almost no twilight, and the changeover from day to night seemed to happen in just a few minutes.

The last part of that journey had been quite spectacular. For much of the way, we had the magnificent sight of Mount Kenya to our right, and we could still see it from the roadside lodge that Joseph had chosen for us. He seemed to be very familiar with everyone working there and was greeted by his name at the door when we arrived.

The next morning, after a good night's sleep and a very satisfying breakfast of cereal, scrambled eggs and bacon, we set off for Maralal, which meant leaving the A2 and settling for a less comfortable road surface, but with the benefit of more to see. According to Joseph, Maralal was four hours away, but how long it would actually take depended on what caught our interest on the way.

As it turned out, the next stop was not that far ahead. A large hoarding came into view. It had the words 'Kenya' and 'Equator', printed in foot-high lettering and set over a huge silhouette of Africa, leaving us in no doubt as to where we were. Joseph pulled the Land Rover to the side and killed the engine. His passengers got out to savour this rare moment and get some souvenir photos, but before Sarah had even got her new camera out of its case, the three of us were swamped by a host of Maasai stallholders, all anxious to direct these new visitors to their respective outlets. The jostling seemed friendly enough, but Joseph, spotting the look of concern on Sarah's face, opened his window and shouted something at the Maasai in an African language that I did not understand. Whatever he said seemed to have the right effect, because they backed off and turned away. "I told them to wait until you've taken all your photos, and you'd be along in a while," he said.

I eyed Sarah, to see her reaction, and was relieved to see she was smiling. Shopping was always dear to her heart, especially with the idea of picking up a bargain. With the thought of more clutter in the already full vehicle, I wasn't too sure whether to thank Joseph or not. As it turned out, I needn't have worried, as we only came away with two strings of wooden beads and a six-inch-high, wooden carving of a giraffe.

A little while after setting off again, it started to rain; the first we'd seen since arriving in the country. Those first raindrops seemed enormous and announced themselves with audible splashing noises on the windscreen. In just a few seconds, that rhythmic pitter-patter became a torrent, forcing Joseph to set the windscreen wipers to fast and turned on the headlights. We had only gone a few kilometres further, when there was a sudden heavy thump from the nearside front.

"Pothole!" cried Joseph, snatching at the wheel to keep the vehicle on course. "Didn't see it: full of water. Made it look like a puddle." He glanced at me and smiled reassuringly. "Don't worry," he laughed. "Everything's under control. I'm used to it but I'm afraid that won't be the last. From now on, it gets worse and worse, but believe me, this machine is built like a tank. It'll take anything this road can throw at it."

I hope you're right, I thought.

After half an hour or so, the rain started to ease off. There was a patch of blue up above, but further ahead we could see more rain clouds gathering. By now, the road had gradually deteriorated from tarmac into not much more than a trail of swept gravel punctuated by occasional tennis-ball-sized stones and well-established vehicle tracks, which seemed to guide the driver into them whether he liked it or not. On either side of us were occasional clumps of low bush, interspersed with dead-looking grass and the occasional acacia tree.

So far we had been disappointed with the sparseness of wildlife, which was much less abundant than expected, but Joseph assured us that it would get better when there were fewer humans around. He was right. Before long we started to see all sorts, way out in the vast savannah lands stretching out on both sides of us. There were elephants, giraffes, three different species of zebra (before then, I'd thought there was only one) and other antelope-type creatures, which Joseph seemed to know quite well. He pointed out several with names I'd never heard of before: Topi, Dik-Dik, Eland, Thomson's gazelle, etc. One group of animals we were all surprised to see were camels: lots of them.

We soon ran into more rain, torrential at times, so Joseph decided we should stop at Maralal for the night, in a Banda, which is a wooden hut with a corrugated iron roof. We were given bedding and dry linen, but the noise of rain on the roof made for a very restless night's sleep (or, at least, it did for me!).

The rain continued for most of the night. We set off to find that the road conditions had become decidedly more treacherous, with a very slippery road surface and occasional areas of flooding which, thankfully, were not beyond the capabilities of the Land Rover. This part of the trip was through an attractive landscape of lush greenery and forest. On the way, we saw several small Maasai villages surrounded by open areas of farmland with goats and cattle.

Eventually the rain stopped, and the sky turned to blue again. We passed through a town called Baragoi, after which the going got a little better as the road (I use the term loosely) started to dry out. As we progressed, the landscape gradually began to lose its lushness, becoming the more typical African scrubland we had fixed in our minds.

Our next stop was a place called South Horr, where we also camped for the night. The terrain had changed yet again, becoming more barren and almost desert-like. From this point on we were starting to see areas of shattered volcanic rock, which Joseph told us were the remnants of ancient lava flow from a mountain way over to the east, called Kulal.

As we drove on, we could see that the volcanic outcrops were becoming larger and more and more frequent, eventually forming great fingers of solidified lava, stretching all the way down from the mountain, which stood out quite clearly above a collar of light cloud in the far distance over to our right. The sheer scale of what we were witnessing was quite breath-taking, reminding me that this whole area was once a raging cauldron of molten lava, engulfing everything in its path as it flowed inexorably downwards from the flame-spitting cauldron high above. Vast as this area was, it was only a very small part of the Great Rift Valley, a huge north-south seismic split in the Earth's surface dotted with many volcanoes, many of them still active, but others, like Kulal, dormant for millions of years.

Chapter 10

Our final part of the journey was through the Chalbi Desert. By this time, I think we had all had enough for one day. There was a strong wind blowing, creating mini twisters which whipped up the loose sandy soil, forming miniature clouds of fine dust, which started to find its way into the cabin. I could feel the grit between my teeth, and it was getting up my nose, making me sneeze.

We finally came upon our goal: Lake Turkana. Gary spotted it first and cried out, probably with relief as much as anything. Seeing it for the first time was probably one of the most dramatic experiences of my whole life. It was like nowhere I had ever seen before. Yes, just as Grayson had said, the water was a stunning shade of pale green, a vivid contrast to the barren desert landscape surrounding it. I could see now why they called it the Jade Sea. That first sight simply took my breath away, just as Grayson had said it would.

We were about a hundred metres or so from the shore, when Joseph brought the Land Rover to a stop and suggested we just sit there for a while to take in the view. It was a good idea. Standing back a little from any great piece of art can give one a different perspective, and here was no exception. If we had gone right down to the water's edge I think we would have missed the chance to appreciate the interplay between the uniquely coloured water and that strange, apocalyptic landscape of blown sand, scattered at intervals with mounds of pumice. And all around us we could see the fingers of that ancient lava field, spreading right down to the water's edge. If it were not for the presence of water we could have been forgiven for thinking that we'd just landed on the moon. Entranced by that unique and magnificent scenery, we decided to stay put in the Land Rover, just to stare out through the windscreen and soak it all in.

But eventually, after having our fill for an hour or so, we decided it was time to head off and get to our destination before dark. Our goal was the village of Loiyangalani, which turned out to be not more than a well-established oasis, formed around a freshwater spring (a very precious commodity in these parts), the source of which was the mountainous area of Kulal, whose peaks we could see quite clearly against the blue sky away over to the east. Joseph told me later that Loiyangalani was the only real settlement on the eastern shore of the lake, which told me something of what we might expect if we decided to venture further north.

We stayed at the Palm Shade campsite, just outside Loiyangalani. It had been a scorching hot day, and discovering that the site had the unexpected luxury of a swimming pool, we took full and immediate advantage of it. Setting up the camp could wait for an hour or two.

The people of Loiyangalani were very friendly. The women were dressed in a very distinctive way, which was apparently quite unique to this region. Their garments were made from animal skins, beaten and treated somehow to make them softer. Many of the women wore brightly coloured beading, often worn on close fitting hoops arranged in groups around their necks, and their hair was styled into tightly woven dreadlocks, dyed with henna, with a goatee-style plug on the lower lip.

Most of the villagers appeared to live in small rounded huts, almost ball-shaped and just about high enough to stand in. They were wooden framed and covered with varying types of broad-leaved plants, to protect from the very harsh (as we were quickly discovering) elements of sun, wind and, presumably, occasional rain.

Turkana is the largest desert lake in the world. It is about180 miles long, from north to south, and about 20 miles across. It is apparently quite salty, and is inhabited by something like 25,000 Nile crocodiles, so not a great place to go swimming, except in very shallow areas where the crocs don't go. It is also well endowed with fish, particularly the huge Nile perch and shoals of tilapia, which are the main catch of the area. Out in the middle of this part of the lake, there is an island inhabited by a people called the El Molo, who hold the distinction of being the smallest tribe in the world. There are about 300 of them, I believe.

The following day, we asked a local fisherman to take us out to get a closer look. We had planned not to land on the island, but just to circumnavigate it and get a feel of the area, but there was a strong and very hot wind blowing, tossing the boat around so much that Gary threw up, much to our fisherman friend's amusement. So we decided to call it a day, and asked him to head back. We spent the rest of that afternoon by the pool, under the welcome shade of a palm tree.

Chapter 11

During dinner that evening, we decided between us that it was time for a change of plan. As much as we had enjoyed our first experience of Turkana, with its dramatic and quite unique scenery, there were other aspects of it that we were having a lot of trouble adjusting to. Maybe we were just unlucky, but since we'd arrived, the temperature had stayed over 40 degrees for much of the day, which was uncomfortable enough, but the worst offender was the very hot wind that blew in almost constantly from across the lake. There were also many swarms of irritating flies to add to the mix. Even Joseph had to agree that the conditions were not too pleasant.

Having made the decision to pack up and move on, the next question was to where. I'd always had it in my mind that we would venture quite a bit further north and perhaps find out more about fossil hunting. After all, the area of North-East Turkana was world famous for it, and presumably that was where Richard Grayson would have based himself.

As I started to talk about my idea, I saw Joseph shaking his head. "I don't think that's a good idea, boss," he said. "The road is not good, especially if it rains, and if you think it's hot here, well I can tell you it'll be a whole lot worse up there. Also there are hardly any campsites and things like that."

Disappointed with his response, I felt I had to put up a challenge of some sort.

"Well, how do all those fossil-seekers and palaeontologists get on then?"

Joseph smiled knowingly. "Most of them fly," he said. "There are one or two small airstrips along the way."

"Of course!" I replied. "Why didn't I realise that?"

"There must be other things we can do?" Sarah said.

Up until now, Gary, still playing on his game and with one ear on the conversation, looked up at me and spoke for the first time. "It's too dry and hot here," he sighed. " To be honest, I don't really like it. What about going in the other direction, towards that mountain? I've heard it rains a lot more there and there are trees and stuff. Might be more fun up there. Cooler too."

I glanced quizzically across at Joseph for his opinion. "Mount Kulal," he said at once. "I think that's a much better idea. Yes, it's much wetter than here, and it's a proper rainforest up there. You can get right up near the top of the mountain. To be honest, I think it'll be more fun for you."

Gary's face lit up at once, and he shut down the lid of his game. "Let's all vote on it," he suggested.

Given all the facts, it was an easy decision, but Joseph did put a slight dampener on the evening when he mentioned that the route we'd take would be very dependent on the weather conditions.

Chapter 12

The prospect of a new adventure had brought Gary back to life. He became unusually chatty all of a sudden, asking Joseph about the journey, how long it would take, and if there was a proper campsite, etc. Eventually, Joseph started to yawn and made his excuses, leaving the three of us to discuss things further.

The change of plan had set Gary thinking. "There's something I don't understand about this fossil thing," he began. "They say that we humans probably began round here, right?"

I nodded. "So the theory goes," I replied.

"And before that, we were apes?"

"Well, not exactly. In fact, I don't think anybody's completely sure what we were, -something different anyway. That's what they're all trying to find out. What we do know is that the chimpanzees are our closest relatives. We share nearly all our DNA with them. More than 98 per cent."

"So we came from chimps then?"

"No, we, and chimps, came from something else. We call it a common ancestor. When the split happened, we went one way and they went the other. They carried on obeying nature's rules and stayed in the rainforest. We broke the rules, and now look!"

He looked puzzled. "But there is no rainforest around Turkana. It's all desert."

"Good thinking!" I replied, proud that he had picked up on that fact. "But what you haven't realised is that the Earth is like a living thing. It's constantly changing and moving things around. There probably was a rainforest here once, millions of years ago, but the Earth has moved on, leaving just scars behind. Apparently this lake hasn't always been here either. I saw somewhere that it's about 200,000 years old. Even much of the UK was tropical at one time."

"Okay," said Gary, "but if humans did start from round here, they would have all looked more or less the same, right? So how come we all look so different now?"

"You mean like dogs? Did you know that they all come from one common ancestor? It was the wolf."

"Wow! But they're all shapes and sizes, so how did they get to be so different from each other?"

"That's a good question, but in the case of dogs, humans have got a lot to do with it. For thousands of years, we've been playing around with them by breeding different traits in and out of them to get the features we want."

Gary was looking puzzled. "So who played around with us?"

"Nobody. We just changed to suit the environment we ended up in. Don't forget, it didn't happen overnight. It would have taken millions of years to get us like this, but underneath we're all the same: same flesh and blood, same brains."

"What made the changes then?"

"It's just a natural process called mutation. Every so often, our DNA gets altered ever so slightly. That's not always a good thing, but when it is, we get a little bit stronger and a little bit better adapted to our local environment. It happens everywhere in nature. It's called 'natural selection'."

"Yes, I know about that. We've been taught it at school. But it was all about plants and animals; our teacher didn't say too much about humans."

I smiled. "I guess that's because he might have thought it's a touchy subject for a lot of people. Skin colour and all that. Once upon a time, it was not much of an issue, because people weren't able to travel very far and everyone around them looked the same. Now it's different, but what I do know is that we're all the same underneath and just as smart as each other, given the chance."

Gary remained silent for a while. He was obviously deep in thought, which was exactly what I was hoping for.

The conversation resumed with plans for tomorrow. Our next destination was a village called Gatab, high up in the rainforest on the way to Mount Kulal, and we spent some time studying the map and trying to guess how long the journey was likely to take, before finally calling it a day.

Chapter 13

Although I was looking forward to this next part of our adventure, I was also a little sad that our visit to Turkana had been so brief. I had the feeling that we had only just scratched the surface of what could have been a very magical and quite unique experience. But for now I realised it was more important, for the sake of the other two members of my family, to keep the momentum flowing. Perhaps we would return one day and take advantage of light aircraft facilities to explore the more northerly regions of the lake, and perhaps we would even have a go at searching for fossils of our own. One day.

The next morning, eager to be on our way, we opted for a simple breakfast of cereal, fruit and coffee, and by eight, we had everything packed up and ready to go. After studying the map for some time last night, I had it in my mind that the journey of around 50 kilometres as the crow flies would take us no more than two hours. My calculations allowed for what I guessed would, even with our very rugged and dependable Land Rover, be a difficult and tortuous route through challenging pumice-strewn tracks and across the many dried-out riverbed tracks I'd noticed on the map.

When I mentioned my estimate to Joseph, his first reaction was to laugh. "I'm sorry, boss," he said. "We've just come out of the rainiest season, and most of those river beds aren't dried out at all right now. In fact, we'd get stuck in the first one we come to." Then he shook his head. "No, I'm afraid we've got to go the long way round this time. It's more than a 150 kilometres and will take us at least four hours if we're lucky!"

So instead of heading east as I had originally hoped, we headed due south, back the way we had come from Nairobi. In a way, I supposed, I was quite glad, because at least the road quality, such as it was in this area, would be more predictable, with less chance of unwelcome surprises like landslides or blocked roads.

We continued south for 60 kilometres or so, back towards the village of South Horr, but some way before there we turned left at a fork in the road and started heading east. After another hour or so I realised the we had changed direction again, because the sun, which had been almost straight ahead of us, was now almost directly behind us and the road was now heading north.

Now, for the first time, we could see the outline of Mount Kulal, with two or three of its highest peaks protruding into the blue sky through a necklace of fluffy white clouds atop a green and hilly landscape gently sloping down towards us. After the dry and barren landscape that we had become used to these past few days, this verdant panorama was a welcome sight indeed.

But there was still a way to go. So far, the terrain had promised nothing new, but now the road was starting to snake here and there as it negotiated its way through the small hillocks scattered all around. To cope with the changing conditions, Joseph reverted to both hands on the wheel, instead of just the one, and even had to drop a gear a couple of times, to deal with the gradually increasing severity of the slopes.

"Hey, there's grass over there, and it's actually green!" cried Gary, stabbing a finger excitedly out to our right. The sight of it made us all smile, because, like coming across an oasis in the desert, this was the first time we'd been so close to anything so lush since we'd first arrived at Turkana. It got better by the minute. Before long just about everything in sight was green, punctuated at intervals by ragged bushy outcrops and the occasional small tree.

A while later we came across cattle wandering across the road, telling us that there had to be people somewhere nearby. Sure enough, a little way further on, we came across two or three clearings on which were bigger versions of the round huts we had seen in the lakeside settlements. In each case the land around the huts was planted with maize, or something very similar, and there were goats tethered within wooden enclosures. Whether these were designed to keep the goats in or unwelcome predators out, I'm not sure. Probably both.

Eventually, as the road became steeper and even more bendy than before, we started to encounter much taller trees, the space between them gradually becoming less and less, until there came a point when the highest leaves were touching those of their neighbours, forming a canopy which blocked out much of the sunlight.

A short while later, we were well and truly in the rainforest, with some of the tallest trees I have ever seen. They looked kind of spooky, with their uppermost branches enveloped in mist and eerily clad with a mossy material, which hung down from them in long spidery strands.

Quite suddenly, from out of the forest darkness, we came to a clearing and much to our surprise the very first thing we saw was a church. Joseph had already anticipated our next question. "The missionaries got here first!" he said, a big smile on his face. "Welcome to Gatab!"

Chapter 14

We drove on slowly through the village, which was quite a bit larger than I had expected for such a remote area. There were dwellings of all kinds, from the usual round tribal huts to the more elaborate concrete and brick houses, indicating European involvement at some time in the past. Joseph pointed out one of the biggest of them and told us it was a former doctor's residence, but was now being used as a guest-house for the odd stray traveller that came this way. "Do you want me to stop and ask if they can put us up?" he asked.

I glanced around at the other two, wondering if they were missing their creature comforts, but saw that Gary was already shaking his head. "Oh, please no, Dad," he pleaded. "I'm getting to like sleeping in a tent under the mozzie net. It's so much fun, even if it is a bit scary listening to all those weird creature noises. If we stay in a house, it'll be like being at home again. We can do that any time." I looked across to see his mother's reaction. To my surprise she was shaking her head as well. "I agree with him," she said. "Being under canvas is what this trip's all about, so let's stick with it."

I motioned Joseph to drive on. "There are two campsites in town," he said, "but I think you'll like the furthest one more. It's nearest to the forest where we'll start our walks from." We passed through what seemed to be the central market area, with stalls and covered walkways alongside the dirt road, and then, at the furthest end of town, we came to another church. All along the route, we were greeted by waving hands and the friendly smiling faces of the people, every one of them curious to see the new visitors in town.

We finally arrived at the campsite at around two. There was nobody about, and only two or three of the sites showed signs of occupation; not so surprising, given the remoteness of the location. Joseph had already told us that the kind of people that came here were mostly adventurers and climbers, keen to tackle the various Kulal peaks. We guessed that's where they would all be right now.

Once the tents were erected and ready for the night, we zipped them up and went off to explore what there was of the village. As soon as we stepped outside the camp's gate, we were surrounded by a throng of tribespeople, who had obviously been there for some time, waiting patiently for us to appear. There were 20 of them at least, nearly all with welcoming smiles on their faces. They were a mixed bag of all sizes and ages, from infants of three or four, to old men with greying hair and beards. And each of them was carrying something he or she was hoping to sell, from strings of beads and wood carvings, to leather-strapped sandals with soles made from what looked like old motorbike tyres. One of the women, wearing a pretty set of beaded hoops around her neck, was holding a large basket of various fruits: bananas, melons, grapes and some others I did not recognise.

At that stage, we elected not to buy anything, but rather to wait until we'd seen what the rest of the village had to offer, knowing all the time that, like a flock of seagulls pecking at a nob of discarded bread, quite a few of them were going to be disappointed.

I've travelled quite a lot in my time, but I've never quite felt comfortable dealing with the enormous rift that exists between the first world and the third. And yet, at the same time, I have to say that, although these people owned little more than the clothes on their backs, they all seemed to be remarkably happy. Perhaps in our inexorable search for a utopia (yet to be revealed) we have lost something very precious along the way.

After wandering around the village market place and picking up a few souvenirs, some of them wanted and others not, but bought anyway as appeasements, we made our way back to the camp to relax for the evening.

As usual, Joseph had lit a fire, and we gathered round to watch him prepare the evening meal: seasoned strips of lean beef, which he was barbecueing. He served them up with jacket potatoes, also cooked on the fire, and green beans. After the meal was finished, we all helped clear up and used the time to discuss plans for the next day.

Chapter 15

Last night, after consulting with Joseph, we had voted to take a trek through the rainforest to the southern summit of Mount Kulal. Our trusty guide assured us that it would take not much more than four hours, maybe less if we did not dally on the way. My main concern was that, including the return journey, it meant being away from our camp for a minimum of eight hours, meaning that there would be no opportunity for a suitable rest.

In this part of the world, so near the equator, the days and nights are pretty much of equal length the whole year round, so if we wanted to be sure to get back to the camp in daylight we needed to set off not much after dawn.

We set out well before seven that morning, but not before Joseph, who must have been up well before daylight, had sorted out and filled our water bottles and prepared snacks and packed lunches for us all. We each had a small rucksack for the food and water and we all wore sturdy walking boots and long trousers to ward off unwelcome biting insects and leeches. As usual, always conscious of my very vulnerable fair skin, I had on my trusty wide-rimmed sun hat.

The forest was just a few hundred yards away and there was a well-trodden track leading straight towards it. We set off in bright sunlight but as we entered the forest it was as if a curtain had been drawn. In fact it was so dark by comparison that we had to tread carefully to avoid tripping over. But very soon, our eyes adjusted to the darkness, so much so that we realised there was not only plenty of light under those tall trees but that it felt kinder to our eyes. We no longer had to squint to block out the sun's harsh rays and it all seemed so much more natural being in there.

At the start, the going was quite easy. The track was obviously well used and there was not much in the way of annoying undergrowth to fight back. We met several villagers on the way, each of them returning with spoils from the forest, including bundles of wood, various types of berries (most of which I'd never seen before), and even strange looking mushrooms which I for one would be too scared to eat.

In sharp contrast to the desert lowlands all around, it obviously rained a lot here. We saw several miniature waterfalls, one of them quite spectacular, with a drop of at least 30 metres. The trees were the tallest I've ever seen, and every now and then we came across a massive strangler fig which had gone about its evil business of climbing up its host tree for support, growing all the while until finally enveloping its dying victim with a mass of hanging roots and branches. To human eyes, yes, this does seem evil, but in nature, it's simply the process of survival of the fittest.

Chapter 16

We had been going for about an hour, when in the undergrowth about 20 yards or so off the track, I noticed a thick clump of bushes, laden with a type of red berry I hadn't seen before. Curious to find out what it was, I suggested to the others to go on and I'd catch them up. My plan was just to break off a few branches, bag them up and check them out later back at the camp.

That was easier said than done. The undergrowth was thick and very unfriendly. Fighting my way through it, and trying my best not to tear my clothes or get badly scratched, I started to regret my decision, particularly as I remembered that this kind of environment is favoured by leeches. The mere thought of one attaching itself to my ankle and sucking my blood sent a cold shiver down my spine. Glad to be wearing my longs, I quickly checked my ankles and arms, relieved to find nothing. So far, at least, I had got away with it.

That bush turned out to be covered with sharp thorns and, with its crown of bright red berries, it reminded me a little bit of the firethorn shrubs we had in our garden back home. I spotted a particularly nice clump of berries towards the middle of the bush and leant in to tear off a branch, taking great care not to get stabbed or scratched in the process.

I don't quite remember exactly how it happened, but suddenly I realised that my walking boots were losing their grip and I'd started to slip. With only the thorny bush in front of me, there was nothing to grab onto, and the very next moment I found myself sliding directly downwards, feet first into the middle of the bush, with the thorns tearing mercilessly at my shirt and arms. And then I began to fall helplessly, straight down and into darkness.

I guess I must have hit my head on something and been knocked out for a while, because the next thing I can remember was coming round to the sound of a familiar voice calling out from somewhere above me.

"Jim! Jim! Where are you?" It was Sarah, but in my semi-conscious state I thought I was imagining it and for a moment or two the whole experience seemed very surreal. As my head started to clear I was horrified to find that my eyes were wide open, yet I could see nothing. This was a place of total darkness. It was as if I had suddenly gone blind.

Or was it something worse? Just for a brief moment, the thought crossed my mind that this was it: the blackness of the afterlife, where there would be no more light but just the sound of an angel in heaven calling out my name.

And there it was again: that sweetest of sounds. "Jim! Jim! Where are you?"

I shook my head to clear the muzziness, and listened again. That angel sounded just like Sarah. And then I heard another voice: Gary's. "Dad! Dad! Can you hear me?" Realising this time, that the voice was real, I breathed a huge sigh of relief, knowing for sure that I wasn't dead after all.

"Yes, I can hear you!" I shouted. "I'm here!"

I listened carefully, but there was no immediate response. At first I thought they hadn't heard me, but

I realise now that they were simply trying to work out where the sound had come from, because they shouted again, this time in unison. "Where?"

"Down here!" I called back, as loudly as I could.

Once again, there was a puzzled silence, then came another shout from Gary. "I've got your hat here. It was stuck in a bush."

I felt the top of my head, and it was only then that I realised my precious hat was not where it should be. I also felt a very large and tender bump, which had developed over my left temple. "That means you must be right above me," I shouted. "But don't go too near that bush again. I think there must be a hole underneath it. That's where I am."

"Oh Jim, how far down are you?" It was Sarah, sounding very anxious. "Have you hurt yourself?"

"No, sweetheart, I'm fine," I lied. "I've no idea how far down I am. It's totally dark down here. All I know is that you don't sound too far away, maybe 30 feet or so?"

"Oh no!" she cried. "If you've fallen that far, you must have broken something."

With an ache coming from almost every part of my body, I wasn't at all sure about that, so I used that moment to check, feeling all over for any new lumps or projections, but there was nothing, except that the skin on my arms felt warm and sticky. Blood, I realised. Probably scratches from that wretched bush. I cautiously flexed each of my ankles and wrists in turn, relieved to find everything working and, with no real pain, I guessed I had got away with it.

With everything apparently intact, I guessed something must have broken my fall. It was then that

I realised that I was lying in a body shaped depression on was a bed of some sort of loose granular material. It was coarse and sandy in texture, probably powdered pumice. Unsure of my surroundings, I remained where I was, lying down with my arms and legs stretched out.

I felt out around me but there was nothing solid to hold onto just that sandy gravel, which to one side felt as if it was sloping downhill away from me. I thanked my lucky stars that I had landed there and not two or three feet further across, where I would have gone rolling down into who knows what.

From somewhere down below I could hear the steady trickle of water, probably from an underground stream. Maybe there was an underground lake down there, into which I could have fallen. I might have drowned.

"Don't worry, darling," I called. "There's nothing broken; just a few scratches, I had a soft landing, so I'm alright. My only problem is getting out of here!" *Very soon, I hoped.*

I'm not normally scared of the dark, but right now I was beginning to find the complete lack of light very disturbing. Usually, even in the middle of the night, there was always some tiny source of light in the house, whether it was the LED on the TV or just from the moon, but no light at all is a very weird experience.

"Don't worry, Mistah James, we'll get you out!" came a call. It was the welcome voice of Joseph, who had now obviously caught up after searching elsewhere. "The only thing is, I'll have to go back to camp and get some rope so we can pull you up. I'll be back as quick as I can."

"Yes please, Joseph!" I shouted, trying my best to sound calm. "And bring a torch!"

Aware that I was going to be holed up there for at least an hour, I told myself that despite my new-found fear of total darkness, I was going to have to remain not only completely calm but also completely still. I was fully aware that until I could see something of my surroundings it would be very foolish, not to mention dangerous, to move at all. I had no idea how deep this cave might be and the further down I went the harder it might be to get rescued. I also had the feeling that too much movement on this unstable surface might start a landslide and take me with it. Drowning or being buried alive were not ways I particularly wanted to end my days.

So I remained very still. The idea of such horrible ways to die brought me out in a cold sweat and I started to shiver. I took a deep breath and reminded myself that right now my only real enemy was negative thought. Deal with that, Jim, and you've got no problem.

I remained there, resting back on my elbows with my legs splayed out. It was quite comfortable really, and reminded me of childhood holidays down on the pebbly beach at Brighton. I would sit there wearing my bathers and with my feet in the water, an ice cream in one hand and throwing pebbles at the incoming waves with the other. This little trick of meditation worked wonders to calm me down. In that totally dark place I managed to conjure up a world of sunshine and serenity, so real at that moment and yet it was all inside my head.

Every now and then there came a call from the anxious two waiting it out up above, but the effort of shouting made the three of us realise it was not possible to carry out a proper conversation so we ended up just shouting "okay" from time to time, either as a question or an answer. All we needed was confirmation.

Chapter 17

I'm not sure how long we had to wait but to me it felt like forever, so that first sound of Joseph's voice breaking the silence was a very welcome sound indeed. A short while later there were scuffling noises, followed soon after by snipping sounds, which I assumed were from Joseph clearing away some of that very unfriendly bush. It was then that I got my first welcome glimpse of daylight. It was no more than a glimmer, but enough to show me the way out of there.

A few moments later I was startled by a beam of light, so strong that I put up a hand to shield my eyes from it. I quickly realised that it was from a torch that Joseph had tied to a rope which he was now starting to feed down through the gap.

"Can you see anything, boss?" he called.

With my eyes gradually adapting to the torchlight, I watched as the rope descended, the torch swinging from side to side and casting weird shadowy shapes on the cave walls.

"That's great, Joseph," I cried. "Keep it coming. You've got another 10 feet or so to go."

The torch was heading pretty much straight down towards me and I hardly had to move to grab it. Joseph had secured it to the rope with a length of string. I reached out, took hold of it and then started to fumble around for the knot with hands that were shaking so badly that, as the torch came free, I nearly dropped it, snatching out desperately to grab it as it started to fall.

With the torch clutched safely in my hand, I quickly shone it around, impatient to get a first proper look at my surroundings. Now, for the first time, I could see how far down I was: about 20 feet or so from the opening. As I shone the beam around, I could see that this place was like a split in the earth: long and narrow up above, with its two walls flaring gradually apart until at my level it was about 10 feet wide. Looking down, I could see that the lower half of the cave was occupied with more of the same pumice shale that I was lying on and which had thankfully broken my fall. There was no sign of the water I could hear trickling, so I guessed there must be a stream some way down there under the pumice.

My only thought now was to get out of this place. I very carefully got to my feet, at once creating a mini landslide which, if I hadn't frozen still right then, might have easily escalated into an avalanche which I'm sure would have taken me all the way down to the bottom. I stood there motionless while I considered my options.

The next problem was how to use the rope. In my younger days, I would have thought nothing of grabbing it and just using the strength in my arms and legs to work my way up it monkey fashion like we used to do in the school gym, but now, after giving the same technique a brief go, I realised my power-to-weight ratio had shifted downwards just that little too much.

I called out to Joseph. "I can't climb it, I'm just not strong enough. You're going to have to pull me out somehow."

"Don't worry, boss. We can do it!" came the response. "Don't forget that there are three of us up here, and I can see your son's got some muscles! Make a loop to put your foot in and wrap some rope round your waist with a knot, and we'll do the rest."

With that he let down more rope, and I did what he asked, but with a double loop for luck. I tucked the torch into my belt, then reached up and gripped the rope tightly, using both hands.

"I'm all set!" I called. "Start pulling!"

They were obviously ready, because in the next moment the slack went out of the rope and I braced myself for what was to come. At first there was no movement at all, and I watched with bated breath as the tension built up in the rope, fearing that perhaps it would snap even before taking my full weight, sending me crashing down to the bottom. But I needn't have worried, because in the very next second, my feet left the pumice and with a slight jerk, I started to rise. I'd gone up about two feet when I came to a halt again. There was a slight pause, then I went up another two feet. I learnt later that they had adopted the tug-of-war technique and were raising me in jerks at the count of three. It worked perfectly. As I hung free in the middle of that chamber, and probably due to the twist in the rope, I started to spin slowly, the light from the torch casting shadowy outlines of my body onto the walls on either side.

It was only then that I noticed something odd about the cave. On one side, the wall was quite rough and pitted with the irregular blow holes that are a well-known feature of volcanic rock, but on the other side there was an area that seemed unusually even and smooth, almost shiny, like the water-worn granite stone I had seen many times on my walks through the Peak

District of Derbyshire. Swinging around as I was, I did not get a second chance to look at it because just then my left shoulder knocked painfully into a rocky abutment, which the rope was sliding over.

And then I saw it: the first welcome beam of daylight, lighting up the rope ahead of me as it passed over a promontory and into a short sloping tunnel, not much wider than my shoulders. I realised then that I must have originally slid down this slope a little way before plunging straight down.

"Stop pulling for a minute!" I shouted, planting both hands on the rock in front of me. "I need to adjust myself." I figured out that to avoid getting ripped to shreds on this last bit, I'd have to keep my body away from the side by using my hands and arms in walking mode. Once set, I gave the okay, and with a couple of more pulls my head was free. At that same moment I was set upon by three pairs of helping hands and dragged unceremoniously to safety.

Squinting to protect my eyes from the unaccustomed daylight, I hugged each of them in turn, aware from their heavy breathing that they had all been working very hard to get me out of that awful place, which without their efforts could so easily have become my tomb.

"Look at the state of you!" said Sarah eventually. "You're covered in blood and scratches!"

How I looked was the last thing on my mind, but she was right. My clothes were torn. Several areas of my body and limbs were coated with congealed blood, and yes, there were scratches everywhere, which, with nothing else to worry about, were for the first time making their presence felt. On top of that I had a splitting headache, a result, no doubt, of that very tender bump on the side of my head.

Needless to say we all decided it would be best not to go any further that day. For one thing this little incident had used up most of the morning, which meant we could not possibly make it to Kulal and get back to the camp before dark, and for another thing we were all very tired, not just physically but mentally as well.

But before we left I had another look at the hole, now much more visible thanks to Joseph's gardening efforts. It was not much more than two feet across and was obscured by the overhang of that wretched bush. No wonder I hadn't seen it. Remembering that I hadn't seen any evidence of plant or animal life down there, my guess was that my weight was the last straw needed to complete the break through, begun in the first instant by the constant erosion from the very frequent episodes of torrential tropical rain.

Back at the camp, my first thought was to have a shower. Blood washes off best with cold water and to use that was no hardship at all in this tropical environment, in fact it was quite soothing. There were only two or three deep scratches warranting a plaster, and once Sarah had sorted that out for me and produced a couple of paracetamols for my headache I felt a whole lot better.

Feeling exhausted (both mentally and physically) by this unforeseen adventure, I decided the best thing was to have a lie down and maybe get some sleep.

Chapter 18

I must have dropped off pretty much straightaway and I think I slept for a couple of hours or more because when I woke up it was already dark outside. For a minute or two I thought it was morning but the sound of chatting just outside the tent made me realise that it was still only evening. Still feeling very achy from my earlier ordeal, I climbed very carefully down from the bed and pulled on my trousers, moving very gingerly so as to test all moving parts. I lifted up the tent flap and saw Sarah and Gary sitting together playing a card game while watching Joseph as he leaned over the campfire, busily stirring something in a large cooking pot. It turned out to be yet another beef stew, the same one he'd made two or three times before, but we didn't mind at all, because it was so delicious.

As you might expect, the rest of the evening was spent talking about the events of the day and how lucky I was to be sitting there with them. I quickly turned that idea around by saying that it was more a question of bad luck that I'd managed to find that hole in the first place. If I hadn't done that, I argued, I wouldn't be covered with all these scratches and bruises and we'd have got to where we were supposed to be going: Kulal. It reminded me of those Chilean miners who were trapped underground for so many days, and when finally rescued, made a point of thanking God for saving them; but I noticed that they failed to curse him for putting them there in the first place.

We all agreed that it was no real problem and that we'd try again, but not tomorrow. Best to give my battle-torn body a rest. After dinner we helped Joseph clear up then played a few more card games before settling down for the night. It took me quite a while to get off to sleep, partly due to the tenderness in my body which prevented me from finding a totally comfortable position and partly due to the fact that I'd already had some shut-eye earlier.

I've read or heard somewhere that the average person has around a dozen dreams every night. I never really believed that because most mornings I wake up not remembering anything at all about having dreams, but if those experts are right then I guess I must do. On the odd occasion when I do remember a dream it's usually because of a call from my bladder or very occasionally the alarm clock (if I hadn't already woken up). Even then I find it very difficult to remember much of the action. The harder I try to recall a dream, the more it seems to slip away. It feels to me a bit like trying to catch the tail of some sort of serpent as it slithers away down into its hidey-hole. Strange really. It's as if there's stuff going on inside my head that I'm not supposed to know about: something I don't understand but which is trying to control me in some way.

But every so often there's that other type of dream: the one that actually wants me to know about it and forces me to wake up and listen. I think we must have those when we are particularly worried about some unfinished business or other. I suspect that these are the kind of dreams the psychologists love to analyse and try to give meanings to.

I had one of those that night. It was about midnight I suppose, -about two hours after I'd fallen asleep. I woke up with a jolt, suddenly wide awake. It was so unexpected that for a moment or two I just lay there listening for any unusual noises that might have disturbed my sleep. But there was nothing. Even my bladder felt comfortable. The only sound was Sarah's deep and regular breathing, telling me she was well away. I felt very hot and sticky all over and my bedsheet was soaked with sweat. I threw it off and sat up to try and cool down. That was when I realised I had not only been dreaming, but for once I could still see all of it, so vividly and clearly, and this time the dream had stayed with me. This time there was no serpent's tail.

I was back in the rainforest with a group of people I did not recognise, and then for some strange reason, I discovered that I could fly. Just by flapping my arms, I could take off, float along up in the trees and just stop whenever I wanted, hovering still, like a humming bird. The people were all just standing there below, watching me in amazement, but nobody tried to copy me, and I realised that I was the only one who could do it. I laughed at them and flew off. The next thing I came across was that bush with the berries, and I dropped down to inspect it. As I got nearer to it, the branches parted, exposing a large hole in the ground, which I flew straight into. I was in a cave again, but this one was different. It was huge, bigger than a football stadium, and filled with so much daylight that I could see everything around me quite clearly.

The funny thing about dreams is that they can create worlds and situations that seem to be beyond our imagination, appearing briefly from the dark side with images our conscious minds would never entertain. It's as if we are constantly being manipulated by some mysterious entity living within us, controlling everything we think and do. We even use the expression "not in my wildest dreams" to describe a bizarre situation or event. I was having one of those wildest dreams right then.

As I flew around in the clouds at the top of the cave, I looked down and saw far below me a tiny stone thatched cottage: the type I'd seen so many times before up in the Cotswold Hills of England. It was sitting all alone in a huge field of green grass. By the front door, there was an old man sitting on a bench, smoking a pipe. He looked up, and when he saw me flying high in the sky above, he immediately stood up and started waving at me, frantically beckoning me to come down and join him. It was as if he had something very important to tell me. Curious and excited at the same time, I started to head down towards him, but as I did so I began to realise that I was beginning to lose the power to fly. Suddenly my dream had turned into a nightmare. I was falling, faster and faster, straight towards the ground below, and to certain death. I tried to scream but there was no sound. Then I woke up.

I sat up there for a while, allowing the sweat to evaporate and cool me off while I re-enacted the dream in my head a few times, trying to guess what it meant. What had that old man wanted to tell me so urgently? Was it something really important, or was it just a silly little trick my subconscious mind was playing on me?

I sat up for more than half an hour, playing that dream back a few more times and trying to work out some meaning but, getting nowhere, I just gave up and went back to sleep.

Chapter 19

After what seemed like just a few minutes I was awake again, but this time there was no sweat and there had been no dream either as far as I was aware. I fumbled around for the torch and checked my watch. It showed 4.30am, which meant that I'd been out for about two hours. I shone the beam towards Sarah, careful not to point it directly at her face. She was still sleeping very peacefully. I then got to my feet and unzipped the tent flap to peer outside.

There was an early crescent moon, horns facing upwards as is usual for this part of the world. It seemed so bright against the blackness of the sky beyond, filled with more stars than I'd ever seen before in those murky skies over London.

As I stood there staring up at this wondrous sight, I thought again about the dream and what it might mean. I already understood that the old man was nothing more than a tool my brain was using to remind me of something, but what? And then it suddenly came to me: it was that wall I'd seen out of the corner of my eye, oddly smooth and rounded and totally out of place in a situation like that. Recalling it clearly for that first time sent a shiver down my spine. I knew then what the dream was trying to tell me: that I would just have to go back there and take another look.

Throughout my life, I've always been very impetuous and not always rational in my thinking, and when something new comes along I'm always very impatient to try it out. This trait has caused me to make many stupid mistakes along the way, and although I've learnt a lot from them I still haven't learnt to curb my impatience. When you shoot first and ask questions later, there's often a big price to pay at the end. I was feeling both impetuous and impatient right now, and also very curious.

I laid back down beside Sarah and put my lips to her ear. "Wake up, sweetheart," I whispered. "I've got something to tell you." But there was no response. I placed a hand on her shoulder and gently shook it. She stirred, opened her eyes and then, startled by the light of my torch, sat straight up, looking fearfully at me. "What's the matter? What's happening?" she cried.

"Don't worry," I said, "There's nothing wrong, but there's something I want to tell you."

She shook her head, trying to clear away the cobwebs. "What time is it?" she croaked.

"It's 4.30."

She stared angrily at me. "What do you mean, 4.30? Whatever could be so important that you'd have to wake me at this time? Can't it wait till the morning?"

She was glaring at me in the same aggressive way I had seen several times before during my previous acts of impetuosity. In the past that look on her face had always been enough to make me back off, but this time I was determined to stand my ground. "No!" I said fiercely, hardly believing that I was addressing my beloved wife like this. "I need to do this now."

"Do what?"

I took a deep breath. "Go back to the cave. It'll be just you and me this time, as soon as the dawn comes up and while the others are still asleep. There's something bugging me about it and I need to check it out, if only to satisfy myself that it's nothing."

She gave me a withering look. "You're crazy," she said. "You're bruised and scratched all over, you nearly got killed down there and now you want to have another go at finishing the job. No, Jim. I'm not letting you do it. Just think of how it would be for me, and the rest of your family, if something happened to you. Yesterday was an accident, but doing it again would be entirely your fault."

She was right of course. Disappointed with her response, I slumped glumly back down onto my bed and buried my face in my hands. Neither of us spoke for a while, acting out one of those stand-offs that most married couples have from time to time. Deciding it was no use trying to persuade her, I sighed and laid myself back down to try and sleep.

"Anyway," she said suddenly, out of the darkness, "if you went down there again, there's no way I could pull you out, not without Gary and Joseph."

That was something I just simply had not thought about. "You're right," I said. "But the real reason I wanted to go now is because I don't want either of them to know. They'll think I'm totally mad."

"They'd be right," she replied, to which I could find no sensible answer, so there followed a long and uncomfortable silence, which made me presume that this was the end of the conversation. But just as I was settling myself back down to try and resume my sleep, she opened up again. "Suppose I went down instead? You could pull me out, no trouble. After all, I'm only half your weight."

I stared at her in disbelief. For a moment or two I was lost for words, stunned that she should even suggest such a thing. That idea had never entered my head, and even now it seemed very alien. Strangely enough, my first thought was not about the forthcoming project, but about my wife and about how much she must love me. Here I was, planning a totally crazy adventure which I was quite sure she did not agree with, and yet here was she, willing to risk everything just to support me. I reacted in the only way I knew how, which was to reach out and grab her with both arms before hugging her as tightly as I could. I said nothing at all. With love like that, words are quite unnecessary.

Chapter 20

With the decision made and agreed, we got ourselves together as quietly as we could, planning to be away at the very earliest sign of dawn, well before the other two were likely to get up, especially Gary who, true to his teenage years, always welcomed a lie in. We left them a note, telling them not to worry and that we'd be back before lunch.

We had quietly discussed what equipment we might need: a couple of bottles of water, a torch and that same rope we had used before, which Joseph had conveniently coiled around the spare wheel bolted to the back of the Land Rover. There was also a small hand shovel tied to the roof rack, presumably as an emergency toilet facility, and I helped myself to it, not really sure why we might possibly need it.

With the first light beginning to mark out the shape of the forest over in the distance, we set off, trying all the while to think of anything we might have forgotten. Somehow, I knew we had, but it was only after we'd reached the edge of the forest that I realised what was missing. "The Coolpix!" I exclaimed, and without a second thought, we turned around and went back for it.

By now the sun was well up, and with a clear plan of action to motivate us we progressed much faster than we had the day before. I'm pretty sure we were there within half an hour and with the recently trampled undergrowth as a marker, it was quite easy to locate the bush (or rather, what was left of it after Joseph's efforts) and the hole.

We wasted no time. I uncoiled the rope, which was about 60 feet in length, and tied one end of it to one of the roots of a nearby strangler fig while Sarah wrapped the other end of it several times around her waist, finishing off in much the same way as I had done the day before, with a step loop for her feet. This, rather than her waist, would be taking most of her weight.

As I watched her readying herself for this little adventure I could not help feeling an immense sense of pride and admiration for her. She seemed so calm and, unlike me, had no fear of darkness, often joking in the past that she could happily sleep in a coffin if need be. And in contrast to me, any action or direction she ever took in life was always done in a measured and carefully considered way. There have been many occasions in our marriage when she has intervened and saved me from messing up on some important decision or other, and right now I knew for sure that I could trust her to complete this little job with no worries at all

With her precious Coolpix in its case and safely strapped to her belt, she came over to give me a kiss, and we hugged each other for a few seconds before she switched the torch on. She then strode purposefully across to the hole and slid herself into it, feet first. I had one loop of the rope around my waist and as she started to descend I took up the tension and fed it out slowly, relieved to find that I could easily cope with her weight, which was somewhat less than eight stone.

With about half of the length of the rope remaining, it suddenly went slack. "I'm down!" she shouted. "It's that loose shale stuff you were talking about. I'm standing on a big slope of it, about half way down. Every time I move, it slips away under my feet like a small landslide."

Until that moment I had been holding my breath, waiting to hear the sound of her voice again. "See anything?" I called, at the same time making sure there was no slack in the rope. For a few minutes, there was no response and I guessed she must be putting the torch to good use.

Then came the answer I'd been waiting for: "Nothing out of the ordinary; not even any spiders as far as I can see." There was another pause and then: "Oh, wait a minute. I've just seen that wall you mentioned. I had to look twice because there's not much of it showing. The pumice is all banked up against it. I'll scramble over and take a closer look."

Once again I had to wait for an update. I could hear the shale as it fell away from under her feet. I'd already prepared her for that, and explained how difficult it would be to move around on such an unstable surface. I held my breath, reminded myself to keep holding on tight and listened intently for any danger sounds. The tension in the rope turned out to be a great way of communicating. It transmitted her every slight movement and I could easily get a fix on the speed of her progress, which was so much faster than mine would have been.

A few minutes went by without incident. I'm not sure how nervous she felt right then, but I was really pumped up. Somehow it's worse when you can't do anything about a situation, especially when the woman you love is involved. Those few minutes seemed like hours.

And then, just when I felt I might boil over with tension, I heard the sound I'd been waiting for. "I made it!" she called. I let out a long sigh of relief.

But just a second or two later, she gave out a loud shriek. It made me jump so much that I nearly let go of the rope. "What's up?" I cried. "Are you okay?"

"Yes, I'm fine, but I just got freaked out. Sorry to scare you, but I just wasn't ready for it."

"Ready for what?" I asked, anxiously.

"This wall or whatever it is," she replied excitedly. "I reached out to steady myself and when I put my hand on it, it just wasn't what I'd expected. It's so smooth, and kind of slippery, like a non-stick pan. And it's not flat. In fact, it's curved, as if it's part of something. It's nothing at all like granite, which is what I was expecting."

"Is it metal then?"

"Well, no, it doesn't seem metallic either; it's more like plastic than anything else," she said.

I shook my head. No, she's got it wrong. No way could there be anything plastic in a place like this. "How could that possibly be?" I shouted.

I listened for an answer, but all I could hear was a dull thudding noise, repeated several times. When it stopped, she called out again. "You're right. It's not plastic, but I don't know what else it can be. It's extremely hard. I tried banging it with a rock, but there are no marks at all. I need to see more of it. Can you throw down that shovel?"

"I might hit you."

"No, you won't. I'm not standing directly under you now. Just let it fall."

I did as I was told and heard the shovel clatter a couple of times before coming to rest. Then I could sense, from the tension in the rope, that she was moving across to retrieve it.

"This section is about a metre high and I think it must go down a lot further, so I'm going to clear away some of the shale. Keep the rope taut in case it all gives way."

"Don't worry!" I assured her, listening intently to the regular scraping of the shovel, punctuated by the sound of the occasional mini-landslide, which, each time it happened, made me tighten my grip just that little bit more.

Tiny as Sarah was (and still is), she made up for it with the kind of determination and focus that I could only dream of, and right now I just knew that, bizarre as the situation might seem, I did not have to worry at all about her safety. Whatever happened down there, she would deal with it. Beware of the little people.

Chapter 21

The shovelling sound continued for quite a while: 10 minutes or so, I guess. I was starting to wonder how much longer this was all going to take when she suddenly let out a loud whoop of excitement. "I've found something!" she cried. "At first, I thought it was just a hole, but now I've cleared more stuff away I can see that it's perfectly round, like a window or something."

"How big is it?"

"About two feet across, and it's so perfect it's just got to be man-made!"

"How can that be?" I queried..

"I've no idea, but I can see now that this is not a wall at all; it's part of something."

"Something? What do you mean?"

"It's part of a complete structure of some sort. I can't see the top because it's hidden under a layer of lava, but the whole thing looks like it goes down quite a bit further under the shale."

"What about that hole you found?"

"I don't know yet, but I'm going to have a look inside when I've cleared some more of this stuff away. And, like I said, it's not a hole; it's a window, or maybe a small door."

"Take photos." I urged.

"I have already."

I could hear that she had started to shovel again, so I let her get on with it.

After what must have been a good quarter of an hour, the scraping noises stopped, and alarmed by the complete silence that followed, I called out.

"What's happened? Are you okay?"

"Oh, sorry, yes," she called back. "I've completely cleared it now, and it definitely is a window or a door. I've got my head through, and I'm looking around with the torch. I can see now that it's a sort of room, quite small. The floor is circular, and the whole thing appears to be cone shaped. It goes almost to a point a few feet above me. There's a lot more shale in here, but only on this side where it's worked its way through the window."

"What's down below?"

"The floor is about 8 or 10 feet down from here. Most of it is covered with this shale stuff. I can't see too well from here, so I'm going to climb in and have a look."

"Be careful!" I warned, trying not to betray my worst fears.

"Don't worry, it's fine. Just hold the rope tight! Oh, and you probably won't be able to hear me when I'm in there, so I'll tug three times on the rope when I want you to start pulling me out."

"Okay," I shouted, but now the initial euphoria I'd had for this new discovery had been replaced by a sense of misgiving. This whole adventure was going much too well.

I've always been a bit of a pessimist. There's an on-going debate we've all had some time in our lives about whether it's better to be an optimist or a pessimist.

At first sight (the argument goes), it would seem better to be an optimist, because you'll enjoy the ride more. But the advantage of being a pessimist is that you can't lose. If it goes wrong, you can say, "There, I told you so", and if it goes right? Well, that's a huge bonus.

I must have been standing in that one spot for half an hour or more, still with the rope coiled around my waist, playing it in and out to match her activity. Right now that rope was my only connection to her and everything was fine as long as it kept moving. But on the occasions when it was absolutely still, I felt my heart miss a beat and I would hold my breath, waiting nervously for it to move again.

And then, just when I thought I could stand it no longer, I felt a strong jerk followed in quick succession by two more. It was the signal that she was ready to come out. With a huge sigh of relief, I immediately tightened my grip and started to pull, one hand over the other.

It was hard work, much harder than I had expected, making me realise once again that I wasn't as young as I used to be. Very soon, after about a dozen pulls, a searing pain started to develop in both of my arms, forcing me to take a rest. I could see from the coil of rope piling up behind me that I had pulled her up 10 feet or so, -more than enough to raise her back through that window. Alarmed by the unexpected pause, she called out. It was the first time in at least 30 minutes that I had heard her voice. "What's up? You okay?"

"Cramp. I'll be all right in a minute," I assured. "Just waiting for it to go away."

But truthfully, I wasn't at all sure it *was* going to go away. Another few pulls and it would be back again.

JAMES H. RUSSELL

I thought hard for a minute. There just had to be another way. I eventually solved the problem by throwing the rope over my shoulder and, using the untapped strength of my leg muscles, I adopted a tug-of-war stance, and by leaning right back on my heels, I was able to gradually force myself away from the hole.

My new technique worked a treat. I still had to stop a few more times to get my breath back, but at least it was all going the right way. It was with a huge sigh of relief that I finally caught a glimpse of her shiny black hair emerging from the hole.

Chapter 22

Two more tugs, and she was out. She let out a shriek of joy, scrambled quickly to her feet and untangled herself from the rope. Then she ran straight over to me, flung her arms around my waist and hugged me more tightly than she had ever done before. We stayed like that, without speaking, for a minute or two, soaking up the secure feeling of togetherness coupled with an immense feeling of relief.

As usual, it was my curiosity that got the better of me. I broke the clinch and pushed her gently back, staring at her face in order to make eye contact. It was only then that I saw how pale she looked, her eyes open unusually wide and her pupils dilated as if in a state of shock.

"What's the matter?" I asked. "Are you all right? You look like you've seen a ghost!"

"Not a ghost, exactly, but..."

I tightened my grip on her shoulders, impatient to find out more.

"But what?" I urged.

"There's a body down there. Well, no, not a body exactly. Actually it was a skeleton. It was lying on the floor face up and half covered in shale, with just the head and torso exposed. It gave me such a shock, because I very nearly tripped over it."

"Oh my God!" I cried. "How could it have got there? You're telling me there was someone here before us?"

She laughed nervously. "There was," she said. "But that's not the only thing."

"Oh, what?"

Her expression saddened. I sensed bad news. "Well, I got the camera out and took lots of photos of it. Then I knelt down to take a closer look and reached out to touch the skull, but as I did so I nearly jumped out of my skin, because the whole thing just fell apart. It was like cigarette ash. All that was left were the teeth and a pile of dust!"

I stared at her in disbelief. "That's very weird," I said. "I wonder what could have caused that? Maybe there's something in the air down there, dissolving out the calcium. Or maybe it's just been there a very long time. How long do bones last, I wonder?"

With that, she felt around in her pocket and produced an unusually large and heavily discoloured molar tooth. "Here, check this out," she said, inviting me to make use of my professional knowledge. I took it and turned it over a few times. The cusps were flat and the enamel on the chewing surface was severely worn, exposing four distinct islands of dark brown dentine.

"This is the most extreme example of attrition I've ever seen." I remarked. "This person, whoever he was made good use of his teeth!"

"Or *her* teeth," she corrected.

"Yes," I continued. "He or she was either very old or very wild, I'm not sure which."

"What do you mean, 'wild'?"

"Well, if he was very old, that would account for the flat cusps, but teeth can also wear down fast if the food needs a lot of chewing, if it's raw for example, or if it's contaminated by sand or grit which will act like an abrasive."

Sarah had a frown on her face. "Raw? That can't be, surely? People haven't eaten raw food since forever."

That was a subject I knew something about. "We've been cooking food for about a half a million years." I said. " Soon after we discovered how to make fire."

"Wow!" she exclaimed. "So if he was around before that, it would make this guy old, very old indeed!"

Chapter 23

Sarah produced a couple more teeth that she had stuffed in her pocket. We made a makeshift seat using the coiled-up rope and sat down together to take a closer look at them. Noticing the many time related shrinkage cracks over all surfaces of the enamel, I now had no doubt that whoever it was down in that cave had been there for a very long time, possibly millions of years. I was totally awestruck with the idea, and sat there, just staring into space.

"Oh yes!" Said Sarah, almost as an afterthought. "There was something else I nearly forgot about." With that, she reached behind her back and pulled out something she had previously tucked under her belt and inside her shorts. "This!"

Her words snapped me out of the trance. I shook my head and looked up to see what she had in her hand and as soon as I saw it I let out a gasp of amazement, nearly dropping the teeth I was holding. The object in question was about the same size as a small plastic chopping board, unusual enough in this environment, but what had made me catch my breath was its colour: orange. Not just any old orange, but the most vibrant shade of that colour I have ever seen before or since. It seemed, in this subdued rainforest daylight, to be almost luminescent.

I could hardly take my eyes off it. When I did finally look up, I saw that Sarah was staring at it too.

"Wow!" We both used the only word appropriate for such a situation.

"It's such a powerful colour," said Sarah. "It almost seems like it's alive! But down there, it was so dark, I didn't really notice. I only picked it up as an afterthought. After seeing that skeleton, I couldn't think straight any more. I just wanted to get away from there."

"It's so bright," I said, "that it gives me the feeling it was just asking to be found. Where was it?"

"It was poking out from a slot in the wall opposite the window. I noticed it because of the colour, but in the torchlight it didn't seem anywhere near as bright as this."

She passed it over so that I could take a closer look. As soon as I took hold of it, I knew this was something quite extraordinary. It felt so smooth, almost soapy to the touch, and had an exquisitely engineered feel about it. It was rectangular in shape, about ten inches long and six inches wide, and it was not much thicker than a pencil. As I ran my fingers over it, I realised that there was not the slightest sign of a scratch or blemish on it. Even the edges were rounded, like those of a well-worn but extremely smooth pebble.

Sarah held her hands out, demanding to hold it. "My turn," she cried. "You've had it long enough!"

"Oh, yes, sorry," I said, passing it over meekly. I realised then that I had just been hypnotized, for the first time in my life, by an inanimate object.

I watched as she fondled it, almost drooling, just as I had done. "It's so beautiful," she remarked at last.

As she spoke those words, I suddenly realised how utterly weird this whole thing was. How could anyone be calling a glorified chopping board beautiful? Yet, in a strange way, because of its absolute perfection, it was.

"I wonder what it's made of," she wondered. "It's so light. I bet it floats on water."

I took it from her and bounced it up and down in my hand. "I think you're probably right," I said, "but it seems so hard, like you couldn't scratch it, no matter how much you tried."

She took the strange object back and tucked it under her belt before checking her watch. "Time to get back." she said. "They'll be wondering what we're up to."

She was right. I quickly rewound the rope, slung it over my shoulder and checked round for anything else we might have left. Then I remembered the shovel. "Where is it?" I asked.

She shrugged her shoulders apologetically. "Sorry," she said, "I left it behind. It was too much to manage with my two hands on the rope."

"We'll just have to make up a story then." I said.

Sarah was busy dusting herself down. "Talking about stories, what are we going to tell them we've been up to?" she asked.

Her words made me stop what I was doing, and I just stood there, trying to think clearly about the whole thing. Whichever way you looked at it, there was a great big mystery going on here and we needed to try and puzzle it out before we told anyone else about it.

"I think we should say nothing right now. Just keep it quiet until we've figured out what's going on."

She nodded. "My thoughts exactly," she said.

Chapter 24

It was around 11am by the time we got back. Joseph was hanging out washing on a line he'd rigged up between two posts near the toilets. Gary was still in bed but awake and playing a Pokemon game on his Nintendo. I used the opportunity to replace the borrowed items back in their homes. I had already replaced the rope and was just fixing the torch back into its bracket when Gary poked his head out from his tent.

"Where have you been all this time?" he demanded,

"Oh, just for an early morning stroll. We thought we'd like to get out and listen to the dawn chorus, and we know how much you like a lie-in."

I could see from his expression that he was not at all pleased. "I do like a lie-in back home," he said, "but not here. If you had woken me, I would have come too."

Sarah came to the rescue. "Okay, sorry," she said. "Next time I'll make sure I wake you, even if you're snoring, and you'd better be happy about it!"

As she turned to leave, I was horrified to see a glint of exposed orange showing just above her belt. I looked over at Gary, but was relieved to see that he had his head back in the Nintendo, and so, using my body to shield her, I ushered Sarah quickly out of the tent. Tapping at the tell-tale shape on her midriff, I whispered: "We need to hide that thing before anyone sees it."

She nodded. "I'll tuck it into the bottom of my rucksack. No one will find it there."

Shortly after that, Joseph came over and asked if we wanted some breakfast. It was only then that I realised I was really quite hungry. On a normal day, with nothing much else to think about, my attention would be drawn to my empty stomach, but not so for today. The lesson is: if you want to stay slim, don't get bored!

Joseph asked us if we enjoyed our walk, and we made up a few white lies to satisfy his curiosity. Luckily, he didn't mention the rope, which I had already returned to its home. I hoped he hadn't noticed, because I couldn't think of a good reason for taking it. The shovel, however, was a different matter, and I still had to work out some excuse for its disappearance; not too much of a problem, because useful things such as that do get stolen from time to time.

Because we had used up much of the morning, we decided we would use the afternoon to explore what there was of the village and perhaps get to know the people and their customs a little better.

So we showered and changed and then sat around chatting about nothing in particular over what was effectively a brunch rather than breakfast. It was only then that I thought about the camera. With my mind still locked in the past, I had forgotten that it was digital and did not require the usual two-week wait for developing. So, when no one was listening, I asked Sarah if she'd looked at any of the pictures. She said yes, when in the toilet, and they'd all come out pretty well, so I took the camera from her and disappeared into the toilet to see for myself.

I don't like spending long in toilets in hot countries like Kenya, because there are always flies and mosquitoes in there. The flies I can deal with, but the thought of a will-o'-the-wisp stealing up on me in the semi-darkness, sucking my blood and possibly passing on a parasite or two gives me the creeps. But as I sat there on the toilet, working my way through those digital photos on that very clever (for those days) Coolpix 700, I forgot all about the creeps.

Sarah, despite all the other things she'd had to worry about down in that cave, had managed to take quite a lot of photos; not all of them were very clear, but with a digital camera, it doesn't really matter, because you can just wipe them whenever you want. The viewing screens on those early digital cameras were much smaller than they are now. This one was about an inch and a half across and without my reading glasses at hand I had to squint to make out any detail. Some of the shots were good and even though it was so dark in the cave the flash had worked very well, showing the outlines of its interior in remarkably clear detail.

Just as Sarah had said, the cave was cone shaped, almost narrowing to a point at its uppermost, and using the prostrate skeleton as a guide, I judged the base to be around eight feet across. There were a few images of the skull, taken at various angles before it had collapsed, and although I thought the features looked a bit odd, the only thing I really homed in on, thanks to my professional bias, were its unusually large teeth. I resolved to have a better look later, when I'd found my glasses.

It was then that I had what seemed at the time to be a completely ridiculous idea. Was this strange contraption actually some sort of alien craft? I shook my head in an attempt to dispel such a crazy thought. After all, it was almost completely enveloped in a layer of lava, so how could it have got there?

Chapter 25

"Are you going to be much longer in there?" It was Gary, sounding desperate.

"No, nearly done. Give me just one minute." I turned off the camera and slid it back in its case, before pretending to flush out the toilet, which I had not actually used. Not wanting Gary to guess what I had been doing, I decided to hide the camera somewhere. Looking up, I saw a shelf loaded with spare toilet paper, so I hid the camera at the back to pick up later, which I did as soon as Gary disappeared into the shower. I returned the camera to Sarah, and she wasted no time in tucking it well out of sight, down inside her rucksack.

"So, what do you think?" she asked, eyeing me quizzically.

I hesitated, considering what I should say. What I had on my mind seemed so ridiculous that I wasn't at all sure whether I should even come out with it. "You're going to think I'm mad," I said at last.

"Why?"

I shrugged, as if apologising in advance for what was going through my head. I opened my mouth to speak, but she put a finger up to my lips to stop me.

"I know what you're thinking," she said.

"How can you know?" I protested. "What I'm thinking doesn't make sense."

She shook her head. "On the contrary, I think it does make complete sense. You think that that machine came from somewhere else, don't you? I agree with you. There can be no other explanation."

I said nothing for a moment and just stared at her, wondering if she had gone crazy too, but then I remembered that this was my very clever, cool, calculating wife talking: a person who never does anything without proper consideration.

"But how come it's down there, underground?"

"You've forgotten something," she said. "This whole area was once one huge volcano."

"Yes," I replied, "but that was millions of years ago."

"About two, actually. If you remember, that guy Grayson told us at the school speech day."

"No, I don't remember that," I replied.

"You were asleep most of the time." she pointed out.

"So you're trying to tell me that thing is a couple of million years old?"

She nodded. "At least," she said.

I shook my head in disbelief. "But what about that skeleton? Is that an alien too?"

"If aliens are supposed to look like us, then he could be, but I don't think we're the first people to come across this thing."

"You mean he discovered it and ended up dying there for some reason?"

"Perhaps he had an accident like you did. If he was alone and fell in there like you did, he would have been trapped."

"Yes, that makes sense. What a way to go! Stuck inside there in complete darkness, with no food and water." I shuddered at the thought of it. "And then the volcano erupted." As I said those last words, I realised my mistake. Of course it wouldn't necessarily have been dark at all before the eruption. The whole thing would have been sitting in some sort of open space, quite probably in the middle of the day.

Sarah frowned, deep in thought. "Why would he have been in there? Exploring, like us?"

"Maybe. But he had to be clever to even get in there when there wasn't any pumice to stand on like there is now. That window is quite high up by the look of things, and didn't you say something about the wall being slippery?"

She nodded. "Very slippery indeed. Are you suggesting it was some kind of deliberate puzzle?"

I shrugged. "Possibly. It obviously required a lot of thought to figure out how to get in there. Maybe it was some kind of intelligence test. When did you first have the idea that it might be a spacecraft?"

"Almost immediately." she replied. "Even before I climbed through that window, I knew, because when I first touched the outer skin, which I expected to be rock of some sort, it felt very weird. It was solid like rock, but it seemed slippery like ice, only not cold. It was like nothing I've ever experienced or seen before. I just knew right then that we were dealing with something out of this world."

"Was that when I heard you scream out?"

She nodded. "Yes, because it was so unexpected: like picking up something slimy, such as a slug. I couldn't help but scream, even though that was the last thing I wanted to do. The thing is, I didn't want you to alarm you, because you couldn't have done anything anyway."

I gave her a hug. "You were very brave. I think I would have dropped everything and started shimming up that rope."

Still in my arms, she said: "Okay, of course I was scared, but by then, the adrenaline had started to flow and I was much too curious to turn back. Now I know why explorers take so many risks. They're driven by something, and somehow they just can't stop. It's like a drug."

I kissed her forehead. "I'm so proud of you, my darling," I said

We resolved there and then to keep it all a secret for the time being, even from Gary and Joseph (particularly the idea of some sort of extra-terrestrial involvement), at least until we'd worked out what the possible implications might be.

Chapter 26

On the third day at Gatab, we all set out again to have a second crack at the hike to the Kulal Peaks. It was much harder going than I had anticipated, and of course, uphill all the way. Climbing the peaks themselves is a task best left to the most experienced climbers, and in any case, that was never our intention, but we still managed to climb to a very respectable height and found a clearing above the treeline where we were able to sit ourselves down for a picnic and enjoy the magnificent views of Lake Turkana, far below us. From up there the lake seemed even greener than before, contrasting so starkly with the barren, rock-strewn landscape all around it.

The trek back was uneventful, and we managed to get back to the camp just a few minutes before nightfall. The only uncomfortable time was when Gary stopped to point out the site of the last misadventure, but luckily Joseph had one eye on the clock and warned us we were running out of time if we wanted to get back before dark.

Two days later, we were back in Nairobi, lining up at the airport check-in. We all felt suitably relaxed and chilled out, and the overall vote was that this had been our best holiday ever. As Gary put it, "Lying on a beach is okay for a little while, but too much of it can be boring, and you can't beat exploring and finding something new." As he said it, Sarah looked round at me, and I saw that she was struggling not to laugh. "You're so right there, Gary," she said. "I like a bit of adventure too. It makes me feel like I've really done something."

"And you've certainly done something this time!" I said it without thinking, and regretted it almost as soon as I'd opened my mouth. I didn't have to look at Sarah to know that she was fixing me with that same admonishing glare I'd seen so many times before when I'd put my foot in it. So I quickly added, "All that camping and hiking and stuff has been a great new experience for us, hasn't it?"

Gary agreed and then said: "Mum, when we're on the plane, can I have the camera so that I can have a look at all the photos?"

I felt my blood run cold. I knew that couldn't happen. How to put him off? "Not a good idea," I said. "It'll run the batteries down too much. Wait till we get back."

I thought I'd dealt with the situation, but to my horror, Sarah interrupted me. "No, that's all right, darling," she said. "I've got plenty more spare batteries."

I frowned and stared hard at her. Why was she suddenly behaving like this and letting the cat out of the bag when we had made an agreement to keep it all secret? But she just smiled back at me and winked. It was only later on the plane when we were working our way along the aisle towards our seats, that she turned and whispered in my ear. "It's okay, my love. You don't have to worry. I swapped the memory cards over."

Chapter 27

I always have very mixed feelings when returning home after a holiday. On the one hand, it's a very comforting feeling to get back inside those familiar walls that have protected you and your family for so long, and to sleep in your same old bed that has gradually moulded itself to suit your body. But on the other hand, there's the inevitable slide back into that same old routine you were so desperate to escape from just two short weeks before, knowing that your life will soon be well and truly controlled once again by that wretched timepiece you wear on your wrist.

And then there's that inevitable pile of mail forming a small mountain in the hallway and trying its best to stop you opening the front door. Every time we return from a trip away, I'm always surprised by the amount of it there is. It's mostly junk, but I cannot resist the urge to open it all there and then, just in case there's something important such as a message telling me that someone's copied my identity and emptied my bank account, or a parking or speeding fine for an incident I can't remember.

This time, to my great relief, there were no unpleasant surprises. With the mail duly sorted, I gathered up the pile of torn envelopes, the inevitable takeaway leaflets and the junk mail (enough to account for the destruction of one small tree), and shaking my head with the usual pang of guilt, I tossed them all in the bin. Remaining on the table were just the usual three or four utility bills and a copy of Gary's school magazine. I picked it up and thumbed quickly through it. Sure enough, there was an account of the speech day, with photos of all the prize winners. I soon spotted Gary, a big smile on his face as he shook hands with the Head while receiving the book he had won as a prize. Among the other photos, I noticed the bearded face of Richard Grayson, the guest speaker who had originally sparked my interest in Turkana.

While I was going through the mail, Sarah had been showering and getting ready for bed, and then she called down to me to tell me the bathroom was free. I checked my watch and saw that it was much later than I had realised: already long past midnight. No wonder I was feeling so tired. I left the paperwork on the table and made my way upstairs, weaving my way through the still-unopened suitcases which were part blocking the hallway. I had left them where they were because I was much too zonked to move them then, and in any case, there would be plenty of time for that tomorrow. Funny how travelling seems to tire a person out, even though most of the time is spent just sitting down, either waiting for transport to arrive or actually sitting in it. I think I fell asleep as soon as my head hit the pillow.

Chapter 28

That next morning with Gary out visiting one of his mates, we decided it was time to review the holiday snaps, particularly the cave shots. I headed into the living room and busied myself connecting the Coolpix to the TV, while Sarah hunted through the rucksack for the memory card she had previously hidden away. As useful as the tiny camera screen was for lining up the subject and composing the balance of the shot, its display for reviewing images was quite limited. It was only when the images were presented on the big screen that they really came to life.

The quality of those early digital pictures, although nowhere near as good as nowadays, was for those times really quite astounding. We were able to view everything in full colour and in even more detail than many prints would have allowed us. We settled down to enjoy reliving the earlier part of our trip, starting with scenes of urban Nairobi, followed by a few posed family shots involving Joseph and the Land Rover. Then there were photos taken on the move, many of which were substandard or blurred, but having already learnt that the beauty of digital is that it doesn't really matter how many you take because there's no extra cost involved, we immediately deleted them. There were some great shots of all sorts of wildlife: zebras, giraffes, various types of antelope and even that herd of camels we encountered on the way up to Turkana.

Eventually we came to the cave photos, the first of which was a blurred image of the shale floor below, partly obscured by a perfect shot of Sarah's left foot. It made her laugh. "I took that one-handed," she giggled. "I was still hanging from the rope at the time."

"Hopefully, it'll get better," I remarked, clicking the button for the next image.

It did get better. The next shot was of the window, perfectly circular in shape, which looked as if it had just been cut out of the perfectly smooth wall with some kind of precision machine.

"There was a door to it on the inside," she commented. "I took a photo. We should see it in the next shot."

I moved the images along to display the door. It was set to the side of the opening and was held by two rails, upper and lower. There were several evenly spaced slots arranged radially around its periphery, matched by the same number of retractable bolts fixed to the inner wall, and it was quite obviously some kind of securing arrangement. "So perfectly engineered." I remarked. "Yes, and I'd like to bet that when it's closed, you can't see the join!" She added.

"I'm beginning to think you're right!"

There were several subsequent shots of the inside of the chamber, and we worked our way through them quite quickly, until we finally came to the images of the skeleton, taken from different angles.

"I'm so glad I took these before I touched it," Sarah said. "Otherwise we'd be looking at a pile of dust."

I took some time to study the skull photos and stopped on the full frontal to assess the features in more detail. I had a funny feeling that something wasn't quite right but I couldn't quite put my finger on anything. At first I thought it was just those oversized teeth, but then I tried to imagine what the face would be like with the skin and flesh back in place. Would it remind me of anyone I knew? The answer was decidedly no. Somehow, the eyebrows were too big and the lower jaw, though large, had a weak chin; too weak, even for the most Neanderthal of my friends and patients

I sat back in my chair and glanced across to see that Sarah was looking just as puzzled as I, with a frown on her face that mirrored mine.

"Weird," she said.

"Very," I agreed.

"Richard Grayson!"

That was all she said, but I knew immediately what she meant. "Richard Grayson!" I repeated. "You're right. We need to get an opinion from somebody, and this kind of thing is right up his street."

"Do we know where he lives?"

"No, but we can ask somebody at the school. The secretary should know. I'll phone her later."

Sarah removed the memory card from the camera and tucked it away in her handbag before loading a blank replacement.

"There's something else in your rucksack we need to look at." I remarked.

She grinned. "I hadn't forgotten, how could I?" She said. "In fact I can't seem to get that thing out of my mind, so much so that I'm almost too scared to see it again, but I really don't know why."

"I think I know what you mean." I said. "That thing is so unique and out of this world, it almost seems supernatural. Here, pass me the rucksack, I'll do it."

There was the usual collection of travel miscellanea, such as the flight bag with the sleeping goggles and the miniature toothbrush set. And then there was the detective novel she had started on the flight out but was still only halfway through. The last thing out of the rucksack was that strange artefact, instantly recognisable, not only from its uniquely slippery feel, but by the richness of its colour.

Even though we were both prepared for it, neither of us could resist gasping with amazement as we set eyes on it once again. The depth of that orange seemed to make the whole thing glow with an intensity that was quite spellbinding, suggesting that it must extend throughout the whole thickness of the body. I simply could not take my eyes off it.

And nor could Sarah. When I finally managed to look up at her, I saw from her trance like stare that she was just as mesmerised as I was. Her face bore the same expression one might see on a young child's face while unwrapping a new present, and she could not seem to resist running her fingers all over and around this new found toy.

"It's so perfect." She murmured. "I have no idea why I was scared."

"I think I do." I said. "It's because we both know this thing's just got to be from somewhere else. There's magic in there somehow, and I get the feeling there's a lot more to it than either of us realise."

She nodded. "Yes, I think you could be right," she said, "but what do you think we should do with it now?"

I thought about that for a few moments. "I haven't got an answer for that just yet." I replied. "But maybe we should do nothing for a while. Perhaps we should hide it away until we come up with a suitable idea."

Sarah looked disappointed. "It's much too pretty just to stick it in a drawer somewhere. Why don't we use it as an ornament? I can find a space in the living room display cabinet. What do you think?"

I shook my head vigorously. "No, we can't do that." I hissed. "Not without letting Gary in on the whole story. Besides, we have no idea what this thing's all about, and once Gary sees it he's bound to tell at least one of his mates about it."

"You're probably right." She agreed glumly. So saying, she took the object in question from me and disappeared upstairs to stow it in her bedside cabinet. When she returned, she started repacking the other items back into her rucksack.

"How about we give it a name?" She suggested.

I frowned. "What do you mean?"

"Well, we can't just keep calling it a thing all the time can we? After all we don't have a clue what it is or what it's supposed to do. It's not a cup, or a plate, or a vase, so why don't we invent a name for it?"

The idea made me laugh, but she was right. Every single object has a name that somebody, somewhere, christened it with: table, chair, knife, fork, just about everything, so yes, it was quite logical to give this thing a name too.

I conjured up the most ridiculous name I could think of.

"How about 'George'? I offered, tongue in cheek.

Her reaction was not what I was expecting. "That'll do!" she exclaimed with a smile. "It's short and sweet, and at least we'll both know what we're talking about without anyone else having a clue."

"They'd probably think we're talking about a person." I remarked. Strangely, it felt right to say that.

From that point on, whenever we said goodnight to each other, we would always finish by adding "Goodnight George" as we turned our lights off.

Chapter 29

The school secretary, April Jones, was very helpful, telling me how much she had enjoyed Grayson's talk. She had to go off and find his details and promised to call me back. She did so 10 minutes later and said that she had found his details but unfortunately, last year's Data Protection Act prevented her from giving out his details. She did, however, volunteer to contact him herself and pass on my details.

A week passed with no response. I was beginning to think I'd have to ask someone else for advice, when the phone rang very late one evening. I recognised that Yorkshire accent immediately. It was the man himself. He was very apologetic, explaining that he had such a busy schedule arranging, travelling to, and giving lectures, that it was all too easy to forget smaller tasks such as making phone calls. When I asked if I could meet up with him to get some advice, he seemed to back off, suggesting that due to the pressures of work, he had little or no time to deal with individual issues. I think he was just about to end the conversation when I quickly interrupted him and explained that we had just returned from Turkana and that I had material that might be of interest to him. It worked like magic. From the tone of his voice I could tell immediately that I'd struck a chord. A few minutes later, after a short debriefing, I had his secretary's phone number safely entered into my address book.

She soon found me an appointment and gave me the address. It turned out that Grayson lived in Hampstead, one of London's richest suburbs: too expensive for me, but only half an hour or so from my more modest neighbourhood. But it didn't really matter how far away Grayson lived, I'd already made up my mind that even if he were on the other side of the world, I'd still make the effort to see him.

Chapter 30

I was born and bred in North London and have always loved its many different facets and faces, but the one area that has always fascinated me is Hampstead, drenched as it is with all sorts of architecture: an eclectic mix of the old and the new, but nearly all of it well outside the limited budget of ordinary folk like me. And the people of Hampstead are a reflection of the property: mostly wealthy and very often with an intellectual eccentricity that somehow only rich people can carry off. Many of Britain's best poets, writers and actors live in Hampstead.

And today I was there again, but this time not in my usual role as a covetous voyeur. This time I had come to visit someone: Richard Grayson. I finally managed to park my car in his street, but not before having to drive up and down it several times in search of a space. After transferring most of the change in my pocket into the parking meter I locked the car and made my way along the street in search of No. 5, which I quickly realised would be at the far end. The houses I passed on my way were typically Victorian, consisting of terraces constructed of age-discoloured yellow London brick under slate-tiled roofs.

Grayson's house had been beautifully maintained and restored. The brickwork had recently been scrubbed and repointed and the woodwork newly painted in the obligatory antique cream. I particularly liked the way the formal Victorian façade had been softened by the clever use of creepers and shrubs. Someone obviously had a deep respect and love for this property.

I climbed the 10 or so steps up to the imposing front door, painted shiny black, and pressed the polished brass doorbell. The door was opened by a woman who, judging by the flecks of grey showing at the corners of her trim wavy hairdo, was around the age of 60. She was quite short, and had to tilt her neck back to look up at me. She had on a striped kitchen apron, tied at the waist over a flowery dress, and blue house slippers on her feet.

She looked at me suspiciously. "What can I do for you?" she enquired. It was then that I realised she might not have been expecting a man, as I had left Sarah to make the appointment.

"I've come to see Dr Grayson. I think he's expecting me."

She frowned and looked down at her watch. "It's almost 12 o'clock," she said, "and it's getting near his lunchtime. He's got an important lecture later this afternoon, so we're eating early. What time did he say to come?" I shrugged and shook my head. "I think his secretary arranged the appointment. I don't think she said an exact time. In fact, as far as I'm aware, she said any time this morning would be okay as Doctor Grayson doesn't usually take visitors on Mondays."

She looked pointedly at her watch again. "Morning ends in a couple of minutes." She sighed, with a look reserved for the long suffering. "Okay, I'll let him know you're here," she said resignedly, "but you know, he's always doing this: making arrangements without telling me."

"Sounds just like me," I said. "But perhaps you should blame his secretary." I smiled feebly in an attempt to defuse the situation. It seemed to work, because she smiled back and went off to tell him, and probably to rebuke him out of earshot.

A few minutes later Richard Grayson appeared in the hallway and judging by the meek expression on his bearded face had been suitably chastised. I must admit that at that point I did not recognise him, having slept through most of his talk on speech night, but as soon as I heard that mellow-toned Yorkshire accent, it all came back to me.

Grayson's receding grey hair was much as I remembered it (if now somewhat more unkempt), as were the goatee beard and the gold-rimmed glasses. The loose-fitting jumper and baggy corduroy trousers seemed to look much more at home on him than the suit he'd worn at the school.

"Hello," he began, shaking my hand. "I'm Richard. I take it you're Jim?"

"Yes," I replied. "Sorry if I've come at a bad time for you. Do you want me to come back later?" Grayson shook his head. "No, no, it's fine," he assured me. "Luckily, my wife is doing a cold salad for lunch, so it can wait. How can I help you?"

I hesitated for a moment. Strangely the question threw me. It was probably because, even though I knew why I'd come today, there was a kind of finality in opening up to a complete stranger. "I hope you won't think me completely mad," I began, "but I'd like your professional opinion about something. The thing is that right now I don't want anyone else to know."

Grayson frowned and studied my face for a moment or two, making me wonder if I'd made a mistake. Perhaps asking for confidentiality so early in a relationship was a bit too much to ask. But then his expression changed suddenly and he began to smile. "Depends what it is," he said. "But, provided it's legal, you don't have to worry. Your secret will be safe with me."

With that, he beckoned me to follow him along the hall. At the far end of it, set at the side and under the stairwell, was a door, and when he opened it I could see that there were stairs leading down to the basement. He made his way down, and I followed. "Mind your head!" he warned, but too late. I had already hit my head on the first riser. I didn't need reminding after that.

As I stepped down into the room, Grayson turned around to face me. "Welcome to my world." he said, with a friendly wave of his hands. "The servants' quarters, or it was once upon a time, but now it's a perfect place for me. It's my own private man cave, and all of my work stuff is down here." He gestured apologetically at the scene of apparent chaos behind him. "Sorry if it looks a bit of a mess. My wife is a very tidy person and she hates coming down here, but believe it or not, I know exactly where everything is. That's why there's a door at the top of the stairs. When it's closed, she can pretend this place doesn't exist!"

A brief survey of the place was enough to tell me that the two original rooms had been fused to make what was now an exceptionally large workspace, occupying almost the whole of the building's footprint, and with windows at both ends there was a surprising amount of natural daylight. Yes, I thought, Grayson was right; not only was it the perfect man cave, and at first sight it did seem to be in a bit of a mess, but both of the long flank walls were completely shelved, all of them fully laden with either books or specimens, most of which were bones or fossils.

Occupying much of the centre of the room was a huge table, about twenty feet long and at least six feet wide. It would have made a good conference table, except that it appeared to have been made from reclaimed floor boards and because of its size I guessed it had to have been built on site. Randomly placed along the centre of the table were what I took to be fossil specimens of all kinds: plant life as well as animal. Towards the middle, there were three or four skulls set out in line, showing a gradual progression of evolutionary development. In pride of place, at the very centre of the table, was what, from my days as a dental student, I knew to be a modern human skull.

There were several separate piles of paperwork on the table, all evenly spaced out around the periphery, indicating to me that there were probably several projects on the go at once. The far end of the table, adjacent to the front door, was given over to the normal essentials of office equipment, including a typewriter, printer, fax machine, etc., and, of course, an office chair.

Grayson pointed to the chair. "That's where my secretary sits." He said. "She's got her own key and comes in and out whenever she pleases. She doesn't keep regular hours, but I don't mind, as long as she gets the work done."

"I can see what your wife means about mess," I remarked. "But I have to say, I quite like it down here. Your own little world." And before I could stop myself, I added, "Where do you keep the beer?"

I grimaced inwardly. That was too flippant. Perhaps I've already gone too far, but to my relief he just smiled and without uttering a word, he turned around to face the tall cupboard behind him and opened the door to reveal a refrigerator hidden beyond. It was liberally stocked with drinks of all kinds. He pulled out two bottles and handed one to me. "Would you like one?" he smiled. " It's an ale, but there are lager types if you prefer."

It would have been impolite not to accept. He motioned me to take a seat on one of the two office chairs while he looked for the bottle opener and a couple of glasses.

We each poured our own and toasted each other. After taking a healthy mouthful of my beer, I put my glass down and surveyed the various exhibits on the table. One in particular caught my eye, and I leaned forward and carefully picked it up to study it more closely. It was fossil set in a base of stone, and it looked a bit like a very oversized woodlouse.

"Trilobite!" said Grayson with an amused grin. "It's a prehistoric arthropod. They were everywhere once, but that was about 330 million years ago. Try and get your head around how long ago that was!"

"Wow, that old?" I marvelled, and yes, I *did* try to get my head around it. 330 million years was a huge, almost incomprehensible, length of time.

"That's what people forget about when they try to downplay the idea of evolution," he said. "Time is the magic ingredient that allows evolution to do its work. Rome wasn't built in a day, as the saying goes."

I decided there and then that I liked Richard Grayson. He had a relaxed assured manner about him and, like me, he looked very comfortable with a beer in his hand. "I've only been here for a few minutes," I said, "but already you've managed to teach me something." He shrugged. "Not really. You probably knew it anyway, but you just needed your eyes opening to understand the reality of it."

He was right. I don't believe that any of us can truly understand how immensely long one million years is, because very few of us expect to see even one hundred of them. If so much change can happen in one lifetime, just imagine how much there might be in a million years, let alone 330 million.

I asked if I could examine the human skull, set as the centre-piece.

"Certainly," he said. "It's a modern skull, so you don't have to worry about damaging it. Plenty more where that came from."

I could see immediately that this was a skull that had been prepared for anatomy teaching, with springs holding the lower jaw in place and the sawn-off cranium re-attached with a couple of hinged brass hooks. I spent a couple of minutes testing my memory, watched by Grayson with an amused look on his face. I undid the clips and removed the cranium to look inside the brain cavity, and slid my finger into the foramen magnum, the opening for the spinal cord.

"This is where I made my first viva boo-boo," I said with a grin.

"I know what you're going to say," he responded. "You told the examiner it was the hole for the oesophagus! You weren't alone, I did as well. So many students make that mistake."

"But they only do it once!" I said.

Laughing, he took the skull from me and turned it over to show the inside of the brain cavity. "This is the most fascinating space in the whole world," he said, "and in many ways, the least understood. We know all about the anatomy of the brain, but there are still many mysteries as to how it works. Some people think they know, but honestly, I believe they're still scratching the surface. For instance, if someone asks you a question, you know instantly if you know the answer. It may take you some time to find the answer, but you know straight away whether it's in there or not."

I hadn't really thought of that before, but I had to admit that it was quite mind-blowing.

"And I'll tell you something else," he continued. "I believe that, although we might have changed physically one way or another, our brainpower is the one thing about us that seems to have remained constant, right from the beginning."

I frowned. "How can you know that?" I asked.

"Axe-heads made from flint in the stone age. Some of the first artefacts we know about."

"What about them?"

"They're extremely difficult to make. It requires a lot of forward thinking to produce anything remotely like an axe-head from a solid piece of flint. It's been suggested that to do such a thing then was just as challenging as building a computer nowadays. In other words, they were just as smart then as we are now. Given the right information, they could have built a computer too."

With that, he replaced the cranium and re-fixed the stays before replacing the skull back in its pole position.

We then sat down on the office chairs facing each other, and Grayson at last got around to ask about the purpose of my visit. I proceeded to tell him how I knew about him, and how his talk at the speech day had inspired me to visit Turkana. On hearing that word, his face lit up immediately. We chatted at some length about Kenya and Turkana, and I told him something of our time in Gatab. It turned out that not only had he stayed in the same village, but it was also at the same campsite as us.

"I loved Gatab," he said. "It was so peaceful, and the views down to Lake Turkana were absolutely breathtaking. I would go there again tomorrow if I didn't have so much work on my plate."

"We loved it too," I agreed. "Especially the walks through the rainforest."

"You did the trek to Kulal?"

"Yes, it was a really great thing to do. And that's the reason I've come to see you."

Grayson looked intrigued. "How can I help you?" he asked.

That was when I reached down and produced the camera from my briefcase. As soon as he saw it, Grayson's eyes lit up. "A digital camera!" he exclaimed. "I've never used one of those. Are they any good?"

I said that I thought so, but that they were still quite expensive and I'd only splashed out because it was for Sarah's fiftieth, and she wanted one. I then went on to point out the various advantages, such as being able to choose instantly which shots were worth keeping, instead of having to wait weeks for the prints to come back and then find out.

I switched the Coolpix on and began scanning through the images until I came to the ones I was looking for. "Most of the stuff on here, you will have seen before in your own travels," I said, "but there are a particular couple of shots I'd like you to look at. I'm hoping you might be able to give me your opinion."

With that, I handed him the camera and showed him how to move the frames along. The picture I had left on the screen was the first of the skull shots.

Grayson adjusted his bifocals and tipped his head back to get a clearer view. He studied the image for what seemed like ages, and then sat back in his chair, shaking his head. "Sorry," he said. "I can't be sure of what I'm looking at. The screen's too tiny. It's only about four centimetres across, and my eyesight's not great. How can we make it bigger?"

I told him that that was no problem; we just needed to connect it to a TV, and he'd be able to see everything. He shook his head. "But as you can see, I don't have a TV down here," he said. "If I did, I'd never get any work done. I can look at it upstairs though."

So the next move, I thought, was that we would be making our way up to his living room, but I saw from the resigned expression on his face that this was not going to happen. Looking up at the ceiling, he shook his head. "I'm afraid that's not possible right now," he said. "I'm already in trouble for delaying my lunch, so suggesting anything else right now will go down like a ton of bricks." "Do you want me to come back later?" I asked, trying hard not to show my frustration.

He shook his head. "Not today, I'm afraid. I've got to be at the Natural History Museum by 3 o' clock, because I'm giving a talk to a group of sixth-formers. Later this week, perhaps? I'll just check my schedule."

With that, he got up and walked over to a calendar, hanging by a frayed string pinned to a bookshelf, and studied it for a few moments. "I've got no spaces at all this week. How about next Monday?" he offered.

It was at this point that my immature tendency for impetuosity reared its head again. I decided there and then that I just could not wait that long. "I'll tell you what," I began. "Why don't you keep the camera for now. I'll show you how to set it up, and you can look at it at your leisure. If you have any news, you can always phone me."

Grayson thought about it for a moment. "Okay," he said with a nod. "As long as your wife doesn't mind?"

I replied that she wouldn't, but to be honest, I wasn't at all sure about that.

Chapter 31

Seeing that thoughts about lunch and a hostile reception from his wife had started to make Grayson anxious, I gave him a brief tutorial and packed the camera back in its case. It was only then that I remembered I'd left George in the car.

"Oh, there is one other thing before I go," I said. "There was something else we found. I think you might like to look at it. If you give me a moment, I'll pop down to the car and get it for you."

Grayson looked at his watch. "Okay," he said, "but I'm afraid the time is catching up on me. I've got to be gone by 2.30, and if I don't leave enough time for lunch, Helen will murder me. Tell you what, I'll come along to the car with you and then I can go straight upstairs for lunch."

He showed me to the door and came out with me, locking it behind him. Then he followed me up the steps and into the street. As we walked hurriedly along, he stopped suddenly, next to a bright blue sports car.

"Do you to like my new Mercedes?" he said proudly, patting the car on the bonnet. The car was a two-door sports SLK convertible, now fitted with a hard top.

I certainly did like it. "Wow, yes!" I exclaimed. "Of course I do! Especially the colour. That metallic blue really stands out from the crowd. What's not to like?"

"Well, for one thing," he said with a grin, "it's no good for taking rubbish to the tip, but at my time of life,

I just wanted to pretend I was young again, and now that I can actually afford it, I wanted a new toy to play with. Come back another time and I'll take you for a spin."

"I'll hold you to that!" I replied.

We walked on to my car, and I produced George from the boot, bubble-wrapped and sealed up in a Jiffy Bag.

"I don't know what you'll make of this," I said, "but we haven't a clue what it's supposed to be. I think it might be some sort of ornament, but I'm not really sure."

He took it from me without opening it and looked at his watch again. "Okay, I'll look at it later, when I've got more time," he replied.

As he walked away, I called out to him: "By the way, we call it George!"

He glanced back at me, a bewildered expression on his face. It was at that moment that realised I might have gone too far once again. In my head, I could hear Sarah's voice repeating what she has said to me on so many other occasions: that I'm too gullible and I trust people too much. With that same uneasy feeling I've had many times in the past, I climbed into my car and put the key in the ignition.

Chapter 32

I don't remember too much my drive back home, because most of my thoughts were taken up with how to explain to Sarah why I had lent out her precious camera. Several ideas came and went, but I knew from bitter experience that she would not entertain any one of them, even if they were true. As I turned the key in the door, I took a deep breath to prepare myself for the verbal onslaught to come.

I was greeted by the mouth-watering aroma of frying onions laced with pepper and other herbs, which told me that she was preparing one of my favourite dishes: lamb stew with barley, like my mother used to make. As I walked into the kitchen, she was indeed standing at the cooker stirring the ingredients. Judging by her welcoming smile, I was very glad to see that she was in a good mood. With the wooden spoon still in her hand, she turned towards me and planted the usual kiss on my cheek. "How did you get on?" she asked.

Passing on bad news to anyone is never easy, but it's even harder when the recipient is one's spouse and there's the prospect of a few frosty hours ahead. But after considering the various alternatives, I had already made up my mind to come straight out with it and take my punishment there and then.

"I've left them both with Grayson," I said, preparing myself for the worst.

"Both?" she said with a start, her eyes narrowing.

"Yes." I replied meekly. "He was too busy to look at either of them straightaway so I decided to let him examine them properly when he had more time."

I held my breath in readiness for a severe rebuke. But to my amazement the expected tirade didn't happen. Instead, she just smiled at me. "Good idea," she nodded. "The sooner we get an answer, the better, and then perhaps I'll be able to get a good night's sleep. I just can't seem to get this whole thing out of my mind, not even for one minute."

"Me too," I said, still thankful that I'd got away with it.

But then I saw her frowning, and I asked her why. She looked at me pensively and said, "Well, you've only just met him. How do you know you can really trust him?"

I shrugged. "I just do," I said. "The vibes felt right; like when you feel you've known someone all your life. In fact, I really liked him almost instantly. It's the same as when you walk into a new house. You know if you're going to like it as soon as you walk through the front door, and anyone who offers me a beer within two minutes of meeting me for the very first time has got to be okay in my books." I think she was happy with that, because she smiled at me again and turned back to carry on preparing the dinner.

The evening went well. Gary came in just as his mother was serving up, having been out playing table tennis with a couple of friends. The meal was delicious, and Gary went back for seconds, making sure that nothing went to waste. After that, he went up to his room to catch up with some homework while his parents relaxed in front of the TV, watching our regular soap, followed by a couple of those inevitable lifestyle programmes about food and property. When the 10 o'clock news had finished, we decided that that was enough for one day and we'd have an early night.

I was just brushing my teeth when the phone rang: a very rare event at that time of night. Sarah took the call from her bedside and then brought the phone into the bathroom. "It's for you," she whispered. "It's someone with a Yorkshire accent. I think it might be Richard Grayson."

Standing there naked, except for a towel around my waist, I quickly rinsed away the remnants of the toothpaste and took hold of the phone with my still damp hand. "Hello again, Richard," I said. "What can I do for you at this time of night?"

"Yes, Jim, I know it's a bit late in the day," came the reply, "and I'm very sorry to disturb you, but there's something I want to tell you."

"Go on," I said.

"Well, I've had a chance to look at those pictures. My wife always goes to bed a lot earlier than me because we have completely opposite body clocks. She's a lark and I'm a night-owl. This evening, she said she was feeling tired and went up even earlier than usual, so I thought it would be a good time to rig your camera up to the TV."

"So, what did you make of the photos?" I asked, all thoughts of sleep suddenly extinguished. My heart started to race.

The line stayed silent, and for a moment, I thought we had been cut off.

"Hello?" I said. "Are you still there?"

"Yes, sorry," came the response, and then another pause. "It's just that I want to make sure you're not just playing games with me. Can you please assure me that these photos haven't been doctored in any way? I've heard that it's possible to play around with digital images so that they can end up looking like something completely different."

"Yes," I responded. "I've heard that too, but I can assure you that neither my wife nor I have the slightest clue how to do it. Those images are real. Believe me!"

Once again, there was a pause. This time, I knew he was still there, because I could hear breathing. It felt as if I was listening to him thinking.

"Homo habilis," he said at length.

"Sorry?"

"Homo habilis. Handy man. They called him that because it looks like he might have been developed enough to use stone tools. He's the only one I can think of with a cranial pattern that might fit the bill. The features are virtually identical. In fact, I've got a plaster cast of one in my office. You were sitting right opposite it today."

"Really? Sorry, I didn't notice. Perhaps I was too interested in the beer!"

"But there's something I don't understand," he continued. "From those photos, it looks like an actual skull. Fossils are more like stone than bone; almost like replicas of the actual thing. Can you tell me where I can see the skull so that I can have a better look at it?"

"I'm afraid that won't be possible," I said apologetically, "because it was my wife who discovered it, and after taking those shots, she went to touch it and it completely fell apart. She said it seemed like cigarette ash. The only things we managed to salvage were the teeth."

I could tell from Grayson's reaction that he was still very doubtful, and I realised then that I wouldn't get anywhere further until I told him the whole story, which I did, there and then.

He listened intently, without interrupting. When I had finished, he said: "Do you realise that Homo habilis goes back two or three million years? Bones just don't last that long, because of weathering and so on. Even exposure to air for that length of time is enough to do it, but if your story is true, I suppose it's possible this thing has been protected from the elements all that time."

"I think that must be the case," I agreed, "because when I fell into that cave, I think it was due to my weight breaking through the outer crust. Until then, it might well have been completely sealed up by the lava."

"Perhaps there was just enough acid in the atmosphere to very slowly decalcify the bone, and maybe your wife touching it was the last straw?"

"Sounds plausible," I responded, relieved that Grayson was keeping an open mind. At last I was beginning to feel some encouragement from his reaction, and instead of just dismissing the whole thing as a joke, he was now trying to justify the almost unthinkable possibility that this whole thing might actually be real.

I started to shiver; I suppose we must have been talking for 15 minutes or more, and I was still only wearing that towel around my waist.

"I'm going to have to leave it for now," I said. "Can we both sleep on it and talk again in the morning? Perhaps we'll come up with some more ideas about the whole thing."

"Okay," he agreed. "Oh, and just one other thing. That orange slab you gave me. Where did you buy it? I'd like to get one. I know it's only a slab, but I just love that colour, and it's got such a wonderfully smooth finish. I think it would make a great ornament for my granddaughter to have in her bedroom. Kids really like bright stuff like that."

"I didn't buy it," I responded coolly. "It was in that chamber with the skeleton. Sarah pulled it out of a slot in the wall."

The phone went quiet yet again. I imagined he was holding it at arm's length and staring at it, not quite able to accept what he had just heard.

"That's unbelievable!" he exclaimed at last.

"I know," I said, "but I promise you it's the truth. You won't be able to buy that thing in any shop. Take another look at it, and keep an open mind. If you come up with any ideas, please let me know."

"Okay," he responded weakly. It was obviously too much for him to take in all at once.

"Please call me in the morning and tell me what you think." I said.

"I will." Grayson's voice was almost down to a whisper.

"Oh, and by the way, just to remind you of what I said yesterday: because we couldn't figure out what it was or what it's meant to be, we thought we'd better name it rather than just call it a thing all the time, so we decided to call it 'George'."

Chapter 33

The next morning, after what Richard Grayson had told me about being a night owl, I decided to wait until I'd got to work before phoning him. I needn't have worried. It turned out that he had been up since 6 o'clock, having had a restless night, thanks to the barrage of new information I had fired at him.

"Firstly, I couldn't get off to sleep," he began. "And then I kept waking up thinking about it all."

I told him I wasn't surprised. A brain like his was never going to let something as crazy as this go quietly.

"If you're right about this chamber thing, and judging by the images on your camera, I think you are, then there can only be one conclusion: that it was some sort of space craft which must have arrived from somewhere else a very, very long time ago. And if that skeleton really was Homo habilis, then the whole deal has got to be at least two million years old!"

I replied that I'd already come to the same conclusion, but for a different reason, which was that there hadn't been any new eruptions in this particular area for pretty much that same length of time.

Just then, Jodie popped her head round the door with a concerned look on her face. Using sign language involving a two-fingered 'V' and a display of throat cutting, she made me aware I had two agitated patients waiting.

"Sorry, Richard," I said down the phone. "I'm afraid I can't talk right now. Too busy."

"Okay," came the reply. "Let's meet up next week, like we agreed. It'll give me a chance to think it through and decide what we ought to do next."

"Give *us* a chance, you mean," I corrected.

"Yes, yes, of course. Sorry. I was getting ahead of myself. See you next week. Bye for now."

I put the phone down, feeling just a touch uneasy. Alarm bells were starting to ring. Grayson's Freudian slip had suddenly made me realise that there were two male egos at work here. I liked him a lot, but the last thing I wanted was some kind of power struggle. Luckily, with the prospect of a very busy day ahead, I was able to push those negative thoughts to the back of my mind.

The best thing about being busy is that you don't have too much time to think. When you have to really concentrate on the job in hand, your brain focuses itself right down and time just flies past. That's where a demanding occupation like dentistry really scores, and there have been many occasions when I've looked up at the clock, disbelieving that it's already nearly time to go home. I'm so glad I didn't have a boring job.

Even the weekend seemed to go fast. Coming back from a holiday always meant there was paperwork to catch up on and bills to pay. Also, like most wives, Sarah is never happy seeing me sitting around doing nothing (as she sees it) and manages to constantly find or invent DIY jobs for me to do. So I spent most of the weekend tidying the garden, cleaning windows and fixing odd bits and pieces around the house.

After an exhausting weekend, I slept very well that Sunday night, and woke up early, refreshed and ready to go, spurred on by the prospect of meeting up with Richard again and exchanging notes and ideas with him. I had cancelled my patients for that morning: something I rarely ever did, but this was a very special occasion.

"What time are you meeting him?" asked Sarah as she poured milk on her cereal.

"I don't think we agreed a time," I replied. "I'll phone him and check. After what happened last time, I'd rather not upset his wife again. I turned up at lunchtime on that last occasion."

She frowned. "That wasn't very clever of you. I would have been the same if I had the table ready and someone rang on the bell. See if you can get there by ten."

"He's a very busy man, but I'll try."

I dialled his number. I'm not sure whether I was just getting too impatient, but the ringer seemed to go on forever, and just as I was thinking of hanging up, the call was answered. It was a female voice. "Hello, Doctor Grayson's office."

"Mrs Grayson?" I asked.

"Er, no. This is Eileen. I'm Doctor Grayson's secretary. I'm afraid he's not here right now."

"When will he be back? I'm expecting to see him sometime today and I just wanted to check on the time."

"I'm afraid I can't help you with that. He's gone away for a few days."

"I presume he'll be back today? He knows he's got an appointment with me."

There was a pause. "Well, in that case, he should be back later, but somehow I don't think so. He usually keeps me up to date on his appointments, but nothing's been mentioned about this morning."

"Do you know where he's gone?" I asked.

There was a moment's pause. "Well, no," she replied. "That's the funny thing. Normally he tells me where he is, so I can get hold of him if I need to. But this time, he just went off somewhere without saying a word."

"When was that?"

"Thursday."

"And you've heard nothing from him since?" I questioned.

"Well, yes I have. We fax each other from time to time, but there's never anything about what he's doing or where he is. It's only ever about his work."

I was starting to sweat. "Have you actually asked him where he is?" I queried.

"No. I'm only his secretary, not his wife," came the curt reply. "He doesn't have to tell me anything. Perhaps you'd better ask her?"

"Yes. Good idea, thanks. I've already got her number, so I'll give her a call."

I put the phone back on its cradle, trying hard to guess what was going on. Why had he gone away like that? Perhaps he was having an affair with somebody or had gone off to some kind of secret men-only conference like Masons do sometimes. Or was it something else entirely: something to do with our conversation last week? I was sweating profusely now.

No sooner had I put the phone down, than I picked it up again, juggling with it while I thumbed through my notebook for the number. In my haste, I misdialled the first time and found myself talking to a woman with a heavy Eastern European accent who seemed to think I was some kind of nuisance caller. She started talking in her own language in a tone that sounded so abusive that

I had to put the phone down on her. For a moment, I had the uneasy feeling that I'd been given the wrong number on purpose, but when I redialled, more carefully this time, I was relieved to hear a voice I recognised.

"Hello. Helen Grayson speaking. Who is this?"

"Oh, hello, Mrs Grayson. It's Jim Russell. I don't know if you remember me from the other day? I'm the one who spoilt your lunch."

"No, don't worry about that." She chuckled, but I detected the faintest tone of sarcasm in her voice. "It happens all the time. I should be used to it by now." And then, after a meaningful pause, she continued: "I suppose you want to speak to Richard, but I'm afraid he's gone away for a few days and I'm not sure when he'll be back. Perhaps you'd better try calling again later this week."

"But I was supposed to see him today, and I really need to speak to him right now. Can I have his number?"

It took her a few seconds to answer. "I'm afraid I haven't got a number for him. I know that sounds a bit strange, but for some reason he won't give it to me. I know he's all right because he phones me every evening and although I've asked him several times, he refuses to tell me where he is. I've even tried call-back but the number's been withheld. He says he has his reasons and not to worry because he's promised to tell me soon, so for the moment, at least, I'm happy to go along with it. All I can say is that I trust him completely and he's never let me down before."

I hesitated for a moment, wondering what to say next. I wasn't quite sure that I believed her. Surely Grayson would have confidence in his own wife? Perhaps there *was* another woman after all.

"Next time you hear from him, could you tell him I called?" I asked weakly.

She confirmed that she would, and with the usual goodbye, I put the phone down, feeling more than a little confused. It was a weird sensation I was getting right then: almost what it must be like when a lover says it's over and I don't want to see you again.

And just like a jilted lover, I was feeling frustrated and more than a touch angry.

Chapter 34

My work schedule was very busy that Monday. In a way I was pleased about that because there was no chance to think about anything else. But the journey home brought everything back to me. Still there had been no word from Grayson. How could he just leave me in mid-air like that? With all sorts of conflicting thoughts and emotions spinning around in my head, I arrived back home feeling something close to a nervous wreck.

Without announcing my presence, I went straight into the living room and over to the drinks cupboard to pour myself a whisky, before sitting down for a while to cool off. I downed the whisky in one, which is something I never normally do. In fact, I hardly ever drink spirits at all. After that, I got up from my chair and went straight into the kitchen. Sarah was feeding dirty washing into the machine. I came straight out with it and told her all about my phone conversations and my misgivings about the situation.

Slamming the washer door shut, she stood back up to face me and said: "Why am I not surprised?" There was more than a hint of sarcasm in her voice.

"He seemed like such a nice guy," I said meekly. "I really felt I could trust him."

When it comes to retracing male weaknesses, like most women, Sarah has a very long memory. "I seem to have heard that from you a few times before," she said, a wry smile on her face.

My memory, on the other hand, is short and selective. It's a male thing. Why dwell on the past? Tomorrow is another day. But on this occasion I still felt I had been right about Richard. I decided to defend my case.

"If we go through life never trusting anybody, then nothing would ever get done," I said. "And, rightly or wrongly, I still trust Richard."

"Maybe you do," she said, "but there's a difference between trust and intuition, and that's a skill reserved for women. I don't think men even know what intuition is."

I could not think of a clever enough answer for that, so I decided to put the ball in her court. "The secretary is going to ring me back if Grayson comes in tomorrow morning, but what do you think I should do if he doesn't?"

She thought about it for a while. "First of all," she began, "I think, as usual, that you're jumping the gun. There's still a possibility he'll turn up."

"And if he doesn't, what's your plan B?" I asked.

"You say he hides his phone number?"

"Yes."

She clicked her fingers, as if to signify a light bulb moment. " I know," she began, "what about the faxes he's sending to his office? They always arrive with the sender's number printed on them somewhere, don't they?"

I had to smile, thankful I was married to someone so much smarter than me.

"So they do!" I exclaimed, and gave her a hug. "I hadn't thought of that. You're so clever! I can ask his secretary. I'll give her a ring."

"Yes, but not before one. Don't forget, you're supposed to be giving him the benefit of the doubt until then."

She was right, of course. In any case, it was too late to phone anyone, and the secretary would have gone home ages ago.

That's when I decided that I was going to have to do something I really hate doing: cancel all my patients for the day. Perhaps, I told myself, I don't need to feel too guilty. After all, I'd only had to do that no more than two or three times in my whole career, and that was when I'd developed a bad cold or something similar. Some other dentists I know wouldn't think twice about cancelling for nothing more important than a game of golf.

The next morning, Tuesday, I phoned Jodie before she left home to give her time to work out her cancellation strategy. I gave her the choice of a cold or a bout of food poisoning as an excuse, realising that either of these conditions could be extended by a day or two, if need be.

I waited at home for the phone to ring. With nothing happening, the time seemed to drag on forever. There were only two calls all morning, both of them from Sarah's badminton friends about fixing up a girls' foursome later in the week, so it was with a sense of deep sadness that, at shortly after one, I picked up the phone and dialled Grayson's office.

"So, I gather you've not heard from him?" I began.

"No, sorry. Absolutely nothing," she confirmed.

"I really need to talk to him about something very important, and I was wondering if you could do me a small favour," I continued.

"What's that?"

"The faxes you receive from him. Can you give me the number they're sent from?" I asked.

She did not reply immediately, and I knew why. She was obviously considering the loyalty factor. I held my breath, willing her to come out in my favour.

"Sorry," she said at length. "I'm afraid I can't do that, not without his permission, and so far he has not given it. The best I can do is tell him in the next message I send, that you want to speak to him. Maybe he'll ring you."

My heart sank. No, he won't, I thought, because he would have done that by now. I told her that I understood her situation and rang off.

True to form, I started to feel extremely frustrated. This was still unfinished business, and it was starting to eat me alive.

Chapter 35

I'm ashamed to say that I went to the drinks cupboard again for another whisky, the second in two days, which was two more than I'd had in the last six months. I took a large gulp and sat there staring at the glass as I swilled the whisky round in it, hoping that by some trick of magic the alcohol would help to prise an idea out of my brain.

Perhaps it *was* the alcohol, or maybe it was just a coincidence, but anyhow, an idea *did* suddenly materialise, seemingly from nowhere. At first, I dismissed it. No one would be that crazy, I thought.

Not only would it be a totally insane thing for any decent person to even contemplate, but to carry it out would mean doing something I've always vowed never to do: I would have to lie to Sarah. I must admit that before I met her, and perhaps fuelled by an excess of testosterone, I had once or twice been less than honest in my personal relationships, ignoring the possible negative consequences and causing irreparable damage. I'm not going to say what sort of damage or to who, but suffice to say that I did not get away scot-free either.

What I was left with in each case was an indelible scar of guilt which, in unguarded moments, comes back to haunt me, and the last thing I wanted was to create any more scars. "Out, damned spot!" as Lady Macbeth would say.

The second problem I had with my new brainwave was that it involved doing something illegal, and if I were to be found out, my name would be removed from the dentists' register and I might not ever be allowed to practise again.

I read somewhere of a group of burghers in Germany a century or two ago who resolved that they would only make important decisions after considering them both while fully inebriated with alcohol, and then again while sober. If they reached the same decision both times, they would act upon it.

Right now, in my case, it was the whisky talking. I decided not to have a second tot, but to wait for the effects of the first to wear off, to see if I still had the same thoughts.

I needed a plan. After dinner that evening, Sarah disappeared upstairs to catch up with a bit more ironing. Bracing myself, I went up to see her. She was halfway through one of my shirts.

"I've just spoken to one of the lads at the club," I said. "They're having a little pool tournament, and they want me to make up the numbers. Okay if I join them?"

She picked out a hanger for the shirt and hung it up on the rail. "I didn't hear the phone ring," she said. "Who was it?"

"No, I phoned him. It was Gerry," I said, trying my hardest not to stammer. "Haven't seen him for a while and I thought he'd like to meet up for a drink. It was just by chance he was playing pool tonight."

I think she believed me, but I could feel sweat collecting on my brow, and I prayed she hadn't noticed. "Don't bother about food for me; I'll get something at the club." I said, trying hard to make my departure look as casual as possible. I gave her a peck on the cheek, careful not to let her face touch mine, in case she noticed my clammy skin.

The car was parked in the drive, but I needed a few things from the garage, so I swung back the up and over, holding onto the handle so that the door would not crash open like it usually did. Even so, there were the usual twangings from the counterbalance springs, noises which I don't usually register, but now they sounded so loud, making me thankful that the ironing room was at the back of the house. Not wishing to test my luck, I quickly grabbed the things I wanted and stowed them down in the passenger foot-well before carefully easing the garage door back down.

My heart was racing, and I could feel it banging against my chest wall as the adrenaline took over. With a quick glance back at the house to make sure she hadn't seen me, I closed the door and started the car up. I don't remember even taking one breath until I had safely turned into the next street. At that point I felt I had to calm myself down and gather myself for the action to come, so I pulled the car over, killed the engine and just sat there for a while, waiting for the thumping in my chest to die down.

My reaction to all this stress made me realise how important it was going to be to maintain control. In that regard I had learnt from my many years in dentistry that, although some adrenaline is good, too much of it can have a very negative effect. It speeds up the heart and increases blood flow to the muscles, which is great for 'flight or fight' but not so good for control, because it tends to make your hands shake and your reflexes just a little too responsive, when in reality, 'steady and sure' is what's really needed. Nobody needs a shaky dentist.

I sat there for a little while, using the power of meditation to steady my breathing and bring my heart rate back down, and I resolved not to do anything further if the palms of my hands were still wet. Happy that I was now back in control, I started the car up and drove on towards my predetermined destination.

Chapter 36

I stopped the car on a single yellow line, some way down from the house and on the other side of the road, so that I could see it clearly. It was around 8.30pm, a time when most people have settled themselves down for the evening, either watching TV or reading, or putting the kids to bed. Being late October, it had already been dark for a few hours, but the street was well lit with sodium lamps, making the row of parked cars appear quite colourless, which I knew they couldn't be.

It was a quiet road, forming part of a large crescent, so either direction led back to the main road, meaning there would never be a lot of traffic. But there were still people about (late commuters and others walking their dogs), so it was not a good time to do what I was contemplating. I was just going to have to sit here and wait.

Grayson's porch light was on and the windows of the first-floor living room were flickering blue. It was probably Helen, watching TV in there. Hopefully she was alone, but I couldn't be sure. The basement was in darkness as, without Grayson around, I knew it would be. I also knew that it would be very foolish to go anywhere near the property until all the lights had been out for at least 30 minutes. In most cases, that would mean waiting until well after midnight, but I remembered that Grayson had said she was a lark and usually went to bed quite early, and as it was now starting to get quite cold, I sincerely hoped he wasn't joking.

With the engine off, the temperature soon started to drop and the cold started to work its way into my body. At first it was just my feet. I tried thumping them alternately against the floor to keep the circulation going, but that only worked for a short while. Slowly but surely the cold began creeping along my arms and legs, making them feel increasingly numb, and faced with the prospect of strenuous activity to come, that was the last thing I wanted.

So I set the heater to max, started up the engine and moved off, realising that a parked car with its engine running would soon attract attention. For the next hour or so I drove around the neighbouring streets, trying not to use the same one twice, and once the cabin had warmed up enough I pulled over for a while until it got too cold again. I had to go through this cycle several times, waiting for the clock to tick down.

It was around 10 o'clock when I finally returned to my original parking spot. The living room was now in darkness, but now there was a light on upstairs (from the bedroom, I assumed), and then a few moments later another light came on. It was the smaller room next door, and the frosted glass told me that this had to be the bathroom.

I don't know if it's just my imagination, but whenever I have to queue to use a toilet, or when I'm waiting for someone else to finish in the bathroom, they always seem to take forever, but when I go in there I seem to be in and out like a flash. Waiting for Helen Grayson to complete her ablutions, particularly as I was starting to get cold again, was no exception.

As the minutes ticked by, I tried to imagine what she was doing: probably having a bath, because a shower could not possibly take that long. First, there would be the process of running the water and getting it to the right temperature, and then there would be the long soak, occasionally topping up with more hot water by stretching a leg out and turning the tap on with the end of the big toe. When I was a teenager, I always used to do that, but I must admit that since showering became popular back in the sixties, I never bother to have a bath. For one thing, I'm too impatient, and for another, I actually quite like the idea of being a good citizen and saving water.

It was a good half an hour before the bathroom light went out. Ten minutes later, the bedroom lights went out as well, at last leaving the house in complete darkness. I read somewhere that it takes on average up to 20 minutes to fall asleep, depending on what sort of day you've had. On that basis, I knew that to be safe I'd have to wait another half an hour, and I used that time to go over my plan.

Chapter 37

I had earlier placed both my home toolbox and some disposable clinical gloves in the passenger footwell. I donned the gloves and sorted through the box to find a couple of wood chisels. I also had a carrier bag containing two pairs of double-suction pads for lifting glass, which I had bought from my local DIY store. This was all the equipment I needed, to do something I had never done before in my whole life: that is, to knowingly break the law.

It was now around 11.30pm. After checking that there were no late dog-walkers in the street, I tucked the chisels under my belt and climbed out of the car. My heart was racing, and I could actually feel it thumping against my ribs. It was time to compose myself -something that as an experienced dentist I was well practised at- so I took a deep breath, reminding myself once again to keep focused and calm, and carefully closed the door, but only up to the first catch so as not to make any unnecessary noise. After pulling my beanie hat down over my ears, I slid my giveaway blue gloved hands out of sight into my zipper-jacket pockets.

As I crossed the road, the thought occurred to me that my furtive attire would probably attract more attention than if I had been dressed more formally, but it was too late to change things now. Keeping my head well bowed, I strode quickly towards Grayson's house, and as I reached the side entrance, I paused to take a last glance over my shoulder, relieved to see that there was no one around. I quickly descended the steps and made my way over to the far window, which was conveniently hidden from pavement level by the privet hedge up above. I paused there for a moment to let my breathing settle down and braced myself for the ordeal ahead.

It was now time to put my plan into action. I was going to break into Grayson's house. On my previous visit to the basement office, I had noticed that the windows had been refitted with double-glazed plastic frames of one of the earlier designs, which meant that they would be far from burglar proof. I knew from watching workmen replacing my own windows, that all it required to gain entry was to prise off the thin plastic retaining strips; a task that was easily done with a couple of chisels.

I set to work. The plan was to remove all four strips and ease the complete double-glazed panel out of its housing using the suction grips. After removing the glass, I would then be able to climb in and search around for recent fax messages from Grayson, take down the sender's details and get straight back out. Then it would be a simple matter to replace the glass and snap the fixing strips back in place. There would be no sign of entry, nothing taken and no one would be any the wiser.

The bottom strip, being at waist height, was easy to work on and came free with little effort. The side strips were somewhat harder to deal with, but after freeing each one at its lower end, I simply had to get hold of it and peel the whole thing out with one easy movement. So far so good. With everything going to plan so smoothly, I breathed a sigh of relief. But it was one sigh too soon, because when I reached up to deal with the last strip, I realised it was just a bit too high for me to reach, no matter how hard I tried to stretch. After several attempts, I sunk back down, cursing under my breath at my lack of forward planning. I stood there thinking for a moment. I had come this far, and I wasn't ready to be defeated by something as simple as this. There had to be another way.

By its very nature, dentistry has a regular habit of presenting the operator with unforeseen problems, whether it's trying to fish out that last little piece of wisdom tooth root or retrieving a broken file from a root canal. The trick I have learnt from this over the years is simply not to panic. Think it through, and nine times out of ten you'll come up with an answer. But if you freak out and allow yourself to start sweating, you'll never do it.

So, although I felt the beginnings of panic trying to invade my space, I resolved to fight it off, just as I had done in the surgery so many times before. I looked around for something to stand on. I only needed a few more inches, but there was nothing suitable down there except a newly built retaining wall, housing soil for the privet hedge above.

Without a moment's hesitation and without really thinking, I aimed a savage kick at the wall, karate style. To my complete surprise, the upper three courses broke loose and fell to the ground, breaking the night silence with a loud and worrying clumping noise. Half expecting to hear a light sleeper somewhere opening a window to see what was going on, I stayed perfectly still, listening carefully for any activity. Thankfully, there was none.

Satisfied that I hadn't been found out, I knelt down and separated out a few of the bricks, stacking them to make a platform to stand on. That extra height turned out to be just enough, and with the last retaining strip gone, all I had to do was remove the glass panel, and I would be in.

But that particular task proved to be more of a challenge than I had expected. A double-glazed panel is really quite heavy and needs careful handling at the best of times, so when you're perched on a loose pile of bricks, anything can happen. I took the two sets of suction pads out of the carrier bag and applied them to the glass, listening each time for the lever to make its reassuring click. Setting myself on the bricks, I braced myself and gave the handles a sharp tug. The window panel came free surprisingly easily, but I wasn't ready for how heavy it was. With my very unstable brick platform shifting around under my feet, I very nearly lost my balance. If I had done so, the noise of a double thickness of glass smashing against concrete would certainly have been enough to waken even the very deepest sleeper. I had to use all my strength, and more, to lower the double-glazed panel gently to the ground.

Once down, the glass was much easier to deal with. I shifted it to one side and took a moment to catch my breath and gather myself for the next episode of my plan. I leaned forward and peered through the opening, but it was too dark to make out anything inside. I tried hard to remember the layout of the room, cursing the fact that I had not paid enough attention to it the when I was there. I knew for sure that the secretary's work station was at this end of the long table and the combined telephone and fax machine was also on the table, to the right. Fingers crossed, there might even be a new fax from Grayson sitting in the machine's out tray, which would make getting the information I was seeking a very simple matter. But first, I needed a torch. This was the most important piece of equipment of all and I cursed under my breath as I realised it was the one thing I had forgotten to bring. How could I be so stupid?

Chapter 38

And then I remembered that I always kept a small pen torch in the car. I climbed back up the steps and made my way back across the road, once again trying not to look too furtive. I scrabbled around in the glove compartment and came out with a variety of objects: pens, sweets, soiled tissues and old parking tickets, but no torch. I swore out loud, enough for the whole street to hear if they weren't already asleep. Luckily for me, they probably all were.

So the torch was not where it should have been. I looked in both door wells. Nothing. And then, out of desperation, I knelt down and felt under the passenger seat, and with a sigh of relief I caught sight of it, only to see that it had successfully managed to make things as difficult as possible by rolling under the slider mechanism of the seat, causing me to lose some skin from the back of a couple of fingers in my efforts to retrieve it. I held my breath as I switched it on to test it, relieved to find that it actually worked, and headed quickly back across the road to my crime scene.

It was only a pen torch, but it was better than nothing and gave me enough light to be able to scan the room and get a fix on where everything was. The fax machine sat close by, on my end of the table, exactly as I remembered, but to my dismay, I saw that the out-tray was empty. No new faxes this evening. There was, however, sitting right next to the machine, an assortment of paperwork in an untidy pile. Maybe that contained a fax or two?

It was time to carry out the dastardly deed. Climb in through the window, sort through those papers, make a note of the information I needed, and get straight out. Simple.

But I'd forgotten one thing: I was older than I used to be. When I was in my early twenties, I was so slim and fit, that I could have vaulted myself into that room in one easy movement, but now in my fifties and with more than a few extra pounds of good living to carry, that same task was much more of a challenge. I had to hook my elbows over the sill and swing one leg up to gain a purchase before heaving my trunk over into the room.

It was at this point, with my body half in and half out of the room, that all hell broke loose. For some stupid reason, I had not anticipated that there would be an alarm. The piercing noise was deafening and so completely invasive that for a moment, I seemed to stop being able to think. But I knew I had to fight it, because in no time at all, that place was going to be swarming with people. This was not part of my plan.

"Shit, shit, shit!" I shouted to myself. "What am I going to do?" Now I really was in a state of panic. Should I just drop back down and run while I had the chance? Yes, of course I should, but to get this far and go away with nothing? That didn't seem like much of an option to me right then, so I took what ought to have been the worst possible decision, and pushing myself hurriedly through the window, I fell with a painful thud on to the floor. Scrambling clumsily to my feet, I raced across to the desk, grabbed a handful of the papers and stuffed them inside my pullover before heading straight back to the window, almost leaping out of it like a cat, with a new-found strength and agility that seemed to have suddenly appeared from nowhere. I raced up the stairs and sprinted across the road, fumbling for my keys, before dumping myself down on the driver's seat. Without properly closing the door, I started the car up and smashed the lever into gear. A few seconds later, I had disappeared around the corner without even looking back.

Heart pounding, I raced up to the next junction, tyres screeching as I took the corner at speed. The force of it made the passenger door swing open, thanks to the fact that it was still on the half-latch. I pulled up to close it and took the opportunity to check my face in the rear-view mirror. It was a bright shade of red, and it glistened all over with sweat. I looked as guilty as hell, and if anyone saw me now, I'd have a lot of explaining to do, especially if they spotted how fast the blood vessels in my neck were pulsating. I knew that the main issue right then was to get cool, then stay cool.

I loosened my collar and drove back home with both front windows wide open and the cooling fan set at maximum, making sure to stay well within the speed limit all the way so as not to attract attention. After all, I was going to have to face Sarah very soon, and the last thing I wanted was to get her worked up.

Chapter 39

It was well past midnight when I finally arrived back home, parking the car as usual up on the drive. I had to ease myself very carefully out of my seat, thanks to a very tender bruise on my right hip, and as I did so, and much to my dismay, I noticed the living room light was still on. After a night out with the boys it was quite usual for me to return at such a time, but on previous occasions Sarah had always used the opportunity to have an early night, thus avoiding the need to suffer any of my alcohol-fuelled ramblings.

Before I put the key in the door I dusted down my chinos and checked that the rest of my clothing was properly in place. It was then that I remembered the stolen paperwork stuffed under my jumper and hastily patted it down so that it wouldn't show.

I was right to feel apprehensive. She was sitting in the living room, staring at the local newspaper, but I had the feeling that she wasn't reading it.

"Did you have a good time?" she said, tight lipped.

"Yes, pretty good," I mumbled, trying not to catch her eye.

She put the paper down and stared hard at me. "I know where you've been." she said accusingly. "I knew even from the moment you left the house."

"What do you mean?" I responded meekly.

She raised a counting finger. "First of all," she began, "when you first told me you were meeting the boys, there was sweat on your upper lip. I knew straight away that you weren't telling the truth.

"Secondly, you took the car, and that's something you never do when you go out drinking. You always order a taxi."

At that point, and to my immense relief, I knew the game was up. There was bound to be a difficult few moments ahead, but at least I did not have to continue this uncomfortable charade any longer.

"And what was the third thing?" I asked.

She smiled triumphantly. I think she was quite enjoying making me squirm.

"There was a phone call for you tonight."

"Who was it?"

"Gerry. He said he hadn't heard from you for a while and wondered if you'd like to meet him for a drink at the club."

That was the last nail in the coffin. I don't know why, but when she said that, I started laughing, and to my complete surprise, so did she. The evidence was overwhelming; I was guilty as charged, and the relief of not having to compound that damn lie any more was like taking the cork out of a bottle of fizz.

Suddenly, the frosty atmosphere between us had melted completely away, and I took her in my arms and gave her a hug.

"So, where do you think I've been?" I said.

She tossed her head back, looked me straight in the eye and replied, "My darling, Jim, don't you think I know you well enough by now? I can guess *exactly* what you did tonight!"

"So, what did I do?" I challenged.

"Given the circumstances, there was only one thing you could do. You became a burglar, right?"

I nodded meekly. Inside, I was amazed (but after all these years, I shouldn't have been) at how well she knew me. "Sorry if I let you down," I said, "but I felt I just had to do it. No way could I let this thing go."

"I knew that." she replied. "It's part of your personality; one of the things that first attracted me to you."

"You mean apart from my hairy chest," I joked.

"It was a toss-up between the two of them," she said with a smile.

"Am I forgiven then?"

She fixed me with a meaningful stare. "As long as you promise never to lie to me again." she said sternly.

I crossed my heart and said: "I promise."

She smiled. "I always knew you wouldn't be able to stand not knowing where Grayson is, and to be honest, I felt the same. When I realised you'd told me a fib, I also knew why you did it. Yes, of course I would have said no to such a crazy idea, but now I've had time to think about it, I realise that there was only one thing you *could* do."

"And I did!" I said triumphantly as I pulled out the stolen paperwork from beneath my jumper. We sat down to go through them. There were about half a dozen sheets of A4, all crumpled and looking decidedly worse for wear, thanks to my frantic efforts to retrieve them. I gave Sarah half, and we flattened each of them out in turn on the coffee table. She picked up the first one, and after quickly scanning through it, she looked up at me and shook her head.

"This one's not a fax," she said. "It looks more like the draft of a speech or talk he was planning to make."

The second page was also part of that speech; and so was the third. As we worked our way through the pile, we began to realise that they all were.

"There's not a single piece of fax paper here!" she said with dismay.

I sat back in my chair with my head in my hands, hardly believing what a stupid fool I'd been. I should have looked more closely at what I was picking up, although with the overriding need to escape, that wasn't an option. Maybe the faxes were all in one of the other piles, and I'd chosen the wrong one.

I explained to Sarah how the alarm had gone off and that I'd had no time to think.

"Well, whatever," she said, shrugging her shoulders. "You can't do much about it now. Anyway, you did the right thing. If you'd have hung about, you'd have been caught, and that would have been much worse. *You'd* be living on prison food and *I'd* be bringing you a cake with a file in it."

Under normal circumstances, I might have laughed at that, but not tonight. "Good job I was wearing gloves," I said.

She gave me a hug. "Come on," she said. "Let's get you out of those stinky clothes and go to bed. After a good night's sleep, we'll be in a better frame of mind."

I nodded but felt too choked to say anything. I filled a glass of water from the kitchen tap and made my way up the stairs while she checked the doors and turned the lights off. When she came up, I was sitting on the bed, still moping.

"Come on," she whispered softly. "Let me give your shoulders a massage. You need to relax or you'll be tossing and turning all night. Take your jumper off."

She started to peel off the garment from the bottom. I held my aching arms up to let her do it. As I did so, a crumpled piece of paper fell out and onto the bed.

She picked it up and flattened it out to look at it.

"It's a fax!" she cried.

Chapter 40

The fax consisted of a series of notes relating to a forthcoming lecture that Grayson was obviously due to give. There were a lot of technical details about Neanderthals and the like, most of which went straight over my head, but I read enough to confirm that there was no mention of George or the photos. But the most important detail for me was in the single line, pre-printed at the bottom of the page. It said 'Bizzeebeez. Number One for Office Supplies' and displayed the fax number, complete with the local code, which I did not recognise. But there was no address.

"That won't be hard to find," said Sarah. "All we need to do is phone Directory Enquiries and get the details."

I did just that, there and then. Even though it was now well past midnight, I had to know. Luckily, Directory Enquiries was a 24-hour service, and considering the time of day, the operator was surprisingly helpful. After just a few minutes, I had the full address and telephone number of the Bizzeebeez shop. It turned out to be in Luton, which is about 40 minutes away from my house, traffic permitting.

"He obviously goes into the shop every day to use their fax machine," commented Sarah, "so he must be staying somewhere nearby."

"I think you're right," I agreed, and then I had a sudden thought. "He won't know anything about my break-in until tomorrow. His secretary's bound to fax him with the news, and as soon as he puts two and two together he'll move on."

"So you've got to get to the shop before *he* does."

"You're right," I replied, looking again at the fax, which was still had in my hand. "It gives the time the message was sent: 12.15pm. If he goes there at the same time every day, then I've got to be there by midday at least."

She shook her head. "No," she said, "You can't make that assumption. You've got to be there when they open, just in case."

She was right as usual, but if I wanted to be in Luton by 9am, I'd have to leave the house no later than 7.30, to allow for rush-hour traffic. With that thought, I yawned and stretched out my arms. It was time to get a few hours' shut-eye.

Not surprisingly, I didn't sleep too well that night. I had set the alarm for 6.15am, but I needn't have bothered. I was up long before that, and dressed and ready to go by seven. Sarah was still snoozing, so I crept in and gave her a very gentle peck on the cheek, which she didn't seem to register, so I presumed she was still well away and took great care to close the door quietly.

In those days, we were living quite near the North Circular Road, which, despite the horrendous build-up of traffic during the rush hours, was still by far the quickest way to get on to the M1 motorway. But today, the traffic was even worse than usual, thanks to a broken-down lorry at the Golders Green intersection. The three-lane carriageway was down to one, slowing everything to a crawl, and by the time I finally filtered onto the M1 motorway, it was already 8.10am.

With the very real prospect of being late, I felt myself tense up all over. My hands felt cold and damp, and it was all I could do to remain inside the unofficial speed limit, which from experience (or was it just good fortune?), I knew to be just under 80mph. The last thing I needed right now was to be pulled over by the police.

Chapter 41

As luck would have it, the rest of the journey was quite uneventful, and by 8.45am, I was turning off from the airport road and heading towards Luton town centre. I had already checked the road map of the area and worked out the location of the Bizzeebeez office supplies shop. It was quite near the police station, close to the middle of town, on a road called Stuart Street. Judging from the map, it looked an easy road to find, as it formed part of the main route, the A505, which led out towards Dunstable.

Sure enough, working my way slowly down Castle Street, I finally hit the junction with Stuart Street. It turned out to be a dual carriageway, and quite a major one at that. The police station was to my left, and as I passed it, I glanced over to the far side of the road and caught sight of an imposing Victorian terrace with shops below. I spotted Bizzeebeez immediately, standing out clearly from the other shops, thanks to its livery of bright yellow paint and with the name boldly displayed on the fascia board above.

On my side of the carriageway, almost opposite the shop, was a row of metered parking, and I pulled over to the grab the one remaining space. After feeding a pound coin into the meter, I checked my watch. It was exactly 9am. They should be getting ready to open right now, and I needed to be there when they did. The only problem was how to get across the very busy road, which had a safety fence separating the two carriageways. I realised that to get to the shop, which was about 50 yards away from me as the crow flies, I would have to walk up to the next junction, about 200 yards away, cross at the traffic lights and then walk back down. I placed the parking ticket on the dashboard and, as I closed the car door, glanced over at the shop. There was a man wearing a grey overcoat and black cheese-cutter hat standing at the door, waiting for it to open. He had his back to me so I couldn't be sure, but he was about the same height and build, so there was a good chance it could be Grayson.

I started to run towards the traffic lights, soon realising from my laboured breathing that I was not as fit as I used to be. Just as I reached the junction, as is always the way, the little red man appeared, telling me to wait. Breathing heavily by now, I pressed the button to register my presence. The road was by now very busy, and I had to wait for what seemed like forever (but was probably only two or three minutes) for the lights to change in my favour. The wait had given my out-of-condition body a chance to recover, and now into my second wind, I took off again at a jog. A few yards from the doorway of the shop, I stopped to catch my breath for a few moments, my gaze fixed firmly on the door. I used that time to compose what I was going to say to Grayson when he came out, and waited for a few more minutes. But in that time nobody went in or came out, so I decided to take the plunge and go in.

To my dismay, I discovered that the shop was deserted.

"Yes, sir? How can I help you?" said the assistant, who was one of two.

I took my handkerchief out and wiped the sweat off my brow. "Was there a man in here just now?" I asked.

"Yes," she replied, "but he's just left. Why, do you know him?"

"I'm not sure. Do you know his name?"

"Yes, it's Mr Wilson. Nice man. He comes in every day to pick up faxes and send them."

"Did he pick up one today?"

"Yes, there was just one. After he read it, he paid me as usual and left. He seemed to be in a bit of a hurry. I saw he had some other papers to send, but he said he would come back later."

"Which way did he go?"

"Same way he always does." She pointed to the left, where I'd just come from.

I cursed inwardly to myself. With my mind set on getting to the shop as quickly as possible I must have run straight past him and if it *was* Grayson, there's no doubt he would have spotted me. A running man stands out like a sore thumb, and all he had to do was duck into a shop doorway or something.

"I think he might be staying in the hotel just up the road," the assistant said. "Is he a friend of yours?"

"Yes, he is," I replied, and despite everything that had happened, I still meant it, because deep down I just knew that when someone as intelligent and focused as Richard Grayson obviously was, does something so bizarrely out of character, there must be a very good reason for it.

Chapter 42

I wasted no more time at the shop and took off in the direction of the hotel the assistant had mentioned. Hopefully, she was right, but if she wasn't, I knew for sure that I'd never be able to find Grayson unless he wanted me to. Judging by his rapid exit from the shop after seeing the fax, he must have put two and two together and realised I would be homing in on him. I imagined that right now, he'd be in his room, wherever that was, hastily packing for a quick getaway.

The reception desk was deserted. I slapped my hand hard on the desk bell and repeated it a couple of times to make sure I'd been heard, but it seemed ages before the smartly dressed receptionist appeared.

"Hello, sir. How can I help?" she asked.

"Do you have a Doctor Richard Grayson staying here?" I asked, knowing of course, that if she wanted to keep her job she wouldn't be able to tell me.

"May I ask who you are?" she enquired.

"I'm a friend of his, and I think he's expecting me. My name is Russell." I couldn't help smiling as I said it. It wasn't *really* a lie. He *was* expecting me, but not in the way she would be thinking.

She ran her finger down the room list. "I'm sorry, sir, but there doesn't seem to be a Mr Grayson staying with us. Maybe you've got the wrong hotel? There is another one about half a mile further on."

My heart sank. Perhaps I was jumping the gun and that guy wasn't Grayson after all. But even so I reasoned, he must be here because it just didn't make any sense to have to walk further than necessary to go to that shop every time.

I was just about to call it a day when I remembered what the girl in the shop had said. "Oh, sorry," I said to the receptionist. "I know it sounds a bit strange, but sometimes he uses a different name when he's away. He calls himself 'Wilson'." With that, I leaned forward to whisper in her ear. "Because he's quite famous and he doesn't want his fans knowing where he is." It seemed like a ridiculous explanation, even to me, but it was the only one I could think of at the time.

She seemed to swallow it. "Oh, is he?" she said, sounding genuinely excited.

"Oh, yes. I know Mr Wilson. He's been here a few days. Not many do that. This is more of an overnight and travellers' hotel and you don't tend to see the same person twice. But I still need to get his permission before I show you up."

She put the phone to her ear and pressed a button on the console. I could clearly hear the dialling tone, and we both waited for a response. There was none.

"No reply," she said finally, putting the phone back on its cradle. "Maybe he's gone out, or he might be asleep. I'll pop up and try knocking on his door. Just wait here for a few minutes and I'll be back."

"Okay," I said, watching as she got into the lift. She pressed the button for the third floor, and as the doors closed behind her, I made the spontaneous decision to head for the stairs. I climbed them two at a time, trying in vain to keep up with the lift. I was halfway up the final flight when I heard the lift door opening on the floor above. I stopped there to catch my breath and listen for any sounds. I heard her knock on a door and the sound of it opening. So there was somebody there after all.

"Sorry to disturb you, Mr Wilson. There's a Mr Russell down in the lobby to see you." By this time, I had climbed up to the top of the stairs and peered cautiously round the corner to see what was going on. She was standing at the open door of No. 34, but I could not see the occupant, so I could not be sure who it was until he spoke.

"Russell?" I heard him say. "I'm sorry but I don't know anyone of that name. There must be some sort of mistake. I think you'd better just tell him to go away."

Despite what it was saying, that voice sounded like music to me. It was the unmistakable Yorkshire accent of Richard Grayson.

"Okay," she replied. "I thought it was a bit strange because he started off calling you by a completely different name. Anyway, I'll tell him you can't see him. Sorry to bother you."

"Okay, thank you."

I heard the door close and waited out of sight at the top of the stairs while she called the lift again. I felt smug, knowing my hunches had been right all along.

That was the moment when the whole thing went pear-shaped.

"Hello, can I help you?" The female voice behind me made me jump out of my skin. I turned to see a thin woman coming up the stairs. She was holding a mop and a bucket.

Why didn't I hear her?

I've asked myself that same question many times since. The only explanation I can come up with is that I was concentrating so hard on what was in front of me that I completely cut off what was happening behind.

As bad luck would have it, the receptionist was still just along the hallway, waiting for the lift. On hearing the commotion, she came along to investigate. She looked horrified to find me there, and in no uncertain terms she told me that since I hadn't been invited up, I was trespassing and she'd have to call security, or even the police, if I did not leave at once.

And with the police station just over the road, I decided not to make a fuss. Out on the street again, I stood there for a minute or two, weighing up my options. There wasn't that much of a choice. I knew for sure that now he realised he'd been rumbled, Grayson would desert his post as soon as possible, knowing that sooner or later I would be back to harass him. He might already be down at the desk settling his bill, and then where would he go? Out the back way, to his car of course, and then take off to some other equally anonymous venue. I knew then that I'd have to follow him, and I cursed as I remembered where I'd parked: over the other side of the damn dual carriageway. Grayson would be long gone by the time I reached my car.

There was a yellow parking ticket on the windscreen. I tore it off and threw it contemptuously on to the back seat for another time. To get back to the hotel I had to drive down to the next roundabout, about half a mile away, and come back on myself. I turned off left, just before the hotel, to access the car park, which was situated at the rear. Just as I passed through the gates, another car was leaving. I recognised it immediately. It was that unmistakeable bright blue Mercedes SLK. As it accelerated away with its rear wheels spinning, leaving a small cloud of dust, I just managed to get a glimpse of the driver's face. It was Richard Grayson.

Chapter 43

Grayson turned left out of the car park and into the side road that led directly on to the A505 dual carriageway at the front of the hotel. From there he could only turn left on to the southbound carriageway, which led to the main roundabout less than a mile away. After that, I would have no way of guessing which way he might go, and I knew I just had to catch him before he got there, or all would be lost.

My car was a Renault Scenic, not exactly the fastest car on the road and certainly no match for a Mercedes, but by now I had become totally obsessed with getting George back, no matter what. Even if it meant breaking the law yet again.

But first, I still had to get out of the car park. As happens so often, it was much too small to cope with the demand required of it and was completely full, except for the one space vacated by Grayson. I used that space to manoeuvre my car, reversing hurriedly into it in order to turn around. I'm ashamed to admit that, in my haste, I made a pig's ear out of the job and managed to put a rather nasty go-faster dent along one side of the Ford Mondeo parked next door. Strangely I did not feel, at that moment anyway, the slightest bit guilty, telling myself that if the owner knew what this was all about he would surely give me his blessing.

The junction with the dual carriageway was about a hundred yards away and the lights were still on green, so I took off, my wheels spitting smoke. But before I was even halfway there the lights had changed to amber. The leading two cars on the main road were already starting to creep forward but with my mind already made up, I kept going. By the time I reached the junction, the lights had changed to red, but I just kept my foot down, snatching down hard on the wheel and forcing my car to lurch dangerously to one side as it turned on to the carriageway, only a matter of inches in front of the lead vehicle. With my right foot still down on the gas, I forced the steering wheel hard over to straighten my car up and glanced in the mirror to see several angry faces behind me, mouthing all sorts of obscenities, along with much gesticulating and shaking of fists. But I didn't care; in fact I felt quite pleased with myself, and probably just because of nerves, I started to laugh.

Normally, I'm quite a sedate sort of motorist. Nowadays, with so many rules and the technology of CCTV cameras to contend with, there's not too much point driving any other way. But in those days it was a lot easier to break the rules and get away with it, and anyway right then I didn't care how many of them I broke because there was only one thing on my mind.

There was no sign of the blue Mercedes up ahead. Grayson had already got too much of a start, and I was going to have to be very lucky if I caught up with him now. I put my foot down as far as it would go, pushing the Scenic up well past 60mph. The roundabout was coming up fast, forcing me to make a quick decision: which way to go? With four exits to choose from, I'd have to take pot luck. Straight ahead on the A505 seemed the most likely option, because it would take

Grayson towards the airport, or maybe to the M1 motorway and back to London. Or would he turn right, down Castle Street, which headed south and was the first part of the Old London Road?

I was only about 20 yards from the roundabout, braking hard while trying to make up my mind, when I had a lucky break. Out of the corner of my eye, heading back along the other side of the carriageway in the opposite direction to me, I saw a flash of blue. Glancing quickly at my wing mirror, I spotted the Mercedes speeding away in the outside lane.

I let out a triumphant whoop and gave the steering wheel a joyful thump, knowing that I hadn't lost him after all. Not only that, but now I even knew which way he was going: North towards Bedford, along the A505. Now all I had to do was double back on myself at the roundabout and follow the road while keeping my speed up. I told myself to be patient, because I guessed that once he felt sure he had given me the slip, he would slow down and merge with the rest of the traffic. Sooner or later I was bound to catch up with him. Unless of course he decided to turn off somewhere up ahead.

Still driving well above the speed limit, I made good progress. There were two or three more roundabouts and a few sets of traffic lights, most of which were kind enough to stay on green, but there was still no sign of the Mercedes. After 10 minutes or so, and after overtaking almost every vehicle on the road, I began to wonder if I really had lost him this time. Maybe he had already turned off down some little side street. That would be easy to do, and I'd never notice. But just when I thought all was lost and I might as well turn back, I suddenly caught sight of him again. He had tucked himself in front of a huge 16-wheeler only about six vehicles ahead of me. No wonder I hadn't spotted him before.

We were well out of Town now, and were heading towards Bedford on what was now the A6. It had narrowed down to a single lane, passing through farmland with freshly ploughed fields on either side. There was no way either of us could overtake, and a slow-moving farm vehicle at the front was conveniently keeping the Mercedes firmly in check.

I couldn't be sure if Grayson would remember my car, as he'd only ever seen it once but just in case, I decided to stay low profile, keeping myself well tucked in behind the Sprinter van in front of me, edging out now and then to keep an eye on my quarry.

The road continued straight on for a few more miles through open countryside, and I had decided that Grayson would be heading for Bedford, which would probably be his next stopping point. No doubt he would find another hotel there, to hide away in and complete whatever it was he found so important.

The Sprinter van did an excellent job of blocking my view, and it was only on one of my 'sorties' out to the middle of the road that I discovered, much to my horror, that the Mercedes was no longer there.

Realising that there was no way it could have overtaken that farm vehicle, I looked over to my left and caught sight of that very distinctive car disappearing fast down a narrow country lane. Almost at that same moment, the turn-off to that lane appeared on my left. Seeing it at the last minute out of the corner of my eye, I snatched hard at the wheel. The Scenic, not built for this type of treatment, did its best to topple over, and I had to grapple wildly with the steering to bring her back on to four wheels. After snaking on a short distance further, I managed to straighten up, and I immediately put my foot down to give chase. I thanked my lucky stars that I'd spotted the Mercedes in time. A few more seconds, and it would have been too late.

I had no idea where this road lead, maybe to a small village or just a farm or two, because there were no clear road markings, and the road itself was overhung by a series of unkempt hedgerows, suggesting it was low priority. There was no other traffic around, which suited me fine because this was my chance to catch up with Grayson and have it out with him, right there and then. I would make it very clear that I wasn't at all angry with him, just very curious about why he had suddenly become so elusive. All I wanted to do was to be friends and share his findings. After all, more than anyone else I had a right to know, because it was I who'd started the whole thing off.

At its widest, the lane was just about wide enough for two cars. I could see Grayson's car in the distance, and by the way he had settled into a more sedate speed, I got the impression that he thought he'd lost me. My plan was to gradually catch up with him and somehow persuade him to stop and talk.

It did not work out that way. I had got to within a few hundred yards of him when no doubt he spotted me in his mirror, because he suddenly took off at speed again. I flashed my headlights in the vain hope that they would somehow encourage him to stop, but to no effect.

I sighed and swore out loud, thumping angrily at the steering wheel. Now that Grayson knew I was behind him, there was no point trying to give chase because I knew my car was no match for his under any circumstances, let alone the challenge of a very bendy country road. I just had to resign myself to admitting defeat.

Chapter 44

Despite feeling so frustrated, I resolved to continue following the Mercedes for as long as I could, but I had to watch helplessly as it got further and further ahead. Soon it would be completely out of sight and that would be it: game over. No way would Grayson make the same mistake again, and I knew I'd never get another chance to find him.

The road took me through a patch of dense woodland, the trees and bushes blocking out my view of the way ahead, and it was only after emerging on to a clear patch of road that I caught sight of the Mercedes again. It was by now at least a mile away and well out of range and still moving very fast. I watched as Grayson approached a sharp right-hand bend at a speed I would have been very uncomfortable with; but then I wasn't driving a Mercedes sports car.

But there was just one thing he hadn't reckoned on. At the precise moment he hit the sharpest part of the right-hand bend, a small deer, a Muntjac or similar, which must have been running along in the field beside him, suddenly darted out through a gap in the hedgerow and straight across his path. I can only guess that, with no time to think, Grayson acted on an age-old reflex to save life.

Unfortunately for him, the life that he saved belonged to the deer. Instead of following the road, the Mercedes continued in a straight line, becoming airborne as it ripped through the hedgerow straight ahead and sailed over a ditch before plunging head first into a grassy bank on the far side. That moment is indelibly imprinted in my mind and will remain so until the day I die. The image that keeps coming back to haunt me is of that car suspended in mid-air: a frozen moment that separates life from death. In fact, it did not so much seem like a moment; it was more like a kind of forever thing, as if time had suddenly decided to stop right there.

The shock of what I had just witnessed sent a sudden wave of paralysis through every muscle in my body, forcing me to bring my car to a halt. I sat there, still tightly gripping the wheel, my mind in a state of total confusion about what to do next. I started to shiver. Suddenly, I felt very scared of what I was about to see, but I knew that I had no choice. I must get there as quickly as possible and try to rescue my friend. Taking a deep breath, I slammed the car into gear and took off as fast as I could.

By the time I got there, I was shaking all over, and I had to take several more deep breaths to steady myself. I stopped the car some way short of the bend and ran, still trembling, towards the gap in the hedgerow. Not sure what to expect, I started to climb up the grassy bank towards the wretched scene, but I was stopped in my tracks by a very strong smell of petrol, accompanied by the sight of wisps of smoke coming from beneath the crumpled bonnet.

The very next second, I noticed flames appearing from underneath one side of the engine compartment. Afraid of what might happen next, I took a step back. I still look back at that moment with mixed feelings, knowing that many people would regard it as a very cowardly thing to do, but on the other hand if I hadn't done it, I might not be here now to tell you the story, because in the very next instant, there was an almighty explosion and the whole car burst into flames.

I threw myself down on to the ground and instinctively curled my body up into the foetal position while covering my face with my hands. I lay there for a few moments, half expecting to be rained on by burning hot shrapnel. Luckily I was just far enough away but I could feel the intense heat of the flames, even from 30 yards. When I opened my eyes again, I stared, hypnotised by the horrific sight of the burning inferno before me. I tried to see through the flames to spot any movement from inside the cabin. Thankfully, there was none. If there had been I still don't know what I would, or could, have done. The searing heat ensured that any rescue attempt would be quite impossible, and if Grayson was conscious after the impact, he would not have been so for very long. I tried to console myself with the idea that such a violent collision would have killed him instantly.

I got up and immediately started coughing uncontrollably from the smoke and noxious chemicals now beginning to fill the air. But even worse than that, came another more familiar aroma, which as soon as it hit my nostrils, caused me to retch repeatedly until I finally threw up. It was the smell of burning flesh; the very same as I'd smelled before at a hundred barbecues. But it was the realisation of its origin that set off the nausea. I cannot go anywhere near a barbecue now.

I stood there motionless, gripped by a morbid fascination, which compelled me to keep watching. It was only with some effort that I managed to shake myself out of it and try to figure out what I should do next.

Chapter 45

Somehow, I did not feel there was any need to rush, because it was already too late, but convention told me that the emergency services should be informed immediately. I had already seen from my mobile phone that there was no signal around there. I'd have to find a house with a landline. I ran back out to the road and looked all around. There was only one house to be seen in any direction, and it was on this road, about a mile further on. I ran back to my car and took off towards it as fast as my Scenic would take me, screeching to a halt on the road in front of the driveway. I threw the car door wide open before sprinting to the front door and ringing on the bell, keeping my finger on it to try to convey a sense of urgency.

I probably didn't have to wait long, but it seemed like forever. As I bent down to look through the letter-box, I heard the latch go. The door swung open as far as the security chain would allow, and I saw the face of a very elderly lady peering enquiringly down at me. She had pure white hair and was wearing a floral housecoat. "Hello, can I help you?" she said.

I stood up and was about to blurt out the details of what I'd just witnessed, when a disturbing thought came into my head. Would what I was about to say incriminate me in some way? I hesitated for a moment, trying to think of a suitably non-committal statement.

"I was just driving along back there," I began, "and I think someone may have had an accident. There's a lot of smoke, and it looks like there's a car on fire. I would have called the emergency services but there's no signal round here. Can you do it for me?"

The poor lady looked quite shocked. "Oh dear, that sounds terrible!" she exclaimed. "Yes, of course. I'll go and do it right now."

"Okay, thanks," I said. "I'll just wait here until you come back."

She wisely closed the door on me. After all, there was no one else around and she didn't know me from Adam.

But I did not wait. I realised that she hadn't seen my car and she didn't know my name. Perhaps it was time to disappear. After all, I had not directly caused the accident, and trying to explain my presence on such a lonely road might create an unnecessary problem. There was nothing I could do for Grayson that would make the slightest difference, so with that thought in my mind, I ran back to the car and headed off.

The road continued on for another mile or so, narrowing down to a single lane punctuated by the occasional passing point, until it ended at a T-junction with the main road. When I finally reached the junction, I turned right and headed back towards Luton, still dazed from witnessing that terrible event, but thankful that I had encountered no other vehicles on the way.

On my journey home, my only thoughts were of Richard Grayson and the tragedy that had befallen him. There's no doubt that given time we would have become firm friends, and if only he had taken me into his confidence, none of this would have happened. The determination he had shown in trying to stay in hiding showed me just how much importance he had attached to this whole thing.

I made up my mind there and then to do all I could to honour his intentions, whatever they were.

Chapter 46

I drove home without stopping off anywhere. It took a lot longer than expected, because I had forgotten about the rush-hour traffic.

The frown on Sarah's face said it all. "Where have you been all this time, and why didn't you call me?" she demanded.

"Come and sit down, and I'll tell you the whole story," I promised, "but first I need a drink."

I grabbed a glass from the kitchen, took it into the living room and poured myself a very large whisky, at the same time feeling just a tinge of shame. This whisky thing was getting to be a habit.

She looked horrified. "No water?"

"Not this time," I replied. "Not after what I've just been through."

She came and sat down next to me. "Okay. Go on."

I told her the whole story, trying hard not to leave anything out. By the time I reached the part about the accident, I saw that there were tears forming in her eyes. I stopped talking, moved over to her side and put my arms around her.

I continued to hug her for a while without saying anything. "That could have been you," she said eventually. "So what did the police have to say?"

I let go of her and took a mouthful of whisky to try and steady my nerves. This was the question I'd been dreading.

"I didn't go to the police. In fact, no one knows I was there, except maybe one little old lady, and she doesn't know who I am."

Sarah pushed me away, staring at me with a look of utter disbelief. "You did what?" she cried. It sounded more like a rebuke than a question.

I shrugged apologetically. "I had my reasons," I said.

"And what reasons could they possibly be?" she asked sarcastically. I thought for a minute. My answer needed to not only be completely truthful, but also to demonstrate that my apparently insane actions had a useful purpose.

"I did it for Richard," I began, "because it was pretty obvious he didn't want anyone to know what he was up to. If I had stayed around, the Police might find out I had something to do with it, and then, sooner or later, the cat would be out of the bag. Anyway," I added, "until we find out more, I think we should go along with his wishes."

She threw her arms in the air and glared at me. "And please tell me, in case I'm missing something, how we are going to do that," she cried.

Just for a minute, I didn't understand what she was getting at. "What do you mean?" I asked, bewildered.

"The fire, you idiot!" she shouted. "It would have destroyed everything. All his notes, my camera and all those precious photos. Everything!"

I sat back in my chair and stared gloomily at the floor. She was right, of course, and somehow, because my only concerns had been for poor Richard and the guilt I was feeling about my role in his death, I had managed to completely forget about what else might have been lost forever in that terrible inferno.

And then I had what seemed at the time to be a perfectly ridiculous thought.

"What about George?" I asked her.

"What *about* George?" she repeated, throwing the question back at me.

"Do you suppose he's gone as well?" I replied. "Knowing how tough he is, I'd like to bet he could survive even in a furnace."

She frowned and shook her head. "Maybe you're right, but there's no way we're going to find out now, is there?"

"Isn't there?" I said, grinning mischievously.

She looked despairingly up at the ceiling. "I don't think I can take any more of this," she said.

I couldn't blame her for feeling that way. After all, she'd just had to absorb, in only a few minutes, everything that had happened to me that entire day. To get that much shocking news all at once must have been totally overwhelming. I think a lot of people would have stopped right there and drawn a very heavy curtain over the whole affair, but I'm not like that. If there's an unanswered question hanging around in my brain I just *have* to deal with it, because if I don't it'll just keep on buzzing around in my head like an annoying blowfly and end up driving me insane.

And at that moment, I realised that George's welfare was an unanswered question. No way could I just forget about it. I had to make Sarah understand that. Even before I opened my mouth, the look of resignation on her face told me that she already knew what I was going to say.

"I'm sorry, my darling," I said. "You know what I'm like. I'm just going to have to find out for sure."

"I know you are," she said. "But how can you possibly do that? By now, there'll be a police cordon around the entire area and they'll never let you go anywhere near the car, or what's left of it."

"I couldn't do that anyway," I remarked, "because they'd get suspicious and start asking me why I was so interested. Somehow, I've got to get at it when there's no one around."

She shook her head. "You realise that if you get caught, your career will be over? You'll never be allowed to fill another tooth again."

I had to smile, because right now, the prospect of being kicked out of my profession seemed small potatoes against the chance of rescuing George.

"I can always do landscape gardening," I quipped. "I'd be quite good at that. It's probably healthier too."

We talked on for a while, during which I filled her in with various minor details of the day's events, and we finally came to an agreement that I would go back tomorrow to reconnoitre the scene of the accident, using her car instead of mine so as to avoid attracting attention.

Chapter 47

I turned into that same country lane, at around 10am, and made my way along at a leisurely pace until I reached the spot from where I had witnessed the accident. From this safe distance, making use of the mini field binoculars that Sarah kept stowed in the glove compartment, I could easily make out the crumpled and blackened mass of the once-pristine but now unidentifiable Mercedes, still forlornly embedded into the bank. The only clues to its colour were a few traces of blue, low down along the rear skirting. The site was fully cordoned off with the familiar black and yellow ribbon. Next to the car was a white forensics tent attended by two figures dressed from head to toe in white protective clothing. There were a couple of police vans parked nearby, and two policemen were guarding the entrance to the site.

I decided that it would be very foolish of me to hang around, but at the same time I needed to keep an eye on the proceedings. With the police vehicles effectively blocking the road and making life very difficult for farm traffic, it was obvious that it would not be too long before they would have to remove the wreck and relocate it to a more convenient site.

Having previously travelled the length of this road, I knew that its sole purpose was to serve the farmers and their buildings. There were only two ways out of it, one at each end, and both led back on to the A6. My plan was to park up near one of the junctions and wait, but which of them should I choose? I was about to toss a coin, when I realised that it really didn't matter, because the lane was too narrow to allow the turning of even a small saloon car, let alone an oversized recovery vehicle. The driver would have no choice but to carry straight on through, so either way, I couldn't miss it. If I saw it go in at one end, all I'd have to do was drive to the other end and wait.

I decided that I'd been sitting there long enough, and drove on past the scene, trying not to appear too interested. When I reached the junction with the A6, I spotted a lay-by only a few hundred yards to the south: the perfect place to sit and keep an eye on the junction. Even better, there was a snack trailer, where I could pick up a cup of tea and maybe something to eat.

That snack bar turned out to be a godsend. Not only did I get a welcome cheese sandwich and a polystyrene cup of tea but, after three hours of sitting at the wheel, I was grateful to be able to go back for seconds. It was the middle of November and it was cold, made so much worse by a strong northerly wind. I had tried to keep warm, not all that successfully, by running the engine intermittently, but that still didn't stop my legs and feet getting cold and numb. I got out occasionally and walked around the car a few times to get the feeling back.

It was around 4pm, and it was starting to get dark. I was queuing up yet again for more tea (not so much to quench my thirst as to help keep my insides warm), when I saw a pick-up truck, with its amber lights flashing, approaching the main road-junction from that narrow country lane. It was equipped with some sort of mini crane and was pulling a trailer. As it came to a halt at the junction, waiting to pull out, I could clearly see that the trailer was loaded with a shapeless mound, securely strapped down under a grey tarpaulin. There was no doubt that it had to be what was left of Richard Grayson's beautiful SLK 230 Mercedes. The sight of it, and the memory of yesterday's nightmare, seemed to root me to the spot. It was as if I was a mourner at a funeral. I watched as the truck began to move slowly out onto the main road, and I suddenly realised that there was no more time to lose. Fumbling in my coat pocket for my keys, I took off and ran back to my car.

Chapter 48

The truck had turned south and was moving off slowly towards Luton. I followed at a discreet distance, knowing that with its flashing amber display lighting it up like a Christmas tree, the recovery vehicle would be virtually impossible to lose in any kind of traffic. Sure enough, the route took us back into the northern suburbs of Luton and down a series of back roads, all jam-packed with parked cars on either side. With so many roads all looking the same, I felt a wave of panic come over me, knowing that if I lost sight of my quarry, I would never be able to find it again. I had to stay close, but not so close as to arouse suspicion. After all, it was a police vehicle I was following.

And then I spotted a familiar blue sign up ahead: a police station. To my immense relief, I saw the truck's brake lights come on. It had finally reached its destination. I held back and slowed right down, trying hard not to attract attention, and watched as the passenger jumped down from the cab and disappeared into the front office. Edging carefully past the pickup, I glanced across just in time to see the two electrically operated yard gates begin to open, allowing the vehicle, complete with its grizzly load, to enter.

I continued along the road for a hundred yards or so and pulled over to one of the few remaining parking spaces, watching the scene in my rear-view mirror with a growing sense of despair, as the gates slowly came together and locked with a loud click. At that moment, I realised that the only thing in the whole wide world I was interested in right now had been taken away and locked out of reach. I felt like crying. Now, it seemed that I would never find out whether George had made it through the inferno.

Feeling totally deflated, I got out of my car and walked slowly up the street towards the station, with my hands in my pockets. I stopped opposite the gates, on the other side of the road, and stood there, staring vacantly across at my quarry while trying to accept the idea that this was finally it. I just had to resign myself to the fact that there was nothing more I could do, so I might as well go home and forget about the whole thing; put it all behind me and go back to what I did best: filling teeth and making crowns.

With my hands in my pockets and staring despondently at the pavement, I turned and started walking back to the car. Just then I heard the sound of a car pulling up some way behind me. I turned to see a police patrol vehicle with its headlights full on. It had stopped in front of the gates and was waiting for them to open.

It was then that I had a totally insane thought. Who'd ever want to break into a police station? No one. Out, yes, but not in. But George might be in there and I had this burning desire to know for sure. This whole thing was bigger than me: controlling me. Somehow, I knew I had no choice. Here was a tiny chance, and I simply had to take it.

The car disappeared into the yard and the doors started to close. In that moment, my mind was made up. Adrenaline suddenly flowing, I took off and sprinted across the road towards the rapidly closing gap. As I reached the pavement, the gap was already man sized and something told me that I had to make a dive, rugby style to get through it; which I did. My momentum was enough to work it. I hit the ground hard, and my whole body slid through just in time, leaving most of the skin from my knees and palms on the ground. But at the time, I felt nothing. Adrenaline mixed with elation is a perfect analgesic. The pain, as I soon discovered, would come later.

Hearing the click of the lock as the doors closed behind me, I quickly got to my knees, crouching low, so as not to be seen. The driver had not yet switched off the headlights, giving me just enough time to get up under the cover of darkness and slip over unseen to the safety of a protruding wall buttress and the shadow it created.

The headlights dimmed, and two flat-capped officers got out of the car. I knew they hadn't spotted me, because they were engaged in a casual chat about last night's football. In any case, I reasoned, who would be expecting anyone to break into a place like this?

I watched them disappear into the main building at the other end of the yard and decided to stay put and out of sight in that dark corner until the banging in my chest had quietened down, using the time to get a fix on my bearings. It was only then that I realised my palms and knees were on fire. I reached down to feel my knees. There were holes in my chinos, and my knees felt sticky. Blood, I presumed. But at least I was in one piece.

I used the opportunity to take a look around. The yard was not as big as I had first imagined, probably about 40 square yards, and there was only enough room in it for maybe six normal-sized squad cars, so it was quite obvious that the recovery vehicle would not be staying there for long. I quickly realised that if I wanted to search it, I'd have to act now, before they decided to take it somewhere else.

Chapter 49

The car park was in total darkness, apart from a thin shaft of light coming from an upstairs window. I guessed that this could be the common room or canteen, because I could hear the steady sound of conversation mixed with occasional bursts of laughter. That was music to my ears, considering what I was planning to do.

With yet another quick glance around to check that all was clear, I crept quietly across the square and around to the far side of the trailer. I gave two or three of the tarpaulin straps a hard tug, but soon discovered that whoever had secured them had done too good a job. The tarpaulin itself, however, was a different matter. I worked my way round its loose lower border and found several areas folded over on themselves. If I could work on one of those and bring all of the gather together, there would be enough slack to make an opening to slip myself under.

But first I had to figure out which way the wreck was facing, because I wanted to get to the passenger side where the glove compartment would be. It was quite obvious that anything important would either be in there or in the boot. I stood back, away from the trailer, to try and get an impression of the car, but because of the damage, both ends looked pretty much the same. It wasn't easy, but eventually I noticed a ridge outlined through the tarpaulin. It had to be the windscreen frame.

Luckily, I was already on the passenger side. I immediately set about working on the tarpaulin. Normally, the task would not have been too much of a challenge, but my raw and bloody palms caused me such pain that, more than once, it was all I could do to stop crying out. It probably took me a full 30 minutes to free that tarpaulin enough to crawl under. Once I'd got my head and shoulders inside, I felt around on the bodywork for the passenger door, which had still more or less retained its shape and was still relatively smooth and flat. Having identified the door, I worked my way up the side of it to where the window would have been, but of course there was no glass there now, just an open void.

The first thing that hit me was the smell: a very pungent and acrid aroma of burnt paint and plastics. It was so overwhelmingly unpleasant -with an ominously carcinogenic aura about it- that my first instinct was to turn back and get out of there. But right now, my behaviour was not being governed by instincts. Right now, there was a much greater power controlling me: the power of a conscious determination to succeed. Having come this far, there was no way I was going to turn back now.

Because it is only humans who have control over their instincts.

Groping around in pitch black, I reached in through the opening, and the first thing I touched was the jagged metal framework of the passenger seat, now without a trace of upholstery, all of which would have simply evaporated in the heat. I reached across to check if it was the same on the driver's side. As I did so, I touched something. Something I hadn't expected: something that shouldn't have been there. I pulled my hand away and shivered involuntarily.

I paused for a moment to consider, sweat breaking out all over. What was it I had touched?

It wasn't metal. No, it felt more like wood. Wood? How could that be? Not in that fire. Wood would have been the first thing to be consumed.

I took a deep breath and reached out to touch it again. This time I was ready, and I ran my fingers over the surface. It was hard and rounded; too hard for wood. As I felt further down, my probing fingertips picked out a double set of promontories, below which were two hollows into which my fingers sank deep inside. I snatched my hand away, realising in horror what it was I had touched. My two fingers had found a pair of eye sockets, and this object could only be a skull: *the burned-out skull of Richard Grayson.*

The shock of that gruesome discovery set off a sudden wave of nausea, which spread rapidly all the way through my body. I had to fight hard to stop myself throwing up and forced myself to take a few deep breaths to try and stay calm. It all seemed so unreal that I really thought I must be dreaming. Surely they wouldn't just leave him here like that would they?

Convinced that I'd got it wrong, I put out my now trembling hand to feel over the skull again, cautiously feeling my way over the smooth domed surface. But there was no mistaking those familiar outlines, which I knew so well from my days as a dental student. I was left in no doubt that Richard Grayson, or what was left of him, was still in here.

I started to shiver again, not only from shock, but also because, now well into a November evening, it was getting cold, reminding me that I had to get on with the job and get out of there pronto. Easing myself back out, I got down on my hands and knees and started crawling closely along the side of the wreck until I reached the boot.

Running my hands over the bodywork confirmed to me that this end of the car was largely intact. Praying that the boot catch would still operate, I fumbled around, trying to locate it, only to discover that the lid had already been opened and was just sitting there in its closed position, held down by the tarpaulin. Realising that somebody had already checked the boot, my heart sank. This could only mean that even if George had been in there, having somehow survived the fire, he would now be under lock and key somewhere and totally out of reach.

With that thought uppermost in my mind, I did not even bother to feel around in the boot. Perhaps it was time to give it all up, admit defeat and get out of there while I still could. So, with a heavy heart, I began to crawl back around to where I had first got in, with a plan to hide out in that same dark corner of the yard until somebody opened the gates again.

I was just about to raise a corner of the tarpaulin and jump down, when the silence was suddenly broken by the sound of a key being turned in a lock, followed by the creak of a door being opened. A moment or two later, the door was slammed shut again and the yard echoed with the sound of voices, the same two I'd heard before, getting louder as they headed in my direction.

They stopped right next to where I was lying; so close that I held my breath in case they might hear me.

"So where are we off to now?" one of them said.

"To the coroner's." came the reply. "We've had instructions to leave the whole trailer there just as it is, and let them sort it out."

"Rather them than me." said the first one. "I wouldn't fancy that job: having to dissect him out of that mess. I heard someone say that his body just melted away in the heat and welded what was left of him into the chair. No wonder they didn't bother to try and get him out on site."

I nodded to myself. Only now did I understand why Grayson was still in the car. Getting his gruesome remains out of here was a job that only the pathologist and his team could do.

"Let's get on with it." said the second voice. "The sooner we get this thing out of the yard, the better. It's taking up half of the parking spaces."

With that, the two of them walked off to get into the cabin. I breathed a sigh of relief but I knew my problems were far from over. Somehow I was going to have to get off this thing without them noticing, and noticing things was what policemen were particularly good at.

Chapter 50

I heard the slamming of doors, followed by the grumbling of a diesel engine as it was reluctantly coaxed into life, and then the driver called up to the office with his walkie-talkie, asking for the gates to be opened.

The clattering of the diesel engine rudely cut into the stillness of the night, made even noisier by the echo from the walling all around. The next sound I heard was a clunk from the gear lever. I suddenly thought that this might be the moment to slip down from underneath the tarpaulin and make my getaway, but at the last minute I realised I would be too easy to spot in the bright glare of the street lights, and thought better of it. When I look back on it now, I recognise that decision as one of the best I've ever made.

I had no idea how long this little trip was going to take: not too long, I hoped. But one thing was for sure: somewhere along the way I was going to have to get off this thing without being spotted and well before it reached its destination. A dimly lit and deserted side street would be ideal, with no curious passers-by to worry about. What I certainly did not want was to end up locked inside another yard, so I decided to make my move sooner rather than later. From my position, lying on the floor of the trailer next to the passenger door of the wreck, I was able to lift the tarpaulin enough to see out and choose the best spot.

We were passing along a narrow street, lined with two rows of terraced houses. At regular intervals along the road there were the usual unfriendly speed humps, but the driver seemed to make no attempt to slow down for any of them, causing the wheels of the trailer to take off for a split second before landing back down with a very unpleasant jolt. Each occasion produced a noisy jangle from the wrecked car, caused by the many loose and untethered pieces of metal clanging together. I think it was at about the third hump that I heard a particularly loud clang from somewhere inside the cockpit. Curious, I knelt up and put my hand in through the window opening, feeling around to try and discover what it was that had made the noise.

It turned out to be the door of the glove compartment that had been shaken loose and was now flapping open. I reached in to feel around inside. The combustible lining of the compartment had completely disappeared, leaving just the metal framework: a skeletal reminder of its former self. I stretched a little further in to feel into the deepest part, and it was then that my probing fingers closed on something totally different: something very smooth and flat with a soapy feel, wedged into the hinge part of the glove-box.

As I touched it, a wave of excitement shot right through me and I could feel the hairs on the back of my neck stand up. Could it possibly be? Surely somebody checked the glove box? Unless, of course, they were put off by the very close presence of Richard Grayson's barbecued remains still sitting there.

With that thought in my mind, I consoled myself with the very fortunate fact that because of the complete darkness created by the tarpaulin, I couldn't see what must in daylight have been a very ghastly spectre.

I grabbed at the object and pulled it out. Almost as soon as I had it in my hand, I knew what it was, even though I could not see it. "George, my beauty!" I cried, forgetting for a moment that I might just be in earshot. I sat back down on the trailer floor with tears of joy running down my cheeks and spent a few indulgent moments examining it all over with my fingers. Just as I had guessed, it felt as delightfully smooth and silky as ever, with not the faintest impression of any damage. My whole body seemed to be tingling with excitement. I just couldn't wait to see George again.

Time to set myself free. Tucking George carefully under my belt, I lay back down again and raised the tarpaulin enough to see out. All I needed now was a nice dark and quiet street, so that I could slip away undetected. I didn't have to wait long. As it arrived at the very next junction, the trailer came to a halt. The road was chock-full of parked cars, extending right up to the corners, and I could just imagine the driver cursing at having to negotiate them with such a long and awkward vehicle as this. As he started to carefully coax the vehicle past the end car, I knew he would be concentrating hard. This was just the right moment to make my escape. Sliding out feet first from under the tarpaulin, and with one final check that George was securely tucked away, I let myself fall silently on to the road and well out of sight of the driver. As the truck began to move off, I quickly picked myself up and darted into the blind side-shadows of a large van.

Chapter 51

After making sure that George was safely hidden out of sight, I spent the next hour or so wandering the backstreets of Luton in search of a taxi. There are always plenty of taxis sitting around at almost any railway station, but try finding one when you're lost in some anonymous suburb and your phone's gone flat (a regular event in those days). Eventually, I came across a phone box, liberally decorated with massage parlour and minicab stickers, and dialled for a cab. They said 10 minutes, which was enough time to speak to Sarah.

It was long past her bedtime but of course she was still up.

"Where the hell have you been, and what have you been up to?" she shouted down the phone. "I thought you were only going over there to take a look! You should have been back ages ago."

I held the phone away from my ear. Not surprisingly, she didn't sound too happy. I couldn't blame her, especially after what she told me next.

"I watched the local news tonight. It was all about the accident and how it could possibly have happened. There was no mention of anyone else involved, so I think you might have got away with it, but please don't push your luck any more."

"I won't, I promise!" I said, and really meant it. "Did they say much about Grayson?"

"Lots. In fact most of the item was about him and how well respected he was. The tributes came in from all over the world. Seems he was even more famous than we realised."

"Makes it feel even worse," I said meekly.

"Anyway, you haven't said why you're still out at this time of night. Your dinner's ruined, so I threw it in the bin."

"I've got George," I said.

"What?" She cried disbelievingly. "How on Earth did you do that?" It felt like an accusation, not a question.

"I'll tell you later. Trust me. It's all okay."

"It had better be. Now just get yourself home as soon as you can. It's already very late!"

Just then, the taxi turned up. I told the driver that I wanted the police station. "Which one?" he asked. "There are two."

Naturally, the first one was the wrong one, but after another tour of Luton's backstreets, I was finally dropped off where I wanted to be, and I walked back up the street to my car. By the time I finally arrived home, it was well after midnight.

She was still up. Late at night is not her best time of day. I got the feeling I was in for a rough ride. Lucky for me, she was too tired to play the game, but she did want a quick peek at George. After watching her fondle and drool over him for five minutes or so, I took him back, wrapped him up in a bin bag and secreted him well away in the back of a kitchen drawer.

May I remind you (and myself) that George was *not* a person, but somehow we both felt that he had a personality, and maybe even something more, locked away within, so looking back to that time, I now know for sure that, not only did his new name quite suit him, but also that our instincts about him were justified.

Chapter 52

When I woke the next morning (sorry, the same morning), there was daylight peeping in under the bedroom curtains, telling me that I'd slept in. I checked my watch and saw that it was well past nine: a full two hours later than usual. Obviously I'd needed that extra sleep. No wonder, after yesterday's incredible goings on.

My thoughts returned to the scene of that terrible accident and how unnecessary it was. If Grayson had only taken me into his confidence right from the start, none of this would have happened. I vowed there and then that I would do my utmost to honour his sacrifice in any way I could.

I'm always the first one up in the morning, and I usually creep out in the dark and let Sarah sleep on, so it was a strange feeling to wake up and find her missing. Donning my dressing gown, I made my way down the stairs with some trepidation, not at all sure what kind of reception I would get. I quietly opened the kitchen door and peered in with an apologetic look on my face. It was a feeble attempt to dampen the expected onslaught.

I needn't have worried. She was sitting at the breakfast table, drinking tea and sorting through the morning mail. She looked up and smiled, catching me off guard. "It's all right," she began. "It's safe to come in." She got up from her chair and came over to give me an unexpected hug. "All is forgiven. I'm sure you had your reasons for doing what you did, and

I trust you. There wouldn't be any point in us being married if I didn't, would there?" I smiled back sheepishly and said nothing. Just an extra big hug was all that was needed to say it all.

I proceeded to relate the details of yesterday's adventure, taking great care to play down (or leave out altogether) some of the more perilous incidents, so as not to create unnecessary alarm. She made little comment, but from the frown on her face, nourished by a generous helping of feminine intuition, I'm quite sure she was reading between the lines. She knew me far too well.

With that enormous hurdle safely overcome, I got up and switched the kettle back on and popped two slices into the toaster.

"Anything in the mail worth looking at?" I asked.

"Usual stuff, by the looks of it." she said. "One of your glossy dental magazines, a couple of so-called special cruise offers and an estate agent informing us that he's got lots of clients on his books, all desperate to buy our house."

"Until we say yes, and then they all magically seem to disappear." I remarked.

"Oh yes. There is one more letter here for you. I didn't open it, because it says 'personal'."

I smiled and gave her a wink as she handed it to me. "I told that blonde nurse at work not to send me love letters!" I joked.

The address was handwritten in an untidy and barely legible scrawl, suggestive of someone who was always very busy, with no time for the niceties of life, such as neatness. I studied the writing for a moment or two, trying to decide if I recognised it, but the only guess

I was prepared to make was that, judging from the messy style, the person was probably male. I tore open the envelope to find a sheet of A4, filled on both sides with that same handwriting. Unusually, the letter did not begin with the sender's address, and the only information at the top was the date, which was for the Friday just gone. The letter began 'Dear Jim'. Now even more curious, I turned the paper over to see whom it was from. The last words on the page read: 'With best regards, your good friend, Richard.'

As I saw that name, I felt as if I had just been shot through the chest. The shock of it took my breath away, and for a moment, thinking I was going to faint, I slumped down on to the kitchen chair.

"What's the matter?" cried Sarah. "You've gone all white. You look like you've seen a ghost!"

I stared back at her, still dazed from the shock. "In a way, I have!" I cried.

We sat down next to each other and read the letter together. This is what it said:

Friday 29 October 1999

Dear Jim,

It was a great pleasure meeting you the other day, and I have a feeling we will be sharing many more beers together, hopefully very soon.

I owe you a huge apology for not getting back in touch. I feel particularly guilty about having retained the camera and the other bits and pieces you kindly allowed me to examine, and I know we had an agreement that I should return them to you on Monday.

By the time you receive this letter, you will already have discovered that I will have reneged on our agreement, and hopefully, you will forgive me when I explain why.

After connecting your camera to my TV, I was able to see the images much more clearly, my close vision having deteriorated somewhat, thanks to my advancing presbyopia.

At first, I could not believe what I was looking at. Those digital images showed in remarkable detail a perfectly preserved example of Homo habilis from the Pleistocene period, which means it must be getting on for two million years old. The only specimens of it that we palaeontologists have at our disposal are fossils, not bones, and these are mostly incomplete and reconstructed.

Although bones are hard, they are composed largely of calcium, which in time, is slowly dissolved away by acids in the air and rain until nothing is left.

Many people think that fossils are bones, but in fact they are petrified reproductions of the original. My only explanation regarding the survival of your specimen is that it was protected from the normal process of demineralisation by the unique atmosphere in the cave, sealed from the outside until you broke through and fell into it.

But blown away as I was by those images, nothing could have prepared me for that amazing artefact that came with them. For a moment, I thought it was a small plastic chopping board, until I examined it more closely. It is such a beautifully smooth and exquisitely finished piece, without a single scratch or abrasion anywhere on its surface. I could not resist holding it and playing around with it, and I soon realised that it couldn't be plastic because it is so hard. My only conclusion is that it must have come from elsewhere. Somehow, I just know it cannot be of this world.

And then, just by sheer chance, I discovered something else. Under the right circumstances, it can identify us, not as individuals, you understand, but as humans. Yes, that's right; it knows who we are! I'm sure you're going to think I've gone crazy, but I can assure you I haven't. I've found out a few other things as well, but I'm not going to talk about them right now. I'll save them for when we get together.

Perhaps you can see now why I had to disappear, because if this thing is really what I'm starting to believe it is, then it's a whole lot bigger than the both of us, and until I've been through every little detail, I think we should keep it all under wraps.

I shall be away in Spain for a few days, but when I'm ready to surface again, I'll contact you, and we can go over a few details. In the meantime, here are some questions for you to consider:

How long had that contraption (a spacecraft, I assume) been down there and what had happened to cause it to be buried like that? Presumably there was a sudden volcanic incident, such as happened with Pompeii.

Was it unmanned? I personally think so. Unless there's a completely new form of transport we don't yet understand, I can't believe it's possible to sustain life long enough to travel and survive the huge distances involved. Even our next nearest star is more than four light years away, and right now with the methods we presently have available, it would take us at least 40,000 years to get there. Try and get your head round that! Quite honestly, I think the only way we'd ever be able to transport ourselves out of this solar system would be in the form of a blueprint involving the use of DNA, or possibly by some other means that we are not yet able to understand.

And what was Mr H. Habilis doing there anyway? Was he just curious, or was it an elaborate trap, part of some kind of scientific experiment? If so, was he the only one, or could there have been others before him?

One last question for you to consider:

It is the question that has troubled us from the very beginning, and which every religion and every philosophy tries its best to answer: What is it that makes us human and so completely different from all other creatures on this planet? I'm beginning to think that it might be nothing more than a sprinkling of fairy dust, brought to us from another world.

Anyway Jim, that's enough for now. I'm looking forward to catching up with you as soon as I've crossed the T's and dotted the I's. We'll make it all up with a few more beers.

Let's hope the sun will be shining when we meet.

With best regards,

Your good friend: Richard.

To find oneself reading the very last written words of someone who has just passed away is an incredibly moving experience, and well before I had reached the end of that letter, I had to stop and wipe my eyes. Sarah was doing the same, and I could see from the downward curl of her lips that she was fighting hard to keep control. There was a lump in my throat. Sarah had finished reading well before me and after I'd gone over it third time to make sure I hadn't missed anything, I looked up at her and took her in my arms. We sat there and hugged each other silently for a while. The only thoughts in my head were guilty ones, born out of my part in Richard Grayson's awful death. After reading that letter and realising its significance, I knew I just had to pay him back or I'd never have a good night's sleep again.

Not only is Sarah a much faster reader than me but unlike me, she usually gets things first time. Quite often, I miss the point because I'm easily distracted and I end up having to read the thing twice. Today was no exception, and with those images of Grayson's last moments clouding my brain, my powers of concentration were at their lowest.

She picked up the letter and scanned quickly through it again, stopping to point something out. "That's an odd thing to say," she remarked.

"What is?" I replied.

"Fairy dust. What on earth did he mean by that? And that last bit, about the sun shining. Sounded a bit weird."

I read the section again. "Yes, it does all sound a bit odd," I said, "but having met him, I can't believe he was just being flippant. I think there must be a message in there somewhere."

She did not look convinced. "I suppose you're right," she said doubtfully.

I took the letter from her and read the whole thing through yet again, this time more carefully. "He had some interesting ideas," I said at length. "Especially the one about Homo habilis. I must admit, I thought originally that he might be part of it rather than being a victim."

"I wonder what it was that Grayson had discovered?" Sarah queried.

I shrugged. "Something big, obviously. Maybe we will never find out. Everything he was working on was there in the car with him, including your camera. It's all been totally destroyed."

"And the photos. No one will ever get a chance to see those images he found so fascinating."

"That reminds me," I said. "I'm going to have to buy you a new camera. But at least we still have George. What we're going to do with him, I've no idea."

"Well, Grayson obviously found out something important. What do you suppose he meant when he said George knows we're human?"

I shook my head. "Doesn't make sense to me," I said. "George can't *know* anything can he? He's just an inanimate object."

We agreed to end the discussion there for the time being. Sarah had a few household chores to catch up on before going off to her fitness class and there were messages on the answering machine from Jodie telling me there was an ever-increasing backlog of disgruntled patients waiting to be appeased.

Chapter 53

After the exhausting events of the past few days, we opted for a few days of normality at home, and our weekdays quickly settled back into the old routine. Sarah busied herself with the usual household chores, interspersed with shopping trips, visits to the gym and coffee mornings with friends, and it was no surprise to me that there was a price to pay for my unscheduled time off work. I was forced to fit emergencies, and other jobs that just wouldn't wait, into non-existent gaps, which meant running over at lunchtime and going-home time. Luckily, Jodie is a very loyal assistant and was quite happy to remember that my absence had given her a chance to catch up on equipment maintenance and ordering. On my return I could not help noticing how fresh and clean the surgery looked, and how tidy and ordered the drawers and cupboards were, with the instruments perfectly arranged for maximum efficiency. She had even taken the initiative to touch up the scuff marks on the surgery walls, something which was well beyond the call of her normal duties, reminding me how lucky I was to have found such a diamond.

We had decided from the beginning not to tell Gary about what had been going on, or anything about George, because the risks of him revealing all or even a small part of our secret to one or other of his friends was just too great. We had moved George into our bedroom and kept him in pride of place on the dressing table. Our bedroom was a forbidden sanctuary, and the only part of the house that Gary did not consider his. In any case, if Gary, or anyone else for that matter, raised any questions about George, we had agreed on a concocted story about finding him in a West End boutique that sold alternative modern art.

Our bedroom is at the back of the house, the front of which faces north-east. On our last property search, which was a very painful and long drawn-out affair, we had made a list of essential features that our new home must have. I think there were at least 10 of them, including the minimum number of bedrooms (four), a utility room next to the kitchen and proximity to facilities, such as schools, shops, doctors' surgeries, and so on. As a keen gardener and lover of barbecues (as I was then), I had also insisted that the back of the house must face south or south-west to get the maximum amount of usable sun. That last condition had hugely reduced the number of properties at our disposal, because, as I quickly discovered, the owners of such homes are much less likely to want to move. So, when we finally came across this house, we snapped it up, not even bothering to negotiate over the price in case there was someone else interested. It was a decision we have never regretted, and we have always been very happy here.

What that all means is, that we get the morning sun (if there is any) in our bedroom. It comes up on the far left of the bay window and gradually works its way round to the right until around midday, when it disappears around to the side of the house. Sometimes in the morning, I curse as those first rays find their way through the gap in the curtains and wake me up by shining directly on to my face and, if I'm not ready to get up just yet, I slip on a pair of eyeshades saved as a souvenir from a long-distance flight.

Have you ever entered a room that you use every day and had the feeling that something is missing or out of place? Like one of the cushions on the sofa has gone, or there's an ornament on the mantelpiece that's been moved. I think that subconsciously we are all aware there is a difference, even though we don't think about it.

I had one of those moments that day. As clear as anything, I can still remember everything as if it happened yesterday. It was a frosty late-November morning, and with frost comes blue skies and the bonus of sunshine, a rare event at that time of year. I had drawn the curtains back to make the most of it and disappeared into the en-suite to have a shower. Then I got dressed in the bedroom and went downstairs for breakfast.

I was halfway through my second piece of toast when it hit me.

"Have you moved George?" I asked Sarah. "I've just realised that I didn't see him this morning."

She shook her head and gave me a puzzled look. "No, darling," she replied. "He's on the dressing table where he always is. I know because I've already picked him up and played with him. It's become a daily routine for me."

"That's funny," I said, "because he's impossible to miss, and I don't remember seeing him this morning."

With that, I got up from the table and headed back up to the bedroom. On my way there, I wondered if

I was just beginning to get a wee bit too paranoid about George, and then told myself that it wouldn't be so surprising after the events of the last few days. As I opened the bedroom door, I breathed a sigh of relief to see that he was there after all, looking even more magnificently bright than ever, thanks to the morning sun which was shining directly on him.

I went over to pick him up, but even before I was halfway across the room, I noticed something so odd that it stopped me in my tracks. That bright orange suddenly didn't seem so bright. In fact, it seemed to be fading away right before my eyes. I rubbed them, wondering if I was imagining things, but when I looked again, there was no doubt that George was getting paler, the deep orange fading into a glassy translucency. In not much more than a minute, the colour had completely disappeared, leaving what looked like nothing more than a slab of crystal-clear glass.

Chapter 54

Rooted to the spot, I just stood there open mouthed and stared at George in a state of utter bewilderment. It was all too much to take in. Now I realised why I hadn't noticed him earlier when I was dressing, because he must have been like this then: almost invisible.

Shaking with excitement but still not daring to move, I called out for Sarah to come quickly. Something about the tone of my voice must have alarmed her, because I heard her fling open the kitchen door, allowing it to bang against the wall in her haste, before bounding up the stairs two at a time. She burst into the bedroom with an anxious look on her face. "What's the matter, Jim?" she cried.

"You've got to see this now!" I shouted excitedly. "George has come out of hiding!"

"Where is he?" she asked, looking all around the room.

I pointed to the dresser. "Right there!" I exclaimed.

She looked mystified, expecting to see that familiar orange glow. "Where?" she said again.

I picked George up and waved him at her. "Here!" I exclaimed.

She glanced disdainfully at me and then smiled as if humouring an idiot.

"Have you gone mad?" she said. "Something can't suddenly change colour just like that."

"Well, yes it can," I replied. "Think of chameleons and octopuses, for example. They can change colour at will, and there are plenty of other animals that can do it."

"Yes, but they're living creatures," she replied, snatching George out of my hand, "and this is just a piece of…"

I think she was just about to say "glass", but as she took hold of George, her expression suddenly changed into one of complete surprise. I instantly knew why: because there was no other substance on Earth that had the same silky-smooth feel as George. She stood there staring down at George and turning him over and over in her hands as if trying to work out what was going on.

"How come this hasn't happened before?" she said at last. "After all, we've had George for a while now, and this is the first time."

I shrugged. The same question was beginning to bug me as well. It was only then that it hit me. George must have changed while I was there in the bedroom getting dressed, and that's why I didn't remember him being there, but when I went back up to find him, he had turned back to his usual self again in my absence. It was only when I went back into the room that the colour began to fade.

"That's it!" I exclaimed excitedly. "It's exactly what Grayson said in his letter. Now I know what he meant when he said that George knows us. I'm guessing he only does this trick when we're around."

Sarah shook her head. "That can't be right," she said, "because why hasn't it happened before? There must be something else."

I had to admit that she was right. Totally baffled, we both sat down on the bed, staring at George and trying desperately to come up with another explanation.

"So, what's different about today?" I said at last. "There must be something that we haven't thought about."

One of the incredible things about the mind is that it doesn't switch off. Even when we're asleep, all sorts of processes are going on in there, doing stuff that we don't really understand, so don't imagine for a minute that your mind isn't still working on a problem you've already dismissed as unsolvable, because I can guarantee that it is. And just when you think you've totally forgotten the question, the answer pops up out of nowhere. That's exactly what happened to Sarah. She suddenly jumped up and clapped her hands triumphantly, making me jump. "The letter!" she cried. "Grayson's last words. Do you remember what they were?"

"Let's hope the sun is shining!" I said.

It was then that the penny finally dropped. "The sun!" I repeated. "That's it; the magic ingredient! Look, the sun is shining on him right now!"

I was overwhelmed by a feeling of excitement such as I've never experienced before, or since. It was one of those very rare eureka moments. I sprang to my feet and gave Sarah a big hug for being so clever. We both realised then that, thanks to the delightful English winter, we had not seen the sun for nearly all of November; but here it was at last, flooding into the bedroom for almost the first time in a month.

As usual, I was carried away with joy at this new discovery, but as usual, Sarah was a little more cautious. "We need to be sure." She said guardedly. "After all, it's only an idea, don't forget."

Even though I was already sold, I had to agree with her. "That should be simple enough," I said. "All we need to do is close the curtains to block out the sun, and then see what happens."

We did just that, and sat back down on the bed in the semi-darkness and watched. It took no more than a couple of minutes for George to return back to full colour. Spellbound, we both sat there in silence, just staring at him in wonderment.

"Looks like he needs the sun even more than we do," I said at last.

The fascinating thing about exploring science and nature is that no matter how much we find out, it is never enough. Answered questions and solved problems are rarely the end, often opening more doors than they close, creating yet another set of questions that need to be answered. And bowled over as we were with this latest revelation, we somehow knew that this was only the beginning. What other tricks did George have up his sleeve?

Chapter 55

Naturally enough, the clouds returned to fill the sky as usual that November afternoon, and judging by the latest weather reports, neither we, nor George were likely see the sun for a while.

With George temporarily out of action, I decided that this would be a good time to pay Helen Grayson a visit. It was deeply troubling me that I'd had a major role in Grayson's death, even though I did not directly cause it. In fact (I argued to myself), if he had not met me in the first place, he would still be alive today. As I have mentioned earlier, guilt is something that never really disappears. It's always lurking there, somewhere in the background, ready to surface at the slightest chance, and if you really want to, you can make yourself feel guilty about the slightest thing. But the subject of Grayson's sacrifice was not the slightest thing, and it was a call that had to be answered.

I realised that there was no way I could ever disclose my involvement to Helen, but at the same time, I needed to let her know how much Sarah and I were thinking of her. So, without telling her I was coming, I turned up on her doorstep with a bunch of flowers. When she opened the door, she immediately recognised me and attempted a weak smile, which did nothing to conceal the sadness she must have been feeling. Despite her obvious grief, she beckoned me to come in and sat me in the front living room while she went off to make tea.

My few minutes' wait gave me a chance to study my surroundings. I was immediately impressed by the condition of the walls and ceiling, adorned with what appeared to be the original Victorian plasterwork, characteristically ornate and yet somehow very tasteful. The walls had been painted with a pale shade of avocado, pleasing to my taste and not at all like that of those awful sixties bathroom suites, most of which have thankfully been discarded.

The furniture consisted of individual period pieces, obviously acquired on different occasions, each tastefully chosen for its own unique character. I noticed that the high-backed single chair I was sitting on was some sort of hybrid. It had Queen Anne legs with brown leather upholstery finished in the classic Chesterfield style and was surprisingly comfortable. The wooden furniture in the room was also an eclectic mix of individual styles and periods, each one an object of interest in its own way.

I felt completely at home in those surroundings. They sent out a message of permanence and stability, as if they had been there forever. They gave me a sense of the previous generations that had lived there through the ages. They had come and gone, but this elderly but very well built house was still there doing its job, and would do so for many more years yet.

The room was very tidy, with spotless furnishings, and I could tell that the woodwork had been recently polished, because there was still the pleasant odour of perfumed beeswax lingering in the air. Looking around, I got the feeling that absolutely nothing was out of place, a fact that made me smile inwardly as I pictured the apparently unruly mess that I knew existed in the basement room immediately below me.

Helen came in bearing a wooden tray with brass handles, placed it on the coffee table and sat down opposite me. The bone china tea set was decorated with a tasteful floral design. After stirring the teapot, she poured tea into a cup and passed it over, gesturing me to help myself to milk and sugar. I stirred in my usual half spoon of sugar and took a sip. "I'm so sorry to hear about your husband." I began. "I saw it on the news last week. It must have been a terrible shock to you."

She pulled a handkerchief out from under her sleeve and used it to wipe the corner of one eye. "It was." She said. There was a distinct tremor in her voice, and for a moment I thought that she was going to break down, but after taking a deep breath, she continued. "Have you known him long?" She asked.

"No," I replied. "In fact, the first time I actually met him was when I saw you the other day, but I had seen him once before, when he gave a talk at my son's school prize-giving."

"Oh, yes," she said, wiping away a tear from the other eye. "There wasn't a week went by when he wasn't giving a talk somewhere or other. He loved telling people about his work, because he always totally believed in it and he thought everyone else should too."

I took a sip of my tea. "He believed in it because he knew it was true and he had the evidence to prove it," I said. "But I'm sure it must be very hard to convince so many people who are fixed in their beliefs."

She nodded approvingly. "Yes, that always used to frustrate him, but he always insisted it would only be a matter of time before they would come to their senses and realise that he was right to go only on facts rather than fairy tales written on manuscripts many centuries ago."

"I think it's going to take a few generations yet to change peoples' attitudes to that idea," I said, finishing the last of my tea.

Helen leaned forward and refilled my cup. "So why did you come to see Richard that day?" she asked.

I suddenly felt hot all over, because I knew from this point on that I was going to have to invent an explanation that didn't involve George in any way.

"O...Oh," I stammered, "It was just that I wanted to know a bit more about where we humans came from, and whether we're really related to apes like they say we are. Having seen Richard at the school, I thought he would be the best man to ask."

"You're not wrong," she said proudly. "That was a subject very close to his heart and he was always going on about it. Did you know that we have almost the same DNA as chimpanzees? There's less than two per cent in it, I believe."

I knew that already, but I decided to play dumb. "Wow!" I exclaimed. "That's an amazingly small amount, considering how different we are!"

"Yes," she said. "And he was working on it right to the end. Funnily enough, he went off not long after he saw you that first time."

"Where to?" I asked.

She suddenly looked very sad, and turned her head away to stare out of the window. "Well, that's the strange thing," she started. "He said he was going up to Whipchester Zoo. He's got a friend from university up there who allows him in to carry out research on chimpanzee behaviour, and for some reason, he left here

in a bit of a hurry. That was the last time I saw him."
She wiped another tear from her cheek and there was a
faraway look in her eyes, making me feel even more
guilty than I was already, about my part in the death of
the man she obviously loved very deeply.

There was a lump in my throat. "I'm sorry," I said.
"I didn't mean to upset you. I know it must be very
painful to talk about him, and I only came here to offer
my condolences. Perhaps I'd better be going."

"No, it's okay," she assured. "In fact, I'm happy to
talk about him. It brings me some comfort, remembering
what a clever and loving man he was and what happy
times we had together."

I stayed there for another hour or so, listening to her
stories about how they'd met and where they'd been for
their holidays, and how many grandchildren they had
and so on. It was good therapy for her, and by the time I
left, she was in quite a cheery frame of mind.

Chapter 56

I remember very little of my journey home from Helen's, such was the level of guilt I was feeling. It was so sad to leave her like that, all alone in that great big house with only memories to keep her company. When I thought about the role I had played in creating this miserable situation, I felt tears welling up in my eyes: something which hadn't happened since the age of 10, when I was told that my father had died. Wiping my eyes with the back of my hand, I decided there and then that I would do my utmost to pay back the enormous debt I owed to Richard and Helen Grayson.

My first step was to try and imagine what it was that had compelled Grayson to disappear like that. The only thing I could come up with was that he had discovered something so completely original and mind-blowingly important about George that it would be enough to create enormous waves of disquiet for somebody, or maybe even everybody. Exactly what sort of something that might be, I had not the slightest inkling.

I read a book many years ago (I think the author's name was De Bono) about the way people think, and how too many of us are trapped by convention and beliefs into only following fixed pathways when we try to solve a problem. The suggestion was that if the usual methods failed to produce an answer, we should revert to what he called 'lateral thinking'. Nowadays, I suppose we would call it 'thinking outside the box'.

There's no one I know who is better at thinking outside the box than my wife, Sarah. I've lost count of the times during our long relationship that she has come up with an answer, often very simple, to a problem that had stumped me for much longer than necessary, simply because I had been too egotistically stubborn to ask her opinion. So today, with these seemingly unanswerable questions spinning around in my head, and having learnt my lessons from those past mistakes, I made up my mind to take my problems straight to the expert.

When I walked into the kitchen, I found her standing by the kettle, waiting for it to boil. Just back from her daily workout, she was still wearing her trainers, gym tights and top. With pretty much the same slender figure she'd had when I first met her, she looked for all the world like a teenager standing there. How lucky I was to have her as a wife.

She took two mugs from the cupboard and dropped in the teabags. "How did you get on?" she asked, adding hot water from the kettle. I proceeded to tell her all about the events of the morning and how bad I felt about Helen's situation, and how all my thoughts were guilty ones. "I need to do something positive about it," I said, "because otherwise I think I'll go mad."

"That won't happen," she said," because you're too level-headed for that. Sooner or later, you'll come to terms with it."

I nodded, but deep down I wasn't convinced. "Have you got any ideas?" I asked.

She sat down at the table, staring at her mug of tea, and said nothing, but I could see from the frown on her face that she had her thinking cap on.

"Who was it that Helen said Richard was going to meet at the zoo?" she asked.

"She didn't give me a name, but I think he's got to be someone high up, because if he went to college with Richard, he must be well educated."

"Well, it sounds like he was the last person Richard saw before he disappeared. Maybe he knows something? Phone Helen and see if you can find out more about him."

I started to laugh, not because of Sarah's idea, but at my good fortune in having her as a wife. Once again, her suggestion, which with the benefit of hindsight was so obvious to anyone but me, had once again hit the mark.

Without even waiting to finish my tea, I went off to dial Helen's number.

It turned out that Helen knew Richard's friend very well. His name was David Kenwright, and he was no less than the director of Whipchester Zoo. The two became friends as fellow students and had remained so ever since.

David Kenwright was not an easy person to reach, particularly as I had to go through the official route to get to speak to him. No doubt, Helen had his private number but I suppose as a friend of his she felt duty-bound not to reveal it to just anyone. I fully respected that, and did not even try to extract the number from her, realising that she could have volunteered it if she'd wanted to.

I left my details with Kenwright's secretary, with a request for him to ring me back when he had a spare moment, which by the sound of his busy schedule was not very often. It was almost a week later when I finally heard from him.

"I'm very sorry to bother you," I began after introducing myself, "but I'm hoping you might be able to tell me something about your recent meeting with Richard Grayson. I believe you may have been the last person to talk to him."

There was a pause, and I imagined Kenwright to be collecting himself after hearing the name of his recently departed colleague.

"Oh yes, Richard," he said at length. "He was probably my closest friend. I was absolutely shocked to hear of his death. Such a brilliant man. I don't honestly think I'll ever get over it. How did you know him?"

"I only met him twice," I replied, "but I liked him from the start. Not only did we get on well, but it turned out that we had something in common. Actually, that's what I wanted to talk to you about."

"Fire away." Invited Kenwright, obviously curious to find out more.

"Okay, here goes. But first, would you mind telling me what it was he came to see you about?" I asked.

"No problem, that's an easy one," he replied. "It was the usual thing: chimpanzees. He was always doing research on them, and we allowed him special privileges to access ours whenever he wanted. I was with him on that last visit, because in the past, he'd always had something interesting to show me. I must say that this time it all seemed rather odd."

"Why was that?" I enquired.

"He had what looked like a small plastic chopping board with him. It was bright orange; quite an unusual colour, I thought. He wanted to see how the chimps reacted to it. He had it in a wooden box with a lid. He put a couple of bananas in there, put the lid back on, placed it in the middle of the group and left them to it."

"What was the outcome?"

"Well, nothing much, really. Chimps are naturally curious, so they soon had the lid off, and the bananas went in a couple of minutes. Then they played around with the chopping board thing for a while. They even tried chewing on it, but they soon lost interest. When they were called over at feeding time, Richard went in to retrieve it and put it back in the box."

"And that was it? Nothing else?" I probed.

There was a pause as Kenwright thought about it. "No. But I must admit that something puzzled me about Richard that day. By the time he left, he was beaming like a Cheshire cat, as if he'd suddenly discovered a hoard of gold or something. I'd never seen him look so excited."

"Did he say anything to you about it?" I asked, pressing for more information.

"No, nothing. All he said was: 'Thank you David, and sorry for the wasted journey.' Those were his very last words to me."

There was another pause, Kenwright obviously deliberating about what else to say. But then he continued: "I must admit I was a bit disappointed, because usually, he keeps me up to date with any new research he carries out, but this time there was nothing, nothing at all. I thought that very strange."

I decided it best to make no comment, other than to thank Kenwright for his time, but just as I was about to say goodbye, I remembered something else. "Oh, by the way," I said casually: "Do you remember if it was sunny that day?"

"That's an odd question," he replied, "but yes, I think it was."

Chapter 57

With those last words from Kenwright echoing around my head, I put the phone down and jumped up from my chair, punching the air with joy. Now I knew what Grayson had been up to at the zoo. With his training as a scientist, he would know that any theory is just that: a theory. It would mean nothing until backed up by proof. He obviously had to find out if George reacted to chimps in the same way as he did to humans, and from what Kenwright had told me, I knew that he didn't. No wonder Grayson was excited when he left that day.

But there was one little detail that was still bothering me: I did not know for sure if the sun was out when Grayson conducted his little experiment. Kenwright had said that he thought it was, but I needed to be certain, so I found the number for the Met Office and dialled them directly. My call was answered by a very helpful woman, who put me on hold while she went off to check. A few minutes later, she was able to confirm exactly what I wanted to hear: that there had been a belt of high pressure over most of the country, and yes, it had been sunny all day. I was overjoyed. Now I knew for sure what Grayson had been able to verify: *that George's little trick works only for Humans.*

But that still left a puzzle to be solved: how did George do it, and what did we have that chimpanzees didn't? I had to find out more. Time to study George a little closer. The first thing needed was the sun. I checked out of the window to see heavy clouds accompanied by that steady kind of drizzle England is famous for. Nothing for it but to just be patient and forget about George for a while.

We had to wait a whole week. Even then, the sun didn't last very long; maybe an hour or so. As before, we chose to use our bedroom, where the sun was brightest, and to make the most of it, we had the curtains pulled right back. George performed as expected, but try as we might, we found nothing new except for the presence of many tiny particles, perhaps thousands, scattered in an apparently random fashion throughout the clear inner matrix. Sarah saw them first, but I had to resort to borrowing her reading glasses before I could see them at all. We decided that they were nothing more than impurities, which I now think was a mistake, because everything else about George was absolutely faultless. If these particles had a purpose, we never discovered what it was. Maybe Grayson did.

But we were convinced of something: George's willingness to reveal himself to us was no accident. Surely there was a message in there somewhere: a message that could only be meant for us.

Chapter 58

Once the clouds closed back in and the rain started up again, we knew that would be it for the day. Sarah sighed and put George back on the dresser, and we went down to have a cold chicken lunch with salad, conjured up from last night's leftovers. Watching her dressing the salad with oil and vinegar, Spanish style, reminded me of the many happy meals we'd shared, sitting in the sun on the terrace at our apartment on the Costa Blanca.

Sitting in the sun. It was then that I realised how stupid we were not to have made more use of that place, especially with the promise of the one thing we really needed right now. Sarah did not need any persuading. I found a couple of suitable flights with no problem at all, and the following Saturday, we were there on our Spanish terrace having breakfast in the surprisingly warm December sun, promising ourselves to do this more often.

That decision to bring George over for a spot of sunbathing was one of the best I've ever made. Later that morning, Sarah made up a couple of gin and tonics, and we sat out there to enjoy them, along with a bowl of peanuts. It goes without saying that we had George there with us, and we took turns at playing around with him, trying to discover something new, just as Richard Grayson had almost certainly done.

Many new discoveries over the centuries have been made by accident. Scientists go looking for one thing, and often end up finding something not only completely different, but also more exciting. The same thing happened to us.

I suppose I was half expecting to see an image of a face or a place, or anything that would reveal something of whoever made George, but all our efforts came to nought. With the midday sun shining brightly, and George turned into glass, we looked along and through him from every possible angle, without success. I was getting so frustrated with it all, that I wanted to pick him up and sling him somewhere very far away.

I give Sarah the credit for the discovery. Having tried everything else, she wanted, by observing the shadow cast on the wall, to see how translucent he was. There was hardly a shadow at all, nearly all the light passing straight through. For some reason, probably pent-up frustration, she shook him, as if to force him to talk. As she did so, I thought I saw a shadowy, dark line dart across the wall, first one way and then the other, in time with the movement of her hands.

It happened so fast that I wondered if I had imagined it. "Hold on!" I cried. "I think I saw something. Do that again, but much more slowly this time."

She obliged, tilting George first to the left, then to the right. As she did so, I saw it again: the briefest suggestion of a shadow, passing quickly across the wall and disappearing almost at once.

"There it is!" I cried. "But I think you need to go even slower."

She glanced at me scornfully, as if to tell me that I was stating the obvious, and then proceeded to reproduce the same movements, but much more deliberately.

The dark shadow came and went several times in quick succession, zipping across the wall too fast to focus on.

"I have to hold him very still," she observed, "otherwise it's gone again. It's a bit like focusing a camera."

"I think George could be polarised or something similar," I remarked, "which would explain why the image comes and goes. It appears only when the light passes directly along the plane. There could be thousands of planes with images there. Keep practising."

Practise she did. It took a while, but she eventually got the knack of rotating George ever so slowly, carefully lining him up with the rays of the sun, until at last a shaky image appeared on the wall, fluttering unsteadily to match the tremor in her hands.

Seeing it for that first time, she let out a shriek of delight, and leaned in closer to get a better view. "Looks like a couple of wiggly worms," she cried.

I saw it too. Those wiggly worms looked familiar; something I'd seen many times before. "It's a double helix!" I exclaimed.

She frowned. "What's that, for heaven's sake?"

"If I'm not mistaken," I said, "we're looking at a strand of DNA!"

I sat back down on my chair and took a large gulp of my drink to settle myself down and help me think. At last we had discovered something new, but what it meant was still a mystery. If that image really was DNA, what was its significance? I had no idea.

"George's trick number two," I said. "I wonder how many more of them he has up his sleeve?"

By now, I could see from the look of excitement on her face, that Sarah was totally captivated by the whole experience, as was I.

"There have got to be more messages," She said. "I'll play around with him for a while to see if I can find anything else."

It did not take long. Now that she had learnt what to do, it took her only a minute or so to find another image, steadying her hand by resting her elbow against the wall. This next image was much clearer and sharper.

We had no trouble deciphering it. It was a series of concentric circles, about a dozen or so, and at their centre was a large sphere. Each of the circles had a small disc on its circumference, and assuming that each of them represented a planet, the whole thing looked very much like the stylised representation of a solar system that we often see in textbooks. I could tell immediately that it wasn't our solar system, because of the number of discs. There were at least 15 of them. One of the discs was picked out by an outer circle of tiny arrows pointing inwards towards it, suggesting that it was more significant than the others.

"That must be where it all came from," I remarked. "Could be absolutely anywhere in the universe: and that's a very big place."

There had to be more messages, but despite trying for another hour or so, we drew a blank. For now, at least, George had nothing more to tell us. I began to think that perhaps we didn't need any more information to make us understand what it was all about.

We spent the rest of that week relaxing in the sun and catching up with the friends we had made in Spain during our previous visits. Most of them were well into retirement age and lived there full time, which was a dream we were hoping to copy once Gary was off our hands. Yes, I know, he is off our hands now, but we've never been quite brave enough to fully take the plunge. Even so, it's still nice to get away there once in a while.

Chapter 59

We got back home late on Sunday. With a busy work schedule that week, I could do nothing further about solving this new puzzle, but when Saturday came I headed off to the local library yet again, and spent a good part of the morning there. In those days, before we all had easy access to Google and the like, the reference library was the best place to go for information.

I needed to satisfy myself that I was getting what George was trying to tell me. What was the significance of the double helix? Was it really a reference to DNA, or was it just a couple of bedsprings joined together? I picked up a book about human genetics and started flicking through the pages until I came across an image of a DNA double helix. It was identical to George's. As soon as I saw it I wanted to shout out loud, and if I were somewhere else other than that library, I would have done.

Satisfied that I was right, I read on further. Much of the material was in a technical jargon that was well beyond my understanding, and I was about to close the book up when I noticed the title of the next chapter. It was headed *Eugenics*. I can't remember the details exactly, but the leader text said something like: *Improving genetic quality by whatever means*. I already knew something about eugenics, but I was interested in finding out more, so I settled back down and continued reading.

Except perhaps for its name, the subject of eugenics is nothing new, having been practised on plants and animals, in the form of selective breeding, by humans for as long as 20,000 years. Thanks to us, the dogs of today are all shapes and sizes. They all have their own set of behaviours and personality traits, yet despite these differences, they are all descended from the wolf.

The chapter went on to describe how the term eugenics covers other more direct methods of genetic modification, processes which I didn't understand, but which were the subject of on-going laboratory experiments with the desire that less desirable inherited traits could be somehow modified, or even removed completely.

I was also fascinated to discover that, as is often the case with any new idea, nature got there first. The example cited in this case was of an organism called the Crown Gall bacterium, which has the amazing ability to transfer DNA across to cells of an unsuspecting host plant, effectively producing new cells that form the gall and producing food specifically for the bacterium.

It was at that moment that the penny finally dropped. Suddenly, I knew what George was trying to tell me. Humans had to have started somewhere; probably from what would have been our own version of the wolf, and perhaps from none other than our old friend Homo habilis (or someone similar), given a kick start by something George had brought with him.

"*Fairy dust!*" I muttered it to myself. That was how Grayson had described it. My voice was loud enough for everyone in the library to hear. I looked up to see them all staring disapprovingly at me as if I'd just committed a cardinal sin. As a matter of fact, I didn't really care, because this was yet another eureka moment.

I had just realised that Grayson's Fairy Dust had to be nothing less than DNA itself. Not any old DNA, but the DNA that makes us human.

I shook my head, wondering how on Earth I could even think of such a crazy idea. This was the stuff of science fiction, wasn't it? Suddenly, George's simple message was making more sense. *Could it be that he was there, not just at the birth of mankind, but also at its conception?* If so, who could have envisaged such a thing, and for what purpose? This was all the stuff of science fiction.

Given time, a lot of science fiction becomes fact, but right now I was beginning to doubt my own sanity, until I remembered again about thinking outside the box. It did not take long to realise that there could well be others, somewhere out there in the universe, who are either smarter than us or have been around a lot longer. They might already know the tricks we have yet to learn, and perhaps, sometime in the distant future, we will be able to understand things as well as them.

Suddenly, it all seemed to make sense. Had Homo habilis been "doctored" somehow, with DNA brought in from elsewhere, to produce offspring substantially different from itself?

I shook my head, hardly daring to believe what I was thinking. On the face of it this was a completely crazy idea, but if it had any foundation in fact, then

Homo habilis would have given birth to Homo sapiens in just one generation.

I was pretty sure that Grayson had come to the same conclusion. To discover something as ground-breaking as this would be a scientist's dream, and to keep it secret would be paramount. No wonder he went into hiding.

I tried to imagine what else Grayson might have discovered. Maybe there was something even more revealing, or did he just simply want to be left alone to formulate and document his own theories? No one would ever know for sure, and that made me sad, because I knew that he would be almost the best person on Earth to make use of it.

Chapter 60

I decided that it was time to share my thoughts with Sarah. After I'd sat her down in the living room and made her a cup of coffee, I proceeded to bombard her with all this new evidence and my crazy interpretation of what it all might mean. As usual, anxious to get the facts and ideas out of my head in case I should forget something, I went at it far too quickly.

I was only halfway through, when she put her hands up to stop me. "Slow down!" she ordered. "You're going much too fast. Just stop and take a deep breath, and we'll start again at the beginning. I get it that George is somehow tuned in only to us and that he's not at all interested in chimpanzees, and I get it that he'll only work when the sun is out, but then what?"

"There's got to be more to it than just a colour change and a couple of images," I began. "George has just got to have another purpose beyond all that. I'm quite sure he didn't just come here for the ride."

She thought for a minute. "I wonder where the ride started?"

"I wonder if they knew where it would end up?" I added.

"And what was it they were trying to achieve?"

"I've got an idea about that," I said, "and I think it's all to do with that Fairy Dust. I'm guessing that Grayson called it that to keep things simple, but I'm pretty sure that what he was really talking about was DNA."

I proceeded to tell her about the piece I'd read in the library. "I think there might be a small part of us that may have come from elsewhere," I said.

She gave me a funny look. "Now you've gone too far," she said.

I nodded. Quite honestly, I couldn't disagree with her. This was all too much to take in and too way out to believe.

Sarah screwed up her face disbelievingly. "And what do you suppose George has got to do with all of this?" she asked.

For a moment or two I was stumped for an answer, trying desperately to think of something sensible to say, and then, out of the blue, it came to me.

"That's it!" I cried. "George is here as a chaperone! His job is to protect the welfare of that precious Fairy Dust, and the only way he can do it is by passing on information."

Sarah was looking decidedly perplexed. "Well," she said. "He hasn't told us very much so far, has he? Just a couple of images; that's not much to go on, is it?"

I wasn't going to give up. "There must be more," I suggested.

"Maybe there is, but it looks like we've already given it our best shot."

"Perhaps our best shot is not good enough." I said. "The society that put this all together was obviously much more advanced than ours. I'm guessing we've still got a long way to go to catch up with them."

"I don't think there's any doubt about that. How long, I wonder?" She sounded as if she was softening up to my idea

I shrugged. "Hard to say, but things move very quickly when somebody invents something new. Take transistors and microchips, for example. Each of them changed technology almost overnight."

That set me thinking. How beautifully crafted was George. Even now, after all the hazards he'd been through, there was not the slightest scratch or blemish on him. Whatever it was, this material was something we knew nothing about. It was so incredibly hard, yet so incredibly light; features that sent out a very clear message, to me at least:

Match me, and then perhaps you'll understand.

My thoughts returned to the cave and the skeleton trapped inside that strange conical contraption. "So what do you suppose was going on there?" I mused.

"It must have been some sort of experiment; and that unfortunate person was part of it."

"Looks like it was a failure then," I remarked.

"You're assuming he was the only one," she said.

I hadn't thought of that possibility. "So you think there might have been others?"

"Why not?" she answered. "Perhaps there were hundreds of others, and this poor soul was the one unlucky enough to be around when the volcano erupted."

"You mean it was some kind of trap? I think you could be right. With those slippery walls and the entrance so high up, it would have been very difficult to get into."

"Requiring a particular level of intelligence to be able to work it out." She suggested.

"There had to be some kind of enticement."

She nodded. "Music, maybe? Or a pleasant smell with the promise of food?"

"Sounds plausible, but how would the unsuspecting victim have been able to get out of there again?"

"Oh yes!" she exclaimed. "I forgot to mention it before. There was another door low down on the other side. Most of it was buried under the pumice, but I could see the upper few inches poking through. It was closed, but perhaps it would open to let the captive out at ground level when he'd been dealt with."

"Which still leaves that same big question." I said. "What was the purpose of it all?

Sarah clicked her fingers as an idea came to her. "Looks to me as if we've been appointed as guardians," she said. "I think we might have been given a job without even realising it."

"What kind of job?"

"To look after the Fairy Dust, of course!"

Her words sent a cold shiver down my spine, and I could feel goose bumps on the back of my neck. In that moment a very disturbing thought had entered my head: if we are only human because of the Fairy Dust, was that it: the end of the story?

Or was there something else? -Something even more mysterious? -Something sinister even?

So there we were, at the end of the twentieth century, trying to work out this crazy puzzle that George had created for us. In the beginning our ancestors were quite happily living in a tropical rain forest: nice and warm all year round, no clothes needed and plenty of food. But now, their offspring are all over the planet and slowly but surely screwing things up for pretty much every other creature and plant.

We had become a species with a split personality: Earth loving animals but with the mind-set of aliens.

Where is all this madness taking us, and what, if anything, did George have to do with it?

It was time to pose the obvious question: "So, what are we going to do with George?" I said.

She frowned. "What do you mean?" she replied.

"Well, are we going to tell the World about him, or what?"

She shook her head vigorously. "No, no, no!" she cried. "That lot out there are just not ready for this right now. We can't let George loose on them just yet can we?"

Suddenly I felt confused. Although we had both become totally obsessed by George, I had always assumed that, as a public duty, we'd have to give him up one day.

"Okay, but you didn't give me an answer, so what do you think we should do with him then?" I repeated.

"Hide him. Put him away somewhere, so no one will find him," she answered.

"Forever?"

She thought for a few moments. "No, of course not. What would be the point of that? We just need to hold on until sometime in the future, when we've become sophisticated enough to be able to speak his language, but I really don't think that's going to be any time soon."

Disappointed as I was to hear those words, deep down I knew she was right. "We're going to have to work out a plan." I said.

She yawned. "Yes, sweetheart, but not tonight, please. I'm ready for my bed, so let's sleep on it and talk about it again in the morning. Perhaps we'll find the answer in our dreams."

Chapter 61

The next morning, the three of us were down at breakfast together, so with Gary present, we didn't talk about our conversation of the previous night. The activity was all about the usual morning ritual of getting ready for work and school, and not too much was spoken by anybody. It was raining very heavily, so I offered to drop Gary off at school on my way to work. Normally, he would catch the bus, but that still entailed a walk in the rain at either end.

As I drove, he thumbed through his homework and rearranged the paperwork into order.

"What lessons have you got today?" I enquired. Anything exciting?"

"No, not really." He answered, with a sigh. "Maths, French and History this morning, and then Geography and Physics this afternoon." He yawned. "I wish you hadn't asked me. Thinking about it makes me feel tired already."

And then, suddenly, he perked up. "Oh yes. There is one other thing. The whole class has got to make a list of things we want to put in the capsule."

"Capsule? What's that?" I asked.

He looked at me as if I were crazy. "Our time capsule, of course! You must have heard of that. Everyone's doing it for the Millennium this year. Our whole class have got our own, and we're each putting in something about ourselves for someone to look at maybe a hundred years from now."

I had forgotten all about that. "Yes, of course," I said. "What are you contributing?"

"I've written about our Turkana trip and the things we saw: the people and the wild animals. I thought it might be interesting for someone in the future. Who knows? They might not be able to do things like that then. In their time, it might all be virtual stuff."

"Great idea," I said, but then an alarm bell rang. "Did you talk about my little accident in the forest?"

He slapped his forehead. "Oh no," he replied. "I completely forgot about that."

I breathed a sigh of relief.

But he hadn't finished. "Don't worry, Dad, it's not a problem," he continued, "I've still got time to add it in. They're not closing the capsule for another three weeks yet."

I tried to appear as nonchalant as possible, but inside, I started to panic. The last thing I wanted was for my little secret to go public. No doubt everything put into the capsule would be closely vetted by the teachers, and some bright spark was bound to home in on it.

"I-I'd rather you kept that to yourself," I muttered. "I think it'll make me look more stupid than I am already, getting myself into a mess like that."

He looked at me quizzically and then gave a shrug. "Okay then. If that's what you want, I won't mention it."

I breathed out again. "Thank you, son," I said.

I dropped him off at the end of the road and watched him as he sprinted along to the school entrance to get out of the rain.

"A time capsule," I said to myself. "Of course! That's the answer."

That evening, I discussed the idea of a time capsule with Sarah. It didn't take her long to make me realise that, for what we had in mind, it could not possibly work. Firstly, she pointed out, the shop-bought capsules are only so wide and were designed for smaller objects, like everyday artefacts, photos and other similar bits and pieces. Almost every one of them would also have a copy of the local paper, dated the First of January 2021. Such a capsule would be too small for George. Secondly, even if we could use one of them, where could we hide it? Somewhere public, like all the others, or somewhere only we would know about? And if the latter were the case, how could we be sure it would *ever* be found? Sarah pointed out the fact that we are still finding artefacts and treasures from thousands of years ago, in places walked over by many generations who had no idea that these things were there, buried just a few feet below them.

"How is this capsule thing supposed to work anyway," I asked. "Is there a set time period to wait, or does it just go on indefinitely?" She told me that they are often put in a communal box, which is then buried in the ground and marked by a plaque inscribed with the date on which the box is to be opened. It might be in 20, 50 or 100 years, or even more. It's really up to whoever sets it up and which generation they want to 'communicate' with.

"And this will happen all over the world?" I asked her.

"Pretty much, yes."

"Then the answer is simple!"

"Go on," she urged.

"We compose an announcement and post it in as many local papers as we can. Not just in England but in as many countries and as many languages as possible. Make it eye-catching, like a boxed advertisement, but with some sort of cryptic clue as to the whereabouts and the importance of George. That way, somebody, somewhere, will get the message and come looking."

"Great idea!" she enthused.

"And we can then hide George wherever we choose. That way, so many more people will have the chance to find him."

"That's all right in theory, but where can you find somewhere that won't ever get dug up or built over?" she wondered.

"Good question," I said, and reached into my back pocket to fish out a folded up scrap of paper. "Here, look at this. What do you make of it?"

I'd written down the following: 51.641359, -0.120083.

She studied the paper for a while and then gave a shrug. "I've got no idea. What are these numbers supposed to mean?" she asked, confused.

"Coordinates. They pinpoint an exact position by latitude and longitude. This one is right in the middle of our local park," I declared.

"Oh, I see. Clever! So that way, you can hide anything almost anywhere. But we can't just hide George away by himself, can we? We need to leave him with some sort of message don't we?"

I had to agree. Whoever found George would definitely benefit from a flying start, so there and then we sat down at the kitchen table and composed a note containing everything we knew about him. I printed it out on a sheet of A5 (a similar size to George), and ran it through the laminator. My plan was to glue it to him, but I should have known better. Nothing would adhere to that ultra-smooth and slippery surface, so after some searching I found a plastic document holder in a stationery shop. It was strong but flexible, with an envelope flap and a fastener, and was the perfect size to accommodate both George and the message. After placing them into the holder, I used a stiff pair of scissors to remove the fastener. Then I sealed the flap all the way along its edge, using glue designed for plastics. I then submerged it in bathwater to check on my work. Satisfied that there were no leaks, I was ready to finish the job.

Looking back on our decision that day, and thinking the whole thing through, as I've done many times before, I'm still happy that we did the right thing in keeping George and his secrets to ourselves. One day the whole world is going to be confronted by some sort of humongous crisis, possibly of our own making. There are all sorts of scenarios for that: climate change, famine, nuclear war, global pandemic, etc. But there could also be an external threat, like a rogue asteroid or meteor strike, or something even more unimaginable, like an alien invasion, for example.

Perhaps that's what we all need: a common enemy to bring us all together as one, and make us all realise that underneath our different exteriors we are all just the same: the same flesh and blood, the same brain.

Whatever that threat might be, one thing's for sure: if something catastrophic did happen to our world, we, as a species, are going to need something very special to help bale us out.

George?

Maybe.

So where did we hide him? I hear you ask.

Sorry, I can't tell you. That's my secret.

GEORGE
PART TWO

Chapter 1
THE YEAR 2117

Mark Peterson shook hands with Raqesh Patel. It wasn't a greeting or a goodbye, but a superstitious ritual which accompanied every change of shift; the passing on of an imaginary talisman to ensure good luck to the next man. Taking his place at the console, Mark felt that familiar nervous quiver as it passed through the pit of his stomach on its way down to haunt the rest of his digestive system in much the same way it always did at this moment. Some things you never get used to.

"Anything?" he asked of his departing colleague, holding his breath as usual. "Nothing," was the short and very welcome answer.

Before starting up, Mark took a quick look around the department. They were all there already, all nineteen of them, heads down and concentrating like mad as if their lives depended on it, which, of course, they did. This was the one job nobody was ever late for, if you could call it a job. The word "honour" would be more appropriate.

The system had already detected his presence in its usual efficient manner. Even before he had sat down, there was a caption on the screen. "Good morning Mark Peterson," it said. He just stared at it, knowing there was no need to acknowledge. Once the geneticode Implant was inserted deep beneath the left scapula at birth (a process that was as easy as ear piercing), it ensured a fool-proof method of identification for life. The electronic tag was chemically linked to the individual's own genetic "fingerprint", and would not function in any other medium.

"Did you enjoy your game of tennis yesterday?" the caption continued, making Mark grimace inwardly as he reluctantly answered: "Yes thank you." Sometimes the system went just a little too far. Before long it wouldn't be possible to have a crap without the whole world knowing about it. Oh well, as long as it was all in the good cause of preserving the future world, he supposed it must be all right. At least all this technology had made some aspects of life a lot easier to manage, -and safer too, by doing away with the tedium of financial exchange, for example. With assured and instant identification, there was no longer any need for money, cheques, or plastic. With one stroke, a whole section of previously very troublesome crime had been completely wiped out.

He adjusted his seat and settled in for the three-hour shift, at the same time making his initial scan for anything unusual. After a few minutes he sat back and quietly repeated that beautiful word to himself: "Nothing." That's the way he liked it. That's the way he wanted it to stay, for ever and ever. That word seemed to magically ease the tension away. The butterflies were going and his arse was tightening up again. Why was it that whenever a person gets keyed up, all he can think about is how far away is the nearest toilet?

He allowed himself a smile. There were millions of people out there who would give their right arms to get to do what he was doing right now: dealing in uncertainties. There wasn't much opportunity to play the game of chance nowadays. Life was perhaps too safe and predictable. You now had to look beyond the planet to be involved in the risk business, and here he was, doing just that.

He felt very proud of himself. After all, close surveillance of near-space was probably the most important job going, and he was one of the chosen few; hand picked on the basis of age, academic achievement, and of course, a proven track record in the science of cosmology, at which he was something of an expert. He had already been on several astronautical expeditions, including a three-month stay at the moon base where he had almost exclusive use of the observatory.

Just about everything on the planet was under control now. They had even struck a deal with Mother Nature, and the two great powers coexisted with a quite unprecedented degree of harmony, thanks largely to the recognition mankind had finally bestowed on the old enemy. She held the key to their survival and they treated her with a begrudging respect. Her ancient rules must be obeyed. This, after all, was her planet, not theirs, and she still had the power to wreak a terrible revenge on the slightest indiscretion. They had not so much tamed her as understood her better, and the peace, uneasy at first, was now assured.

This job would have appeared very boring to any of those old timers who could still remember what it was like to work, but to Mark it was excitement itself. After all, where else could a person have the opportunity to be directly involved with the future of mankind? Yes to be honest, it *was* quite boring, but there was a kind of primeval thrill, -hard to achieve in this safe world, -attached to the knowledge that each day was spiced with uncertainty.

Nobody knew for sure that it wouldn't happen again, and by the law of averages it shouldn't happen for another thousand years at least. But laws were made to be broken, and who could say with any certainty that the last asteroid wasn't just the first in a cluster? As it so often did, Mark's mind began to wander back to that truly momentous day.

The fourth of April, 2067, just over fifty years ago, was a date that was as indelible in most peoples' minds as their own birthday. It was the day the world woke up. Yes, it was a holocaust, but most people nowadays saw it as a blessing in disguise. More than just a warning, it was their saviour.

Up until that time it was beginning to appear as if the whole world was wrapped up in a perpetual round of petty territorial squabbling; so much so, that the biggest thing around was the United Nations Force. Originally set up as a cooperative international peace keeping organisation, it had become a powerful automaton, which had grown to an immense size in an attempt to control local aggression. The whole problem, of course, was about over population confined within political boundaries. The human race, at one time nomadic and opportunist, was now being hemmed in by its own enormous success.

All this was to change on that fateful day. The asteroid hadn't seemed all that big, six kilometres across, but it was travelling at nearly thirty kilometres per second, and that was enough to give it one hell of a punch. Like a speeding bullet to a Rhino, it stopped them in their tracks. They had known it was coming, of course, and they knew it would be a problem, but they hadn't reckoned on how much. Some experts had said it would burn itself out. Others said this was it: the end. The human race was doomed to meet the same fate as the Dinosaurs. Both were wrong.

It hit home in central Mongolia, burying itself several kilometres below the surface and creating an explosion many thousands of times the size of anything seen before. The crater it formed was several hundred kilometres across and the soil it displaced created a cloud of dust which rose into the upper atmosphere and spread itself as an even mantle over two thirds of the globe. Probably only twenty thousand people were killed by the initial impact, but over the ensuing months more than two billion succumbed to starvation, disease, and exposure to the elements, as temperatures around many parts of the globe plummeted to intolerable depths.

Surely, they had thought, this was the worst disaster ever to have befallen mankind. But although it had seemed that way in the beginning, no-one today would dispute that it was actually the best thing that could have happened to them, as if God had enough of their foolish ways and had sent His messenger down to bang their heads together, like an angry schoolmaster dealing with squabbling pupils. In the event, they had woken up to the realisation that here was something more powerful than they. One more asteroid like that would be curtains for them all, every single one of them. It didn't take too long to figure out that the only way the human race was going to survive was to work together as one global nation against a common enemy, an idea that would have seemed quite inconceivable not so many years before.

Which was why Mark Peterson came to be sitting at this chair.

The job was simply to ensure that such a thing could not happen again, or leastways, there would be plenty of warning if it did. The whole thing was virtually automatic. There were eight geostationary observer stations positioned way out in space, sending a constant stream of data which was received and monitored each minute of the day by the department's very powerful computers. Mark was part of a large hand picked team of experts whose collective task was simply to ensure that all was in order with the system, a second line of security in case of breakdown.

The whole set up was overlorded by Tony Chen, obviously of the old Asian stock. He was a solidly built man, not Sumo but near enough, and had a rounded unsmiling face with narrow eyes, made inscrutable by the heavily folded lids which encased them. All queries or possible emergencies had to be reported to him for analysis and assessment. Therein lay the sting. Tony Chen had a very short temper and did not suffer fools gladly. If you took your problem to him it had better be a good one. He had better things to do with his time, like playing Magnetoball.

After carrying out the usual preliminary checks, Mark sat back in his chair and stretched his arms back over his head, yawning deeply in an attempt to clear the sleep from his head. The other day he had nearly nodded off, and he knew full well that if Chen had seen him he wouldn't be sitting here right now. As he stretched back, he was startled, as somebody behind him grabbed hold of his wrists.

"You're not thinking of dropping off again, are you?"

Mark breathed a sigh of relief as he recognised the familiar voice of his friend, Joe, the one who had saved him from a similar fate just the other day.

Mark spun round in his chair and smiled at his old buddy. "Just the opposite. I was getting some oxygen in my lungs, that's all," he said.

"Well, just make sure you don't fall asleep again, because I won't always be around to bale you out!"

Mark grinned sheepishly. "Surely that's what friends are for, to be there when you need them," he joked.

Joe's mood became more serious as he sat down at the assistant observer's chair. "Since you owe me a favour, perhaps I can ask one of you now," he said.

"What's that?" said Mark guardedly. A favour for Joe could mean almost anything.

"Would you cover one of my shifts for me?"

"No problem!" Mark managed to make his relief sound more like enthusiasm. "When?"

"Next Tuesday, ten till one. I've booked a week on a Pacific sub."

"You lucky bastard!" Mark didn't try to hide his envy. "How did you manage that?"

"Oh, easy. I've been saving up my points for ages. Don't forget it's been nearly five years since the moon trip."

"You're kidding!" exclaimed Mark. Yes, he *had* forgotten. Was it really that long? Everybody earned leisure points, and most were quite happy just to use them up on local trips, but Joe preferred to save his points for more exotic adventures. Most places in the world could be recreated in the comfort of one's own home, including the sounds and the smells, so there wasn't really any need to travel any more. There were some exceptions: space travel and submarine exploration were two. Joe's last trip was a three-week odyssey to Mars. It obviously left a lasting impression on him, because he could not stop talking about it for ages afterwards, boring everyone in the department nearly to death.

Sometimes experiences can't be put into words. The only way to really understand them is to be there. Joe was so deeply affected by his trip that the indifference shown by some of the others to his descriptions caused him obvious frustration. But there was one thing he had said about it that remained very clear in Mark's mind. It was to do with Joe's impressions of the meaning of his home. He had always placed it in the narrow context of a building that he lived in and the people who lived there with him: his family. But looking back on the earth from so far out in space he had started to become confused. From that distance he could not see his home, not even his home town. In fact the only man-made thing that could be made out with the naked eye from space was the Great Wall of China.

But he was entranced by the object of great beauty before him, a shining ball of blue and brown, laced over with white, and if he made a circle with his thumb and forefinger, he could look through that small gap and appear to be holding the whole world in his hand. Suddenly, as he did just that, he became confused, mainly about the meaning of the word "home". Surely, from that distance, it was wrong to call anything but the whole world home? Now home didn't just mean his house and family, or even his town, but that round orb in front of him which, from such a distance, seemed so very tiny and yet was all he could offer as evidence to any passing alien.

So what was his home? Was it the house or was it the planet? Joe had driven everyone mad trying to get an answer that would satisfy him. And that wasn't all. As he got further out in space he watched the earth become progressively smaller until finally it was no longer the biggest thing in view. Suddenly he could see it in a different context altogether, as nothing more than an insignificant pinhead to which he was having serious trouble relating. For a little while he even admitted losing all sense of belonging to it, instead feeling like a tiny part of something much greater, like a drop of water in an ocean. Strangely, he did not feel any less important, in fact, quite the opposite. Now he began to feel as if he really were an integral part of the universe all around him and that, in some peculiar way, it could not possibly function without him.

Although he could not fully comprehend the full meaning of Joe's thoughts, Mark knew his friend well enough to accept everything he had said. The whole affair had left him with the distinct impression that although travel does broaden the mind, it should not be undertaken without a proper understanding of the threat it imposes on one's perspective of life. There is something to be lost, as well as gained.

With that thought in mind, Mark gladly accepted Joe's request. "Sure," he said, "I'll cover for you. No problem." And then as an afterthought, he chuckled: "I know why you want to go sub-marining. You're obviously trying to redress the balance. Perhaps the weight of all that water above you will really help to compress your thoughts and get you down on the ground again!"

Chapter 2

Mark's first stand-in shift was on that next Tuesday morning. As the electrocar carried him swiftly and smoothly to his destination, he could feel his stomach churning over as usual, but he was also aware of another, deeper-set feeling: a gut feeling, warning him that perhaps today was going to be different. He shrugged. It was probably just an irrational superstition about changing a winning routine.

The shift started at ten. As he strolled towards his console, Mark exchanged the usual pleasantries with today's colleagues. Several of them were complete strangers, but there were three he knew quite well: Bob the bearded bachelor, a quiet man of about thirty with a pleasant smiling face, Christine, a short and well rounded woman who had a young daughter and was very gifted in mathematics, and then there was Geoff, probably in his fifties judging by the greyness of his hair, and who was married with no child, nothing unusual nowadays. Geoff was very keen on sailing and had tried many times to get Mark interested in it, but without success. Mark had always refused his invitations on the grounds that sailing had become too automated and there was no challenge left in it any more. One might just as well go and stand in a wind tunnel.

He stopped to say hello to Christine. "How's your daughter?" he asked.

"She's fine now. She was back at school the next day."

"I'm glad to hear that. What was the matter?"

"Oh, just appendicitis," she said, casually. "We had to leave her at the hospital for an hour or so, that's all. Her biggest complaint was that she couldn't go to netball practise that night!"

Mark laughed. "She doesn't know how lucky she is! Just imagine what it must have been like in the old days, before we had nanosurgery."

Christine nodded. "Yes, the youngsters take everything for granted nowadays, don't they?"

Mark agreed, and moved off to man his post, still thinking about what had just been said. Yes, technological achievements were so commonplace these days, it was easier to become numb to them than to try and take in the truly mind-boggling pace at which they occurred. Who would have believed, two hundred years ago, that it would ever be possible to "service" the bodily systems by means of minute, totally automated robots, no larger than small blood vessels that were able to explore almost anywhere in the body with complete safety, correcting any abnormalities they found? And yet, here we were today, having all sorts of surgical procedures carried out with no more discomfort than the tiny injection needed to introduce these minute robots into the system.

He took his seat, and after returning the mandatory niceties with the screen, glanced across at the next console to see who was to be his neighbour for the next three hours. It was Sue Collins. As soon as he saw her, his heart skipped a beat. Where had she been all this time? Joe must have seen her but he never mentioned her, crafty swine. He was probably keeping her for himself.

All at once he began to get that same feeling back again: the sick stomach and the drainpipe colon. But this time it wasn't apprehension; it was something else, something quite new. His mouth had gone dry for no apparent reason, and yet he hadn't even spoken to her. He suddenly realised he was staring at her, fascinated by every little movement she made with her head and hands as she went about her work.

To his disappointment she did not look up, acknowledging his verbal greeting with a barely imperceptible nod of her head. He sighed quietly to himself. Either she was deeply involved with her work or, worse, she was deeply involved with somebody else. He preferred to believe in the former right now. As he went through his set-up procedure he could not resist the opportunity to steal more than the occasional glance across in her direction.

She was beautiful, made so by an indefinable something that seemed to have clicked with him the moment he first saw her. With her eyes firmly fixed on the display in front of her, he took the opportunity to study her features, trying to figure out why it was he found her so attractive. She had thick, honey-blonde hair, so soft and shiny, which she had allowed to grow to the statutory limit so that it almost reached her shoulders, and she had the bluest eyes he had ever seen, with a cute, well formed nose. He watched her hands as she tapped on the keys. There was something very graceful and serene in her movements, even in the expression on her face, which, whenever he had seen her speak, seemed to break easily into a friendly smile. These were reflections of her mind, not her body. He realised It was up there in her head where the real beauty lay.

Sensing his stare, she looked up at him, catching him unawares. He turned away, not quickly enough, and felt a guilty flush spread across his cheeks, a Peeping Tom caught in the act. Now it was her turn. He imagined he could feel her eyes on the back of his head as he pretended to be concentrating on his screen. For that moment he was wishing he could miraculously disappear. Dammit, he was going to have to be careful not to get caught out like that again. Why was he being so furtive anyway? With anyone else he would be making all sorts of small talk by now, but with her it was different. He was scared to open his mouth for fear of saying something stupid.

He continued staring blankly at the screen. How could he possibly feel that way about somebody he hardly knew, he who was so well up on all the behavioural aspects of mankind? Didn't he hold a masters degree in that very subject? And besides which it wasn't as if he weren't well acquainted with the opposite sex. God knows how many girlfriends he'd had in his thirty-five years. It must have been hundreds. And didn't he know all the right things to do? There could not have been a single one of them who didn't leave his flat feeling satisfied. One thing was for sure: nowadays nobody was too shy to let a need as important as sexual satisfaction go unanswered.

Although he had always enjoyed sex, he did sometimes wonder whether the whole thing hadn't got a little bit out of hand. What was it supposed to be for anyway? Nature only had one purpose for it, but nowadays the power to procreate had been taken out of their hands by the system. Nowadays sex was for a different purpose entirely. Orgasm was the gift of nature that they had exploited to the Nth degree for the sole purpose of reconnecting their intellect with their primordial roots in that flashing moment of orgasm.

There was something else troubling him. Here he was, mister wonderful in bed, everybody went away happy. So why did he never feel that great about it? True, it was very nice, but there still seemed to be something missing, like you'd peeled the best looking orange you'd ever seen in your life, but when you came to eat it there was nothing; no taste. That's what sex was beginning to feel like. There was more pleasure in having a piss. At least you got the feeling you had produced something.

He glanced across at her again. Again that same feeling shot through him: something like insecurity, as if she was holding the key, and he was on the outside, looking in. There was a kind of fizz about her that nobody else seemed to have, and he decided there and then that he was going to have to do something to get a share of it.

Conscious of his stare, she looked up. This time he did not look away. "Do you like oranges?" he asked.

She started to laugh. "Yes I do, but that's a funny way to start a conversation!"

Her warm response put him immediately at ease. "Sorry, I was just thinking about something."

"It must have been your stomach by the sound of things!"

"N..No, it was nothing really, I..I was just thinking I haven't had one for a long time."

She looked at him curiously. For the first time he got a really good look at those eyes: such a deep shade of blue.

He swallowed hard, uncharacteristically lost for words.

"I wonder if you could help me?" She said.

"S..Sure, what's the problem?"

She pointed to the display above her screen.

"My alert beacon is flashing again."

"What do you mean, again?"

"Oh, sorry, of course, you weren't here this morning. I'm doing a double shift today. Earlier this morning it started to flash without any apparent reason. I surveyed the whole field, but couldn't find any evidence of activity."

"Did you contact the Director?"

"No. I thought it would be better to be sure of my ground first."

"Very wise. He can be a real bastard when he wants. Sometimes I think he forgets we're just volunteers. So what did you do?"

"I called in a service robot. It turned out there was a blown circuit and everything was fine for a while. But now it's just started again and I'm not too sure what to do."

"If it's a fault then perhaps you'd better get the whole system renewed. Better that than be caught out by a faulty machine. Once these things start going wrong they keep going wrong."

She nodded. "You're right," she said, pressing the service button.

While they were waiting for the robot to appear, Mark decided to make full use of the opportunity. "Have you been working here long?" He winced inwardly as he said it.

"About six months."

"I've hardly seen you. We must always be on different shifts."

"I'm Tuesdays, Thursdays and Saturdays, but I'm covering today for Rachel."

"No wonder then. I'm Mondays, Wednesdays and Fridays, how can you stand working Saturdays?" It was a loaded question. He held his breath for the answer.

"It's all the same to me, I don't have any commitments."

It was just what he wanted to hear. He let his breath out very slowly in case she noticed.

"No child?" It was always said in the singular nowadays.

"No husband either." There was just a hint of a smile.

"How come..?"

She stopped him, anticipating the question. "There was somebody, but he upped and went one day, about a year ago."

"Must be crazy..." Too late, it slipped out. Damn, he hadn't meant to play any cards just yet. She just smiled.

Just then the robot came along. It was already carrying a new set-up. "It looks like they read our thoughts," said Mark.

"It's probably standard procedure to replace anything that goes wrong more than once. There's no point taking a chance in this sort of business."

They both laughed as they realised what she had said. This was just about the only place left on Earth where chance had any say at all.

The new system was up and running in ten minutes, but within five minutes the warning beacon was on again. Sue ran a check, working her way through the grid for anything unusual. Mark watched the proceedings over her shoulder. One set of co-ordinates would not shut down.

"You'd better run an enhancer program," he suggested.
"Good idea."

They studied the screen again for a while. There was definitely something there but it was much too far away to get a positive reading on size or speed.

"There's no way out of it. You'll just have to call him," sighed Mark, sounding quite apologetic for having to say it. Sue nodded dejectedly, her eyes still on the screen. "I'm afraid you're right," she murmured. "Tony Chen or no, a Category One can't be ignored. Here goes!" so saying, she defiantly stabbed at the call button.

Chapter 3

Tony Chen was already two games ahead with three more to play. He had not been playing Magnetobowls all that long, but he was certainly getting the hang of it, much to his opponent's annoyance. It was all about getting the right static charge to match the amount of swing required. He was using his supreme knowledge of physics to full advantage. Just as he was getting down to fire off his shot, he heard that irritating electronic voice in his left ear. "Urgent call for Mister Chen. Level one priority."

"Oh shit!" exclaimed the director to himself. He chose to ignore the message for a minute, at least until he'd played the next shot. After all, nobody else could hear the message. That was the great beauty of these ear implants: you could have the volume at any level you wanted and nobody knew. The worst thing about them was, as right now, you were instantly accessible.

He let the ball loose. As it snaked its way around the tortuous circuit, he let out a great whoop of delight and turned triumphantly to his opponent to shake his hand. Both men already knew that shot was a winner. "Better luck next time, Bob!" exclaimed the Director, patting his crestfallen opponent on the back. "Keep on practising!"

Without further hesitation he raised his left wrist to his mouth. "Chen here. Who's calling?"

The female voice in his ear said: "Susan Collins, monitor three. We have a Category One situation here, sir. We think you should come and check it out."

The director chewed at the corner of a fingernail. "Who's we?" He said sharply.

"I have been discussing the situation with Mark Peterson on number two, sir."

"What's the matter, can't you handle it yourself? And anyway who's looking after number two while you're having your cosy little chat?"

"Sorry, sir. I thought..."

"You know the rules number three. You make your own decisions, and you talk to me if you've got a problem, but I'll tell you something right now, this had better be something good!"

What he really meant was: it had better be nothing at all.

He ran out and dumped himself into the first waiting electrocar and slid his emergency one swipe across the sensor. The machine was thus automatically programmed to take him to his destination with absolute priority, clearing all intersections on the way. With speeds of over a hundred and twenty it never took more than five minutes to get right across the city in an emergency; and in complete safety. In fact there had not been a single accident since the system was perfected more than twenty years ago.

He burst into the department like a wounded rhino, intent on doing some kind of damage. The whole place went quiet as all eyes followed his determined march along to number three.

Sue knew it was Chen as soon as she heard the door slide open but she did not look up. There was no way he was getting any satisfaction out of seeing her submit to his aggression. He came up to her chair and paused there for a moment, obviously thrown by her lack of response. Suddenly he became aware the whole room was watching him. Normally people just slid away from him and simply blended with the furniture like the nonentities he perceived them to be. But this was different. Now he was being challenged to break into her world, and with all eyes upon him he began to feel just a little vulnerable. He hesitated for a moment. To rise to the bait and show aggression now would only be seen as a sign of weakness.

"Miss Collins, I believe you sent for me?" The tone was polite and even a little guarded. She turned and fixed him with a calm stare. "Yes, there's something here you ought to see. I'm getting a persistent signal from this section of the grid and I think it ought to be investigated." Although she spoke softly, everyone heard her. Strangely, the listeners were not so much interested in the cause for her request as the reaction from Chen. The sweat on his upper lip indicated he was fully aware of that. Somehow this slip of a girl had managed to make his truculence seem very immature. His stern expression softened into a faint smile. "We'd better have a look then, hadn't we," he said quietly.

As he ran through the system, Sue used the moment to update him. "I've had the system checked out for faults. In fact this is a whole new one, and the readings keep coming out the same." He nodded but said nothing, his face a study in concentration as he tapped in various commands. After several minutes he raised his head to look at her. She already knew what he was going to say.

"Miss Collins," he said slowly. "I think I owe you an apology. Not for what I said, but for what I thought. I've been brought back here on so many wild goose chases in the past I'd began to assume that's how it always would be. But I was wrong." He slumped back in the chair, gazing at nothing in particular. "I've never been more sorry to be wrong as I am right now," he said solemnly.

It was a message that every person in that room immediately understood. They looked around at each other in dismay. This was not supposed to happen was it? Lightning was not supposed to strike twice in the same place. The whole thing had been a game up till now, like being in the army. It was all great fun until the war really started and then it was a whole new ball game. For a short while the whole room was stunned into silence, not wanting to believe what they had just heard, and then, almost as one they broke into a nervous chatter, still with their eyes fixed on the Director.

Tony Chen rose slowly from the chair and turned to face them. "Yes, ladies and gentlemen, you have understood me correctly. There is cause to believe that this object is on a collision course with the earth. Whether it is of sufficient mass to be of concern to us remains to be assessed. By tomorrow we should have an answer to that question, and until that time I'm sure I don't need to remind you this information is totally confidential. Please return to your duties until further notice."

He was right; they did not need reminding. This was probably just another false alarm like all the others. So far, in more than forty years of surveillance, only one of these had needed to be followed up, but even that was found to be more than two million miles off target.

Chen thanked Collins as graciously as his ego would allow, and proceeded to brief her on what to do next. She was to call in a team of analysts specially trained to sift out the vital information, and report back to him as soon as she had a result. With that he turned and walked off as briskly as he had arrived, but not before shaking her by the hand.

Chapter 4

As he watched the director's stubby frame disappear through the door, Mark stood up. All throughout, he had divided his attention between what Chen had to say and how Sue dealt with him. Somehow the determination on her face seemed to emphasise her beauty even more. He went over to her desk. "You were great," he said. "I wish I had the courage to stand up to him like that." She grinned. "He's a softie really. That's just a front he puts on." Her face became more serious. "You shouldn't need courage if you believe you are right," she said, frowning at him. "Surely you would do the same thing in those circumstances wouldn't you?" Mark tried hard not to appear sheepish. "Of course," he replied, hoping she hadn't noticed the waver in his voice.

The moment seemed right. There could not possibly a better time than now, while she was on this euphoric high he had a chance. "Can I take you out to dinner tonight? I think you deserve it after that." He held his breath in the moment of silence that followed. She studied him for what seemed an age before answering. "What do I deserve?" She asked. "Dinner, or being taken out by you?" Her expression was dead-pan, her question a challenge. He had to meet it headlong, or die right there. "It could be both," he smiled. "But just take the dinner right now and you can make your own decision about me later." She made him sweat again as she paused before answering. Finally the slightest grin began at the corners of her mouth. "Okay," she murmured. "What have I got to lose?"

"Chinese?" He was trying desperately hard to conceal his excitement.

"Sounds great. In fact it seems appropriate!"

"Have you been to Mr. Wong's?"

"No, but I've heard it's very good."

"I'll book it for eight. Is that okay?"

She nodded. "That's fine."

He called for her at seven forty-five. Mr. Wong's was about twenty miles away, so they had plenty of time to get there. As the electrocar parked itself effortlessly and silently into Sue's guest parking bay, Mark felt a tingle of excitement on suddenly hearing her honey voice in his left ear. "Come right up, the door's expecting you." Sure enough, as he approached it, the door slid silently open, already programmed to accept his geneticode implant.

She was standing in the hall wearing a snugly fitting black dress which, as Mark was quick to observe, did her already near perfect figure no harm at all. It was obviously a compudress, there not being a bulge or ripple to be seen. Perhaps it wasn't the dress; maybe her figure *was* that good. That was the only trouble with compudresses. So well engineered were they, you just could not tell what you were getting. With any luck he would find out the truth one day. Soon, he hoped.

Mark gave out a long, low whistle. "You're beautiful," he murmured. "It's a good job you don't wear that to work. I'd never be able to concentrate."

She grinned. "You don't concentrate anyway. I've seen you looking."

He felt suddenly hot. "What do you mean?" He said, trying to sound innocent.

"You know." She said pointedly.

He was silent for a moment, and then looked up at her eyes. They were dancing with unconcealed amusement.

"Sorry," he said sheepishly. "I just couldn't help it. I guess I was just fascinated by you. Some people you can read like a book, but you're different. I was just trying to work you out."

She laughed. "I'm very simple really."

Her tone made him relax. "I don't believe that for a minute," he said.

She looked inquiringly at him. "I thought you were never going to ask. At first I thought you kept looking at me because you liked me, but when nothing happened, I started to wonder if I simply had some strange affliction that was fascinating you."

"Not at all; quite the opposite. I was just too shy to say anything, that's all." He said nothing for a moment, appearing to wrestle with a thought. "You know, I'm not really shy with anyone else. There's obviously something about you..." He stopped mid sentence. Damn, he hadn't wanted to say that. Not yet anyway. It made him feel too vulnerable and weak, which was not something he was used to.

It was time to change the subject. He looked at his wrist. "It's getting late," he said. "I think we ought to be going."

He reversed the electrocar out and set it on auto. The display lit up with the request: "Destination please?"

He spoke the name of the restaurant and sat back. The computer would do the rest, finding the name in its directory and matching it with the coordinates. Almost without pausing the vehicle set off, the route already planned. "E.T.A. eight oh five," an electronic voice said. They sat back to talk as the machine moved smoothly into the line of traffic, automatically maintaining the appropriate distance from other vehicles as it conveyed the occupants to their destination in complete safety.

The restaurant was very popular. The word was that the food was authentic and prepared by hand, a rare thing nowadays. Certainly the car park was quite full, but the electrocar had already earmarked a space, setting itself neatly as ever right over one of the ubiquitous recharging terminals. Nowadays there was never any fear of "going flat". By the time they moved off again the machine would be fully charged, and so would Mark's bank account. It was not a thing he ever thought about. It just happened, like so many other everyday processes.

The waiter showed them to the table and left them to study the menu. It was fun to eat out in the old-fashioned way and try to relive the atmosphere of the culture as it was more than a hundred years ago. Even the menu was a novelty. It was probably the only time they ever saw print, other than on some form of electronic visual display. The print was on plastic; paper having been banned almost seventy years ago.

They ordered three dishes. Sue decided to have the Peking Duck, and Mark chose the house speciality: a variation on chilli beef. They shared a plate of Singapore noodles and Mark ordered Chinese tea for two. The waiter bowed, more out of irreverence, than deference, to the bygone age, and the couple laughed as he left to fetch the meal.

"There's nothing like the real thing," said Mark as he watched the waiter retreating. "This is far more fun than just touching icons on a screen." Meanwhile, out of sight, the waiter was doing just that. Nothing was quite what it seemed in this artificial world.

The meal, of course, was perfect, a predictability that people took for granted nowadays, and which offered the only cause for complaint. Chance had been taken out of almost everything, including cuisine. Planes never crashed, ships never sank. Nearly everything that moved was controlled and monitored by computers, so that mistakes were never made. Mark often wondered whether life wasn't just a bit too safe. Since money in any form had been made obsolete by electronics coupled with the certainty of identity (thanks to the geneticode implant) you couldn't even rely on the possibility of a good mugging to get your adrenaline flowing.

Their talk was lively. They were both well educated, like most people nowadays, and there was no shortage of subject matter. But despite the flowing conversation, Mark found himself becoming more and more uneasy. His stomach seemed to be tightening, and even with all this superb food in front of him, he could not eat. Something was happening to him, something that he couldn't control. It was her. Every movement of her mouth, every flicker of her eyelids seemed to send a sharp, but strangely pleasant pang through his stomach, the same kind of feeling he'd experienced when the adrenaline starred to flow before an exam, as if he was being launched into some new world which was completely out of control

He laid his chopsticks across one edge of the plate and looked into her eyes, knowing that now was the time to say what he felt. He tried to speak but his tongue was too dry to work. Nervously taking a sip of tea, he worked it around his mouth trying not to make it too obvious. He swallowed hard. "I...I just want to say... that I find you very attractive," he wavered. Even though he knew he was speaking the words, he somehow seemed to be listening to them with her, as if they were coming from someone else's lips. He could feel his cheeks getting warm as he awoke to this new-found commitment which he was hearing but hardly believing.

She listened intently, her eyes inscrutable, studying his, still nervously flitting from side to side. After what was for him an agonising pause, she said: "Thank you," very softly and deliberately.

They took their time to enjoy the meal. Mark's only thought was that this evening was going to end sometime, and already he wasn't sure he could cope with the prospect of being away from her for one minute, let alone a night. At the same time he felt anxious not to give her the wrong impression. Funny, he wouldn't have thought twice about asking anyone else back to his flat on the first night, but this was different. It felt like he was on a tight-rope. One false move and all would be lost.

The waiter came to ask if they would like coffee. Mark was just about to say "Yes", when Sue put up a hand to stop him. "No thank you," she said, and then leaned closer to speak to him. "This has cost you enough points already," she whispered. "Why don't we go back to my place?"

Mark swallowed hard. "Okay," he said, trying his best not to sound too eager, and feeling eternally grateful that the suggestion had come from her and not him.

That next morning he woke with a start. He opened his eyes to see a ceiling and walls of a colour he did not recognise. He jerked his head to one side. She was laying there next to him, still fast asleep, her face as beautiful as ever, untarnished by the night. He pinched himself to make sure it was really happening, and with the truth confirmed, slumped his head back on the pillow, smiling contentedly to himself.

She woke ten minutes later. He watched as she opened her blue eyes and started to gently stroke her hair. "You're even more beautiful in the morning," he murmured. She snuggled up closer to him. "You know you'll have to marry me now, don't you?" she purred.

"I knew that from the moment I first saw you," he said. "How could that be? Nobody else has ever made me feel that way."

"Me neither. Just old fashioned chemistry, I guess."

Chapter 5

For perhaps the one and only time in his life, Mark had not the slightest desire to go to work, just as Sue had no desire to let him. He contacted Chris to ask if he would sub, but bit his tongue when he realised the latter was speaking from his fishing boat way out in the ocean somewhere. To expect anyone to turn that in would be too much to ask, even for someone as easy going as Chris. So it was with a heavy heart and a laboured foot that Mark finally and reluctantly entered the department. The first thing he saw was that very unmistakable frame of Tony Chen, seated at number three and staring intently at the screen. Standing behind him and following his every move were three other men, all strangers, or at least they were to Mark. The trouble-shooters he guessed; their grim expressions telling him quite clearly that yesterday's little problem had not gone away.

He stopped at number one to ask Mohamed Aziz the latest. "It looks like it might be the real thing this time," his friend whispered. "They've run all the standard checks plus a few more, and everything keeps coming up positive."

Mark was wide eyed. "Jesus!" he breathed. "That'll really give us all something to think about!"

The Director looked up sharply, distracted by the noise. His hostile glare was not lost on Mark, who wasted no further time in making his way to his position. He completely ignored the screen's persistent promptings and just sat there staring blankly into space. He was still dazed by the realisation that this was not, after all, just another false alarm. After a while he sighed out loud and shook his head despairingly. Everything seemed to be happening so fast. Last night the whole world had been opened right up for him and now it was in real danger of being closed right down.

He was finally dragged out of his daydream by the unit's second line of attack: the audible prompt. It said: "Please wake up, Mark Peterson, and talk to me. Did you enjoy your Chinese meal last night?" He wanted to throw something at it, but instead managed to squeeze out a "Yes thank you" through clenched teeth.

It was another two hours before the men at number three stood up, the solemn looks on their faces advertising their grim conclusions quite clearly. Nothing was said, nor needed to be said, neither was there any need for secrecy. Like any other important discovery, this sort of news was already public property, and as such, the rest of the world had as much right as they to know all about it.

The official announcement came at three in the afternoon. Despite everything, Mark had decided to keep his previously arranged engagement, which was to meet up with a couple of friends down at the beach and catch up with some practise for next weekend's power surfing competition. It was one of his favourite pastimes. With the addition of a remarkably powerful micro-motor, the stunt variation was truly amazing. He was just trying unsuccessfully to master one of them when a ten-footer came up and dumped him unceremoniously to the bottom. As he began clawing his way back to the surface, he heard the official confirmation of the dreaded news coming through in his left ear.

"It is with regret that the World Administrative Council has to announce the presence of a large asteroid of unknown origin which is on a confirmed collision course with Earth. This is expected to occur on the Seventeenth of July, in the year twenty one twenty nine, a little over twelve years from now. A further update will be given at Eighteen hours Standard Time, after which the Council will be taking all suggestions for an appropriate course of action, the most practical of which will be decided upon in the normal way during the usual Sunday Plebiscite."

Mark flopped his aching body down onto the surfboard and listened attentively to the message while allowing the micro-motor to cruise him gently back to the beach. Once ashore, he picked up the board and made his way hurriedly back to the electrocar, aware from their serious expressions that everyone else on that beach was also deep in thought. As he folded the board and stashed it away in the boot, the only thing in his mind was to get back to Sue as quickly as possible, and share his thoughts with her and nobody else. He pressed a tiny button on his wrist console and spoke her name.

Within twenty seconds her voice came through in his right ear. "Hi, Mark, I was just going to call you. What are we going to do?"

There was no need for Sue to explain what she meant. When she said "we", she was using that word in a truly collective sense. Communication all around the world was virtually complete, with everyone kept up to date with events almost as soon as they happened, thanks to their lifetime earspeakers fitted within a few weeks of birth.

"I was going to ask you the same thing," said Mark, drying his hair with a towel. "We'll have to get together and talk about it. How about coming over to my place tonight?"

He didn't have to ask her twice. She was there precisely at seven and as he greeted her at the door, she kissed him softly on the cheek, catching him off guard and bringing a colour to his face. Surprised at his own reaction to her touch, he guided her into the lounge and sat her down on the sofa before fixing her a drink. Before the gin had a chance to cover the bottom of the glass she held her hand up in protest. "Whoa! That's quite enough! I want to be able to think tonight, not fall asleep!"

He carried on pouring. "Don't worry," he chuckled, "I'm using one-hour gin. It'll be water by eight o'clock. Anyway you should know it's not wise to make important decisions when you're totally sober." He paused and grinned at her. "Or at least, if you do, then make sure you reassess them again when you've had a few, to see if the answer's still the same. If it isn't, then don't make a decision!"

"In vino veritas!" she rejoined with a smile, holding her glass up to him in salute.

They took their drinks into the entertainment lounge. "Let's just relax for a while and watch a holomovie," suggested Mark, switching on the display for the latest update.

"Sure, how about something historical? I can never get enough of those."

"Suits me." he shrugged. It didn't really, but this was no time for friction. He paused the control on a thing called "The Family."

"I've heard this one's pretty good."

"It's okay by me," she agreed, with a nod of her head. "I haven't seen it. But there's just one thing..."

"What's that?"

"Do you mind if we watch it quarter size and turn off the smellosim. Sometimes those old aromas are a bit *too* authentic for my liking!"

He laughed. "I know what you mean! All that sweat and flowers is a bit much isn't it? It's a bit like having a perfumed piggery in your living room! They had a funny idea of what was nice in those days, didn't they?"

"You're not kidding! Three cheers for the guy who came up with bottled pheromones, they're much more fun!"

They were totally captivated by the holomovie. It was a period piece, set in the early part of the twentieth century, about the fortunes and misfortunes of two generations of a family, as they became caught up in the two world wars and the technological revolution. How incredible to think of the changes, largely brought about by the increasing use of electricity and the amazing acceleration of scientific discovery it had facilitated.

As he switched the system off, Mark turned to Sue and kissed her on the cheek. She smiled, but it was a vacant smile, her eyes were staring blankly ahead.

"What's the matter, sweetheart?" he asked softly, half guessing already.

At length, and still with the same bemused expression, she said: "I wonder what it must have been like to have brothers and sisters?"

"Noisy, I should think."

"Sibling rivalry. It must have been a great character builder."

"Yes. That was the way it was meant to be, of course." He put his arm round her shoulder, sensing she needed comforting.

"If it was meant to be, then why aren't we doing it now?" There was a hint of despair in her voice.

"You know the answer to that as well as anybody. There's already way too many of us. We've got to keep the numbers down somehow, and short of going out and culling the masses, there's nothing else we can do but accept the Fertility Quotient. It would be great if they *could* get it above one again, but I honestly don't think it's going to be possible in the near future." He paused and shrugged apologetically, as if somehow it was his fault. "Until then, the world will just have to be content with less than one child per couple."

She looked deep into his eyes. "Don't you get the feeling that the more in control we become, the further we get from nature?" she sighed. "It's as if we're gradually trying to disown our animal past in the search for something better."

He nodded. "Do you believe there *is* anything better?"

She thought for a moment, and then shook her head. "I don't know, but if there is, we haven't got much time left to find out, have we?

At that moment, the robobutler brought them coffee, and they sat talking for a while. Mark was trying desperately hard to think of something cheerful to say.

"It must have been pretty soul destroying to have to go to work every day," he began. "No wonder so many people weren't all that creative, they just didn't have the time to be. It must have been a full time job just trying to make ends meet!"

Sue nodded. "So many people lived their lives through their children, hoping maybe they could figure things out a little better than their parents ever could."

"They were playing pass the parcel, just like we do, hoping that the last one to open it will win the prize."

"Which is?"

He gave a shrug. "Complete happiness, I guess. Whatever that is."

"We'll never know the answer to that until we get to that last box!" she cried, a wry smile on her face.

Mark finished the last of his coffee. "Since we've started on the crystal gazing, we'd better continue," he suggested. "Got any ideas for the Sunday Plebiscite?"

They spent ages talking about various possibilities for saving the world, but eventually had to narrow their options down to just two. That rogue asteroid was going to have to be either blown out of the sky, or given a friendly nudge to persuade it to go elsewhere. There was really no other choice.

Sue was getting fidgety. All this talk of doom and gloom was making her anxious. "What if nothing works and they can't stop this thing?" she said, the colour draining from her face.

"Of course it'll work," he replied, trying hard to sound reassuring. "It's got to."

Secretly, he was not so sure. But the thought of all humanity being extinguished by such a holocaust -something much worse than contemplating one's own death- was unthinkable, particularly to an optimist like Mark.

Sue was not convinced. "Yes, but supposing it didn't?" She said nervously.

"Then we perish; never more to exploit this poor old planet. R.I.P. the human race!" His tone was flippant, but his eyes were humourless.

"Don't joke. You know it's not funny!"

"Sorry. I guess I was just using humour as a defence."

His chilling words had sent a cold shiver through Sue's body, making her move closer to him. He put a reassuring arm around her, but somehow it wasn't enough to thaw out a feeling that seemed to have invaded the depths of her marrow. Her hands felt like ice, despite the perfectly functioning optimoclime heating system.

"There's got to be something to believe in," she croaked. "Surely it can't all end just like that." He said nothing, but sensing the pitiful tremor in her voice, pulled her towards him and hugged her tightly. Over her shoulder, he stared unseeingly into the distance, trying to think of something positive: Eco-colonies on the moon, or Mars maybe? No, they'd already abandoned that idea as any sort of permanent solution. The ones they set up before had only really survived because of constant supplementation from Earth. It was like the idea of perpetual motion: nothing more than a dream.

But an even bigger problem was the unexpected emergence of a strange neurosis during the later stages of each and every one of the projects. It was a kind of melancholia, experienced with disturbing regularity by volunteer colonists. Sufferers had reported feelings of great panic, similar to that which a small boy when he loses his mother in a crowded place. In each case it was quickly followed by a sense of extreme hopelessness, very much akin to that experienced during the very worst bouts of home sickness. Even the best of the hand picked and seemingly well balanced individuals succumbed to it, as if a basic driving force in their make-up had been denied to them.

And the idea of men leaving this solar system to colonise another was still just that: an idea. The distances were just too great and the time factors so enormous as to make such a project completely untenable. And what chance of actually finding a habitable planet -a twin for Mother Earth- amongst the countless numbers out there? Almost none.

They spent the rest of that evening listening to relaxing music and drinking wine, before ending the evening sharing a relaxing duobath, which was followed by a very satisfying session of lovemaking, made even more special by Sue's foresight in spending five extra minutes on the vibrosaddle. Peaceful sleep followed.

Mark was suddenly woken by a familiar voice in his left ear. Opening his eyes and blinking hard to clear away the sleep, he saw the faint grey of dawn seeping through the curtains. It must be about five, he guessed, still too feeble to raise his wrist. The voice, synthetic and monotonous, and heard by each individual in his or her own language, was the information service at level three. It was only level one that stayed on all the time but, apart from the daily test, was almost never used. It was reserved exclusively for very urgent matters concerning world security, and therefore nowadays hardly ever interfered with sleep. But level three was optional, and Mark cursed to himself as he realised he had forgotten to switch it off last night.

"This is the latest update on suggestions submitted to the World Security Council up to now, twelve hundred hours Standard time," the voice was saying. "The two most popular suggestions are for the destruction or the deflection of the asteroid, or a combination of both."

He grunted disparagingly. "Surprise, surprise," he muttered to himself, and made to switch off that irritating voice, but at the last second, something stopped him. Who knows what variety of crackpot ideas there were out there? It might make for some entertaining listening.

He was right. It *did* turn out to be a comedy show. But it was fascinating to see how ingenious some of the ideas could be, even if most of them were more than a little naive. They ranged from projects to search for new solar habitats, to an idea for forming colonies at the depths of the ocean and staying there until the turmoils on the surface had subsided, if they ever did. The idea of suspended animation was very popular, but no-one had come up with a method of bringing it back to life again.

Most of the rest was pure science fiction, including the freezing of human ova and sperm tissue, deemed to be a logistic impossibility, since it would involve incubation and rearing of individuals by purely mechanical means. Some obviously very impractical person had even suggested that, since we really only needed to be assured of the survival of our human spirit, then why not just isolate the DNA responsible, and send it off minus the rest of our DNA baggage (which we already shared with chimps), then release it later, like a genie from a bottle, into some other living world, so that it could unite with and control the best example of whatever form of life could be found.

Mark yawned and pulled the plug on the talk. It was all getting a bit silly now and anyway he was still in need of some more sleep, apart from which he was quite clear in his own mind about which was the way to go. He turned over and snuggled up close to the sleeping Sue, sliding his arm under the sheets and around her waist, a gesture which she accepted with a peaceful murmur.

Chapter 6

That Sunday the options had been short-listed to just five. They were tabled according to the numbers of individual suggestions in their favour, and alongside each, there was a feasibility forecast, formulated by computation and augmented by commentary from panels of hand picked experts. Way out in front on both counts was the suggestion to destroy the asteroid, using a series of nuclear explosions. This was given a feasibility forecast of sixty-nine per cent, which, as Sue was quick to point out, meant that it stood an almost one in three chance of not working.

The next three were also fairly predictable: the deviation plan with fifty-five per-cent feasibility, the Lunar colonisation scheme with forty-nine per cent, and the cryogamete plan with thirty-one per-cent. But what had really astounded Mark was the fifth placed idea, and why it should even be a consideration. Only a few hundred people had made the original suggestion, but what had really kept it in the running was the staggering feasibility quotient of sixty-four per cent. Who, in their right minds, would ever have believed that the genie-in-the-bottle theory would have any practical application? There was obviously something he did not understand.

What was even more remarkable was the fact that only projects with a feasibility quotient of more than fifty per cent could be voted on, which suddenly put this complete outsider in the running. At the very worst it would come third. It turned out that Mark and Sue were not the only people to be intrigued by this very unlikely newcomer. They stayed in that afternoon, anticipating a great afternoon's sport. They were not disappointed. The viewing room buzzed incessantly with debate from all corners of the globe.

The main thing on everyone's mind was to be given a fuller explanation of the remarkable feasibility score of the "Genie" theory, as it came to be called. The simple, but not entirely satisfactory, answer was that, although (subject to the development of suitably durable materials) it could soon be technologically possible to construct a spacecraft capable of reaching other solar systems unscathed, it was not possible to transport even the smallest of life forms and hope to maintain their vitality over such long periods of time. This principal had come to be known as the "Veevee Catch". Given that viability and vitality, (from which the idea derived its name) were not compatible in this context, then the alternative was to try and transport the essential information in some other, non-vital form: a form that would last indefinitely, many millions of years even, but could be reconstituted at the appropriate time. Computer analysis had shown that this was indeed theoretically possible. Practically speaking, however, it was still a very long way off.

"Perhaps they should have made a distinction between feasibility and practicability," sighed Sue as she read the explanation. "This Genie thing wouldn't have got a look in."

Mark was sitting on the floor next to her, his elbow on her knee. In response to her comment he leaned back to think, clasping his hands behind his head to make a pillow.

"It's funny hearing you say that," he remarked at length. "You were the one who was worried about saving our souls and now you're rejecting the opportunity to do just that."

"No I'm not," she protested. "It's just that I wish there were something more concrete to vote on than just a totally wild idea like that."

He nodded, but could think of nothing comforting to say. Sadly he had to agree with her.

The vote was duly cast at twenty four hundred hours Standard Time which for Mark and Sue was five in the afternoon. The world worked with two time systems: Local and Standard. It was the only sure way of synchronising important events, such as the Weekly Plebiscite. They had adopted the old International Date Line as the starting point for the Standard Day and all times were given out in both formats with red for Standard and blue for local. The only place the two times correlated was, of course, along the line itself (which was coloured purple).

Voting was simple. The alternatives were displayed very clearly in the appropriate language on one's own personal wrist monitor, and it was simply a matter of tapping in a priority number against each, within twenty four hours of the start time. As each vote was tagged with the individual's geneticode the system was tamper proof. Mark and Sue voted the same as virtually everyone else: 1 for destruction, 2 for deviation, and 3 for "Genie".

All three proposals were thus duly adopted, but with a descending budget. With so much at stake it would have been folly to put all of the eggs in one basket. On the other hand it was only logical to invest most heavily in the surest project. Consequently three times as much was allocated to project one as to project three.

The general mood that following week was strange, to say the least. It was as if people had already started to build their own personal defence mechanisms in order to be able to cope with the enormous mental stresses the future had in store for them. One way of dealing with a problem is to artificially diminish its significance in one's mind's eye. The very next evening Mark and Sue had a first- hand experience of this when they went along to "An Armageddon Party" with an invitation that read: "Eat and drink yourself silly, as if there were no tomorrow!" If you can't handle it, make a joke out of it.

The atmosphere was distinctly bacchanalian, with the best one-hour champagne and delicious food, impeccably served by an army of androwaiters poised waiting to fill the empty glass or offer the most delicate and tasty bite-sized morsels. Mark and Sue arrived quite early, but already the noise level was well above the usual permitted maximum, something quite rare nowadays. With the ubiquitous ear speaker implants and the virtually silent electrocars, sound pollution was a thing of the past, and it was now possible to turn off and bask in a world of comparative silence, save for the more pleasant sounds of nature.

Sue was immediately caught up in the atmosphere. She grabbed Mark's arm, making him almost choke on a smoked salmon roll. "Come on, let's dance before the floor gets too crowded!" She begged excitedly.

"Okay, okay," he relented. "Just give me a second to finish this!" He hastily downed the last of his champagne and as she dragged him towards the dance floor, he dumped the empty glass on the nearest androwaiter.

The floor was already crowded, but holodancing was so exciting it did not matter how many there were. Spinning round and round to the music, Sue felt her heart skip a beat as she suddenly came face to face with Rik Stone, her teenage heart-throb. There he was, as large as life, right in front of her and beckoning her to dance. She screamed with delight and reached out to touch him, but her eager hand encountered nothing but thin air, passing right through his body and making her recoil in horror. But she soon began to laugh as she realised she had been duped by an amazingly real holoprojection.

When the number finished they left the floor for a break.

"I could have sworn it was really him!" said Sue, struggling to catch her breath.

"So what's new?" responded Mark, a broad grin on his sweating face. "It's just an illusion, like most other things in our lives. We left reality behind centuries ago." He wiped his brow with a handkerchief, and pointed to the far side of the hall. "Hey, there's a couple of seats over there. Let's grab them before anyone else does!"

They made their way quickly across to a table for four, part occupied by one couple. Mark made the usual polite request to join them. "Of course," the other man said, smiling. They helped themselves to a couple of drinks from a passing androwaiter and stood by the table toasting themselves. As he made to sit down, Mark became aware that the other man was staring a little too intently at him, a quizzical look in his eyes. At length, he said: "I know you, don't I? It's Mark Peterson, isn't it?" Mark peered at the man blankly for a moment and then suddenly a glint of recognition came into his eyes. "Of course!" he exclaimed, "You're Tony Marchetti! I'm sorry, I didn't recognise you. It must be that beard. How long have you had that?"

They shook hands warmly.

"Oh, at least five years now," came the response. "It dawned on me one day that if we were meant to shave we'd have been born with a razor in our hand, and since we weren't, I decided to let my whiskers do their own thing! I can tell you it's a lot easier. You just have to watch out for birds' nests, that's all!"

Still grinning, Marchetti turned to introduce his attractive partner. "Darling, this is Mark Peterson, we were at College together, over ten years ago now. Mark, this is Elizabeth, my wife." Although Mark returned the introductions and repeated the names, Sue forgot them almost immediately, fascinated more by the couple's obvious similarities. Both about the same height and colouring, with jet black hair and lightly tanned skin.

Even their facial expressions were similar. It struck her that they could easily pass for brother and sister; so much so that anything but a totally happy relationship seemed quite inconceivable.

Her intuition turned out to be quite accurate. Tony and Elizabeth had been married for more than eight years. They had been one of those couples lucky enough to have come through on the right side of the fertility quotient, and their son, Adam, was already three years old. They were both keenly involved in research, which, like so many occupations nowadays, was voluntary. They worked together on the same project at the Human Research Institute, but when Sue asked what the research was about, neither of them seemed too keen to respond.

"Genes and DNA," said Tony at length, but not before exchanging glances with his wife, almost as if he was requesting her approval.

"Sounds fascinating," remarked Sue.

"Yes it is."

"Is it laboratory work or field study?" asked Mark, slightly puzzled by their reticence.

"Oh, nearly all lab work. We don't get out all that much."

"Genetics is an enormous subject isn't it? Do you have a special interest?"

"Yes, we certainly do, but we don't seem to be getting very far at the moment."

"Blind alley?"

"Not quite; more of an endless maze. Somehow you know there's a way out, but it's just too hard to find."

"Keep trying. Anyway, you haven't told us what it is you're looking for?"

Tony eyed them doubtfully for a moment, once more glancing across to his partner. She gave him a nod.

"Well..." he began, combining the word with a sigh. "I suppose you already know we're less than two per-cent away from the chimps?"

"Not in intelligence, surely?"

"No, of course not. No, I was talking about our genetic make-up. Ninety eight point four per-cent of it is exactly the same."

"No kidding? And the one point six per-cent?"

"That's the bit we're interested in. There's only about sixteen hundred genes involved. Do you realise how small an amount that is, considering how vastly different we are?"

"Tiny," gasped Mark, amazed. "After all, we're a whole universe away from them, aren't we?"

"Just about!"

"So what's your problem?"

"Well, firstly, just being able to identify them. As you must know, we already know the DNA sequencing of each and every one of them, and have done for more than a hundred years, ever since the completion of the Genome Project. But being able to separate them into functions and origins, well that's something else altogether! We've always had to rely on malfunctions and mutations to give us clues."

Mark shook his head. "A real needle in a haystack job, eh?"

"You're telling me!"

"But why do you need to separate them?"

"Because, somehow contained within that amazingly complex chemistry, is the elusive secret of our intelligence, our consciousness, and our very souls. It's the only part of us we really care about; the part we all want to last for an eternity."

"Wow! That's pretty mind blowing stuff! And secondly?"

"What? Oh yes..." Tony hesitated for a moment. "Look, you're both probably going to think us totally mad, but if we *could* manage to crack it, then the Genie project would no longer be just pie in the sky."

"Crack what?"

"Well, just imagine if we did manage to get all that DNA sorted out, the only problem left is how bring it all back to life again."

Mark sank back into his chair and eyed Sue with obvious dismay. "Oh is that all?" he groaned, unable to disguise his sarcasm.

"Seems impossible, doesn't it?" murmured Elizabeth, obviously used to the reaction.

"Quite beyond us, I'm sure. You'd need some special kind of superhuman magic to make that one work."

"That's exactly what *we're* beginning to think."

"What do you mean?"

"Well, the computers have already suggested it can be done somehow, but we can't make any sense about how they come to that conclusion. There must be something else; something other than just pure chemistry that we haven't yet thought of."

"Magic?"

"Who knows? Maybe!"

"So the Genie project's not just a fairy tale?"

"Not at all, but I think it should be renamed the Gene Project, don't you?"

"By the sound of things, I still think "Genie" is more appropriate!"

Sue was looking puzzled. "But I still don't understand how the idea could be made to work," she sighed.

"DNA transference."

"That's impossible isn't it? And anyway, what do you mean, transference? Between what and what?"

"No, it's not impossible at all. Like all the best so-called clever man-made ideas, it already happens in nature. Have you ever heard of the Crown Gall bacterium?"

They shook their heads. "No, I can't say I have," said Mark.

"Well, to cut a long story short, this is a clever little organism which makes a present of a splice of DNA to an unsuspecting host. By doing so, it alters that host's cell activity to suit its own ends, getting it to grow abnormally and even produce food specifically for that bacterium to live on. A very devious little trick, don't you think?"

"Sounds amazing. But how can we put it to use?"

"We do the same thing, somewhere else, using our super soul genes."

"Where else?"

"We don't know but that's not our problem. Our job is just to try and make it work."

"Hold on, let me get this straight. You mean to tell me the idea is to transfer our special DNA to some totally unimaginable creature, somewhere out there, and in effect, become something else?"

"Yes, something like that. But it wouldn't be as grotesque as you might imagine. After all, our souls would still be the same, wouldn't they? And without any prior knowledge of what went before, there wouldn't be a problem."

Mark and Sue stared at each other in disbelief, left speechless by the horrific thought of existing in another creature's body.

"Believe us, it's the only way," said Tony, anxious to placate their looks of horror.

Mark finally found his tongue. "It's all about distances really, isn't it?" he said. "There's no way we can transport living tissue so far for so long, so all we can hope to do is rely on chemistry to save us."

"That's right, and don't forget that whatever host we use will be perfectly adapted to its own environment."

Mark sat back and nodded furiously. "Now I see why the feasibility factor was so high!" he cried.

He felt a tugging at his sleeve. Sue, obviously overwhelmed by the morbidity of the conversation was getting fidgety. "Come on, Darling," she whispered. "Let's dance. This is supposed to be a party, not a scientific convention."

Chapter 7

It was a crisp, clear, January morning, with a sky so deep blue; as blue as it ever is anywhere in the world. That was nothing unusual for this area, which was the main reason it was chosen in the first place. With a virtual guarantee of more than three hundred days of clear weather each year, it had to be one of the best places in the world for the site of the biggest and by far the most important launch pad ever to be built.

This really *was* going to be the biggest, and quite possibly the last, so it had to be just right. It had been designed to take all three of the projects. Despite their different objectives, they all had remarkably similar payloads, which made the planning just that little bit easier. The site was also very conveniently situated, close to a sea port and positioned just about midway between three important astro-aeronautical manufacturing regions. The climate was also ideal, with more than three hundred days of clear weather every year, and increasing all the time, thanks to the irrepressible progress of global warming. The only slight drawback was that they were having to do away with Newport, a country town slap bang in the middle of it all. The locals did not seem to mind too much, especially as most of them had left town long ago.

Newport had certainly seen better days. Most of the land round here was second only to desert. At least it was now. Once upon a time they used to boast you could grow almost anything here, but that was when they still had topsoil. What hadn't blown away in those terrible dust storms was washed away by the very occasional torrential rains and taken far out to sea. The only way you could even guess there ever had been any topsoil was if you ever got a chance to take a look from the sky. From up there you would see a great scar of silt and sand pushing its way through a beautiful turquoise green pond of shallow water and spilling out like a huge yellow tongue into the deep blue of the ocean. Trust Mother Nature to go and make something so beautiful out of something so bad.

So what locals *were* still here must have secretly jumped for joy when it was announced they would have to be relocated, even if they did mouth hollow complaints about being deprived of their heritage. Certainly they all got a pretty good deal, with apartments by the sea, *and* in the location of their choice.

And when they had all gone, there was the clearing away to be done. That was where Chris Jones, the chief demolitions supervisor, came in. He was a short, stubby man of sixty-three, with greying, thinning, short cropped hair, matched by a walrus moustache which gave him an unjustifiably fierce look. From the general disarray and dishevelment of his clothing, it would have been quite obvious to any passing observer, had there ever been one, that Chris Jones' interests in life, whatever they were, had nothing to do with himself.

Pausing for a moment to take in what for most people would have been a truly startling scene (but for him was quite routine), he produced a plastic bottle from the small bag at his waist, and took a large swig from it; not to swallow, but to rinse round and spit out in a quite futile attempt to rid his mouth of that all-pervading dust and grit which seemed to form a permanent coating on his teeth.

Yes, it was very familiar sight for him: a landscape of relentless destruction, which was being carried out faithfully and very efficiently by his robot minions. There were several different kinds, each a specialist in its own particular task; a veritable teamwork of crushers, bulldozers, sorters and carriers, together quite capable of seeing the job through to completion without any outside assistance. There certainly wasn't much that Chris Jones needed to do, but legislation demanded that an overseer be present at all times that robots of this status were working. It kept them in their place and ensured there would be no monkey business. All he had to do was throw a switch and they'd all come to a dead stop.

It was not the sort of position many people would want to volunteer for, mainly because it was very lonely, but Chris Jones liked it. For one thing there was the sense of great power in being able to control those machines. Sometimes he would just turn them off for the heck of it, just to remind them who was in charge, and sometimes, as now, he would turn them off for another purpose altogether. This was the other reason he applied for the post: to search for souvenirs, and maybe even treasure.

Stopping those machines was not something he was supposed to do, and no doubt he would have got into some kind of trouble if anyone had seen; but there *was* no-one else. That was the down side of the job: having nobody at all to talk to. But it was compensated for by a big upside; or at least it was for Chris Jones, because of his singular obsession for collecting things: relics, mementos, any kind of souvenir that would put him in touch with a bygone era. His main interest was in the twentieth century, so today he was particularly keen to get out there and root around. And what better place could there be for anyone who wanted the chance to hunt for souvenirs from the past than this old town left neglected and virtually abandoned by progress?

Amazing what you could find under these circumstances, so long as you knew what you were looking for. In those days, people often put perfectly good and serviceable things in their lofts, not because they didn't work but because they were getting old-fashioned. In fact almost everything he found functioned perfectly. Such a waste, he could hardly believe it. If it had carried on like this for another century he felt pretty sure he wouldn't be standing here right now. There would be nothing left.

Today had been very disappointing so far. Despite searching amongst all the woodwork, in lofts and spare rooms, and even cupboards people obviously didn't know they had (judging by the way they'd been wallpapered over), he hadn't managed to find one new thing. There was all the usual stuff: heaters, toasters, irons, microwaves, hi-fi equipment with those great big floor speakers they used to have; it was all here, all junk as far as he was concerned. He'd seen it all before, -had some really good examples already, all renovated, working, and as good as the day they were made. One day his son would have them: something to treasure and hand down to *his* child, if he was lucky enough to have one.

He shook his head with disappointment and took an extra hard chew of the now tasteless wad of Cocagum he kept tucked in his cheek. With nothing worth salvaging, he pressed reluctantly on his remote control and stood watching as the faithful team stirred back into life and lumbered away to continue on their task.

The system was amazingly efficient. Robots don't stop to talk, or have tea breaks. They just charge along, doing exactly what they should, in any weather, night and day. At this rate the whole town would be cleared away by Friday. Right now it was the turn of the Cinema and the Courthouse. The Town Hall went yesterday, leaving just a marble floor on which Chris Jones was now standing as he watched the mechanical grabbers tearing at the Courthouse walls.

The building had a certain late Twentieth Century feel about it. Six stories, so-called matchbox style, originally in concrete and glass. Although quite charming in its own way, it was also very dated in appearance, tending to stick out like a sore thumb against the softer, more natural look of the more modern buildings. Public opinion nowadays deferred increasingly to the wisdom of nature, softening those very practical, but also very harsh straight lines into a more harmonious and subtle fusion with the surrounding countryside.

As the layers started breaking away, Chris Jones could see that the building had been given several face-lifts in its time, the most recent of which must have been about seventy years ago when the solar skin was added. Nowadays, of course, the entire external surface of every building was constructed in this material, which could be moulded into any shape or style, and afforded the building maximum exposure to the sun's rays, thus creating precious electrical energy. What must it have cost, he wondered, to heat a building like this *and* supply all the hot water? He marvelled at the sheer profligacy of life in those days.

Even the floor he was standing on right now seemed to symbolise that same attitude. Marble slabs, probably Italian, and which must have cost a small fortune to import. Who footed the bill for that? Probably the poor local tax payer. Thank heavens those days were long gone. He walked slowly across the floor, trying to imagine what it felt like to come in and pay your local dues, or get permission from some faceless bureaucrat just to put a shed in your own back yard.

Just then he stubbed his foot, cursing out loud as a sharp pain shot up his leg, nearly causing him to topple. He turned round angrily, ready to give the offending article a punishing kick, but stopped himself as he caught sight of something bright there, shining up at him through the dust he had just disturbed. It was a metal something; a brass strip set into the marble floor. He knelt down and brushed more dust away with his hand, following the strip along. Intrigued, he carried on dusting, exposing more and more of the strip. After three feet or so, he came to a right-angled bend and followed it on for a couple more feet, where it returned again. He soon realised the strip was forming the outer border of a rectangular slab of marble; a different colour from the rest. With mounting excitement, he knelt right down and began brushing away feverishly, using both hands at once. Finally, he could see that the slab had been secured in position by means of four large brass screws.

There was a small brass plate set in the surface. He took out an already dirty handkerchief and polished the remaining dust away. There was an inscription, still clearly visible. It read: "Time Capsule, made up of contributions from the people of Newport on this, the first day of the Twenty First Century, January One, Two thousand and one."

Chris Jones read the inscription again, after which he read it a third time. In fact he kept on reading it for at least another five minutes, wondering if it was really real or if he wasn't just dreaming. How come it was still here? How come they hadn't opened it when they vacated the building? He looked closely at the screws. There was a solid layer of verdigris around each one. Nobody had touched this thing for a very long time.

"Jesus!" he screeched, loud enough for the whole world to hear. "Jones, you finally did it! This has got to be it, the big one after all these years!" He thrust both arms triumphantly skywards as if to give praise to the Almighty, and began dancing round in circles, Red Indian fashion. If anyone had been around to see him now, they would have undoubtedly assumed that Chris Jones had finally gone over the edge.

After a minute or two of this he stopped to get his breath back. The whole place was spinning. He sat down for a minute and started laughing loudly, partly because of this new-found euphoria and partly at himself for behaving so much like a child. "Hey! Take it easy, old man," he muttered to himself, "You're not as young as you used to be!"

He sat still on the ground for a while, waiting for his complaining heart to settle. His forehead was feeling cold with sweat, and his hands were getting clammy, but the only thing on his mind was getting that thing open. Lucky he always brought tools with him just for times like this, enough of them to make him rattle when he walked. The thumping in his chest subsiding, he began fumbling around in his pockets, trying to remember where he'd put the screwdriver. Finally, after first drawing out a pair of pliers and then a small hammer, his shaking fingers closed round that elusive article, which had been residing in his left inside pocket. By now the shaking had progressed to his whole body. No wonder! This had to be the most exciting thing to happen since that time he found a stack of porno tapes hidden under some floorboards more than five years ago.

His hand shook so much it took him a couple of goes to home the screwdriver in the slot, and then only after he'd steadied it with the other hand. It was not going to be easy. With his first effort the screwdriver jerked out of the slot, but not before gouging a sizeable piece off the head. He cursed out loud at his own stupidity. Better be careful, any more of that and he wouldn't be able to undo it at all. Don't forget this thing has been sitting here for more than a hundred years so it's not going to give up its secrets that easily.

The next time he was more cautious, making sure the instrument stayed firmly in its slot while he slowly increased the load. Nothing happening, he shook his head and reminded himself to have patience. Somehow, it needed more force. Taking a deep breath, he applied both of his big hands together on the screwdriver, and leaned forward over it to make the most of his considerable weight, at the same time jerking hard on the handle. This time it worked. With a sudden movement the verdigris seal gave way and the reluctant screw yielded with a jerk. The rest was easy. Once started, the screw turned as smooth as silk until it was all the way out, like the well-engineered piece it had promised to be.

The other three screws were much the same. After triumphantly removing the last of them he stood up for a minute, to get the ache out of his knees and set himself up for the excitement to come. Right now his only regret was not having somebody else around to share this moment with him. Somehow, without a witness to record it, an event, however momentous, does not really seem to happen. Just like the passage of time. His solitude was making him feel as if in some way he were betraying those that laid this capsule. He had the uncomfortable feeling they were watching his every move, angry at his selfishness. This was not how it was meant to be. Even now, he could visualise the ceremony when the capsule was closed, and the hopes those people might have had. If they could see him now, a kind of furtive magpie, they might not be so pleased.

Chapter 8

"Chris Jones, you're a stupid old fool," he said to himself as he took a good look around. "There's nobody here. No-one's gonna care. Just go ahead and open it!" He heard his own words but he tried to pretend they were coming from some other lips, maybe God's, telling him everything was all right. Wherever he believed they came from, they were just what he wanted to hear. Without wasting any more time he bent down again and slipped the screwdriver under the brass rim of the cover plate. It was heavy, but it moved just enough to tell him all he had to do was take it easy, and sooner or later...

Sure enough, after not a little effort, he managed to raise it sufficiently for the screwdriver to slide in further and act as a wedge. There was just enough space now to get both sets of fingers under the slab and, with one mighty pull, he tipped it right back, causing it to crash down under its own weight and crack in two. No matter, he didn't need it any more. With a cloud of dust still rising, he knelt down and pushed his head anxiously through it, impatient to see inside. As the dust cleared, he let out an excited gasp of delight, for there, looking as clean and shiny as the day it was made, was a stainless steel box with an inviting handle at each end.

He took hold of one handle and tested the box for weight. It was heavy, obviously designed for two people.

But there weren't two people here, so he positioned himself firmly over the opening with feet astride, and heaved with all his might. He didn't quite make it. With the bottom of the box just a few inches from the rim, the pain in his fingers was just too much and he had to let go, causing it to fall back with a resounding crash. Was that sound glass or metal? He cursed himself for being such a fool to do it all by himself. That could have been something really precious in there and it might be in a thousand pieces by now.

He stood there, looking at the wheals on his lily-white hands and wishing he did more physical exercise. At this rate there soon wouldn't be any need for arms and legs. The robots would be doing everything, including brushing your teeth and wiping your arse. That's what it was coming down to: the final outcome. If evolution had its way, humans would end up as one big brain with vestigial limbs barely strong enough to push a button. He smacked himself on the side of the head. "You idiot!" he shouted to himself. "That's all you've got to do, push a button!" So saying he took opened up the mini-panel on his wrist and did just that.

Not far away a small excavating robot sprang into life and began immediately to pick its way through the rubble and head directly towards him. Once within earshot it was able to respond to his voice commands and in no time he had it positioned above the casket with two grab hands at the ready. The casket came up as if it were made of balsa wood, and the powerful machine placed it gently at his feet without the slightest trace of a jolt.

The casket was not locked, merely secured by a small bolt. With trembling fingers Jones pulled on it, and to his great surprise, it slid back as if closed only yesterday. With unbridled haste he swung back the lid, making it crash against the side of the casket. That first stunning sight froze every muscle in his body, allowing the unbelievable truth to sink in. He drew his parched lips together and let out a long, low whistle, at the same time slowly shaking his head in recognition of this incredible piece of good luck.

The casket was crammed right to the top with items of all shapes and sizes, neatly packed like a suitcase. Jones took a deep breath, still not quite believing his luck. Everything was wrapped in sealed plastic bags, presumably once clear, but now clouded by time. Nevertheless it was still quite possible to make out some of the contents. There seemed to be one of everything: everyday items, most of which had long gone out of use. There was all types of kitchenware, including an old fashioned can opener, a potato peeler and a scouring pad, things that were never used nowadays. Cans could be opened with the flick of a thumb, potatoes had been genetically modified to grow perfectly round and smooth, and all cooking utensils were perfectly and permanently non-stick.

There were even items from the office, including an amazingly bulky personal computer that must have weighed at least half a pound, and only just fitted into the palm of his hand. He stood there bouncing it in his hand to try to guess the weight, and marvelling over how they could have managed in those days. There was also a so-called personal radio with earphones and cables trailing back to a large receiver about three inches across. "Try going swimming with that!" he murmured, feeling inside his ear canal for the outline of his speaker implants, barely detectable under the surface of the skin.

And there was a message. Written in capital lettering and etched on a sheet of stainless steel, it said:

"To the people of the future world. This is a gift from the citizens of Newport. A gathering of everyday items, to show life as we live it today, the first day of the twenty-first century. We send this to you in the hope that life for all peoples of the world has continued to improve, for your world is still our world, and we are as much a part of it as you. Please do not forget that, although our bodies are no more, our spirit lives on through you. Enjoy and savour the contents of this capsule and try to get a sense of the soul of our people, which has been passed on to you for safe keeping."

He *did* savour that moment. He had been feeling guilty, mainly due to his intention to keep the best souvenirs for himself, but the message in that casket had instantly cleared his mind. He closed his eyes, imagining he could feel their presence, right here and now. In a strangely comforting way, he knew they *were* here, their spirit was somehow already within him. He was their messenger, and he dare not let them down.

All the same, he might just as well have a look at everything. After all he was the first here. Once he had passed the casket on he might never get another chance to see it again. Tucked in at the sides were some newspapers. There were three nationals and a local, "The Newport Times." Sending the robots back to work with a touch of a button, he sat down to read the papers. It was so strange to read the print that way. Somehow it seemed so much more meaningful and positive to see it in solid form, instead of on a display. The headlines were about the new millennium celebrations. They were to have street parties and barbecues that day, plus a parade through the main street. Just a few yards from where he was sitting right now, he guessed.

The ads were rather quaint. There was one for a car. A great cumbersome "gas guzzler". Strange, he mused, how they all knew perfectly well those things were slowly but surely choking them to death, yet they still went out and bought them. So much better now that all vehicles had been removed from private ownership. And there was another ad for headache pills. It was a wonder any of them survived over fifty with all that pollution and all those drugs they had around. Must have been some kind of death wish, he concluded. He tried to remember when electrolytic endorphinogenesis came in. Yes that was the proper name, but now they just called it EEG for short. Just the right amount of stimulus in the right place and your pain was gone instantly. No drugs, no side effects, just a logical application of a basic principal, and let nature do the rest. So obvious and so very simple, and yet it had taken them so long to discover it. Like so many other things, discovery was largely a matter of luck.

On page fourteen his attention was drawn to a very strange looking advertisement. In fact he decided it was not an advertisement at all. There was no product. It looked more like an announcement than anything, probably one of those crackpot religious groups they used to have so many of. He read the words through a couple of times, trying to make some sense of them. The heading was: "*Know where you are going,*" in big bold letters. Underneath was a message written in plain text. Smaller print but still eye-catching, it said: "*When the time for reckoning finally arrives, our future will depend on knowing what to do and where to go. Be assured there is an answer to these questions, and the answer lies with Karl Marx. The direction is left and the colour is red. Seek and ye shall find. Remember: The key to our perpetuity lies with Karl Marx.*

Do not ignore this message. It may be our last chance."

Chris Jones read that notice a third time. Something about it was bothering him, but he couldn't think what. Somehow it seemed out of context with the rest of the newspaper. Everything else he had read was full of fun and gaiety, but here right in the middle was somebody putting a damper on things. "Oh well," He said to himself, shrugging his shoulders as he turned the page. "There's always one."

The rest of that afternoon slipped by almost unnoticed, so engrossed was he in those newspapers. Eventually he began to realise he was squinting. He looked up to see that it was getting dark and he was beginning to feel quite cold. A gust of wind made him shiver, at the same time pulling on the page he was reading. The thin paper started to rip, making him grab at it quickly, and reminding him it wasn't his property. It was time to put it away. As he started to fold it carefully, he glanced around to see what progress his obedient robots had made, astonished to find that the nearest one was at least a half mile away and the ground in between was totally clear. He looked at his watch. Jesus, it was nearly six. Allenby would be along in a minute to take over the next shift. He stood up quickly and unceremoniously bundled everything back in the casket. The sorting out would have to be done later.

Chapter 9

It was only another three weeks before they were living together. If you're a mature adult, and you'd had as many relationships as they had, it doesn't take too long to figure out whether you're compatible or not. In fact you don't have to figure it out at all, it just happens. Maybe it can happen in you're very first relationship; some people are lucky that way, but there's always the risk they'll eventually begin to wonder whether any other fruits have a better taste. Perhaps they're really the unlucky ones, always fantasising and living in a dream world of unreality. If they're faithful, they'll take that nagging uncertainty to the grave with them. If they're not, they will quickly discover that the penalties for indiscretion are extremely severe. Best to sow those wild oats before making that final decision.

Mark and Sue had no such problems. They had, of course, still to pass the compulsory compatibility test before being allowed to marry, which they did with flying colours. There being no detectable rogue gene mutants showing up, a ten year procreation licence was issued, during which time it was permissible in theory to have as many children as you could. In practice it was hardly ever more than one, due mainly to the well-managed Fertility Control Program, which tackled the population problem at source, using a gene modification technique. The only obvious drawback of the system was that any adjustment had to be planned a whole generation ahead.

There was also the mandatory counselling session, designed to ensure the couple had a clear understanding of the nature of the commitment, particularly with regard to the well-being of any offspring. Obvious incompatibilities in this area would have had to be resolved before a licence could be issued.

It was Mark's turn to prepare the dinner. They had planned on a quiet night in, just to enjoy each other's company. Sue was in the viewing room, catching up on the day's news. There were the usual reports on the progress of the Three Projects, as they had come to be known. It had been decided at the last plebiscite that the deflection rocket should be sent off first. It was, after all, almost as practical as the destruction plan, but if it worked it could avoid the need for so much unnecessary pollution of the solar system.

The Genie Project was still a source of amusement to most people, appearing to be more of an intellectual exercise rather than anything useful and practical. Nevertheless it had become the main topic of so many after dinner conversations, probably because it was more fun to fantasise than be involved in practical realities. In most people's minds the idea was doomed to failure from the start, simply because nobody had yet come up with any tangible evidence of life elsewhere, so the prospect of blindly heading off out there with only the faintest hope of stumbling across a vital planet, seemed absurd in the extreme.

The rest of the discussion was based around the other technical impossibilities of the Genie project, particularly the need to develop a new material which would not only need to be at least five time tougher than the strongest known alloy, but also had to be extremely light, and have a melting point high enough to withstand the rigours of entry into who-knows-what kind of atmosphere. It was beginning to appear as if this particular project was going to be forever consigned to the drawing board.

Just then, Mark appeared at the door of the viewing room. "Supper's ready," he announced. "It's Gazpacho, followed by Seafood Lasagne. Hope you're hungry!"

Sue stood up quickly. "Sounds good," she said. "If it tastes good too, I'll give you a permanent job!"

Mark couldn't resist a chuckle. That particular job would not be too taxing. Preparing the meal consisted of simply touching a few icons on the menu display and letting Francois (as they had affectionately nicknamed him) the robochef, get on with it.

As she moved to turn off the holoscreen, he held his hand up to stop her.

"No, wait, I just want to see what they were saying," he said. "It sounded interesting."

The scene was of a middle-aged man, with short-cropped hair and a greying walrus moustache, holding open the lid of a steel box. He was removing articles from it one by one, taking his time to describe each in turn. Apparently he had found the box, labelled as a Time Capsule, in a sealed underground compartment he had unearthed while supervising demolition works.

Chris Jones had packed everything back just as he found it, even to the extent of carefully re-wrapping the various items back in their own plastic sleeves. He wanted the whole world to share in the moment as if this was the original opening ceremony. Wanting to savour this moment of unaccustomed glory to the full, he worked his way slowly, and much more deliberately than he had done previously, trying with each one to sound as surprised and as knowledgeable as he could. Even though it was the second time for him, he was still fascinated, taking time over each piece and trying to explain how it could have been used in those days. Finally, after more than half an hour, during which time Mark had to go out and rescue the food, Chris Jones produced the newspapers from the bottom of the casket, and held them up so that the headlines could be seen.

Mark watched, spell-bound. It was one thing to go back in time through holovision, but this was real. He glanced up at Sue, his eyes wide with excitement. "Gee," he enthused. "I'd really like to have a read of those newspapers. I wonder if they'll be made available..."

He stopped, mid-sentence, to hear what else Chris Jones was saying. "In a short while there will be a transmission of each page in turn, to enable you to save the data if you so desire."

The supper was delicious but Mark hardly noticed. Right now he was doing a fairly poor job of hiding his impatience, staring with apparent nonchalance at his empty plate, which he had managed to clear in the same time it had taken Sue to enjoy two mouthfuls. She took her third, and began chewing very slowly, conscious that he was watching every movement of her jaws. The fourth forkful was slowly gathered up with precise attention to shape and quantity, and as she solemnly took the bite, she looked up to see him staring mournfully at her mouth, obviously wondering how long this one was going to take. At that moment she exploded, sending seafood lasagne in all directions. He got up quickly to pat her on the back, only to find there were tears of laughter pouring down her cheeks.

It took her a few minutes to recover. "I'm sorry," she giggled, wiping stray lasagne from her chin. "It was just so funny seeing you trying to be patient, I couldn't resist winding you up!" She gestured to him. "Well, go on then. Go and read those papers before you crack up!"

"You're completely mad!" he laughed. Taking the joke as it was intended, he went off to the viewing room, a sheepish smile on his face.

He planned to read the paper from end to end, setting out to absorb every word. But before long he was yawning, as his interest started to wane. The paper had obviously been produced as a special souvenir edition, and the heavy stuff like the murders and rapes, so prevalent in those days, had been laundered out for the benefit of the occasion. He started scanning through the pages, looking for more interesting headlines, and just like Chris Jones had done a few days earlier, he stopped on page fourteen to see that same announcement that had puzzled Chris Jones and, just like Chris Jones, he read it over and over again.

"Sue!" he called. "Come and have a look at this!"

The urgency in his voice made her hurry straight in, still with a mouthful of salad. "What is it, Darling?" she spluttered.

He was pointing to something on the display. "This!" He cried excitedly. She leaned closer and read the message out loud. "Karl Marx...Karl Marx... I know the name, but I just can't place it."

"He was the Author of The Communist Manifesto. Not a bad idea in theory, but it tended to ignore the fact that people are individuals who like to have at least some say in how things are run. The State becomes too much of a parent in the end."

"So what does that message mean? Is it just some political extremist having a final fling, a joke, or what?"

"That's what's puzzling me. There's no address or telephone number of any organisation. It's almost as if it's got some other meaning, like a message or something."

"The key to our perpetuity lies with Karl Marx." Sue said it over and over, three or four times. "If it's telling us to take up Communism again, then I think it's come a bit too late!"

Mark's face suddenly lit up. "Just say that again!" he cried. Something in that last statement had just touched a nerve.

Sue paused to read it through for herself once more, and then repeated what she had just said. "If it's telling us to take up Communism again, then I think it's come a bit too late. But I can't see..."

"That's it! That's it!" he screeched excitedly, cutting her off in mid sentence. "You said if it's telling us?

Well maybe it *is* trying to tell us something. I mean us *now*, not us *then*!"

"Don't be silly, how could it be? Whoever wrote that couldn't possibly have known we'd be sitting here reading it, more than a hundred years later, could he?"

"Oh yes he could! Don't you see? There must have been thousands of these time capsules put down then. After all it was a very special occasion, wasn't it? It's the obvious thing to do at the start of a new millennium."

Sue understood at last. "I get it!" she cried. "And what do they always put in those things? A copy of the local newspaper of course! But I still don't understand why somebody back there would want to tell us about Karl Marx."

Mark shook his head and stared at the floor as if trying to find an answer there somehow.

At length he said: "Let's read it through again. There's probably something we've missed."

They did read it through, silently and out loud, trying to emphasise different parts of the message to see if it might make more sense to them.

"There's something in that last line," said Sue. "Say it again."

"The key to our perpetuity lies with Karl Marx."

She snapped her fingers. "That's it! It's all in the word "lies"! Where would Karl Marx be lying right now?"

"I wouldn't have a clue," he said with a shrug. "But it wouldn't take a minute to find out."

He tapped at the holovision icon on his wrist-band. A menu flashed up with the caption: "You are on line to the encyclopaedia service. Please state the information you require."

"The whereabouts of Karl Marx," said Mark, slowly and clearly.

There was just a two second pause before a synthesised voice answered. "Karl Marx. Russian, but lived in exile in London, England. Father of Communism. Died 14th of March 1883. Buried in Highgate Cemetery, London. Is there any further information you require?"

"No, thank you," replied Mark. He turned back to face Sue. "Well, my love, there's your answer. So what do you make of that?"

She took a deep breath, puffing her cheeks out and letting the air escape slowly though her lips, whilst she considered. "It *could* be something. On the other hand, it could be nothing. I don't know. But one thing's for sure..."

"What's that?"

"If we don't do *something* about it, we'll be forever wondering."

"But what *can* we do?" he said, despairingly.

She didn't answer. Instead she gave him an impish grin.

He shook his head and frowned deprecatingly. "Oh, no. Surely you're not thinking of..."

"Why not? How else are we going to find out?"

"But there are too many problems. Surely we should just make it public and get an opinion?"

"And you know what the answer would be to that. There's not enough evidence. No, the only way we're likely to get an answer is to do it ourselves."

"But we'd never get away with it. You know we need a special permit to travel to London, especially when we can see all the sights right here in our viewing room."

"Ah, well it just so happens I've got an aunt living in London, and that means I'm entitled to a permit every once in a while. Not only that, I'm allowed to take a companion with me!"

"But are you seriously suggesting we go all the way to London to desecrate a grave? People just don't *do* things like that any more."

"No, I'm not saying that...Well, not at the moment, anyway! All I'm saying is we go and have a look...and, well, take it from there. If we do take it any further, it'll be easy -for precisely the reason you just mentioned- because people just don't do that kind of thing any more."

He was silent for a while, pretending to study a picture on the wall. She sat watching him, patiently waiting for the great man to respond. Finally he looked at her, stone-faced.

"You know what I think?" he said. She opened her mouth to speak, but he carried straight on. "I think you're crazy. Only a complete idiot would go along with an idea like that." He paused, and the faintest trace of a smile began at the corner of his mouth. "On the other hand, I've always wanted to see London!"

Chapter 10

They arrived in London on a grey day in February. It was cool, but not nearly as bad as they had expected. There was a strong wind blowing, apparently a regular feature now, due to the gradual polarising of weather patterns over the years. The population density of these islands had been moderated several times since the asteroid disaster, to tie in with local food and energy production. It was hard to believe that at one time there were seventy million people living here, almost three times as much as now. Surely even in the good times that was too many.

Aunt Julie lived in one of the older parts of Hampstead, a six minute electrocar ride from the airport. The house was over three hundred years old, retained by a heritage order for its historical value. It was an enormous rambling affair, constructed of London brick with a slate roof, but had been suitably modernised to meet current energy control regulations. So well had the conversion been done, that it was almost impossible to detect the difference. That external "brickwork" was actually solar skin, and those great windows were not made of glass at all, but the much more energy efficient "Permaplastic".

Aunt Julie was real enough, and had as much character as the house. She was getting on in years -about eighty,

Mark guessed- but there was still a gleam in her eye and plenty of sparkle in her conversation. That first afternoon was spent in animated chat, during which time she left them in no doubt that some things at least, were better in the old days. "We're all getting too much alike. There's no room for individualism any more. People all seem to have the same thoughts and ideas nowadays." These were the main topics of her conversation. It did no good at all to try and convince her that this was the inevitable consequence of progress, and that there was far more sharing of ideas now than there had ever been. Nevertheless, there was enough richness in Aunt Julie's character to make Mark wonder if she might not be right.

That next morning they set off for Highgate Cemetery. With plenty of time on hand they decided to walk, always a worthwhile occupation in any of the big old cities, many of which were built before any form of mechanised travel and were therefore eminently suitable for exploring on foot. As the two lovers strolled along, hand in hand, they tried to imagine how it all would have sounded in those far off days, with children playing in the streets, and just the occasional sound of horses' hooves and metal cartwheels on cobbled roads. It was pleasantly reassuring to think of the generations that had passed this way, each leaving their own invisible, yet quite indelible, footprints on the pavements.

The cemetery was well cared for, obviously still considered important enough to warrant a maintenance order. They stopped at almost every stone to read the inscriptions. It was fascinating to see the lifespans of the residents, some tragically short, and some hardly begun, judging by the size of the headstones, which at times were no more than the length of a new-born child.

Eventually, they came to it. Constructed from marble slabs and standing some twelve feet high, it was capped by a stone bust of the man himself. They stood there for some while, staring at the inscription, and wishing they had X-ray eyes. Mark walked round to the side, studying the monument in detail and looking for any deficiency in the surfaces, but there was nothing obvious. The whole structure was complete, and the marble-work had been re-pointed not so long ago.

"I don't think we're going to get anywhere with this, do you?" sighed Mark. He saw from Sue's glum expression that she was thinking the same.

"This was either one sick joke," she murmured, "or we're missing something. Let's just check through the wording again."

With that, she produced a fold-up miniscreen from her back pocket and brought up the message again.

She frowned. That strange remark about Karl Marx was puzzling her.

She read it out loud. "*The direction is left and the colour is red*. What is that supposed to mean?" she said.

"I presume it's to do with socialism. In some parts of the world they were nicknamed 'Lefties' and red was the colour they adopted after the French Revolution."

"Yes, I knew that, but there's got to be more to it. I think it might be telling us where to look."

Mark was staring at Marx's stony face, willing him to come alive and let them in on the secret.

"Left is easy," he said at last, "but what is there that's red? They just don't do red in graveyards."

Sue agreed with a nod of her head. "No," she replied, "but if you look behind you there are a couple of coloured burial sites right here."

"They're not exactly red are they? More like a subdued shade of pink, but I guess you could say there's some red in the mix."

The nearest of the two memorials was directly in front of Marx's tomb. It consisted of a conventional headstone set behind a raised marble sided container, which seemed to be full of soil and was, no doubt, intended for the planting of flowers but it was now overflowing only with weeds.

The other monument was about twenty feet away. As Sue quickly pointed out, this structure more closely matched the requirements of that puzzling message because it was well over to Marx's left. It was a much grander affair than the other grave and was constructed of a very high quality rose pink marble, which gave one the impression that it was meant to last forever, just like Marx's tomb. The centrally place obelisk was truly impressive, being about fifteen feet high and set on a marble pedestal, itself about four feet square and supported by a rough slab of concrete of the same size. The foundation for the structure was another huge rectangular slab of concrete, guarded on all sides by ten smaller identical obelisks, each about two feet high and spaced three feet apart around the periphery of the concrete base. They were joined together by heavy loops of iron chain, sending out a clear message to keep off.

The couple slowly circumnavigated the whole structure, trying to find any sort of deficiency that might make a good hidey-hole, but there seemed to be absolutely nothing out of place, thanks to the inescapable fact that this was the work of a master craftsman.

With a sigh of disappointment, Mark rested his foot, perhaps a shade disrespectfully, on the front of the concrete slab and leaned forward to get a better view of the inscription. As he began to read it he was distracted by the sight of an unexpected imperfection in the form of the concrete slab on which the obelisk's pedestal was set. It was the same size as the pedestal (about three feet square) but its much more basic and uneven construction had left an untidy gap, no wider than the thickness of a pencil, which was clearly visible and ran the whole length of the side. It had previously been quite poorly repaired with cement some long time ago and the now crumbling mortar had defects in several places along its length.

"That's the only fault anywhere on this whole structure," sighed Mark. "It's not much to go on but as there's nothing else, I'm going to have to check it out. We'll just have to get some tools from somewhere and come back tomorrow."

Sue looked unconvinced. "I think you're clutching at straws," she said with a wry smile.

He returned that same smile, knowing full well she was probably right.

Chapter 11

It was around four-thirty as the couple retraced their steps, trodden earlier that day along the same gravel pathway. The damp autumn air hung heavily about them, laced with the not unpleasant seasonal smell of fungus and decaying leaves. The crunching of their footsteps was the only sound to be heard in this still and silent place, preserved now just as it had been for more than a hundred years. Glancing carefully around to make doubly sure they were alone, they stopped again in front of that same rose coloured monument.

This time Mark had a small plastic case with him. Setting it down on a nearby flagstone, he proceeded to open it, and produced the compact, but exceedingly efficient Ultrachisel he had acquired from the local hobbies centre.

Sue was beginning to have misgivings about the idea of desecrating a sacred monument.

"I'm scared that someone might see us," she whispered. "Before you start hacking away, I'll walk up to the next corner and keep watch. I really don't want to try and explain what we're doing if someone else should turn up."

He nodded his head vigorously. "You're right!" he exclaimed. "I'm so wrapped up with this thing I hadn't given that possibility any thought. Just give me a call if you see anyone."

He stood there watching her as she made her way up the path in the direction of the main entrance, and then, anxious not to waste any time, knelt down at the base of the obelisk with the ultrachisel in his hand and offered the razor thin ultrasonic tip of the machine up to the crumbing grout line before turning it on.

With just a couple of passes, the irresistible ultrasonic vibrations had reduced the mortar to a fine dust. Mark then took out a small jet duster to blow away the debris and then, taking a torch from the case, leant down low to peer into the small gap he had created. Something glinted. The sight of it made him catch his breath.

"It's metal!" he croaked, and began searching in the case for anything narrow enough to work into the gap. After scrabbling around for a few moments he came out with a long thin screwdriver. It was the perfect instrument for the job. Mark pushed it into one end of the gap and used it with a sweeping motion to try and shift whatever it was in there. He felt something move. Encouraged, he tried again and after two more side-swipes with the screw driver, the leading edge of a flat strip of metal began to appear. He caught hold of it with his fingers, working it from side to side until it came free. The next minute he was on his feet with the object in his hand and as he held it up like a trophy he couldn't resist letting out a loud cry of triumph, which would have been heard in every corner of the cemetery.

At her lookout post at the top of the lane, Sue had been daydreaming. She had been trying to imagine what it must have been like to be a common criminal. Quite a lot of fun, she decided. Her heart was beating faster than it had ever done, except, perhaps during love making, but this was a different kind of thrill. Maybe that's what was missing in their lives: the raw thrill of uncertainty and a peculiar inability to recognise the animal within. Perhaps life was getting altogether too safe and clinical, as if they were trying to divorce themselves entirely from that ghastly primitive.

The sound of Mark's sudden cry snapped her abruptly out of her daydream, urging her to turn round and run back down the lane.

As she got closer she could see that he was holding what looked like an oversized ruler, about eighteen inches long and four inches wide and coated with a thick layer of grime. She came up to his side and watched from over his shoulder as he began to scrape away at it the surface of the strip, using the screwdriver he was still holding. The metal was the unmistakable colour of brass, and as he continued to remove more of the coating, the letters "S" and "u" started to appear. "It's some sort of inscription" he murmured. Eager to find out what it said, he carried on scraping feverishly until it was possible to read the whole thing.

The message said: "Surgery hours: Monday to Friday 9am to 6pm. Saturday 9am to 1pm."

Sue took the strip from him and read the inscription out loud. "What on Earth is this supposed to mean?" she cried.

"Looks like it was a sign -probably from a doctor's or dentist's surgery like they use to have way back then.

That was long before Technomed came along. In those days people would have to actually see a real person for diagnosis and treatment, and a lot of it was just guesswork. Don't forget they didn't have nanorobots to go in through the veins and sort things out like we do now."

"Gee, and just look at those hours! Did people really have to work like that? Must have been really awful. If we did that now we'd have to spend the rest of the time sleeping!"

It was time to get out of here. Every minute spent in the cemetery would, like every other movement they made, have been noted and recorded, thanks to the constant monitoring of their geneticode Implants. Any excessive lingering in any one place would trigger a flag and demand an explanation. Failure to give a satisfactory answer would result not only in the reduction of subsistence points but precious travel allowance as well.

Without further ado, Mark produced a tube of quick drying mortar grout which he used to repair the gap. After cleaning away the excess he stood back to inspect his handiwork and allowed himself a congratulatory nod, satisfied that nobody would ever guess that anything had ever been touched.

They spent the rest of the evening at Aunt Julie's, listening to stories about how things were in the old days and were things really any better now that almost every human activity was accounted for in some way or other. The way she talked about things gave them the impression that she actually liked the element of uncertainty that seemed to prevail in the olden days, things as basic as whether that wine you've just bought was drinkable, or whether the souffle you'd just made was going to rise as it should. Such events were quite unthinkable now that the human element had been taken out of the equation.

Fascinating as Aunt Julie's comments were, Mark found his concentration wavering, his thoughts constantly returning to the events of the afternoon. What was the idea of leaving that brass strip in the tomb? Was there some sort of message in something as mundane as a statement of business hours, or was he missing something? Perhaps he should just forget about it for now and sleep on it.

But that next morning, after further lengthy discussions with Sue, their joint conclusion was that it had all been one huge joke by somebody unknown and they were the unfortunate victims. The only consolation to be had was that the perpetrator of the joke was not around to enjoy the fruits of his (or maybe her) misdeeds. The two positives to emerge from the situation were that it had given Sue what might well turn out to be the one last chance to see her very elderly aunt and give her the one thing denied to so many nowadays: a great big hug. The other good thing (if they could call it that) was, that once cleaned up and polished, that brass strip would make an attractive living room ornament and a future subject of conversation.

They decided to show their trophy to Aunt Julie. Her first reaction when offered it to inspect, was to recoil with a look of disgust on her face. "I can't touch that thing," she said. "It's filthy! Why don't you go out to the kitchen and ask Cedric to run it through the ultraclean. That'll bring it up like a new pin." Cedric was the name Aunt Julie had given to her robobutler. She called out for him and when he appeared at the door Mark passed the strip over to him with instructions as to what to do.

A few minutes later Cedric returned, holding out a tray on which the strip had been placed. As soon as they saw it, Sue and Mark cried out "Wow!". That ultraclean machine had done such a good job that the strip looked pristine, pretty much as it would have done on the day it was made. "It'll make a great ornament," commented Sue, "I can just see it now, pinned up on the wall on that space next to the 3D Velasquez holo. It'll really stand out."

Mark couldn't resist picking it up and running his fingers over it. Nowadays as with almost everything else, most ornaments were facsimiles, no more than representations of the real thing, so something real like this was precious. After taking a few minutes to examine the script more closely, he looked up at Sue and shook his head.

"Nothing new," he murmured,

"Have you looked on the back?" she asked.

He turned the strip over and caught his breath. "Oh wow!" he cried. "There's some kind of writing. Looks like it's been done by hand, with some sort of drill."

"What does it say?"

He held it up to the light to get a better look. "It doesn't say anything. Its just a lot of numbers."

She took the strip from him to see for herself and read it out loud:

"50.554173, -4.608950." A puzzled frown on her face, she repeated the numbers. "What on Earth is that supposed to mean?" she said.

Mark rested one arm on her back to look at the strip from over her shoulder.

"Maybe it's a manufacturer's code or something?"

"I doubt it. Too many numbers."

Up until now, Aunt Julie who, watching the two all the while from the comfort of her adaptachair, had preferred to remain silent, decided that now was the time to intervene.

"Why don't you ask Cedric to do a search for you?" she said. "If those numbers mean anything, he'll find out in just a few seconds."

Her suggestion made Mark smile. "Why didn't I think of that?"

Aunt Julie returned the smile. "You're not as old and wise as me," she said. "don't forget I've been round the block a few more times than you!"

Cedric was duly summoned and put the strip up to the scanner built in to his chest. "These are coordinates," he announced, in a voice so perfectly human it was hard to believe he was actually a machine. "They give an accurate global position to within a metre or two. This system is no longer in use, having been replaced by the latest geosat system. I can tell you, however, that this location is in a place called Bodmin Moor in the West Country of England."

Mark's joyful expression said it all. "Now it makes sense!" he cried, and gave Sue a hug. He turned to face Aunt Julie. "How far is that from here, and how can we get there?" he croaked, unable to control his elation.

"Well, I suppose it's about 200 miles away. The best way to go is by helitaxi, but don't forget it'll cost you quite a few subsistence points. You won't be able to eat anything fancy for at least a month."

"I think we'll manage." grinned Sue. "It would do us good to go without once in a while. After all most people are vegans already. Perhaps we'll end up joining them."

Aunt Julie had a frown on her face. "I have a question for you." she began.

"What's that?" said Sue.

"Have you any idea about what it is you're looking for?"

They exchanged sheepish glances. "To be honest, no," Mark replied. "But we just have a funny feeling it must be something important. Maybe we're wrong, but having got this far we both know that if we don't follow it through now, we'd both go crazy."

"Is it something above ground or could it be buried?"

They looked at each other once again and shrugged in unison. "To be honest," said Mark, "I hadn't thought about that either. Perhaps we should take a few tools with us, just in case."

So later that day they were standing on the roof pad and waiting for the helitaxi to arrive. Mark was carrying a compact tool set in a small case, and Aunt Julie had come up to tearfully wave them goodbye, knowing that, because they'd used up their visitation points, it would be a long time (if ever) before she would get to see them in the flesh again.

Cedric had already programmed the positional details into the geosat. With this latest system there could be no doubt that they would be taken to exactly the right spot. The journey took a surprisingly long time, about twenty minutes or so, and the landing was easy, thanks to the fact that there were no buildings of any sort for almost as far as the eye could see. The vehicle, expertly manoeuvred by its robopilot, landed as smoothly as ever on an open patch of grassland and exactly on the predetermined square metre.

They disembarked and surveyed the landscape for a while, but there was nothing obvious to pick out from the usual moorland terrain of grasses, heather, gorse and bracken. "I think if there's anything to be found here it's got to have been buried." said Mark with a sigh.

Sue nodded in agreement. "And the best place to start is right under the helitaxi. If those coordinates were accurate then what we're looking for has got to be there."

"Agreed!" said Mark and began collecting a few stones to mark out the spot, before ordering the robopilot to move his machine away. Once that had been suitably parked, Mark wasted no time in attacking the spot with the fold-up electroshovel.

After digging down about a foot or so and finding nothing but soil, he stood up and shook his head. "I think we've drawn a blank." he sighed. "I can't imagine that anyone would want to bury something any deeper than that."

"You're forgetting something. If whatever it is has been there for any period of time there could well have been a build up of soil. It might be a lot lower down than you think. Keep digging!"

Mark acknowledged her wisdom with a smile and carried on digging. In any case it was no big deal because this electroshovel required almost no effort. He could go as deep as he liked without getting tired and it was made even easier because the soil was actually quite soft and peaty, thanks to the many generations of decaying plant life incorporated into its structure.

At around three feet deep the blade suddenly hit something hard, causing Mark to nearly lose his grip as the machine kicked back violently.

He leaned right down into the hole. "It's getting difficult to see, but I think I've hit a rock. It's getting in the way and I'll have to free it and lift it out by hand. Pass me that trowel and I'll scrape away the soil so I can get at it."

Sue put the trowel into his outstretched hand, shaking her head as she did so.

"If you've got down to rock level I really don't think there's much point going any further. You're not going to find anything any lower down are you?"

Mark looked up at her and sighed glumly. He knew she was right of course, but they'd come so far...

Using the trowel, he continued to scrape more soil away to expose more of the rock. "That's funny," he said suddenly.

"What's funny?"

"This rock. I'm not getting the usual clanging noise when the trowel hits it, but it must be rock because it's so hard."

"What does it look like?"

"I can't really see it. Too dark down there and still a lot of soil in the way."

He carried on excavating for a few more minutes, eventually resorting to bare hands to clear away the final clods of soil clinging to the edges. He could feel the outline of the obstruction quite distinctly now. "It's flat. Doesn't feel like stone. More like plastic. I can get my fingers underneath and I'm getting it to move. One more tug and it should come loose."

The next minute he was back on his feet, the object in his hand. They both stood there staring. It was not a rock at all. No, this was definitely man-made, a kind of envelope, made of a thick plastic, probably once translucent but now clouded by time so that the contents were no longer visible. The plastic had been punctured in a couple of places, no doubt caused by that first contact with the electroshovel. His hands trembling with excitement, Mark went over to the tool case and retrieved a sharp-bladed knife with which he proceeded to cut open the envelope. As he lifted the flap and felt inside, his fingers closed on something hard and flat, with a slippery feel to it. With Sue peering over his shoulder, he pulled the object free to inspect it.

For a just a moment there was silence, both of them too stunned to react in any way. The object was coloured a deep shade of orange, the brightest orange either of them had ever seen.

They looked up at each other, wide eyed with astonishment and cried out "Wow!" in unison. It was the only appropriate word.

She took the object from him and started to examine it. "Strange," she said, "It's just a flat piece of plastic but somehow it's so beautiful. It's so delightfully smooth and there's not the slightest mark or blemish on it."

Mark shook his head. "How can that be? I smashed into it a couple of times with the electroshovel." So saying, he took it from her and then proceeded to run his fingers all over it on both sides, looking for the slightest sign of damage.

But there was none.

"You're right!" he exclaimed, a look of utter astonishment on his face. "There's not a single flaw anywhere. How come? And another thing: it's got a funny slippery sort of feel. It's definitely not plastic."

Sue noticed the envelope lying on the ground where he had dropped it. She picked it up and realised there was something else inside.

"There's a note here. It's in English." She cried, and started to read it out loud.

It said:

Hello! Congratulations on discovering me. My name is George and I am more than two million years old.

I am almost indestructible. Try and scratch me, and you will see for yourselves.

I was discovered in the year 1999, by James and Sarah, of London.

I have many secrets and they are just for you and your kind. Place me in the sun and you will see.

There are things I know about you that you don't know yourselves. Perhaps I even hold the key for the salvation of you and your kind?

But understand this:

You will never discover all of my secrets until your technology matches mine.

Use me now, but only if you think you are ready, or hide me once again.

I can wait. Time is on my side.

Mark took the note from her and read it through again.

"This is all so weird!" he cried. "Who would call something like this, 'George'? And how could it possibly be two million years old? It looks brand new!"

Sarah was holding the object and was already starting to play around with it, fascinated by its soapy feel and perfectly smooth finish. "George sounds like quite a good name to me," she said. "Gives it a personality. Whoever named it must have had a good reason for choosing a name like that."

Mark shrugged. "Maybe it's just a big joke?"

Sue shook her head and held the strange artefact up close to his face. "It can't be a joke, Mark," she cried, "Just look how perfect this thing is!"

He took it from her and studied it closely again, turning it over several times and holding it up to the light in search of any imperfections. "That's quite amazing," he admitted, "there really isn't a single mark on it. Perhaps we'd better reserve judgement."

"At least until the sun comes out!" She suggested, looking despondently up at the cloudy sky. "And by the way, don't forget its name is George!"

It was time to go. The helitaxi was booked for two hours; any longer and there'd be more subsistence points deducted. No point living on survival rations for a whole month just for the sake of a few minutes.

Mark set about refilling the hole and replacing the greenery and after quickly checking all was as it was, they boarded the helitaxi for the twenty minute trip back to London.

Chapter 12

Wallace Feldstein stared hard and thoughtfully at the control switch, his trembling finger poised and ready to press. He took a deep breath, trying without success to subdue the violent pounding of his heart, and wearily shook his head. Why was he still so up tight? After all, this was hardly the first time was it? No, more like the thirty-first time. He paused for a moment to work it out, and smiled grimly as he realised that figure was about right.

And here it was yet again: that same moment of truth he had relived all those many times before. All that hard work, all that worry and all those sleepless nights; they could all suddenly be brought to nought by that one slight movement of his finger. But on the other hand....

This is the stuff from which dreams are made, and nightmares. In one split second a lifetime's work could go up in smoke and mean nothing at all. Nobody ever remembers the losers, only the winners. To get so far and yet fail was like gambling with your life and losing: the sudden death of Russian Roulette.

But with the stakes as high as this, there is no other course than to go for it; to go for broke, double or quits, because every scientist's dream is to reach the absolute threshold of his own ability and knowledge, and for all that hard work and sacrifice to culminate in just one sweet moment of pure ecstasy, -a moment to treasure and relive through each day until death: the very pinnacle of achievement that seems to mean so extraordinarily much.

He had known from the very beginning of this project that he was taking a big gamble. He could have just ridden out the rest of his life in the middle lane. Looking back, he'd certainly done his fair share. Take all those little improvements and discoveries he had made in the world of metallurgy, for example. Weren't corrosion and metal fatigue now just things of the past? Strange how easy it had become to solve them once the stifling demands of the market place were lifted. It was almost as if they'd always known the best ways to do so many other things before, but had been keeping them a closely guarded secret, purely to satisfy the avaricious needs of private enterprise. A perfect example was the ubiquitous and publicly owned electrocar, now the only permissible method of transport for the individual, and invented so long ago. How incredible to think it had only been in general use for not much more than fifty years.

A material five times stronger than steel, yet able to float on water: that's what they desperately needed right now. It was a very tall order indeed, and yet various independent computer studies had shown it was possible, but how? To Wallace Feldstein it was a challenge, perhaps the ultimate challenge, like Mount Everest to a climber. But he was a scientist, and as such his lot was to keep on probing and searching and opening little boxes to see what they contained, in the hope that one day he, or someone like him, would open that ultimate box and find what they'd all really been looking for if they did but know it: that elusive secret of eternal happiness.

Until that wonderful day comes, all a person can do is to set himself a goal and set about trying to achieve it. Whether that goal is raising a child to one's best ability, climbing the highest mountain, or discovering the ultimate material, it doesn't really matter, but if it *does* all work out, then *maybe* that person will discover what "happy" means. But whether dealing with children, mountains, or materials, it's worth remembering that the price for failure can be very high indeed.

But there was something else about this project which meant so much for Wallace Feldstein. The whole thing was absolutely fundamental to the success of Project Genie. Without the right material there was just no way to reach out into those vast distances of space and to be able to survive for a vast amount of time, a fact that (to Wallace Feldstein at least) seemed more than just coincidence. It was as if these two ultimate problems had been locked into each other by design. He knew that right now the whole of humanity was relying on him as it had never relied on one person before. He clenched his teeth and rubbed his brow nervously. This time it just *had* to work. This time he just *had* to succeed.

He closed his eyes and kept them shut tight, offering a silent prayer as his finger came down on the button. All at once his head seemed to fill with a multitude of conflicting sensations: the sensations of a suicide as he squeezes the trigger, an unbearable acid tension sweetened by the prospect of certain relief from all anguish and uncertainty.

There was a sharp electrical crackle as twenty thousand volts surged across the terminals. With his finger still on that button and his eyes firmly closed, Wallace Feldstein took a deep breath and held it while waiting for the sound to die away. He opened his eyes again. Now it was time for the worrying to stop. Whatever was done was done.

"Remove the safety pins please Raymond." he commanded, a croak in his voice, and as his obedient robot did so, the spring loaded lid opened smoothly, releasing a cloud of acrid grey smoke which cut into the back of Feldstein's throat and made him gasp for breath.

He waited for a while for the smoke to clear, hardly daring to look. After all, there had been more than thirty failures so far, so why should this time be any different? No reason at all really, but hope springs eternal, so who knows? Taking a deep breath, he got up from his chair and started across to the crucible, his eyes now fixed firmly upon it. And then he saw it: an amorphous blob of grey still with wisps of smoke escaping from its shiny surface. Feldstein's heart was beating so fast it seemed to be banging against his ribs. Was this the one at long last?

But it was early days yet, and nobody would know that better than Wallace Feldstein. He'd been disappointed too many times before. He cooled the amorphous blob of grey with a jet of water and eagerly picked it out of the crucible. Yes it was light, lighter than even he had expected, more like the weight of pumice than metal. He carried it carefully over to a sink, which he had already filled up with water, and carefully dropped it in. Sure enough it floated, just like pumice. With that, the tension written all over Wallace Feldstein's face simply melted away, replaced by a huge smile of contentment. His new toy had passed its first test.

If it turned out right, this substance would be unique, a one-off. He had discovered the way to triple the intermolecular bond strength, and at the same time blowing the particles far apart to form an immensely strong and stable material. Grabbing a small pair of pliers from the work-top he stabbed the pointed beaks at the grey mass. They slid off the shiny surface without making a mark. Hands still trembling, Feldstein took hold of the mass and held it up high above his head, like a trophy. There were tears in his eyes: tears of happiness.

Still hardly daring to believe, he felt weak all over from this sudden release of emotion and had to sit down for a minute. He took his glasses off and leaned forward in the chair, resting his chin in the cupped palms of his hands as he tried to take it all in. For centuries people had been searching for the perfect material and here it was at long last, right there in front of him. He began to chuckle, softly at first, and then gradually louder until it had become a crescendo of almost hysterical laughter, filling every corner of the laboratory with sound. If only those other doubters could see him now.

Chapter 13

Mark and Sue stayed in London just one more day. At any other time they would have grabbed at this golden opportunity to see the sights first hand, so as to compare real life against holovision, but the grey London skies were making them impatient. This kind of dull, overcast weather could last a week or more, -just about the last thing they wanted right now.

They realised that someone had already personified George, because he had been given a name, so it seemed only appropriate to always refer to him in the same way. That vivid colour fascinated them both, seeming to have all shades of orange wrapped into one, and so incredibly bright that Mark was quite sure it would be luminous, but on examining it in the dark later that evening he was both surprised and disappointed to discover that it was not. He also used the opportunity to test its strength. Although very light and with a smooth soapy non-stick feel, it refused to yield to any form of abuse that Mark threw at it, including trying to scratch it with a diamond set into Sue's favourite dress ring.

The journey home was twenty minutes quicker than the trip out, but even four hours seemed a long time for a five thousand mile journey. Although air travel was quite fast nowadays, the changeover at the airport was still the main cause for delay. Luckily it was becoming more and more unnecessary to travel anywhere outside one's own neighbourhood, apart from which it seemed like such a tedious and wasteful pastime. No wonder they nearly went broke, back in the early part of the twenty first century.

By the time they arrived home it was getting dark. They were tired and felt dirty. All they wanted to do was shower and go to bed, maybe with a warm drink while catching up with the latest news. To keep George safe from prying robotic eyes Mark had tucked him well out of sight at the bottom of his hold-all.

The warm flow of the shower was very welcome and relaxing. How great it felt to be clean and rid of all those unpleasant body odours. How did they manage to cope in those olden days when they only bathed once a week? They must have really stunk to high heaven, just like animals, he thought, but at the same time he had to laugh at how absurd some aspects of modern life had become, such as the need to wash so often. Maybe humans were really trying to deny their primordial origins by flushing them down the drain.

He climbed onto the bed and turned on the news channel. Sue came in a few seconds later with a hot chocolate drink and they lay there together studying the list of items. It was possible to choose them in any order you wished, or just let the programs run automatically. Michael had selected the weather report for tomorrow. The forecast was for early rain, clearing in the afternoon.

"That's just typical," he groaned. "Just when we need sun, we get the first rain we've had for weeks!"

"Its only for a few hours, darling. The sun will be out in the afternoon. Surely you can wait that long!"

He sighed. "I suppose I'll have to. What else..."

He stopped, mid sentence, his attention caught by the next news item. They were interviewing a white haired man with glasses about a new discovery he had made. "I have known for some time that it was theoretically possible," he was saying, his voice croaking with emotion, "but putting theory into practise is quite a different story. This was only one of many attempts, and it was only the knowledge that this research was so fundamental to the viability of the Genie Project that kept me going. Otherwise I'm sure I would have given up long ago."

The interviewer commented that the sample was very small and asked if there were likely to be a problem reproducing it on a larger scale. The old man smiled. "Surely you should know by now that man is capable of almost anything. I have done the hard part. The rest is easy by comparison. One thing is for sure though: that without our current state of technology it would have been absolutely impossible to fabricate this product. This is quite definitely a material of the future!"

"Hey, that sounds interesting," said Mark. "I wonder what's so special about that stuff? Can we just hear that interview again from the beginning?" Before Sue could reply he picked up the control and touched the rewind icon.

He had not missed very much. The reporter started by announcing that a new material had been invented and it appeared to fit the requirements of the Genie project. It had been provisionally been called Triple-bonded, Ultra-expanded Ferralloy, or TUF for short. Not only did it appear to live up to its new name, but it was also so light that it could float on water.

Those words made Mark sit up suddenly. He grabbed the control and stabbed at the freeze icon. "Did you hear that?" He almost shouted it, leaping out of bed as he did so. "C'mon, let's put some water in the basin!"

"Careful! Oh now look, you've made me spill my hot chocolate. Just warn me next time you do something silly like that!" She snapped, frantically wiping her sleeve.

"Sorry, love, but this could be important. Come on, bring George!" He was already in the bathroom.

"What for?"

"You'll see! Don't worry, I haven't gone mad. Not yet anyway!"

George was still in the hold-all. Sue retrieved him and took him through to the bathroom where she found Mark filling the washbasin with water. "Drop him in there." he said. Sure enough George floated.

Sue was not so impressed. "So what?" she said. "He's made of some sort of plastic isn't he?"

"No, how can he be? You saw for yourself how strong and hard he is, and anyway, it says in the message that he's indestructible."

"Yes, but I didn't really believe that."

"Nor did I, but now I'm starting to think there's something in it. Perhaps I'm just dreaming, letting my imagination get the better of me."

She smacked him hard on the buttock, and gave him a mischievous grin. "Did you feel that?" She asked, not needing a reply as she saw him wince. "No, you're not dreaming!"

He sat back against the edge of the bath, staring at nothing in particular.

"I'll tell you one person who's not going to like this," he said at length.

"Who's that?"

"That scientist we just saw. Wallace Feldstein!"

Chapter 14

Wallace Feldstein was feeling great. This was cloud nine and he was in no hurry to come down. After all, when you'd put as much effort into something as he had, you'd feel you were quite entitled to a bit of self-indulgence. That was precisely what he was doing, revelling in his new found fame and glory. There was tremendous satisfaction in just achieving the impossible, but all this new found stroking from his admiring peers was the icing on the cake. This was something he would cherish every day for the rest of his life. Even if he were alone on a desert island, nothing could ever take the memory of this moment away from him.

The security light was flashing. Somebody was outside, probably some other admirer come to pay his respects. "Who is it?" He asked.

"Mark Peterson and Sue Collins. We called you earlier today."

"Oh yes. Come right in. There have been so many calls today, I'm not sure who I'm supposed to be seeing any more, but I do remember your names."

He greeted the couple with a warm smile and shook them both vigorously by the hand. "Can I get you both a drink?" he offered, pressing a button on his wrist console. The robobutler glided silently in and waited obediently for a command. "Oh, er..thank you," said Mark. "A gin and tonic and a beer please."

As the robobutler slid away, Feldstein turned back to face his visitors. They seemed a pleasant couple, well suited physically, either married or living together, he guessed.

"Well, I suppose you've come to see me about my latest little venture. Suddenly I've become the flavour of the month. I can't deny I'm enjoying it, but I wouldn't want all this publicity too often, I hardly get a minute to myself."

"You must be feeling very proud," said Sue, taking her gin and tonic from the robobutler's outstretched hand.

"Yes, but the greatest thing is knowing that what I am doing is putting us that much closer to achieving our goal." Said Feldstein. He sat back and seemed to be contemplating something that had just come into his mind. "You know," he said after a pause, "This Genie scheme might appear to be rather far-fetched, but I've got a strange instinct about it. I just know it's going to work. I can't explain why I feel so sure, I just do"

He stopped to study the couple for a moment, conscious of the fact that he had been doing all the talking. "So, what brings you here? Not just a social call I presume?"

It was only then that he noticed the package his visitors had left over by the wall and stared curiously at it, making Mark feel suddenly very uncomfortable. It was all right before. Before, Feldstein was just a name, someone they'd never met, but now it was different. He had shown them hospitality and his nature was friendly. And right now he seemed very much at peace with himself: the great achiever. Now there was a real possibility of spoiling it all for him. Pride comes before a fall.

"I.. I..We...," Mark hesitated for a moment and took a deep breath. Like it or not, it just had to be done. "We've found something which we have reason to think is more than a hundred years old, maybe very much older than that, and which we think you ought to see before anyone else, especially as you're probably more qualified than most to understand what it might be."

The expert stared at him blankly for a second or two, not able to comprehend. "Well, you'd better show me, or I'll never be able to guess."

"Oh, er..Yes, sorry," mumbled Mark, and got to his feet to pass George, still wrapped up, over to his host..

He watched as Feldstein started to peel off the brown paper. "Be ready for this. It's a very unusual colour," he warned.

"Feels a bit like Christmas," grinned Feldstein.

That comment made Mark cringe. In a few moments from now, for Feldstein if nobody else, it might feel very much *unlike* Christmas.

As the final layer came away the expert let out a gasp. "Wow!" he exclaimed. "You weren't wrong about the colour! I could do with a pair of sunglasses!" He took the last of the wrapping off and ran his fingers over that seductively smooth surface. "It's beautifully made, whatever it is," he remarked, tilting his head back to study George more closely through his bifocals. After a minute or so, he looked up to eye his guests. "So what is it?" he said, looking puzzled.

Mark coughed nervously. "We thought you might be able to tell us," he said, "and by the way, this thing's got a name. We call it George."

Feldstein frowned. "That's a funny name to give a piece of plastic." he remarked.

"Er, well, I don't think it's plastic," replied Mark, "because it seems much too hard for that. That's why we're here, we thought you might know."

Feldstein stared hard at him. "What did you say?" He said, making it sound more like a rebuke than a question.

"I'm saying that it's hard, very hard indeed. Why don't you test it for yourself?"

Feldstein did not answer. Instead he gazed down at George, staring at its unblemished surface. His mouth was open and his faced creased with a look of utter disbelief. He did not test the surface. The sincerity in Mark's voice was enough to convince him this was no joke.

"Where did you get this?" he croaked, after what seemed to be forever.

Mark looked inquiringly across at Sue. She shook her head. "We...We'd rather not say just at the moment, sir," he said, "but we're pretty sure that it's old, very old indeed."

Feldstein sat down in the nearest chair, the colour gone from his face. As he took a sip from his whisky, Sue put a steadying hand on his shoulder. "Are you feeling all right?" She asked anxiously.

"Yes.. Yes thank you my dear, it was just a bit of a shock, that's all. It's not every day you get told that something you've just invented has been around for years!"

"But you don't know for sure. You'll have to test it first." Mark was trying desperately to give the expert some crumb of comfort.

Feldstein managed a weak smile. "I don't need to test it," he said quietly. "There's only one material with those properties. Don't you see, it's the *ultimate* material, the one and only. There cannot be anything better!"

It was uncomfortable, almost painful to watch Feldstein having to deal with this incredibly disappointing situation that they had suddenly landed him in. There he was, basking in the glory, and now he had to accept that there was someone, somewhere, -who knows how long ago- who had already beaten him to it. Coming second in a race doesn't seem to count.

"I think that what you've managed to do in inventing this material is a quite incredible achievement," said Mark, desperately anxious to revive the expert's spirits. "Maybe it is the same material, but there's no doubt that only someone as clever has you could possibly have done it. We both think you're amazing."

Feldstein smiled. "Thank you for saying that." he responded. "To be honest, I'm so hardened to setbacks, I'm quite sure I'll be bouncing back with something else in no time at all. In any case George, or whatever he's called, would not have been able to give me any clues as to his composition. I would still have had to find that out for myself. The great thing is, we now have the right material to enable us to go ahead and complete this Genie project. Without it, the whole thing would never have got off the drawing board."

Chapter 15

Feldstein's reassuring remarks came as a great relief to his guests, so much so that Mark decided it was now safe to impart some more stunning information. "Oh, by the way, there *is* another thing, sir. Apparently it's sensitive to sunlight in some way. We haven't had a chance to test that yet."

Feldstein's eyes widened. "How many more surprises have you got for me? I don't think I can handle many more!"

Mark smiled, but he said nothing. He didn't know the answer to that one himself.

The robobutler brought in another round of drinks and the three sat there facing each other in silence, while desperately trying to find some inspiration. After a few minutes spent just staring at the cube of ice in his glass, Feldstein, his forehead deeply furrowed in thought, was the first to break the silence.

"If this thing is as old as you say it is, then the obvious questions are: where did it come from, and who made it?"

Mark gave a shrug. "We've got no idea, but whoever they were, they had to be very clever."

Feldstein smiled. "Well, at least as clever as me!" he chuckled. "But the message I'm getting is, it's so beautifully made that it seems to be throwing out a challenge."

"What could that be?"

"I am the pinnacle of perfection. Match me if you can."

Sue was staring out of the window. "The sun's *just* come out!" she cried. "Let's get out there and see what happens!"

In no time at all Mark had propped George up against the wall in a sunny spot, and the three of them stood there gazing expectantly at him, but with no idea of what might happen.

George did not disappoint.

"Holy shit!" gasped Mark, hardly believing his own eyes as he watched the colour start to drain away.

The three of them watched spellbound as, in no more than a minute, George turned into glass, the colour completely gone.

"How on earth did that happen?" murmured Feldstein, mystified.

Mark went and picked George up to examine him more closely. "He's crystal clear," he said, holding him up to get a better look.

And then, as if bitten by a snake, he let out a startled cry and jerked his head backwards without warning, nearly knocking the approaching Sue headlong.

"What is it?" she cried, just managing to regain her balance.

He made no sound as if suddenly rendered mute, and stabbed a finger at the shadow cast by George on the adjacent wall.

The other two peered over his shoulder to see what had had made him react so strangely. Peering boldly back at them as large and as real as life and smiling gently, was a face. The three of them stared back at it, wide eyed and stunned into silence.

Mark was the first to find his voice. "I can't quite believe what I'm seeing," he gasped. "It looks like there is life out there after all!"

The face was not one of a human, but nevertheless there was something curiously familiar about that expression. It was the eyes: the windows of the brain, so bright and alert and conveying the inescapable message that this was indeed a very intelligent being.

"It's certainly no-one I know," remarked Feldstein, using flippancy to mask his astonishment.

They continued to watch in silence, rendered speechless by the amazing sight of this incredible revelation. They were all at once spellbound and almost hypnotised by the intensity of that stare, so much so that the other strange features went almost unnoticed, features that in essence were not so vastly different from their own. The complexion was pale, on a hairless skin, but everything else was there: the nose was small, but with large nostrils, giving the impression of two large puncture holes in the middle of the face. The ears were two little walnuts, which appeared to have been stuck on as an afterthought. The head was pear shaped, the upper part obviously housing an enormous brain, and tapered down to a tiny pointed chin.

"If it weren't so perfect I'd think it was some kind of joke." said Mark, suddenly finding his voice. "It's like all the caricatures of Martians and other aliens I've ever seen, rolled up into one!"

Sue nodded in agreement. "It's as if those fiction writers knew already. Perhaps it's just a question of logic. They got one thing wrong though: he's not green!"

"Funnily enough he doesn't scare me at all," said Mark.

"Me neither." enjoined Sue. "In fact, it's more like seeing an old friend than anything else."

"I know what you mean. I think its something to do with the eye contact. You can feel the intelligence can't you?"

"Yes," she agreed "It's as if we already know each other. Like recognising like. I wouldn't be surprised if we had the same sort of I.Q.!"

Feldstein, quiet up until now, suddenly came to life. "Can I have George for a moment?" he asked. So saying, he took him up and held him in the sunlight, copying Mark's movements so as to keep that fascinating image displayed on the wall. And then, suddenly inspired, he used the slightest of movements to rotate George fore and aft.

A kaleidoscope of images flashed across the wall, causing the three spectators to gasp in unison.

"We haven't got just one picture here," mused Feldstein, " It looks like we've got a whole story!"

"It must be a series of images set on different planes," suggested Mark. "What a brilliant idea! All we need to do is rotate him little at a time to get a new picture."

Feldstein's hands were starting to shake, making it difficult to maintain a steady image. "This is too much excitement for an old man," he said, and passed George back to Mark, who copied the same movements to get that face back again before moving on to the next image. This one showed several of them, standing in a group. There were young ones too, from all age groups. It was just like a family snap. Sue was secretly relieved to see they had two arms and two legs. Anything else would have been too much to handle right now. They were huddled close together and waving collectively with their long thin arms held high, in a gesture that was unmistakably friendly.

"No language required," murmured Mark, after studying the scene for a while. "What a great way to communicate!"

The next hour seemed like five minutes. Each time a new scene was revealed, they turned to stare wide-eyed at each other, mouths open and totally gobsmacked. Here was a complete story in the universal language of pictures, made believable by the superb realism of the images. At the end of it they were all feeling quite numb.

Judging by the first few images, it appeared that the lifestyle of these beings had been nothing less than utopian. If the seemingly bounteous vegetation was anything to go by, there was always plenty to eat, and the climate must have been equable since they wore no clothes in any of the pictures. They always portrayed themselves in happy groups, not of two or three but always ten, twenty, or even more, as if this was their normal behaviour. In each group there were always children, but it was impossible to make out any definition of sex within the adults.

But as the three slowly worked their way through the pictures, a different story began to unfold. From scenes of total harmony, there began to emerge a pattern of increasing disharmony, accompanied by a gradual reduction in the quality and quantity of the previously lush vegetation. With each new frame the numbers in the groups began to fall, reducing each time until finally there were only two or three in each group.

"It's trying to tell us a story," said Sue, a tear welling up in the corner of her eye. "Something's happening to them, something dreadful."

While she was speaking, Mark had moved onto the next picture. It was a scene of death and starvation: a kind of holocaust, not just for them but also for the plants and wildlife all around.

The very next image was a scene of utter desolation: a barren landscape, totally devoid of life of any kind. It was followed by another one, even more dramatic and depicting a very modern and futuristic city, encapsulated within an enormous artificial dome.

"It's as if they've gone to live on Mars," commented Mark, sadly.

"Or maybe Mars has come to visit them," said Feldstein.

"What do you mean?"

"An ecological disaster of some sort. Possibly the same as we are threatened with: a giant asteroid or something. Or it could be an unusual burst of solar energy." He shrugged. "Who knows what it might have been. Perhaps they'll tell us in a minute."

It was a cue for Mark to tilt to the next image.

The next scene showed a launch vehicle seemingly being prepared for blast off. Along its length were a number of discernible compartments, some of them still open and ready to accept their identical cargos, each one a kind of cone shaped capsule.

"I wonder what they had in those?" remarked Sue.

Mark shook his head. "I wouldn't have a clue, but they're all alike, so they must all do the same job."

The next image was different from the rest in that it was not the real thing this time, but a scaled-down model of the launch craft, roughly the same height as the people themselves. The same person they had seen in the first image was standing beside the model, and was pointing straight out towards the viewer.

"It's as if he's pointing directly at us," said Mark.

"Perhaps he is," murmured Feldstein.

There were five more pictures left, all depicting the same scene, but this time, they were illustrations, rather than true images, of the real thing. The first showed that same barren landscape as before, but this time it was followed by scenes of a gradual and progressive reclamation of the land by increasingly lush vegetation, until at the end it had become a veritable jungle, showing all sorts of weird and wonderful plants.

In the last picture, that same person appeared again, this time superimposed in front of the last illustration. There was a friendly smile on his face, and he was holding his hands out, in a kind of beckoning gesture.

Mark laid George down on the table and worked his aching arms. Until now he hadn't noticed how tired they were getting, so absorbed was he in the picture show. "So what do you make of that?" he said at length.

There was a blank, glassy expression on Feldstein's face. Just for once he was lost for words, but a shrug of his shoulders said it all.

"Hope," murmured Sue. She considered for a moment. "Yes, that's the feeling I got from it. Despite everything that happened to them, they still had hope. Those last illustrations must have been to show what life could be like once again."

"I've just realised something," said Feldstein.

"What's that?"

"We are looking at something that might have happened millions of years ago. It's like when you see light from a star, you're actually looking at history."

"So it's more than possible that they don't exist any more?" suggested Sue.

"We'll probably never know," murmured Feldstein, and then he clicked his fingers. "Something's just occurred to me," he said. " Let's leave George out here in the sun and go inside for a minute or two. I just want to see if anything happens."

Back inside, they watched George through the glass. Sure enough, he was back to full colour within a couple of minutes.

"That's it!" cried Feldstein triumphantly. "He only works while we're there with him."

Sue stared out at George through the window. "I don't understand," she said. "How can it be? There must be something we've overlooked."

"What do you mean?" asked Mark.

"I mean, how can George possibly know about us?" she said heatedly, annoyed by his obtuseness. "He's supposed to have come from somewhere else, isn't he?"

"She's right," agreed Feldstein. "It can't be just coincidence that he knows. Maybe he's been programmed that way. I'm guessing there's got to be a link between those little people in his pictures and us!"

"Hey, that's really spooky!" cried Mark. "If that really is the case, then what is it about us that he can recognise, Wallace?"

Feldstein thought for a while. "It would have to be chemical, I guess. There is a chemical aura circulating around every one of us, consisting of a whole cocktail of our proteins. That's how leeches and mosquitoes are so adept at finding us. It wouldn't be that difficult to find out exactly which protein is the culprit."

"Do you know anyone?"

"Yes, as a matter of fact there's an excellent chemist right here in the Institute. I'll just go up to my office and see if I can get him on to it tomorrow."

With that, Feldstein disappeared out of the door. Fascinated by all of those amazing images, Sue decided she wanted to have another look. She picked George up and stood over by the window to make sure he was in full sun, before rotating him side to side just as Feldstein had done. Mark was relaxing in an armchair catching up with his messages coming through in his right ear.

She looked puzzled. "That's strange." she remarked. "I can't seem to all get those images up any more, only two of them. One shows a couple of wiggly lines joined together and the other one is just a collection of rings, but all those people have disappeared. Perhaps I'm not holding him right?"

Mark got up and came over to check for himself. "Here, let me have a go." he said. "You've probably got him at the wrong angle."

"I don't think so, but see if you have any better luck."

He took George from her, repeating the same movements as before, but try as he might, he could only bring up those same two images. "That's very strange." he remarked. "What are we doing that's different?"

She shrugged. "Maybe we're allowed only one throw of the dice?"

He shook his head. "Surely not?"

Just then the laboratory door opened and Feldstein walked back in. "I've fixed up a time to see my chemist friend." he beamed. "First thing tomorrow."

It was then he noticed the puzzled looks on their faces. "What's up?" he enquired.

"Looks like George has stopped performing," replied Mark.

"Oh no, really? Let me try," said Feldstein. As soon as he held George out in front of him they could all see those missing images again.

"That's weird!" cried Mark. "I did the same as you. How come it didn't work for me? You must have the magic touch."

Feldstein passed George back to him. "Try it again."

This time it worked. Mark frowned and shook his head. "I don't get it," he said.

But Feldstein did. "I've just realised the trick!" he exclaimed, clicking his fingers. "It needs three of us to be present to make it work. Seems like it's the sort of information that must be shared. Three heads are better than two. Very clever!"

It was time for a break. Feldstein called the robobutler in to fetch them celebratory drinks, and they sat around for a while unwinding.

During a lull in the conversation, Feldstein rested his head back in the armchair.

In less than a minute he had fallen asleep.

It was the signal that now would be a good time to leave. Sue pulled herself up close to Mark, and rested her head on his shoulder. "I think we should go home now, darling. I think Wallace has had enough for one day. All this excitement's finally getting to him."

Mark yawned. "He's not the only one!" he whispered. "You're right, let's call it a day. It'll probably be a good idea to sleep on things anyway."

They gathered up their belongings, including George, and left quietly without waking the sleeping metallurgist.

Chapter 16

When Wallace Feldstein opened his eyes again it was dark and getting cold. It was the cold that woke him, and his left leg, which had gone to sleep. It must have been like that for some time, he decided, because he couldn't feel it at all. He shook his head and blinked a few times, trying to convert his brain to the wake mode as quickly as possible.

He eased himself forward in the chair, at the same time raising his left buttock to ease the pressure on the dead nerve. Gradually the feeling started to return, bringing with it that almost unbearable tingling he hated so much. He sat there for a while, gritting his teeth as he waited for the leg to return to normality. As that sensation finally passed, he became aware of something else, an unfamiliar pain in his arm. Probably a muscle cramp from the way he'd been sitting, he decided.

With a vocal command the lights came on. In no time the room would be warm as well. The robobutler brought him a cup of hot chocolate, which he sipped slowly, while contemplating the events of the past few days. He chuckled to himself as he thought back to last week, and the sense of hopelessness he had felt. Who would have guessed it would turn out like this?

He finished the chocolate and checked the time. It was eleven-thirty, really time for bed, except now he felt wide awake. Perhaps it would be a good time to catch up on a little research into the remarkable physical properties of TUF. He'd already been given a head start by that amazing thing called George but maybe there were other secrets to discover.

That was one good thing about having a flat on the institute campus. It meant he could dabble at any time he liked, and with a generous supply of robots to assist him, there were none of the limitations that humans would impose. Anyway some of his best work was done at night, when there was little likelihood of any interruptions.

As he made his way across the quadrangle, he stopped to look up at the stars. It was a cloudless night and the moon was in its first quarter, giving him plenty of opportunity to search for the most familiar constellations. He spent quite some time out there. All of a sudden that dark roof was taking on a whole new meaning. Somewhere in amongst that mass of twinkling it was there, the place where George must have come from. Who knows, maybe he was looking at it right now. For the first time in his life he had the strange sensation that instead of looking out into the universe, he was looking in.

After a while he gave a shrug and carried on walking. Okay, so they may have been out there once upon a time, but nobody could prove there was anybody out there right now, could they? Even a positive signal could mean nothing at all, only that somebody was out there at some time, but not necessarily now. The vast distances involved made it more than possible that whoever made

George had perished long ago. Perhaps they sent him off as their own version of the Genie project. The idea of that made him chuckle. How ironic would that be? He studied the ground in front of him and shook his head as he realised the chances of finding some other suitable solar system, let alone the right planet, were absolutely nil in a universe whose other name was infinity.

The whole thing seemed completely hopeless, but without hope a scientist is nothing, and somehow he instinctively knew there had to be something. It was not a rational feeling, just that small voice, deep inside, telling him he must go on whatever: the same voice that drives the intrepid explorer ever forward to who knows what, even when he knows he is bound to die.

He took out his small sample of the TUF he had made in that first successful experiment, and placed it on the table in front of him. He stood back for a minute, arms folded, admiring the amorphous grey blob, which for him was the second most beautiful thing he'd ever seen. Not only that, it had passed all tests with flying colours, exceeding his wildest expectations.

But there was still one particular test he hadn't carried out. He had realised that with so much energy input during its creation, this material could easily have oversubscribed energy bonding, resulting in a highly positive intrinsic energy value. Such instability, by his calculations, should result in a very low grade energy release, spread out over an extremely long period of time, and not unlike that which occurs in radioactivity.

If there was any such energy release, the biggest problem was to determine the type of energy, for without knowing that it would be impossible to make any further assessment. After working intently for more than three hours, Wallace Feldstein stretched back in his chair and rested his head back in the cradle of his interlocked hands, his forehead deeply furrowed in thought. He had worked his way through the complete range of known electromagnetic wavelengths without the slightest sign of any activity. He sighed with disappointment, having to accept that he must have been wrong all along, perhaps there was no energy release after all. What a great pity! He could think of so many applications for something like that. Maybe it was just *too* much to ask, on top of all the success he'd had lately.

He stood up and slowly paced the full length of the laboratory, vainly hoping to intercept some invisible or errant thought wave, which might just inspire his imagination. Passing by the fish tank, he paused for a moment to stare in at its occupants as they moved lazily around without a care in the world. He fingered the switch on the wall next to the tank. With one flick of his finger he could cut off their heating and air supply, condemning them to a slow death. That fish tank and its contents were a microcosm of life on Earth: the natural world versus man, the arch-enemy.

A Blue Gourami swam lazily up to the glass and appeared to be eyeing him disdainfully. Further back, a school of brightly coloured Neons darted by, suddenly to change direction in one smooth movement, all together like guardsmen on parade controlled by some unseen commander. He watched, entranced by their graceful movements as they gradually lulled him into a hypnotic stupor. It was then that he had a sudden wild thought. He looked down at that precious sample of TUF, which he was still holding in his right hand, and with one illogical and impulsive movement, reached out and dropped it into the tank.

It sank down for a moment, but quickly rose to the surface and floated there, like a small grey iceberg with just the tip exposed. The disturbance made the occupants dart hastily for cover to survey it cautiously from a safe distance. After a while they began to become more curious, inching forward to peck at it and then darting away to examine it from a safer distance.

Feldstein watched with interest. He had assumed they would soon settle down again and lose interest in this inanimate object, but to his surprise they gradually became even more restless. The tiny Neons in particular were darting haphazardly about the tank, sometimes hitting the glass wall and sometimes bumping into each other: movements which were quite out of character with the usual graceful harmony of these fascinating fish.

He stared at his precious piece of TUF as it floated, motionless, in the middle of the tank. Could it be that he was right after all, that this new material did really possess some kind of energy emission capability, and that these humble fish were picking it up? He could hardly dare to believe what he was witnessing. Whatever properties this material possessed, it was quite obvious that those little fish understood them far better than any machine ever could.

He sat down to think for a while, sending out a verbal order for tea, which was duly brought to him by a laboratory technorobot. As he took the first careful sip from the cup, he looked up to see the orange glow of dawn outlining the window and with it he began to sense the first vestiges of an idea forming in the back of his mind.

Chapter 17

Tony Marchetti's wristcom was flashing. "Dammit," he muttered to himself, annoyed that he'd forgotten to turn it off earlier. Too often he'd been disturbed right in the middle of some important experiment, the caller usually getting the short end of Tony's Latin temperament. This time, however, the other party was a little more fortunate because Tony was still in the setting-up stage. He cancelled the call light, and brought his wrist up to his mouth. "Hi, Mark. What is it?" He asked shortly.

Mark caught the tone clearly enough. "Hi, Tony," he breezed. "I'm sorry if I've called at a bad time. If it's not convenient now, I'll contact you later."

"No,..No. It's okay. There's no panic right now. Look, I'm sorry if I sounded a bit touchy but I'm getting myself psyched up for my next experiment. When it's getting near the time I start to get scared I'm going to forget something. But that's enough of my troubles," he continued, his tone now more relaxed. "Tell me how are you, It must be at least six months since I last saw you."

"More than that, I think. Look, Tony I won't hold you up. I guess you must be the man of the moment right now. I was just wondering if you could spare me ten minutes some time in the next few days?"

"Well, if it's only ten minutes you want, then there's no time like the present."

"Thanks," said Mark, "I'll come straight to the point. I was just wondering if you've been getting anywhere with your project. I know it's really none of my business, and you can tell me to go to hell if you like, only there doesn't seem to have been any news update release for some time."

"No, you're right, there hasn't been, "sighed Tony quite audibly, "and that's because we haven't really made any progress since I saw you last. The only crumb of comfort I can offer you is that we have been able to categorise our specific genes one stage further. About half of them show characteristics that lead us to believe they are mutational descendants from similar ones found in the chimps."

"And the other eight hundred?"

Tony sighed. "Well, I must admit we're puzzled. They don't seem to fit into any pattern at all. In fact I almost get the impression that they shouldn't even be there, as if they don't belong."

"You're kidding?"

"No, I'm quite serious. I'm sure there's a simple explanation, but I'm damned if I know where to look for it. The whole thing is getting to be very soul destroying."

"I'm sure it must be," said Mark, "but don't give up. This whole project would be nothing without you."

"Oh, and that's the other thing..."

"What?"

Tony hesitated. "...Well I guess we're all getting somewhat disillusioned at this end, because we can't see where it's all leading to. So far no-one has said anything to make us think otherwise."

Reluctantly, Mark had to agree. "Funny, I had a feeling you were going to say that," he said. "It must be pretty depressing to think all that work could be for nothing."

"It is. Okay, so we get our end of the deal completed, with everything sorted and categorised, and then what? They're just going to blast it all out into space in no particular direction, and hope that one happy day the planet Serendipity will appear out of nowhere for our intrepid little explorer to just float down and surreptitiously infect the brightest inhabitants with our cargo of human soul."

He gave a contemptuous grunt. "This is just a little diversion to give people some kind of hope for the future, some kind of meaning to their lives. You know as well as I do it doesn't have the remotest chance of succeeding"

"Well I must admit that up until a couple of days ago, I would have agreed with you," replied Mark, "but something's happened to make me change my mind. That's why I'm talking to you now, to give you some kind of hope."

"Don't tell me," came the mocking response, "you were looking through your telescope one night and there, as clear as anything was this nice little solar system very much like ours that somehow had previously been overlooked. Not only that, you could even pick out planet Serendipity, with clouds and water, and even cows grazing in the fields!" By now there was a distinctly hysterical pitch to his voice.

"Not quite," said Mark, calmly, "but I may have the next best thing."

"What's that?"

"Positive proof that there is, or should I say has been, life out there somewhere."

"You mean you've found a half empty tin of alien baked beans only slightly charred from re-entry!"

"Tony, I'm being serious. I've got something to show you which I know will change your mind. At least wait until you've seen it before you make any more wisecracks."

There was a pause as Tony thought it through. Why was he being so sceptical? Surely he knew Mark well enough by now to know when he was being serious, and this was certainly no time for practical jokes.

"Sorry Mark. I guess the pressure's getting to me. Apart from anything else it would be good to get away from this place for a while. Is it all right if I bring Elizabeth?"

"Of course. There's no point in only having one half of the team, is there?

Chapter 18

They had arranged to meet at Sue's apartment around lunchtime. Mark already had George set out on the table like some glorious ecclesiastical centrepiece, designed to draw the casual observer inexorably towards it. So as to ensure the maximum effect of that powerful orange colour, Mark had closed the curtains to keep the bright autumn sun at bay.

Perhaps it was the suddenness of the introduction, or maybe it was just the overwhelming magnitude of the revelation but whatever the cause, the effect was to send both of the unsuspecting visitors into a speechless trance from which it took them a full five minutes to recover. Their reaction started Mark wondering whether in future, he should not issue shock warnings before introducing others to his new toy.

After the stunned silence came the usual deluge of questions, which were patiently answered in turn until there was nothing more to tell. At the end of it there was a puzzled look on Tony's face. "I can't understand," he began, "how they can take us so far and then suddenly pull the shutters down. Why bother to go to all the trouble of finding us without telling us of their whereabouts? Okay, you could argue that if they have perished, then there wouldn't be much point looking for them, but at least it would be nice to have something to home in on."

"It's almost as if we've been set a puzzle on purpose. Like it's a test to see how smart we are," commented Mark.

"There is one other possibility," said Tony, making the others look up.

"What's that?" queried Mark, speaking for all of them.

There was a gleam of excitement in Tony's eyes. "-That George arrived the same time as we did," he declared, "and now I'm starting to wonder if we ourselves weren't the result of somebody else's Genie project!"

Mark looked horrified. "You mean those same set of genes could have been brought here all that time ago, and grafted on to whatever was living here already? Are you suggesting we could be half and half?"

Tony nodded. "Something like that." he replied. "To my mind, everything seems to fit. The whole thing's going round in one big circle and back to the beginning again. That's a perfect definition of eternity!"

"But when was the beginning? Where was the somewhere else?" Sue was looking confused.

"Who knows?" said Tony, shrugging his shoulders. "But I'll tell you one thing: There's no way this planet could have been our original home, could it? What other creature would shit on its own doorstep like we do? Ever since the very beginning we've behaved like a band of lost souls who can't find our way back. Perhaps that's why we've always been so restless, searching and probing, not just the world around us but ourselves as well. We always seem to be analysing who and what we are, and why we are here, without ever finding a completely convincing answer, when all we really need to do is go back home."

"Are you trying to suggest that it was all planned from the very beginning, that from the word go it was just a matter of time?"

"That's right. And if I'm not mistaken, George is just sitting there, waiting for our ingenuity to catch up with him. My guess is there's still a few secrets we haven't yet unravelled, but now I'm beginning to think there's a good chance we'll actually get there in the end."

"If you're right, then we'd better get moving. There's less than twelve years left to sort things out!"

Chapter 19

"Do you realise we've had George for nearly a week now and we still haven't made him public?" Mark was beginning to feel a touch guilty.

"Yes, I know, darling, but it's not as if we've just been sitting on him, is it? After all, we had to make sure he wasn't just some kind of twentieth century hoax. By all accounts they were quite fond of them in those days."

"You're right." he agreed. "I guess it's just my sense of community getting the better of me."

"Oh darling, I'm so glad you said that. I feel the same way too. It's great to feel that we're actually part of everything that happens nowadays."

"It's called democracy."

"Yes, but we never really had it before. Once the politicians got voted in they could more or less do what they liked and we all had to put up with it. That wasn't democracy was it?"

Mark nodded. "It's so different now, and it's all down to technology. Everyone knows what's going on and they all have a say in it all the time. It was never like that. Now we're like a colony of ants; we're all talking to each other, and we're all heading in the same direction for just about the first time ever, thanks to our friend the asteroid."

"But what about George?" said Sue, changing tack. "Don't you think we ought to tell the others first before letting him go?"

"Yes, perhaps you're right, after all, Wallace must have a special interest in it after having his sails deflated like that."

"Why don't you give him a call after breakfast?"

"Okay, I will."

Feldstein beat him to it. Mark was just draining his second cup of coffee when his call light started flashing. A tiny electronic voice in his left ear said, "Doctor Wallace Feldstein wishes to speak with you."

He pressed the speak button on his wrist. "Hi Wallace. Sorry we didn't say goodbye yesterday. You seemed to be sleeping so peacefully we thought it would be a shame to wake you."

"That's okay, Mark. No, really I should thank you. Yes I was enjoying that nap, so you did the right thing. In fact that's the reason I'm calling you."

"Oh?" Mark sounded intrigued.

"Well, I must have really needed that sleep," Feldstein continued, "because when I finally woke up I felt really refreshed and wide awake, so much so that I decided to carry out some more research..." He paused. "..I'm really calling to ask if I can borrow George for a few days?"

The request made Mark sit up. Like everyone else who had ever had contact with George, he was starting to get uncharacteristically possessive. "What for?" was all he could think of saying at that moment.

"I think I may be on to something, but I need a little time."

"As a matter of fact I was just about to call you," responded Mark, "because, sad as we are to have to let go of George, we thought it about time we made him more public. If we keep him quiet for too much longer we could be getting ourselves in to serious trouble. The last thing I want is to lose any more leisure points."

"Yes, I understand that, but it's just possible I may be able to get some quick results. How about twenty-four hours?"

Mark hesitated. "Would you give me one second please, Wallace?"

"Sure, you can have two if you like!"

Mark pressed the secrecy button and went out to the kitchen to consult with Sue. "Why not?" she said with a shrug. "What harm can it do?"

Comforted by her approval, Mark wasted no further time. "Okay, Wallace," he called, "but would you count us in too? We're so much part of it now, we'd really hate to miss out on anything!"

"Of course, my friend. I was going to suggest that myself, anyway. I'll be over in thirty minutes."

Chapter 20

"Where are we going?" queried Sue, as she climbed into the back of Feldstein's electrocar. Mark stowed George, carefully wrapped in black plastic, in the boot.

Feldstein was setting up the auto-controls for the trip.

"I've got a good friend who is carrying out an intensive study of dolphin behaviour," he began. "I've got a strong hunch he may be able to help us in some way."

Sue was intrigued. Since way back, humans had always been fascinated by dolphin behaviour, and the interest was still as much alive today as it had ever been.

"I know they're clever creatures," she said, " but what could dolphins possibly do to help us?"

"Maybe nothing, but I think we shall just have to wait and see," said Feldstein mysteriously.

Pedro Lopez was a short, dark and very cheery individual with a relaxed smile that revealed a perfectly straight set of gleaming white teeth, made to look even whiter by his Mediterranean complexion. He greeted the visitors at the side entrance to his laboratory, which had a plain and deceptively modest facade to it. Nobody would have guessed that a place like this would have anything to do with marine animals. After the usual introductions, he quickly ushered them through to the back, which opened out onto a large pool area, divided into sections.

There were four bottle-nose dolphins in the pool, and at first sight of the visitors they swam across to greet them, holding their heads well out of the water, their excited squeaks making everybody smile. Sue was trying to decide whether this was a genuine show of friendship or just a display driven by some ulterior motive, such as the hope of receiving a titbit.

She decided to give them the benefit of the doubt.

"They're so friendly, they seem almost human!" she exclaimed, as she knelt down to pat one on the snout.

"Surely that's a contradiction in terms!" laughed Mark.

Sue looked up at him disapprovingly. "That might have been true once," she chided, "but things are different now."

"Yes, you're right of course. I'm sorry I didn't mean it," he apologised.

They sat by the pool for a while, filled with admiration at the superb skills of these magnificent creatures as they put on a spontaneous show, seemingly just for their guests. At the end of it Mark was deep in thought.

"It's fascinating how they seem to react to humans, isn't it? As far as I know, they always seem to regard us humans as friendly, and yet they're quite capable of killing sharks if they have to. It's as if there's something different about us that they can recognise."

"Well, there is, of course," said Pedro. "It's our intellect. They seem to be able to identify with it, but exactly how we're still not sure. They certainly have a very large brain themselves, but it only seems to be that way because of their much more advanced sensory skills. That's what I'm doing at the moment, trying to unravel the mysteries of the dolphin brain. In fact…" He paused to study his guests for a moment, "…In fact I think I can allow you to come and have a look at my latest experiment, so long as you can promise to keep it to yourselves."

"Don't worry, Pedro, I can vouch for them," said Feldstein. "They're good friends of mine."

The words seemed to satisfy Lopez. "Well, what are we waiting for, then," he smiled, "Let's go!"

He led them through a door and into the darkened laboratory. On one side was a large window, which overlooked the dolphin pool, and from it the occupants could be seen quite clearly. They were swimming lazily around, occasionally allowing their shimmering backs to break above the surface of the water as if to confirm their awareness of the happenings beyond.

The room was not over large, but was so crammed full of monitoring devices and viewing screens that Mark could not help but gasp in amazement. Not even at his own asteroid monitoring station was there as much electronic equipment as this. It was quite obvious that dolphin research still carried a very high priority in the order of things.

Lopez seated himself at a console. In front of him was a viewing screen on which was displayed the word "Sheila".

He half turned to face his guests, and pointed towards the screen.

"I would like to introduce you all to Sheila," he began. "She is one of the four dolphins you can see through the glass. Sheila is no ordinary dolphin. We have made her very special by wiring up all her sensory pathways, so that we can get an idea of what she is experiencing through her sight, her hearing, and whatever else she's able to do. As you can see there is no external evidence that she is any different from any of the other dolphins, because we have been able to use the latest implantation techniques to place the devices within her body, exactly where we want them."

"Nanosurgery!" interrupted Mark.

"Neuronanosurgery." corrected Lopez. "The whole process, as you probably know, is totally humane and painless, and Sheila is quite unaware of any sort of intrusion."

"So how do you go about analysing the results?" asked Sue.

Lopez gave her a wry smile. "Ah, that's the hard bit," he said. "But we think we've finally cracked it by means of a series of very sophisticated software programs we've been developing, and which have enabled us to produce a screen image of what Sheila is experiencing." With that he touched a button on the console, causing the screen to come to life.

Mark gasped as a moving image appeared on the screen, showing under-water shots and blue sky above. It was a much speeded-up version of what he had seen many times from the bottom of a swimming pool, but it was only when he saw a dolphin leap from the water outside, a movement synchronous with the image on the screen, that he could accept what was really happening.

Open-mouthed in astonishment, he turned to look at Sue, only to see that her expression was mirroring his.

Lopez had been watching them with amusement. "That's right," he chuckled, "You're not dreaming. It's real!"

"You mean...we are actually seeing what that dolphin is seeing? That's incredible! It's as if it had a camera on board!" Mark was unable to suppress his astonishment.

Lopez touched another icon. At once the room was filled with the sounds of rushing water and the constant echo clicks made by the animals.

Now Mark was grinning, like a little boy who had just been shown how to work a new toy. "I suppose you're going to show us what she can smell next!" he joked.

"Not quite," replied Lopez, suddenly more serious, "but there is something else we've been working on. Stick around for a while. You never know, you might just be lucky enough to see a bit of scientific history in the making."

"I thought we already did!" exclaimed the stunned observer.

All throughout this, Feldstein had remained quiet. Having seen this all before, he was enjoying watching the reactions of his friends, but now was the time he had been patiently waiting for. Moving himself up next to Lopez, he put a hand on his friend's shoulder. "Do you think it'll work?" he murmured.

Lopez shrugged and looked up to the sky, his palms flattened together in a gesture of mock prayer. "Who knows?" he said, eyeing Feldstein meaningfully. "After all, it's only guesswork, but I've just got a hunch about this one. There's a whole bunch of nervous pathways in there, all humming away with activity, and without any obvious function, but you can bet your life old Mother Nature didn't put them there for nothing!"

Feldstein listened thoughtfully. "I guess the other problem you've had, is in interpreting what they mean?" he said at length.

Lopez nodded. "You got it in one. To begin with, we didn't have a clue." He shook his head. "I'm telling you Wally, it's been an absolute nightmare for us. Can you imagine trying to pin down something you don't really understand, because you've never experienced it for yourself?"

"What do you mean?" said Feldstein, puzzled.

"Well, supposing there's some other sense that we don't know about?"

"Like a sixth sense, you mean?"

Lopez smiled. "In the dolphin's case it would be a seventh sense, wouldn't it? They've already got sonar, don't forget!"

Feldstein looked puzzled. "But what else *could* there be that would be of any use to a dolphin?"

Lopez shrugged. "Maybe nothing, but there are a whole lot of different energy patterns all around us all the time, covering an enormous spectrum. Sensory perception doesn't just have to stop at light and sound does it?"

"True," agreed Feldstein, "but if there *is* something, how can you possibly hope to capture it?"

Lopez nodded resignedly. "You're right, of course," he agreed. "All we can really hope to do is get some sort of understandable interpretation of what's going on.

Right now, I've decided to opt for the visual approach. It's the best we can do at the moment."

"It could be like trying to get a picture of a smell!" mused Feldstein. "Sorry I didn't mean to sound so negative, but it does sound like a pretty long shot doesn't it?"

"Even long shots hit the target sometimes!" said Lopez, a wry smile on his face.

"So when are you going to test it out?" asked Feldstein, suddenly feeling guilty about being so sceptical.

Lopez smiled softly. "Right now, my friend, right now." he said quietly.

Outside, the three assistant robots were placing several small plastic hoops in the water. There were three different shapes, circular, triangular, and square, floating at random on the surface. One of the robots was positioned at the far end of the pool, to begin a sequence that had obviously been rehearsed many times before. The only dolphin remaining in the pool had been fitted with a set of tailor-made blindfolds, each with a motorised visor, which were presently set at open.

From his chair at the operating console, Lopez turned to address his guests. "I'm going to ask Sheila to perform her best party trick for you right now. It's probably one you've seen before, but it demonstrates very well one very special skill she possesses." With that he tapped in a command to the end robot, which sounded a high-pitched note, instantly bringing the dolphin to attention. The robot held aloft a triangular hoop and sounded another note. The dolphin responded immediately by diving and methodically swam around the tank collecting all the triangles, which she took straight to the robot in return for her reward of fish.

The three spectators applauded loudly, the sound probably unheard through the thickness of the glass. "That's very clever," said Sue, "they're so intelligent aren't they?"

"Yes," replied Lopez, "but did you notice something else?"

"What?" asked Sue, looking puzzled.

"Sheila was blind when she picked up those hoops. I closed her visors before she took off."

Sue stared at him, wide eyed. "You're not serious?" she cried.

Lopez just smiled at her and then nodded very deliberately.

"Sonar. Echolocation. Many different animals can do it. It's very handy when there's not enough light."

He pointed to the monitoring screen. "We've got that on record, too," he said casually.

He tapped in a few commands, causing the monitor to light up. The three visitors gathered round to watch as he replayed the action. The picture was not in colour as before, but a black and white, almost surreal, version of the same thing, except that objects appeared to be thrown into very sharp relief, appearing much blacker than expected, against a whiter than usual background. The individual shapes of the floating hoops could easily be made out as Sheila homed in on them with her usual unerring accuracy.

"That's very neat," remarked Feldstein, impressed. "But I know you've got something else, haven't you? After all, this is very much akin to vision, so it's almost the same decoding program, I would imagine."

Lopez nodded. "You're right," he said, producing a small package from his pocket. "But this little beauty could change everything!"

"What is it?" queried Mark.

"This is our latest little brainchild," began Lopez proudly. "It's a software program we've been developing to try and analyse any uncharted neural pathways, and make some sense out of them. We're going to try it out on Sheila right now!"

With that he pulled a tiny cartridge from the package and plugged it into a small aperture at the front of the console.

"I've got to tell you," he said, "I've got no idea what we might see, so don't raise your hopes too much. It'll probably be nothing more than a bunch of squiggly lines."

He was wrong. What came up on the screen did very little to excite anybody. The picture was foggy, and the images were blurred. Lopez studied it for a while, his subdued reaction betraying his obvious disappointment. Eventually he shook his head. "Oh well," he sighed. "It was worth a try. This is nothing more than just a second rate visual image. Perhaps these nervous pathways are just there for standby, in case of damage to the main ones."

"Sounds logical," agreed Feldstein.

For a while after that, Lopez was uncharacteristically quiet. Mark gave Sue a nudge, and suggested with a whisper, that perhaps this would be a good time to go. She was just nodding her approval, when Feldstein suddenly jumped up out of his chair. "For Heaven's sake!" he cried. "I nearly forgot why we came here! George!" he beckoned to Mark. "Be a good chap and go and get him would you? I want to see what Sheila makes of him!"

Although very warm and sultry, it was a cloudy day, with the prospect of heavy rain and possibly a storm to come sometime later in the day. Mark was back in a very short while, unwrapping George as he walked. Lopez gasped when he saw him. "What in the name of hell is that?" he croaked. "It looks like some sort of very shiny chopping board!"

"No, it's not a chopping board, it's something much more interesting than that," laughed Feldstein. "But it's a long story, so I'll tell you later. Just believe me when I say it's something very special."

"I *do* believe you," Came the stunned reply.

Mark started to make his way out to the pool. With George in his hand he said: "Would it be all right if I just throw this into the water and let Sheila play with it for a few minutes?"

Lopez was scratching his head. "Why not?" he shrugged, gesturing towards the pool. "Be my guest!"

Nobody, not even Feldstein, was ready for what happened next.

As George hit the water and came to rest, more or less in the middle of the pool, Sheila, who had been lazily cruising out of sight, suddenly took off as if frightened by something and began racing around in circles at breakneck speed, causing a startled Lopez to go running out. He was just in time to see her take a mighty leap, which was so close to the side it was something of a miracle she did not end up marooned on the walkway. She repeated the same frenzied actions several times until finally the very worried looking Lopez took it upon himself to dive in and recover the offending article.

With one mighty pull, he grabbed George, and threw him as far as he could, watching as he sailed away to land well clear of the side. He waited for a few minutes for Sheila to calm herself down, and then pulled himself out of the water to retrieve the mysterious object. The others came running over to join him.

"I'm really sorry, Pedro," apologised Feldstein. "I didn't expect her to react as much as that."

Lopez's expression darkened. "Are you trying to tell me you knew something was going to happen?" he demanded, angrily.

"To be quite honest, I wasn't sure," stammered Feldstein. "But I really didn't expect her to behave like that. I thought she might just show just a bit more than the usual amount of curiosity, that's all."

Lopez appeared to accept the explanation. "Anyway, you still haven't told me what that thing is supposed to be."

Feldstein glanced across at Mark, who decided to take over the conversation. "It's something very special," he said. "We think it might have come from somewhere else."

Lopez frowned, not quite believing his ears. "What do you mean, somewhere else?"

"Another planet. We think it may well be alien."

Lopez, eyeing Mark with suspicion, walked over to George and examined him more closely, turning him over a few times, fascinated by his exquisite smoothness. "There certainly is something very weird about it," he declared at length. "I've never seen anything so smooth. And what a crazy colour!"

"It's certainly a very unique material, probably the ultimate," said Feldstein. "And I had an idea there maybe some sort of energy emission going on. That's why we brought him along, to see if the dolphins could detect anything."

"Obviously they can," remarked Lopez, passing George over to Mark. "Here, Mark. You stay out here with this thing, and we'll get Sheila to run through her act."

With that, he began walking back to the laboratory, beckoning the others to follow. "Let's see what we can make of it," he called.

Lopez announced that he would just be a few minutes changing into the spare set of clothes he always kept for such an emergency, and disappeared through a side door. The other two went over to examine the imaging screen for a while. The last program was still running, showing the same foggy picture and fuzzy images. Feldstein went over to the door to tell Mark to move to the edge of the pool, and on his return, found Sue giggling to herself.

"Something funny?" he asked.

She pointed to the screen, still giggling. "It's Mark. It makes him look like a ghost, and the picture's so distorted, it makes his head seem three times too big! No wonder Pedro's disappointed with the quality."

Feldstein leaned over to take a look. But the expression on his face was more of astonishment than amusement. Just then Lopez came back. They made way for him to examine the screen. He looked even more astonished than Feldstein.

"There's no distortion there," he announced, solemnly. "Those images are for real."

"What do you mean?" Feldstein cried in disbelief. "How can they be?"

Lopez shrugged. "I don't know, but believe me, they are!"

Feldstein stared back at him, aghast. "But the head is out of proportion, it's three times bigger than it should be!"

"Maybe the program works after all!" said Lopez, a tremor of excitement in his voice.

"So what are we looking at?"

"I'm not sure, but did you notice George? It's the same for him!"

They hadn't noticed, having been too involved with the sight of Mark. They peered at the screen again. Sure enough, George, still lying on the side where Lopez had left him, had that same strange halo around him too.

Lopez had an idea. "I wonder if an enhancement would give us a better picture," he murmured, tapping in a few instructions. In a few seconds the picture quality had improved quite dramatically.

They could now identify Mark quite easily, and the extreme contrast of the image gave his face a weird, almost unearthly effect. But it was not the ghostly expression on the face that caught Lopez's attention, so much as the bright halo which surrounded it. Most intense above the head and around the upper part of the face, it disappeared completely at the neck.

Lopez scratched his head and looked quizzically across at Feldstein. The latter just stared blankly back. "Don't look at me," he declared. "Your guess is as good as mine!" Lopez shrugged. "Well, I know one thing for sure," he said. "This is turning out to be a hell of a lot more than I ever bargained for!"

"It's obviously not sonar," said Feldstein, thoughtfully. "Sheila seems to be picking up emissions rather than rebounds."

"Yes, but emissions of what?" puzzled Sue.

"Energy, but what kind, I'm not quite sure." Said Feldstein.

"Whatever it is, it must be all around, like light." Lopez added.

"What makes you say that?"

"Because everything else on the screen was lit up dimly. It just seemed to be so much brighter around Mark's head and that chopping board thing."

"Perhaps they are both actually emitting energy," suggested Feldstein. "By the way that board's got a name. We call it George."

As he spoke he put his fingertips up to his head, running them over the surface as if feeling for something. "Do you know," he continued. "When I've been thinking a lot, I often do this. I sort of imagine my brain's getting hot and it's glowing somehow."

"Perhaps *you* can't physically feel it," remarked Sue. "But maybe dolphins can actually *see* it!"

"Sounds incredible doesn't it?" mused Feldstein.

Lopez was smiling broadly. "Not to me!" he exclaimed. "This is exactly what I was looking for!"

"Well if it is true," said Feldstein. "Then we must appear very weird to them, - almost supernatural."

"Like angels." added Sue.

"Perhaps that's why they treat us with so much respect," said Lopez. "That's something that's often puzzled me. Do you know, I've always had the feeling they know something I don't!"

Just then Mark came back in, carrying George. "I seem to have been out there a long time," he said. "Have I been missing something?"

Chapter 21

Lopez persuaded Mark to let him keep George for a while. He had become very curious about the nature and source of this mysterious new energy form, but after two days of exhaustive investigation, he had to admit defeat, and decided to give Feldstein a call.

"Sorry, my friend," he apologised gloomily. "I've really tried my best, but only Sheila knows the answer, and she's not telling. There's no response at all from any other detection equipment."

"Don't worry, Pedro," Came the reassuring voice from the other end. "I'm sure you tried your best. I guess some problems just aren't meant to be solved. Anyway, I'll come round later and pick George up. We've held on to him far too long already."

"Okay, Wally, see you later. Oh yes, there is just one thing..."

"What's that?"

"The energy patterns of the halos around Mark and George. I'm pretty sure they're identical."

There was a pause. "Do you know what you're saying?" There was a distinct tremor in Feldstein's voice.

"Not altogether. But it does seem to be quite a coincidence, don't you think?"

"You're telling me! If what you say is right, and if George really *is* from somewhere else, then I would say it's *too* much of a coincidence! Thanks, Pedro, you've been a great help. I'll see you later."

"You're welcome." was the bewildered response.

From the comfort of the electrocar, Feldstein called up Mark to tell him the news.

"We've got to see Tony and Elizabeth as soon as possible. I've got a feeling there's something here that may interest them."

"What's that?"

"Something Pedro came up with. How are they getting on with their research?"

"Okay, I think, but they still can't see how it can lead anywhere."

"Maybe they will after today."

"What do you mean?"

"It's only a hunch at the moment, but it might just be a piece of the jigsaw. But don't build your hopes up yet, we'd better wait and see what the Marchettis make of it. Knowing me, it'll probably turn out to be nothing at all."

Just then a synthesised voice in his right ear told him there was a call from Tony. He touched a button on his wrist console to open up the line. "Hi, Tony, your ears must be burning, we were talking about you. What can I do for you?" he said, warmly.

"Sorry to bother you, Wally, but Mark tells me you might have something to interest me?"

"Quite possibly, but I can't make any promises. I've had an idea, but it seems so crazy, and yet I can't seem to get it out of my mind. Maybe you can put it to rest for me?"

"Don't worry, sometimes the craziest ideas are the best. Shall I come over now?"

"Okay, I'm at Pedro Lopez's Oceanographic research lab. There's something here I think you ought to see."

Tony was there in ten minutes, Elizabeth by his side as usual. Feldstein wasted no time with pleasantries. "How's your project coming on?" he began.

They both nodded. "Pretty good." said Tony.

"But you're still chasing the big one aren't you?" probed Feldstein.

"If you mean the final mechanism, then the answer's yes, I'm afraid." admitted Tony, glumly.

"That's the ultimate achievement isn't it? The secret of life itself." continued Feldstein.

"For a scientist, I suppose it is. But why are you asking?" responded Tony, with barely disguised impatience.

Feldstein studied the couple for a moment. "Well," he began. "It may be nothing, but..." he paused, wondering whether what he was going to say wasn't just a bit too far out.

Elizabeth read his mind. "Don't worry," she assured. "We're clutching at straws at the moment, so quite honestly, no suggestion would be laughed at, no matter how crazy it might sound."

Feldstein smiled. Encouraged, he continued: "Well, what you're looking for is the ultimate catalyst, aren't you? The one that finally brings all your strands of DNA into line and converts them from just mere chemicals and into life itself."

The two nodded, but remained silent, hanging expectantly on Feldstein's next words.

"I suppose you've been going down the chemical pathway, haven't you?" guessed Feldstein.

Tony frowned. "Why, yes," he admitted. "What other way is there?"

"I'm not sure," said Feldstein guardedly. "But have you ever heard of Morphic Resonance?"

"Yes, of course we have," said Tony. "It's an idea that's been around for a very long time, but there's never been anything positive. It's just an idea, that's all."

"Hold on, darling," chided Elizabeth. "Let Wally finish before you start getting dismissive."

"Well," continued Feldstein. "Just suppose it *does* really exist, and that life is some kind of all-pervading ethereal force, constantly present and keeping our chemistry working, and that, somehow, it can transmit essential information from one living being to another..."

"Like having green fingers?" Tony was being facetious.

"Why not?" defended Feldstein.

Elizabeth scowled darkly at her husband. "Tony, will you just shut up for a minute and give Wally a chance?" she ordered.

Encouraged by her support, Feldstein continued: "And suppose you could use it to stimulate the formation of life itself?"

"Then all we'd need to do is bottle it, send it off into space with our little collection of chemicals, and then introduce the two to each other when the time eventually came." said Tony, hardly attempting to subdue his scorn. "It's a very sweet idea, but I'm afraid it's all wishful thinking. Like spiritualism and all the rest of it, I can only believe in what I see, and I see nothing."

"That's why I've brought you here," said Feldstein flatly. With that, he turned and beckoned for the bemused couple to follow him.

Lopez put on a very good show for them. At one point, after Lopez had adjusted the enhancement program to give the halos a maximum effect, the stunned Tony was heard to say: "I see it, but I still can't believe it!"

Feldstein was having the same difficulty. Even though he'd seen the show a few times before, there was something so unreal about those images. They seemed to make humans appear almost unnatural, especially alongside the other creatures Lopez had introduced (including his own cat and dog), none of which had the slightest trace of a halo.

"So how do you know this is Morphic Resonance we're seeing?" said Elizabeth thoughtfully.

"I don't, of course. That's for you to discover, but he only way you'll find out for sure is to use George in your experiments."

Tony was still looking doubtful." You make it sound as if George is the answer to all our wildest dreams!" he scoffed.

Feldstein remained quite unperturbed by the taunting. "Do you know," he smiled, "I've been seriously wondering whether he isn't!"

Chapter 22

The Marchettis took George away with them that day. A week later Feldstein was visited personally by Tony, alone this time except for a magnum of the best champagne which he meekly presented to the astonished metallurgist. Tony managed a weak smile as Feldstein came to the door to greet him.

"I've come with my tail between my legs in humble apology," he muttered. "You were absolutely right, and I was wrong to be so sceptical." So saying, he proffered the champagne.

Feldstein took hold of the heavy bottle with both hands. "I don't blame you," he smiled. "Even now, I still have to pinch myself occasionally to make sure it's not just a dream."

He eyed Tony inquiringly. "I take it the idea worked then?"

Tony's face cracked into an enormous smile. "You're damn right, it did!" he beamed.

During the course of those next three years, the Marchettis overlorded a series of closely coordinated nuclear construction programs, during which they able to show that George did indeed emit what was still a completely baffling form of energy, but which nonetheless was able to actively catalyse DNA bonding to form the elusive double helix formation of genes.

Feldstein's intuitive predictions had proven to be totally correct.

The exact nature of the energy was to remain a mystery, and everybody soon came to realise that nothing would have been possible without George. The nearest anyone ever got to understanding the energy was to align its nature to psychic energy, which, according to Lopez's dolphins, had enough strength to exist beyond the physical confines of the body.

In accordance with the overwhelming wishes of a recent plebiscite, the actual fabrication of human life by totally artificial means had been banned, much to everyone's relief. Playing God to a generation of living artefacts would have proved altogether too much of a responsibility for mere mortals to sustain.

Chapter 23

When Mark and Sue heard the news from Feldstein, they were not altogether surprised.

"I just knew there had to be more to it," said Sue. "As I said before, why would anyone go to all the bother of sending something all that way from wherever it was if they hadn't given it a specific purpose?"

"I'd like to bet there's even more," murmured Mark.

"Like what?"

"Well, it's already shown us the secret of how to turn chemistry into life, but why? It's as if somebody already knew we would need that information."

"Seems very philanthropic," mused Sue. There was a touch of sarcasm in her voice.

"What do you mean?"

"Oh, well.." she sighed, "I suppose I'm just being cynical, but I just get the feeling it wasn't just for our good. Nobody's going to go to all that trouble if there's nothing in it for themselves, are they? It's one of the failings of human nature."

Mark studied his feet, considering for a moment. "You're right!" he agreed.

And then it hit him. Jerking his head up to look at her, his eyes wild with excitement, he cried: "That's it! You just said it!"

She stared back at him, baffled. "Said what?"

"Human nature!.... Human nature!...Why did you say that?"

She shook her head with bewilderment. "I..I don't know what you mean," she stuttered.

"You were talking about aliens, weren't you? But you referred to them as humans!"

She shrugged. "That was just a figure of speech, nothing more."

"I know, but all of a sudden, it makes sense. Don't you see? Somebody out there had an incredible amount of interested in us...because they *are* us!..Or should I say, *were* us! Without even realising it, you've just confirmed what Tony was suggesting the other day."

Sue gazed at him as if questioning his sanity. "Are you trying to say we came from somewhere else?" she derided.

"I don't know, exactly, but there's some sort of connection. There's got to be, otherwise how did they know so much about us?"

Sue frowned. "Wait a minute," she cautioned, "there's something that doesn't fit."

"What's that?"

"Chimpanzees. They're our cousins. We share more than ninety eight per cent of the same genetic material. That can't be just a coincidence, can it? You're not going to tell me *they're* aliens as well?"

"No, of course not. But that can only mean one thing."

"What?"

"DNA: the two per cent. That's where we've got to look. The answer's just *got* to be in there!"

Chapter 24

"Tony?..It's Mark. Those essential genes you're trying to identify. I think I know how you can do it."

"Oh, really?" came the sceptical response. "Well you're a better man than me, if you can!"

Mark stood his ground. "I know what you're thinking: another meddler. I don't blame you Tony, but I really think it might be worth a try."

"Okay, shoot."

"It's just a calculated guess. Why don't you try separating out the sequences and try using each of them in turn to activate George while he's in direct sunlight? I've got a feeling he will select the right ones for you."

"How did you come to that conclusion?" Tony sounded mystified.

"I don't really know. It just seems to add up, that's all."

Tony sighed audibly. "Oh well, what can I lose? I suppose it's as good a suggestion as anything else. I'll call you later."

Mark ended the call wishing Tony good luck, a satisfied look on his face. Somehow he already knew it was going to work. In no time at all, Project Genie would be up and running. No longer a figment of anyone's imagination.

Chapter 25

The great brooding monster sat steaming on its launch pad, the final preparations for take-off now complete. They could all relax now and enjoy this one. The previous launches were far more fraught with tension, every single life on Earth depending on a successful outcome. They had finally chosen a belt and braces approach, using a lateral explosion to push the asteroid off course, followed in quick succession by a direct hit from the second payload. Happily for the whole of the living world, Project Intercept was a total success, and the asteroid was reduced to a million pieces, nearly all of them directed harmlessly on a new course to nowhere. The few bits of shrapnel that did continue in Earth's direction burned out during entry, giving everyone a free firework display which lasted for several more days.

The Genie Project delivery system was by far the most powerful rocket ever built, almost half as big again as Intercept, because, to improve the chances of completing its mission, it had been redesigned to carry six mini landing craft instead of just the one as originally planned. Not only was it powerful, but it was virtually indestructible too, thanks to a skin made entirely from Feldstein's TUF, which could easily see it through a few million years of intergalactic exploration. Maybe it wouldn't have to go that far to find what it was looking for, but it really didn't matter how long it took, because chemistry without life is permanent.

Many people had questioned whether there was any real need for the Genie project any more, particularly as the unthinkable asteroid disaster had been dealt with, but the romantic element of sewing seeds in some far flung corner of the universe seemed to appeal to so many, and by a very narrow majority the plebiscite vote was finally cast in favour. The winning argument was that nobody could be really sure that such a situation would not occur again, and, if it ever did, it would be at least comforting to know that some kind of effort had been made to preserve the human spirit and ensure its continued journey into perpetuity.

It was a public holiday throughout the world. Parties were being held everywhere, and the mood was festive and optimistic. The launch was scheduled for two hundred hours world standard time, which in Mark and Sue's area was eight in the evening. They were at a party being given by, of all people, Tony Chen, whose formerly aggressive nature had mellowed remarkably in those years since Sue had made that first discovery of the asteroid.

Everyone from the department was there. Chen had decided it was all right to leave the monitoring system running on auto for just one day, any unusual findings to be stored for later analysis. It being very much a family day, the Petersons had brought their four year old daughter, Tanilba, along with them, and they watched with pride as she ran off to make friends in the electrofun enclosure Tony had the foresight to hire for the day.

The Marchettis were also there, with their son, Raymond, now twelve. Seeing how tall he had become gave Sue a momentary pang of horror as she realised how quickly these last few years had passed. Feldstein was there, his pure white hair plainly visible on the far side of the hall. As usual, he appeared to be engaged in a deep and meaningful conversation with someone of similar years, no doubt on some technical matter or other.

Tony came over to greet them. "How are you?" he began warmly, "Haven't seen you in such a long time."

They all shook hands and exchanged kisses. After the usual preliminary small talk, Tony took Mark aside.

"I just want to thank you once again for sending me in the right direction. Without your help, we would never have made it. Who'd have thought everything would be tied up with George like that? Even now, when I think back, I'm still amazed how lucky we were to get that break."

"I used to think it was luck too," said Mark, "but now I can't help feeling it was all inevitable, like the whole thing was preordained."

"You mean we would have worked it out, no matter what?"

"Yes."

"But how?" Tony was looking puzzled.

"Instinct. I believe we are being driven by it: not just any old instinct, but one very special one that only humans have. It's called *achievement*. It's been in our DNA from the very beginning."

For a few moments Tony remained silent and just stared back at Mark, letting the idea sink in. "Makes complete sense," he said at last, "so you're telling me that when you came up with the idea of using George, it was no accident?"

"That's right. But this time the feeling was so much stronger than usual, as if something else was acting on me, giving me that final push."

"Morphic Resonance!" cried Tony.

"That's what I thought, but it seemed so way out I thought you might think me crazy."

"Where was George when that happened?"

"Right next to me."

The smile on Tony's face said that he had already guessed what the answer would be. "I don't think you're crazy at all!" he exclaimed. "George is such an amazing piece of ingenuity, you need to guard him with your life!"

"I will do, when I get him back."

"Why, where is he?" asked Tony, concerned.

"The launch team were curious about him for some reason. They had come up with another theory they wanted to investigate further, but they wouldn't tell me what it was. They promised I'll get him back when it's all over."

Tony shook his head doubtfully. "Don't hold your breath." He murmured.

Chapter 26

It was almost eight o'clock. Tony Chen had set up the holovision and the assembly reorganised itself into a large circle so they could all get a good view of the launch.

"Well this is finally it, eh? I really hope it's worth it after all that time and effort!"

The sound of Wallace Feldstein's familiar voice made Mark swing round to greet his old friend.

"Hi, Wallace!" he cried. "Don't worry about a thing. I just know for sure it's going to work."

"How can you say that?"

"Oh, I don't know, really. There's just a little voice, deep down inside of me, that's all."

At eight o'clock precisely, a great white plume of steam shot out from the lower burners of the mighty machine, causing a great cheer to erupt from the watching crowd. Amid wild whoops of excitement, the beautiful craft eased itself away from the launch pad, seeming almost to hang there motionless for a while before gradually gathering power until, in no time at all, it was just a burning, crackling streak of white, silhouetted in reverse against the deep blue sky.

"Funny, I've got a lump in my throat," murmured Sue.

Mark put an arm around her shoulder. "Me too," he said. "Parting is such sweet sorrow, as Shakespeare would say. The worst thing is, we know for sure that we are never going to see this particular friend again."

"It feels like something even more than that to me," she added, "something good."

"What do you mean?"

"Like it's the beginning, not the end, as if we're finally going home."

"Who knows? Perhaps we are!"

"There's one thing still puzzling me," said Sue with a frown.

"What's that?"

"The universe is such a huge place. How can they possibly know where to go?"

Feldstein overheard their conversation. "Didn't you hear?" He said.

She eyed him curiously. "No... Hear what?"

"George... He's on board the spacecraft of course, because they need him to activate the chemistry when the time comes, but that's not all. They finally managed to figure out what all those tiny so-called imperfections in the matrix were for. They even built a laser machine with the capacity to read them."

She stared at him, wide eyed. "You're kidding!" she cried. "So what were they?"

Feldstein peered back into her big blue eyes and smiled. There was a look of complete satisfaction on his face.

"They weren't imperfections at all," he murmured, "they were directions."

THE END (or is it just the beginning?)